SONG OF THE SWORDS

"There can be no Light without Dark
and no darkness without light.
Heed these songs well, for without them,
Alinae is lost."
~Tyranon the Artagh
Fourth cycle of the Craedr Age

SONG OF THE SWORDS BOOK TWO

THE TEMPLE OF ARDYN

TAMERI ETHERTON

TEACUP DRAGON PUBLISHING

Cover design and interior artwork by Carol Phillips

Library of Congress Control Number: 2015902895
ISBN-13: 978-1-941955-04-8
ISBN-10: 1-941955-04-5
ISBN (ebook): 978-1-941955-05-5

To Alexzandra and Michael.
For being you.

THE WORLD OF
ARINAR

Tolmaran Islands

SEA OF JADEN
JANSEN STRAIGHT

Ullan Desert

THE WEIRREN

Pendrian Wastes

The Narthvier

LIN GYLDWELLE

Ilorian Sea

ISLE OF GWRDYN

DENK SCARBOG

Spine of Orin

Lake EION

LAKE PADERAU

MOUNT MADRENE

RAVENWOOD

LAKE OSTER

CAER IDRIS

CELYN ERYRI

STONES OF KALDAAR

TALAITH

CAER DANURI

GAARENDAHL

Ankar

Summerlands

Danuri

Havisham

Provence

Sea Kingdom

Sturi

Chapter 1

DESTROYER. Betrayer. Lover. You are eternally mine.

A voice, deep with the rasp of one not accustomed to speaking, twisted in her thoughts. Shards of fear raked across her skin, leaving indelible marks visible only to her. Taryn scanned the room, forcing a bored expression while taking in every courtier, each servant. A slight flare to her nostrils was the only outward sign of distress as she fought to slow her breathing, to warm the ice chilling her veins.

Thrice now the voice had disturbed Taryn. Each time entreating her to find him, to be his, but Taryn had no idea who 'he' was. Fresh slivers tore her thoughts. That wasn't entirely true. She pressed a hand beneath her heart and took a long drag of air to calm her unsteady pulse.

"All is well, Taryn. I am well." Sabina's encouraging smile did little to help Taryn relax. "Have some tea." Her gentle voice held a hint of steel and Taryn knew better than to argue.

She sipped the tea Sabina handed her, hiding the shaking of her fingers beneath a shock of silvery hair. Sabina had every right to assume Taryn's anxious behavior stemmed from concerns about her health. After all, she'd rarely let Sabina out of her sight for the past several weeks, but that morning Sabina couldn't have been more wrong.

"We must not dwell upon the events at the Stones of

Kaldaar. You can't spend your days worrying over me. I am alive because of you. Now, you must turn your focus to other matters."

Despite her brave words, Taryn knew Sabina could never forget the horrors of that morning. Nor would Taryn ever forget the way the phantom had used Herbret as his living entity to rape two other women before nearly succeeding with Sabina. If Taryn and Hayden had been even a few minutes later—Taryn shuddered and squeezed her eyes shut against the memory. It should've been enough that they were able to save her friend, but she was haunted by the images of the innocent women Herbret and Celia callously destroyed.

To her knowledge, the court knew nothing of the attack except what Lliandra wanted them to know. The true events of that morning had been buried beneath a shining account of lies and propaganda, all of which made Marissa appear to be a hapless victim in Herbret and Celia's schemes. Taryn's role was downplayed to being nothing more than a convenient bystander.

Even so, everywhere she looked, accusatory stares and whispered innuendos followed her. The courtiers feared her more now than they ever had. Feeling sorry for herself would solve nothing. Fearing a nameless voice would help even less.

"You're absolutely right." Taryn set her cup aside and retrieved her playing cards. With a wink she knew wouldn't fool Sabina, but her friend playfully returned, she said, "Now, where were we? I believe I was walloping your arses in Pift."

The chill persisted regardless of the warmth of the room and she wrapped herself in a protective layer of ShantiMari. The rasp of the voice taunted her, the words lingering in spite of her efforts to replace them with cheerful volleys with her sisters. She fidgeted in her seat, staring without seeing the cards in her hand. The crowded room closed in on her, simultaneously suffocating and alienating her from the others. She had to get out of the palace before she lost her bloody mind.

Eliahnna placed a hand on Taryn, startling her. "Look what you've done."

Taryn's fingers had methodically shredded the once beautiful playing card and left the evidence of her unease scattered like confetti across the table. "Oh, sorry." She scooped the mess into her palm, folded her fingers tight, and with a flourish opened them. "Here." Taryn offered the restored card to Eliahnna.

"It's not the same, Taryn. It will never be the same." She stuck the offending square into the deck and shuffled. "Once ShantiMari touches something, it's forever altered."

Truer words were never spoken. The phantom had touched Taryn with his Black ShantiMari. She couldn't explain how or why and refused to speak of it, but before she banished the phantom, he'd reached into her soul and placed a chill that refused to abate. It was his voice she feared now mocked her thoughts. Somehow, he'd gained access to her without her knowledge or permission and she had no way of removing his presence. The court had good reason to be frightened. Whatever had happened at the Stones would alter everyone's lives and Taryn could neither protect them, nor comfort them.

"Taryn, it's your turn," Eliahnna prodded and Taryn placed a card on the table. "That's the wrong suit. Where is your mind, dear sister? Oh, look! It's stopped raining. Perhaps today you can visit the docks for Rhoane's gift." Eliahnna offered, her hand grazing the pendant she wore beneath her gown. Her ShantiMari made it invisible, but Taryn saw the telltale wisps of power encircling the snippet of wood.

She glanced out the huge windows that allowed for a view of the ocean and nodded. "I think I will. Do you want to come with me?"

"And meet an Artagh? I do!" Tessa jumped up to stand expectantly beside Taryn.

Always one for adventure, Tessa had been devastated to learn the others left without her Harvest morning. Taryn was glad Tessa hadn't seen the brutality of Herbret's attack on the young women. She was still young enough to believe in her own innocence and Taryn wanted to keep it that way for as long as possible.

Tessa pulled at her sleeve, a pleading look in her eyes. "Yes, fine. You can come along. Eliahnna? Sabina? Would either of you like to join us?"

Kaida stretched lazily, her tail thumping on the rug. She'd been cooped up in the palace far too long. They all had. It was time to shake off the past and move forward.

Sabina sniffed the air and frowned. "You should stay here, Taryn. But if you insist on going, take Baehlon."

"You know, since getting your ShantiMari, you're kind of bossy."

"It's only been three weeks. I'm fairly certain my power has nothing to do with my concern for your well-being." An impish smile marred Sabina's haughty look.

"You know, you're right. You've always been bossy." Taryn grinned at her friend. "Are you sure you don't want to come?"

"I promised Marissa we'd have tea. This business with Kaldaar upsets her still." Eliahnna answered with a shake of her head.

Tessa's face scrunched with a look of indecision. "But Taryn vanquished the phantom. Surely she isn't worried the banished god will return?"

"I think she mourns Celia, but Mother forbade her from speaking the name," Eliahnna said in a whisper.

"Should I stay? I would ever so like to meet an Artagh, but if our sister needs cheering, I will gladly accompany you." Tessa looked to Eliahnna for an answer.

For Tessa to give up the chance at adventure to raise Marissa's spirits tugged at Taryn's heartstrings. Her youngest sister was forever trying to win Marissa's love. "You stay, Tessa. I'm sure Marissa would appreciate your company. I'll take you to the docks another time."

"Promise?" Tears shimmered in her eyes.

"I promise." Taryn bent low to whisper in her ear, "Not only will I take you to the Artagh, we'll have lunch in a tavern."

Her sister's grin nearly reached each ear. Lliandra was too protective of her daughters. She rarely let them leave the palace, and when they did, made certain they had a royal guard. To dine in a tavern would never be allowed on Lliandra's watch.

Tessa held out her little finger. "Pinky promise." They intertwined their fingers and gave a firm shake. "You said that was stronger than any oath."

"It is." Taryn glanced around the room, looking for invisible dangers. "I think I'll visit Ebus first."

"He isn't there." Eliahnna gave her a meaningful glance. "I saw Tarro this morning. When he woke up, Ebus was gone."

After the attack at the Stones, when Carina found him unconscious, Lliandra had demanded to know who he was, and why he was there. Rhoane fabricated a lie that made Ebus a minor servant who was in the wrong place at the wrong time. Since he was discovered unconscious, Lliandra wasn't able to question him, but upon their return to the palace, she demanded Ebus be placed under arrest and imprisoned in the dungeons.

Instead of taking him to the dank cells, the captain of Lliandra's guard turned Ebus over to Baehlon, who hid the thief with the tailor. It was the last place the empress would think to look and a week later, when Lliandra inquired of the prisoner, she was told he'd died of his wounds and was given a pauper's burial.

A grin broke the seriousness of Taryn's features. Ebus was truly the most skilled spy she'd ever met. Not that she'd met many, but Ebus was gifted in being untraceable. He was most likely, at that very moment, somewhere in the palace.

"Then I suppose there's nothing preventing me from going. If you'll excuse me, I'm off to see an Artagh about a birthday gift."

She left her sisters, Kaida silent beside her, and was joined by Timor and Carina, two of her guards who had taken to shadowing her every move. She didn't mind the company, but their jittery looks and constant scanning of the streets and buildings put Taryn on edge. It was the first time since the attack she'd been out of the palace gates.

A chill whipped beneath her coat. The heaviness of summer had long since disappeared and with Harvest came shorter days and colder weather. Taryn welcomed the crisp air and took a deep breath, filling her lungs. She'd missed the hustle of people and the smell of the city filling her nostrils. The salty tang of the harbor competed with the sweet scents of fresh pastries from several bakeries; even the horse manure and body odor of those they passed refreshed her spirit.

She wasn't raised to be confined in a stodgy palace. Brandt had instilled a sense of adventure in her that couldn't be quelled, even if the walls around her were decorated with gold and silks.

"Your Highness." Carina nodded her chin at a nondescript building. "I believe your Artagh can be found here."

Taryn searched for a sign above the door but found none. Either Carina was wrong or the Artagh didn't want to advertise his presence. "Stay close," Taryn said before steeling herself for what lay beyond.

She pushed open the heavy door, made of rough-hewn

oak planks six inches thick. It creaked like a dying crow and Taryn winced. The sound reminded her of the feiches on the road to Paderau. The fetid stink of their blood assaulted her senses as assuredly as it had all those months ago.

A shortish man, in his late forties perhaps—or it might be early nineties, she could never tell—with long chestnut hair and a dour expression, squinted up from where he worked at a bench. He surveyed Taryn and her companions before snorting a grunt and continuing his work.

Whatever preconceived ideas Taryn had about Artaghs, the distant relatives of the Eleri, were dashed as she stood at the counter, patiently waiting. The man had the same delicate features as the Eleri, without the silky hair and barely pointed ears. Beneath his skin, she detected a muted shimmer, but it was nothing like Eleri Glamour. When he finally halted his work, he glanced at her, judgment clear in that one look.

"What do you want?" If a man could growl, Taryn was certain that's what he did.

"I'm in need of a special gift, and I'm told you are the only one who can accommodate me."

"I don't make trifles. Be gone with the lot of you." He waved his hand and bent his head back to his work. Cases filled the small room, stocked with easily concealed weapons. Displayed on a shelf were four ornately carved pendants, covered in glass and protected by a coating of ShantiMari.

Ignoring his obvious lie and rude behavior, she placed a sketch on the counter. "I would like you to craft this *cynfar*." Circular in shape and framed by a laurel wreath with a single diamond set in the center of a crystal plane, the image had come to her in a dream long before she'd met Rhoane, or even set foot on Aelinae. But she knew it belonged to her beloved. "It needs to be made out of godsteel."

Without looking at her sketch, he barked a laugh and Taryn wondered if Artagh were half-man, half-dog.

"Godsteel? What's a slip of a thing like you need with godsteel? Takes a mighty heart to control the mineral. What makes you think you can?"

"What makes you think I can't?" She laid her sword on the counter just to watch his response.

"Well, suck my balls. Heard a rumor you were in Talaith. Didn't believe it, did I? But then, Artagh aren't as taken with shiny things like the Eleri, so it makes no matter to me."

His hand reached lovingly for her sword, hovering just above it. Even an Artagh wouldn't touch Ohlin's blade.

"Can you pay?" He held out his grubby palm and Taryn counted out the coins he demanded.

"I need it in five days."

"Impossible."

She placed a gold crown on the countertop. "Not for a skilled artisan like yourself. Five days. Godsteel. You can do this, Sulein of the Lorn Clan."

His eyes widened and then narrowed to tiny slits. He bared pointed, yellow teeth at her; a low growl came from deep in his throat. "You do not call me this, witch."

Carina slowly removed her sword from its scabbard. "At ease," Taryn commanded her guard. Kaida sat beside her, ears pricked forward, eyes trained on the Artagh. "Sulein," Taryn purred, running her fingers along his jaw to the tip of his ear. She used the pads of her fingers and not the backs. Doing so would be a complete breach of Eleri/Artagh etiquette. As it was, she was certain the intimate gesture broke several forms of protocol.

His shudder started at his scalp and traveled to his bare feet. Overgrown toenails scraped the floor. "You do not have my consent to touch me." Even as he said the words, he swayed closer, inviting her to stroke his hair.

"I know." She leaned forward until she could smell the rankness of his breath, see the pores of his skin, and look into the depths of his soul. "But you want it all the same, yes?"

"Yes." The word slowly unraveled from his lips, lingering overlong on the last sibilance.

"Do this for me and you will have my gratitude."

He snapped out of his stupor and jerked his head from her touch, glaring at her with the hatred of his people. Theirs was a chaotic history, the Lorn Clan, one Taryn would unravel, but not that day. First, she needed him to make Rhoane's birthday gift.

"Five days," she insisted yet again.

"Your gold is all I need. You may keep your gratitude."

She straightened, a wide smile on her face. "I am honored." She lowered her head and winked at Kaida. That went far better than she'd hoped. He hadn't tried to turn her into a gargoyle, for a start.

As they exited the shop, Taryn spied the Artagh placing his hand over the spot she'd touched, a traitorous, wistful smile on his gruff features.

Timor scanned the buildings outside of Sulein's shop and scowled. "We should return to the palace, Your Highness."

"Not yet. I'd like to explore the docks a little." Her guards wore twin looks of apprehension and she laughed. "Seriously, the two of you need to lighten up. It looks like a storm is moving in and I'd like to enjoy my freedom for as long as possible." She angled toward the harbor, where dark clouds hovered several miles out to sea. A storm meant seclusion in the palace and that was the last thing Taryn needed.

She'd been in Talaith for several months and had yet to tour her hometown properly. The parade on her crowning day had given her a glimpse of the capital city, but Taryn longed to know every detail about the place. Timor and Carina followed her as she wove her way between stacks of crates down a narrow passageway. The cries of men shouting from the ships anchored in Talaith's huge harbor mingled with the sound of seagulls calling out to the flock. Taryn paused, letting the sounds and smells envelop her.

"Is something wrong?" Carina's hand went to the hilt of her sword.

"It's wonderful, isn't it? The city. Sweet spices and the brininess of the ocean. It reminds me of a place I visited many times before coming here." The memory of a trip she'd taken to Egypt with Brandt slammed against her thoughts and she reeled from the heartache of missing him.

An idea formed and she embraced the memory, sending a silent kiss to Dal Tara before she spun to face her guards, both of whom looked less pleased with the city than she did. "Didn't Tabul, the spice merchant in Paderau, say he had a brother in Talaith? Let's find him. We'll surprise Sabina with a gift from her homeland."

A movement to their left, followed by loud cursing and the sound of several boxes being knocked over, had Taryn and her guard unsheathing their swords. A man, tall, with dark skin and eyes that marked him from the Summerlands, stepped out from behind the mess with his hands held before him. "I'm unarmed. Don't hurt me."

His speech and features were familiar enough Taryn lowered her sword. "Why are you following me?"

"I am the spice merchant you seek. My brother Tabul asked that I watch over you should you ever leave the palace. When I received word you were in the city, I followed you here." He bowed his head and placed his right palm over his heart. "I am Adesh. Please. No swords."

Taryn signaled for Timor and Carina to sheathe their weapons. She held hers with a loose grip, wary. "Why would Tabul want me watched?"

Adesh glanced to his left, then right and shook his head. "Not here. Please. Follow me."

His long legs made short work of the distance from

the docks to his tent in the main marketplace. When they entered, a young boy scurried from the space, only to return moments later with tea for Taryn and the others. Curiosity danced in his large brown eyes.

Taryn thanked him in his language, using the opportunity to practice what Sabina had taught her. It wasn't much, but enough to offer gratitude to a young boy. A slight blush brightened his cheeks. Adesh dismissed him and sat with his legs crossed. A protective barrier of ShantiMari rose around them, ensconcing the group in a dome of privacy.

"Tabul was there the day you were attacked in Paderau. Since then, he has asked all of his brothers, some from blood, others by marriage, to learn what we can about the assassin. And you."

"But why?"

Adesh poured four cups of tea. "It is a special blend. You will enjoy, please." He waited for Taryn to take a sip before drinking from his own cup. "Tabul said you were kind to him in Paderau. You introduced him to our princess, who is most keen to help us with our taxation problem."

He lost Taryn on the last part. She'd have to ask Sabina about it later. "What have you found about the assassin?"

"Not much, I'm afraid. After the attack, he fled the city. There has been no sighting of him since." Adesh snorted. "But then, there won't be, will there? Not with his abilities." As if remembering himself, he bent forward, touching his head to the mat. "Forgive me, Your Highness."

"Adesh, please call me Taryn and always speak freely." She touched his arm and he glanced at her with a look of deference. His ShantiMari belied the look, swarming beneath her fingers with tempered savagery. She removed her hand, disturbed by what she'd experienced. "What do you mean, 'abilities'?"

"Through his connection with his master, the assassin is

able to see, hear, and smell, but his sole reason for existence is finding you. Without his master, he is nothing. Without his need to hunt you, he has no purpose. He feeds on fear. From you, people on the street, anyone near enough he can sense their anxiety. A great city like Talaith is a banquet for one like him. But you, Princess…to you, he is drawn like a mowbat to nectar. Your fear sustains him."

A protest rose to her lips, but she did fear him. More than she ever wanted to admit.

Adesh continued, taking her silence for acceptance. "When your betrothed fought him in Paderau, he bled. This should never happen. Yet it has. Your assassin draws life from you as easily as you draw breath. If you don't end him, he will destroy you."

Taryn jerked at the words, spilling her tea. She hadn't expected this from the spice merchant. The room darkened, the air becoming as thick and stagnant as the void. Her breathing deepened, her lungs laboring with each inhale. Scenes flashed through her mind, of a desolate world devoid of life, charred stumps of trees dotting the landscape. Plumes of smoke rising toward a charcoal sky.

You did this, the voice rasped in her mind. *You are the destroyer.*

Taryn rose from the mat on shaking legs. "I must go. Thank you, Adesh, for the tea." She rushed from the tent, not caring if the others followed, needing only to shut out the taunts. Outside, the boy stepped in her path, a hand outstretched, a pouch resting atop his palm.

"For our princess." He spoke Elennish. Then, in his native tongue, "Protection."

Taryn took the pouch and thanked him, but he darted off before she finished the words. Carina and Timor joined her, scowls on their faces. Kaida silently padded down the street, sniffing the air. Adesh's words had rattled not just Taryn, it appeared. She tucked the pouch into her pocket, not quite knowing if the boy meant her or Sabina, and followed the grierbas toward the palace.

A familiar tingling from her pendant preceded a chill running up her neck. A heartbeat before she saw the hooded figure in the shadows, Kaida lunged.

Chapter 2

A BRIEF glimpse of terror crossed the assassin's pale face before he disappeared. Kaida darted after him and clambered up a crate, snarling with every vicious snap of her jaw. Carina and Timor raced to where the assassin had been, with Taryn a step behind. She clearly saw the dark outline of his body as he pulled himself over the ledge of the roof.

Timor reached the rooftop first and paced along the shingled edge, sputtering curses. Carina joined him while Taryn helped Kaida up the empty stretch between the crate and building. The city sprawled out before them, a kaleidoscope of colorful tents mixed with drab shingled structures and dun-colored thatched roofs. One thing caught Taryn's attention—the rooftop's emptiness. Not even the silhouetted form was in sight.

She scanned the sky, looking for a bird that might be the assassin, knowing full well even if she spotted him, there was nothing she could do to follow.

"Fuck!" she screamed at the dark clouds that hovered just above their heads, perfect camouflage for someone wishing to escape unseen. "I don't fear you. Do you hear me? You or your master." The last she said more to herself, willing the words to be true.

"Princess." Carina eyed the threatening sky. "We should

return to the safety of the palace."

If anything happened to the Eirielle, it was Carina's life on the line, Taryn knew. But there was an urgency beneath her warning that went beyond the weather. For once, Taryn didn't argue. Adesh's words tumbled through her thoughts, chilling her. The assassin fed off her fear. She was his banquet. Yet how did she stop herself from fearing a demon?

Where did he come from? she asked Kaida.

He has been tracking us since the docks.

Taryn glared at the animal. "Why didn't you tell me?"

Kaida returned the look, an intensity to her golden eyes that disturbed Taryn. *I wished to know what he wanted. He was observing, nothing more. I will not let him harm you.*

Kaida would do everything in her power to stop the assassin, but what could a grierbas do that the others could not? It was far too easy for the assassin to find her and far too difficult for her to follow him.

As much as she hated to admit it, she couldn't rely on the others for her safety, which meant she had to overcome her fear and do what was necessary to control her Dark ShantiMari.

They walked quickly, without drawing attention, through the marketplace and up the hill to the palace gates. Once through, Taryn took a deep breath and released some of the tension she'd been holding. Instead of going inside, she directed them toward the gardens, pacing along the seawall, orienting her thoughts.

She'd been surprised by Adesh's admission that Tabul had people following her movements and shocked to learn he knew about the assassin. He knew, in fact, more about him than Taryn did. There was more to the spice merchant, much more, and she was going to find out everything she could.

Carina interrupted her pacing with a gentle, yet firm placement of her body in Taryn's path. "Your Highness, I know you are trying to be brave, but please, you must tell Prince Rhoane and Sir Baehlon. As your guard, we are honor bound to you, but your safety is our concern."

"If I tell them, they'll just double the watch on me, and I'm sure it's no fun following me around all day."

The guard's frown served as an answer. They were of equal height and similar build, which made them excellent sparring partners in the training ring. From Taryn's earliest days at Paderau, before she or anyone else knew her true identity, she'd trained with Carina and earned the woman's respect. When Duke Anje handpicked Carina to accompany Taryn to Talaith as her personal guard, it was with a sense of relief on Taryn's part that her friend would accompany her.

As she stood in front of Timor and Carina, she was thankful they answered to her and not her mother, which meant as long as she stayed alive, whatever happened would stay between the three of them. Except Taryn knew she'd stretched their loyalty by chasing the assassin.

From the other side of the garden, Rhoane approached and by the look of thunder on his face, he knew where she'd been and what transpired.

Taryn pierced her guards with an accusatory glare. "How does he know?"

"Not by me, I swear it to you," Timor said, placing his hand over his heart.

"Nor me." Carina echoed the gesture. The two stepped behind Taryn but stayed close in case they were needed.

Feigning ignorance, Taryn greeted Rhoane in a cheery voice. "Good day, my beloved."

"What the hell are you about? Sneaking off to the docks?" He scowled at Carina and Timor. "With so few of your guard? Where is Baehlon? Does he know you left the palace grounds?"

Kaida sat at Rhoane's side, her tail thumping expectantly.

"I hear it was you who saved the princess today," Rhoane said, kneeling to scratch Kaida behind her ears. He put his head against hers, holding her for a moment before standing to confront Taryn. "If my sources are correct, Kaida chased off the assassin before any harm could come to you."

The cold grip of anger crept up her spine. "If you have so many spies watching my every move, I don't really need a guard, now do I?"

"He was not watching you."

"Oh."

Rhoane addressed her guard, his voice low, full of authority. "If I hear of you allowing the princess to leave without my knowledge again, I will personally see to your punishment."

Carina swallowed hard and said, "With all due respect, Your Highness, we take our orders from Princess Taryn."

Taryn stifled a laugh. "Carina, you are so getting a raise." To Rhoane, she said, "I appreciate the thought, but you don't have to threaten my guards. I won't need to leave the palace again for a while and when I do, I'll be sure to let my babysitter know."

He moved closer to her, saying in Eleri, "You are far too careless of your safety."

Anxiety clouded his eyes and she responded in his language. "I had hoped the danger was gone. I am sorry." Since the attack at the Stones, Rhoane had taken to speaking to her almost exclusively in Eleri. She understood far more than she could speak, which generally worked in her favor, but not so much when Rhoane was angry and his words came in a clipped rush, as they did then.

Kaida's ears perked forward, a low growl deep in her throat. A moment later, she raced toward the orchard.

"Stay here," Rhoane commanded before sprinting after her.

Taryn ignored him, following close behind, her guards on her heels. As they neared the orchard, Taryn heard Rhoane whispering to Ebus. She motioned for Carina and Timor to wait. "There's no danger, but keep watch all the same."

Kaida sat patiently by Rhoane's leg with her eyes trained on the thief. "I told you to stay with the others," the Eleri prince snapped.

"You cannot keep trying to protect me by leaving me out of things," she retorted, hands on hips, her jaw set.

Ebus interrupted them with a dramatic clearing of his throat. "If you're going to argue, and not even in a language I understand, I have better things to be doing."

"Yes, like resting until you're well enough to continue your duties." Taryn knew better than to expect Ebus to sit around all day, but he'd come too close to death and even Faelara wasn't sure what ailed him.

The phantom had knocked him unconscious, but more than that, Taryn suspected Celia and Herbret had bled the little man. When they found him at the Stones, he had several deep slashes on his arms. Ebus had no memory of the events that day, remembering only the previous morning when he'd spoken to her at breakfast. Even when she prompted him, there remained a blank space in his timeline.

He cut her a glare, but there was little malice in his eyes. "I was bored. Do you wish to continue discussing my restoration, or perhaps you might like to know the assassin has left the city?"

"Are you certain? Where has he gone?" Rhoane asked.

"I followed him to a boarding house near the docks. There, he spoke with his master for a few minutes. After that, he shifted into a bird and flew off to the north."

Irritated Ebus could follow him when she could not, but not willing to let Rhoane know how far she'd gone to pursue the assassin, she directed the conversation toward identifying the one controlling the assassin. "Were you able to hear the conversation?"

"Only part, Great Lady. I did garner that he has a wound slow in healing and is terrified of your grierbas."

"Did you happen to see how it was the assassin spoke to his master?" Taryn asked. "Why wouldn't they just use a more private method?" She tapped her temple. "In here."

"Your assassin might be deadly, but he isn't too gifted, if you know what I mean. I doubt he's all there in the head."

"Could you recognize the sound of his master's voice?" This was the break they needed to uncover the master's identity.

"Nay, it was tempered, as if someone were speaking through a door. I'm sorry."

"Thank you for your help, Ebus." Defeat leaked into her voice. She rested her hand on his shoulder and his Dark Shanti swirled under her fingertips. Mutated and twisted—not Aelan or Eleri, it sparked a similar sense of unease as Adesh's had, yet it wasn't suppressed, just…wrong. Like Sabina's had been before the attack.

Out of habit, she sent a healing thread of her own power through Ebus. He was nearly mended, with only a slight bruising on his skull where they'd knocked him unconscious. A stain, blurred but perceptible, pressed against her ShantiMari.

"I don't do this out of charity. It's your gold I value." He jerked away from her touch and trotted off a few feet before disappearing.

Taryn searched the area, her gaze roving over the trees. A black silhouette of his form moved nimbly from one branch to another until he was out of sight. "I think I know how the assassin can appear and disappear on command."

Rhoane glanced at her, concern tight in his features. "Were you able to follow Ebus just now?"

"Sort of." What she saw, or rather, didn't see, worried her. Before the ordeal at the Stones, she hadn't been able to see the assassin when he vanished. But that morning on the docks, she was certain the silhouetted form *was* the assassin "disappearing." Same with Ebus just then.

How they made their body become a dark shimmering outline that blended into the surrounding area, she had to find out. If it was a trick of the Dark, perhaps she could use the power to follow the assassin. And if it wasn't? The thought burned through her sternum. If it wasn't the Dark, then she shouldn't be able to see it at all. A shudder of revulsion coursed through her veins, chilling her.

Rhoane stepped close, his hands resting on her shoulders before sliding down her arms. He placed his forehead against hers. "You frightened me today." His caress was hesitant but full of yearning. Since returning to Talaith, and after what happened at the Stones, he'd spent as much time with her as he could, touching her as much or as often as she would allow. It was his unspoken apology and Taryn accepted everything he gave her.

She tilted her head until her lips met his. The tremble of desire that always flared at his touch coursed through her. Her ShantiMari spun in a controlled tempest. Rhoane's hands tangled in her long silvery hair, coaxing her closer until her body melded into his. Heat scorched her in the most delicious way.

Her nails scratched up his neck to the tips of his ears but skimmed past the sensitive area to rake through his hair. She toyed with the tightly woven braids, the need to loosen them and stroke his tresses strong. Never before had she understood his fascination with her hair until his had grown out in silken waves that tempted her each time she looked at him. The feel of his locks on her flesh made her ache to be wrapped in his arms, skin on skin, their bodies a tangle of passion.

Rhoane's lips parted, inviting her in, and she grazed his tongue with hers, tasting him. Tart apples and mint. Rhoane. She sighed a moan, delighting in the feel of his erection against her thigh. Her nipples hardened against the leather tunic she wore and even that roughness felt good. So good.

Their power circled them—his moss green, hers every color of the rainbow.

A polite clearing of a throat brought Taryn out of her lust-filled fog. She glanced behind her to where Timor and Carina stood with their backs to them. Kaida whined toward the palace and Taryn spied the group that approached.

Her mother had the worst timing and she was in no mood to be scolded yet again by the empress.

"Unless you want a royal lecture, we should make like Ebus and disappear," Taryn joked.

"But we have neither the skill nor knowledge of how he did so." If not for the sincerity in his voice, Taryn would've laughed.

"We'll talk about that later. Let's go." They ducked under the sargot trees, bereft of their delicious fruit in the chill weather, and managed to avoid her mother by entering the palace on the far side of the garden. At the entrance to the great room, Baehlon intercepted them and Taryn steeled herself for his reprimand.

"Faelara would like to see you, Rhoane. She wants to discuss Taryn's lesson for this evening." His almond-shaped eyes were like slivers of burnt cedar as he glowered at her. "If the princess wouldn't mind, I would like to know what transpired on the docks this morning."

Taryn refrained from rolling her eyes, but she did cast him a baleful glance. He didn't have to make everything a bigger deal than it was, and yet he did.

"Actually, I have some information you might find fascinating. Give me about a bell, and then I'll meet you at

Faelara's and share what I learned on my outing." She pivoted toward the library. "Ask Hayden and Sabina to join us."

Rhoane caught her hand. "You will not leave the palace again?" The fear lurking in the depths of his eyes cut her heart and she staggered at the realization she had to stop thinking only of herself and remember he cared for her. The wounds of the past few months were slow to heal.

"I promise." Her lips brushed his and even that slight touch inflamed her blood. His ShantiMari slipped up her arms, caressing her, and she fought off the desire to skip the meeting and take Rhoane to her rooms. Again she hesitated. They had yet to share their bodies and Taryn was to blame. Damn her apprehension and fear of her own power. "I'm going to the library, that's all."

He stroked her cheek with the back of his hand and grazed the tip of her ear. Her uncontrolled shiver brought a smile to his lips, but concern remained in his steady gaze. "Would you like me to accompany you?"

"I would, but Faelara is waiting and I won't be long. Go. I'll join you soon." She pushed his chest playfully and he relented.

Kaida trotted at her side, with Carina and Timor following a few paces behind. Despite their closeness, Taryn was alone. Vulnerable. The Shadow Assassin was in the city and no one could keep her safe.

Chapter 3

THE storm that threatened all morning finally broke, sending a deluge of rain cascading down the library's thick glass windows, casting eerie shadows in the already darkened room. The familiar scent of musty books greeted Taryn when she entered the small space she'd once claimed as her own. Scrolls and scraps of paper no longer littered the large table she'd used as a desk. All of her quills and ink jars now sat on the desk in her rooms. She missed the quiet of the library but required the privacy and security of her apartments.

She ignored the pang of longing and searched the stacks for a scroll she remembered from a previous search, trying to recall if the parchment was in the library or Tessa's hidden stash. The morning of the attack at the Stones, Tessa had proved to be an asset. While the others were away, she'd snuck into Celia's rooms and removed most of the documents the girl had taken from the library, cleverly hiding them in a trunk at the back of her dressing room.

Tessa's quick thinking had secured the documents; later that afternoon, Lliandra had Celia's rooms emptied and her personal items packed and given away—to whom, Taryn didn't know. By the following morning, it was as if Celia had never existed. Every scrap of paper was taken to the library, where they were dutifully catalogued and returned to the stacks.

Before the empress sent Herbret's belongings to his family south of Talaith, Tessa searched his rooms as well and found a curious dagger she placed amongst the papers. Much later, after the funerals and feasts, Tessa shared with the others what she'd discovered. Eliahnna spent bells copying the texts before she and Taryn returned the scrolls to the library. The copies she hid in her rooms, where she could read them at her leisure. She needed to understand what prompted two of Lliandra's courtiers to commit such a heinous act of treason.

With Myrddin out of town, Rhoane took the dagger for further study. Ancient, with etchings on the blade similar to the Seal of Ardyn and Taryn's sword, he suspected there was more to the dagger than it simply being a weapon.

Learn the words had echoed in her mind when she held the dagger.

"Learn the words," Taryn said aloud to the empty room. "That's what I'm trying to do, you fickle gods."

Her hand hovered above a shelf as she scanned her memory for what Tessa had taken from Celia's rooms. Confident the item she sought was not there, she resumed her search amidst the dusty papers.

Once found, she returned to her rooms and tossed the scroll on her desk. Several hastily scrawled notes she'd written to herself lay atop a stack of parchments she'd been meaning to read. The list never got shorter, always longer.

She sat at her desk and carefully unrolled the first paper. As she read, she made several notations on a blank sheet. Only after reviewing her notes did she realize she'd written in English. Even after more than four months in this new world, it was a hard habit to break.

Frustrated, she threw the quill on the table and rubbed her eyes. The meeting with the others was in a few minutes and she was no closer to understanding how the assassin manipulated shadows than she'd been a bell earlier. If it was a trick of the Dark, Duke Anje would've told her about it. Or perhaps not. He claimed to be too long in the Light to remember much. But surely Hayden would know. Then again, maybe not. He was, after all, raised by Anje and Gwyneira at the Light Court.

Myrddin might know, but he was off on an errand for the empress. To date, she'd not consulted with him, for no other reason than pride. Myrddin's quiet confidence intimidated her. Once he returned, she'd seek him out, explain everything she'd learned and beg him to help. He claimed his ShantiMari was too antiquated for what she required, which was probably true, but a man who had lived as long as he had would surely know something, anything.

She rubbed her eyes and leaned back in the chair. No amount of Myrddin's help, or anyone else's, could hide the fact she needed a high-ranking noble who understood all the facets of Dark ShantiMari intimately. She needed her brother or father.

Even though Rhoane agreed she should seek them out, Taryn stalled. The letters asking permission to visit sat on her desk, unsent. She couldn't bring herself to send them, even though it was the only way to unlock all of her powers. Her arguments were many and varied, but all centered around a common theme—Zakael and Valterys frightened her far more than the Shadow Assassin ever had.

For all she knew, they were behind the demon trying to kill her.

If she went to them unprepared, she'd be unable to stop them from overpowering her and using her for only the gods knew what.

Her hand shook as she raised a cup of tea to her lips. The altercation at the Stones of Kaldaar had left her changed. Not necessarily in a good way. The dark cold never left her. Even wrapped in a fur blanket and sitting in front of a fire, a tiny chill spread from her heart to her thoughts. It was infinite, the blackness inside her. As expansive as the void.

"Your Highness?" Ellie stood beside her, a warm hand on Taryn's arm. "It's time for your meeting."

Taryn shook the gloomy thoughts from her mind and forced a smile. "Yes, it is." She placed her hand over the girl's and the small amount of ShantiMari Ellie had vibrated beneath her touch. Ellie's power was slight but fierce. On impulse, Taryn rose and kissed the girl's cheek. "Thank you, Ellie."

The maid blushed a furious shade of crimson, a confused smile on her lips. "For what?"

"For believing in me."

It was Ellie who made Taryn see that being the Eirielle was more than just an obligation. On that day, so long ago it seemed now, when Taryn was given the title Keeper of the Stars and Nadra had placed the elaborate moonstone and stardust crown on Taryn's head, Ellie had confided in Taryn that in all the world, there was no one finer to wear the mantle.

Taryn hadn't believed in herself that day, nor for many days after. Not until Sabina's life was threatened did Taryn start to truly believe she could be what Aelinae expected of her. But doubts continued to dog her confidence.

"Always, my lady." Ellie curtseyed low to the ground before rising slowly to kiss her thumb and place it over her heart.

"I won't be long. Let Kaida rest. If the rain lets up, will you take her outside?"

"Of course." Kaida lay snoring on a thick rug in front of the fire, her paws twitching with her dreams, and Taryn couldn't bring herself to disturb the grierbas. "Be safe."

Ellie's words haunted Taryn as she hurried to Faelara's

apartments. How could she be safe in a world where people could appear and disappear on command? When she was hunted by an unseen demon controlled by someone who, at that very moment, might be within a hand's reach of her?

"You look as foul-tempered as the weather. What has you so despondent, my sister?" Marissa's cheery tone did nothing to alleviate Taryn's mood. To date, she'd managed to avoid her older sister, but like her trip West, knew it couldn't be postponed forever.

"Marissa," Taryn drawled, her quick gaze taking in the group of women twittering behind the crown princess, "you're positively glowing. Your visit with Tessa and Eliahnna must've done you good."

A minute frown tugged her sister's lips toward the ground for just a moment before Marissa recovered. "Yes, you were missed. I do hope you'll come visit sometime soon. We really should be allies, my darling." She grasped Taryn's hands and squeezed a little too hard. "We've so much in common, you and I. Please say you will."

Marissa's ShantiMari was off. The same calculated coolness she'd felt numerous times before was hampered by an entity Taryn couldn't quite define. The persistent chill spread through her, but it came from Marissa's grasp. Shocked, Taryn realized the phantom had touched Marissa as surely as he'd afflicted her. The sword sang softly in her mind, its dulcet tones those of mourning.

Since the encounter at the Stones, her sword had yet to sing a joyful tune. Most days Taryn tuned it out, but right then she listened carefully to the melody. Three words echoed in her thoughts—betrayal, darkness, forgiveness. The last gave Taryn pause. The sword urged her to forgive Marissa?

"Yes, I will. Thank you." Taryn leaned in to kiss her sister and breathed in the scent of her. Lilies and lye. Her lips touched Marissa's cheek and her sister flinched. "I look forward to it."

Marissa clearly hadn't expected Taryn to agree to a visit. She blustered to her ladies-in-waiting something about being late for an appointment and rushed off in the opposite direction. Taryn turned away from her sister's hasty retreat to catch the wry smiles her guards tried to hide.

Hayden and Sabina were waiting for her when she arrived at Faelara's rooms. By the looks on their faces, they had been discussing her errand that morning and were not pleased. She sat through half a bell of recriminations not only from the pair, but Faelara and Baehlon as well. Rhoane stayed silent, having already voiced his displeasure that morning.

"Fine. Okay," Taryn said when she couldn't take one more dramatic sigh or feigned snarl of anger, "I'm sorry I left the palace without alerting Baehlon. I won't make that mistake again. Ever. But really, there are more important issues to discuss here. Like, what's going on with the taxes on the Summerlands?"

Sabina took the change of subject in stride. "From what I can discern, Lliandra's not just taxing our goods, but Danuri's goods as well. Although, not to the same extent. She has serious levies attached to spices, textiles, and lime coming from the Summerlands. Danuri is only being taxed on their liquid resources."

"What does the king have to say about the taxes?" Baehlon asked.

"He has issued an edict to prevent Lliandra from charging more for our supplies, but she's ignoring him. I'm not sure if this is punishment for my choosing Hayden over Herbret, or if she truly wants war, but my father will not ignore this blatant extortion."

Hayden sat with one leg resting atop the other, his long fingers stroking the beginnings of a beard. "I broached the topic in council this past week and was met with silence.

What I don't know is if the other members are aware of this illegal taxation, or if Lliandra is doing this on her own. I've tried to meet with several members, but they're being cagey."

"What I've been able to uncover," Sabina started with an apologetic look to Hayden, "is she's granted a special dispensation to Ulla to trade with merchants from both Cacr Idris and Haversham."

"What would the Artagh want with Ullan goods?" Faelara mused. "And why Valterys?"

"Do you think they are forging an alliance? Perhaps the threat of Kaldaar's return has Lliandra more frightened than she'd like to admit. These are his lands, after all, and he's been gone a long time," Taryn offered.

"Nadra would never let him interfere with the Light Throne. No, there must be something in Caer Idris Lliandra needs. Same with Haversham, Danuri, and the Summerlands. Except she is trying to weaken the latter, but why?" Rhoane traced the runes on his hand, a frown pinching his brows dangerously close together.

"Hayden, is there anyone on the council you trust?"

Her cousin smirked at the question. "Not with my life, but there are a few who I'm sure I could compel into friendship if that's what you're suggesting."

Sixteenth bells chimed and Faelara stood suddenly. "I must help the empress dress for dinner." A glimmer of panic crossed her pretty features. "Since the Stones, she's kept me on a short leash." At Taryn's hopeful look, she said, "No, darling, I can't get any information from her. She barely speaks to me as it is, yet insists I be there to help with the preparations. I'm doing all I can to get back into her good graces in the hope we'll learn something. Anything."

"I'm sorry, Faelara," Taryn said with genuine concern. When Lliandra learned Faelara had known Taryn was researching Kaldaar and didn't share the information with her, she'd been livid. At Taryn, at Faelara, at Rhoane, and even Baehlon. No one was spared her anger. But it was Faelara who bore the brunt of the empress's punishment. Lliandra effectively demoted her, making her duties on par with a servant most of the time; other times, she was little more than a lady-in-waiting.

"Not to worry, my love. All will be well in time. If you'll excuse me?" Faelara rushed from the room.

When the door clicked shut, Taryn said to no one in particular, "Lliandra will pay for what she's doing to Faelara. She was only trying to help."

"Yes, help *you*, Taryn, not the empress." Sabina's ShantiMari whizzed around her in a frenzy. A dark shadow lined the deep brown threads. Taryn stared at her friend's Mari, an uncomfortable realization taking shape. "What is it, Taryn? You look like you've seen death himself."

"I just recalled I promised Marissa I would meet with her. Will you excuse me?" She said her goodbyes, giving hugs to Hayden and Baehlon, and a kiss to Rhoane. To Sabina, she whispered, "Come to my rooms after dinner. We need to talk."

Taryn hastened to Marissa's rooms, turning over what she'd witnessed, an idea forming that excited and disturbed her. She arrived at the painted doors edged with real gold and knocked softly. When no one answered, she knocked again, louder. Even if Marissa were out, a maid should be present, but no one appeared. Taryn turned the ornate handle and pushed open the door several inches.

"Hello?" she called out to the empty air. The hairs on the back of her neck stood to attention, but her pendant and sword remained silent. Taking that as a good sign, she sidled into the room and closed the door behind her.

In the sitting room, two of Marissa's maids lay on the sofa, unmoving. Her heart bumped against her ribcage as she bent to check their pulses. She saw no obvious signs of trauma, but a telltale thread of Marissa's ShantiMari hovered over them both. Her sister had put the maids to sleep on purpose, but why? Taryn had heard the rumors of what Marissa did with her ladies, the sexual exploits and games of pleasure. Surely there was nothing she had to hide from them.

Her breath caught. Whatever Marissa was doing, if she wished to keep it from her maids, Taryn needed to know.

She crept to her sister's bedroom and listened for several moments before discerning it was empty. As she was about to leave, a moan came from the balcony. The curtains whipped against the open doors and Taryn padded through the lavishly decorated room. Golden candelabra and chandeliers held candles that glowed softly, illuminating the huge bed covered in stark white damask and framed by crimson velvet panels. An image of marble and blood assaulted Taryn, and she looked away.

Marissa's ShantiMari glinted from every surface, its lavender hue laced with inscriptions. Each time she focused on a thread, the image would fade, but she was certain words were woven into the powerful wards. Her hands twitched with a desire to touch the threads and she balled them into fists, keeping them close to her body.

Marissa moaned again, louder, more urgently. Taryn hid behind the curtain and peered through a gap, suppressing a gasp at the sight before her.

Her sister hovered above the floor, her naked skin dusted with a smattering of black glitter. Rain slashed through the air, battering the palace walls relentlessly, but Marissa was oblivious of the raging storm. A cocoon of ShantiMari enveloped her, protecting her from the wind and cold. She writhed in the empty air, her arms clasping at nothing, her leg hitched at an awkward angle.

Vomit roiled in Taryn's gut. She'd vanquished the

phantom. It couldn't possibly be the same one. And yet, if it wasn't, that meant there was more than one. She blinked back tears and swallowed the acrid bile that rose in her throat. She squinted, focusing on a faint, barely perceptible outline of black amid the swirling motes of rain and glitter. The phantom, Taryn was certain of it. From her sister's movements and the sounds of desire she made, they were having sex.

A compulsion she couldn't deny forced her to watch. Violent in its scope, the coercion immobilized her, sending painful shocks of heat throughout her body. Taryn twisted as much as she was allowed, but it wasn't enough. Her sister's head jerked from side-to-side, her heavy breasts swayed against her quivering body. The sound of slapping echoed off the stone walls. Red welts marred Marissa's buttocks in the shape of a man's hand. Her sister cried out several times, not quite screams, but close, and then shuddered with a revolting display of satisfaction. Taryn gagged. Marissa knew how to use her body. A little too well.

"Show me." Marissa panted. "Now."

A terrible growl came from the invisible lover. Not human. Not animal. Otherworldly.

Marissa nodded intently, her focus on a spot several inches before her. "Yes, yes, and then?" A wide smile broke out on her face. "I see." She flourished her wrist and a thread of lavender ShantiMari swirled around her. It was edged in black.

Then, to Taryn's astonishment, Marissa's feet disappeared, followed by her legs, her torso, and finally, her head. The same hazy silhouette was all that remained of her sister.

A triumphant laugh came from the empty air. "My exquisite lover, you shall be rewarded."

The compulsion released Taryn with a slithering discharge that left her drained of energy, of thought, of emotion.

Instead of fleeing, she stayed rooted in place and watched, fascinated, as the two contours merged and separated time and again. Taryn studied the coupling with scientific scrutiny, noting every movement, every inflection of shadow within the space. When finally Marissa screamed at yet another climax, Taryn had gleaned information on not only the elusive "disappearing", but her sister and the invisible lover as well. Marissa released her cloaking shadows and tossed her long curls. A dusting of glitter shimmered a glow of deepest night before subsiding.

Only after Marissa commanded the phantom to be gone and disappeared into her dressing chamber did Taryn dart for the door. Once in the hallway, she leaned against the wall until her heartbeat calmed and ragged breathing leveled. A few servants scurried past, keeping their gazes lowered, some making a figure eight above their heads.

Unsure of what, exactly, she'd witnessed, Taryn started toward Faelara's rooms. After several steps, she stopped. Too many questions begged for an answer and only Marissa could provide them. She spun around and knocked on her sister's door.

A disheveled maid answered and bade her wait in the small foyer. Marissa arrived a few moments later, dressed in a simple gown, the glow Taryn noticed earlier shimmering brighter. The black glitter was all but gone from her skin.

When she saw Taryn, her eyes brightened with a dangerous glint. "Sister, please come in." She motioned to the sofa where her maids had been passed out. "Sit. I'll have Marina bring us some tea. Would you like anything else? You look a bit flushed. Perhaps some broth?"

"No, thank you, I'm fine."

Marissa sent the maid away before sitting beside Taryn. "My dear, you are anything but fine." She twisted a strand of Taryn's silvery hair around her finger and pulled Taryn's face closer to hers. "Did you enjoy watching?"

Taryn's breath stilled and her heart stopped for two heartbeats.

"I know he enjoyed having you there. He wants you, and he always gets what he wants."

The compulsion returned, stronger than before. "Who is he?"

Marissa's cruel laugh cut the thick air. "I don't know. Nor do I care. He gives me something no one else can." She released Taryn's hair and traced a finger down her tunic to her breast. "He is my god." Marissa's voice held a dreaminess Taryn didn't recognize. "Right now he's weak. When you vanquished him, it nearly destroyed him."

Her lovely lavender eyes met Taryn's. "We could overpower him, you and I. Think about it, Taryn. The power we would wield. It's greater than Zakael ever dreamed."

Desperate fanaticism edged Marissa's words and features.

A part of Taryn yearned for the phantom's touch. Yearned to feel Black ShantiMari slip around her naked body, dusting her with its power. That part of herself terrified Taryn.

Marissa's face was an inch from her own, flushed still from her encounter, with that eerie glow emanating around her. "You want this, Taryn. I can sense your desire. I saw it in the way you watched with absolute longing." Her eyes narrowed and she grinned like a feral cat come upon a barge rat. "He will have you, in the end. You are the vessel he craves. Sabina was nothing but a distraction."

Anger sparked in Taryn, but she kept her face blank, her breathing even. "He will never have me. I vanquished him once. I'll do it again. Now that I know he is weakened, I'll find him and destroy him for good."

"You poor, simple girl. He can't be found. He is everywhere and nowhere. Even I don't know how to summon him." A look of panic flickered in her eyes for a brief moment, and then was gone. She'd given away too much.

"Why are you telling me this? What do you want from me?" The compulsion made her thoughts sluggish and hard to form into words.

Marissa's pink tongue darted out and stroked Taryn's lips. Her sister's touch revolted Taryn, and she jerked away, but her body wouldn't cooperate. Whatever had her in its grip forced her mouth open for more. The taste of sweet wine teased the bile rising in her throat. The sensual warmth of her sister's kiss left her dizzy. When Marissa ended the kiss, the compulsion lifted, again coating her with a layer of filth and leaving her weary.

"We are more alike than you'd care to admit, Taryn. Someday you'll know this is true. As for what I want from you, isn't it obvious?"

Taryn shook her head and flexed her fingers, testing her flailing energy.

"I want what everyone wants from you. Your power."

A blur of silver studded with sapphires plunged deep into her midsection, ripping skin and muscle. Taryn staggered to her feet, jerking the blade free. The pain drained what little strength she had left, but she kept moving forward, away from Marissa. Her sister sat on the sofa, laughing and calling taunts to her as she stumbled, disoriented.

Rhoane, help me.

Blood seeped from the wound, over her hand, to drip onto the thick carpets.

Hayden.

Her boots thudded on tile and she lunged for the door, her vision narrowing as she fumbled with the doorknob, her hands slick.

Baehlon. Faelara.

Finally, she managed to grasp it enough to yank open. Marissa's laughter burrowed like a worm into her mind;

confusion muddled her thoughts. *Why, Marissa?* But no answer came to her.

Brandt, I need you. Please.

She stumbled into the empty hallway, blinking at her surroundings.

Sabina. Please hurry.

The light from the wall sconces hurt her eyes and she turned away from the glare. Her rooms were at the far end of the palace, away from Marissa. She focused on setting one foot in front of the other, making slow progress. Stars teased the outer edges of her sight.

Kaida.

The sound of footsteps approaching spurred Taryn to move faster. Marissa was coming to finish what she'd started. She had to get away from her sister.

The last of her strength gave way and she collapsed, a discordant ringing in her ears the final thing she heard.

Chapter 4

RHOANE sprang from the comfortable chair and sprinted toward the outer room, ignoring the cries of his companions. He'd no more than reached the door to Faelara's suite when Baehlon joined him, his face full of concern. A moment later, Hayden and Sabina were rushing through the palace as well. They raced down the hallway, dodging servants and courtiers, Rhoane swearing at both. Taryn's call had been faint, but full of urgency.

He took the stairs two at a time, vaulting over the banister at the top. From close behind he heard Baehlon grunt, but kept up his pace. Rounding the corner to Taryn's apartments, Rhoane almost tripped over Kaida, who lay curled around an unmoving Taryn. Terror-fueled dread gripped his heart, but his mind cautioned patience.

Rhoane knelt beside his betrothed and smoothed the hair from her face, searching for signs of trauma. No visible marks could be seen. He placed two fingers along her neck, relief flooding him at the faint pulse of her heart. It skipped several beats but was constant enough. Strained breathing came out between white lips.

The others crowded around him.

"Is she alive?" Sabina asked, between gasps of air.

"She lives, yes. Baehlon, help me get her inside."

Sabina opened Taryn's door and he and Baehlon gently lifted Taryn from the floor, making certain not to jostle her overmuch. Saeko rushed toward them, and then, seeing her mistress in his arms, hurried to Taryn's bedchamber to pull down her blankets. Rhoane set Taryn on the soft sheets and bent to kiss her forehead. A chill passed from her skin to his lips and he shuddered.

Taryn moaned, her hands grasping her abdomen. Kaida bounded onto the bed before Rhoane could stop her.

Faelara arrived as Rhoane lifted Taryn's tunic. "Taryn called for me." She arched over Taryn to inspect her belly. "Was she injured? I see nothing."

Taryn's eyelids fluttered open and she looked from one worried face to another. "Am I dead?"

Ellie ran into the room, panting.

"I'm sorry, my lady. Kaida ran off and I chased her, but she was too fast." When she saw the gathered group, she stopped her apology. "Has something happened?"

"That is what we are trying to discover." Rhoane beckoned Ellie to wait with the others and turned to speak softly to Taryn. "Can you tell us what caused you to call out?"

One hand absently stroked Kaida and the other patted her midsection. A look of confusion muddied the deep blue of her eyes. A moment later, panic cut across her face. Both hands poked and prodded her body, from her throat to her thighs.

"I was stabbed. Dying. Did you heal me?"

"Taryn, darling, you have no injuries." Faelara sat on the bed with Taryn, stroking her hair and speaking in a soothing voice. "Can you tell us what happened?"

Sabina stepped beside Rhoane and took Taryn's hand in her own. "Perhaps she needs a moment to collect herself. You should wait in the sitting room." When no one moved, Sabina looked at Hayden, Baehlon, and Rhoane directly.

"That wasn't a request."

"Go," Taryn said, meeting his gaze. "I'll be out in a few minutes."

Rhoane followed the others to the sitting room and paced around the sofa. Ellie sat with Saeko and worried a thread on her chemise while Lorilee busied herself with lighting candles and closing the drapes. When finally Faelara joined them, the men stood expectantly.

"She's confused. According to her, the phantom returned and stabbed her, but I found no sign of trauma or injury. It's as if the event happened solely in her mind. Yet to her, it's very real."

Rhoane's back teeth ground together with the clenching of his jaw. He forcibly relaxed his mouth before speaking. "Do you believe the phantom was here?"

Faelara shook her head. "I don't know. Did you sense anything?"

"Nay. But then, she was not long departed from your rooms and I was intent on the discussion with Baehlon and the others." He took in Taryn's maids. "Did you hear anything? We found her outside her door. Hayden, you are close to Taryn—was there any hint of danger?"

"Nothing more than usual." Hayden glanced at the maids. "You?"

Lorilee stopped her fussing and stood behind Ellie and Saeko. The three shook their heads, muttering apologies they had not.

Sabina joined them and motioned to Rhoane. "She asked for you."

Taryn was sitting on the balcony with one leg dangling over the side, her head resting against a pillar. He paused for a moment and studied her movements—her slender fingers burrowed in Kaida's fur, the way her throat constricted with each swallow, the gentle rise and fall of her breasts with each breath. He braced himself and opened his mind to her thoughts and emotions.

To his surprise, she was calm. He'd expected a tempest of confusion, but she held herself in check.

She turned her head and smiled at him. "Hey."

Pewter storm clouds hovered over the ocean, silhouetting her against a dark illumination. A moment later, it was gone. Unsettled, he strode to the banister and swung his leg up and over to sit facing her. Panic lingered in her eyes.

"Faelara says you were attacked by the phantom."

Her gaze drifted away from him, toward the open water. "She says it didn't happen. That I made it up."

"No, she said she could not find a wound. There are many ways to assault someone, as you know. If he accessed your mind, that is just as damaging as a physical attack." Rhoane leaned forward and took her face in his hands. "Look at me."

Taryn bit her cheek, her eyes narrowing slightly before she turned her face to him. "It was real, Rhoane. I saw the phantom and—" She stopped abruptly, once again looking away from him.

"What, Taryn? What else?"

"Nothing. It doesn't matter."

His hands remained on her face, strengthening the connection between them. Her *cynfar* hummed in his mind, startling him. Whether she was letting him in or it was her pendant, he wasn't sure, but he saw what Taryn had experienced. Saw Marissa with the phantom, saw her taunting Taryn, saw the blade impale his love's sternum. Saw her collapse in the hallway. Saw the blood.

The vision ended and Rhoane pulled Taryn into his arms. "I should have been with you. I am sorry, Taryn."

Muffled sobs disturbed the already unsettled air. He stroked her hair, twining her braid through his fingers, desperately wanting to release the silken strands. His lips rested on her forehead, tasting the saltiness of recently fevered skin.

"Am I going mad, Rhoane?" She pulled back to look up at him, tears streaking her cheeks. "What if I didn't really see the phantom? What if somehow he can make me think I've done something? Or, what if he can make me do things?"

"No one can make you do something against your will. You are stronger than that, Taryn. You are stronger than you realize. Whether you saw the phantom and Marissa does not matter. If you believe it was real, then we must treat it as such."

A chill passed between them and she moved as far from him as the pillar would allow. "I never said anything about Marissa."

Confused, Rhoane shook his head to recall the vision. Marissa had been there. Most definitely. "I am mistaken then?"

She wouldn't meet his eyes.

"Taryn, tell me everything that happened. Please, I am only trying to help."

"It doesn't matter. It's like you said, whether it happened or not, we have to believe the phantom can get into my head. We have to stop him." Her challenging look dared him to defy her.

"If you are feeling strong enough, Faelara and I can begin now."

They returned to the others, whose worried faces brightened when they saw Taryn unharmed. Pale still, Taryn held herself with sturdy confidence. She hadn't shown him the vision, and adamantly avoided naming Marissa's involvement. For the time being, he had to assume she had a good reason to keep it from him. A nagging voice in the back of his mind told him it was his own fault. He hadn't believed her before when she tried to warn him about her sister; why would he believe her now? But he shuttled the thought to the deep recesses where denial lurked with complacent consistency. They'd worked past that after the incident at the Stones.

At least, he thought they had.

With the others seated around them in a protective circle, he and Faelara gripped Taryn's head in their hands. The other woman's ShantiMari flowed over him and he sensed her nurturing spirit. Her love of Taryn was greater than any mother's. Their eyes met above Taryn's head and the concern in Fae's eyes echoed his own.

Beneath Taryn's apprehension, a stain shadowed her thoughts. The utter blackness wove through her ShantiMari until he couldn't separate one from the other.

They worked in tandem to free the phantom's grip on Taryn, but it became evident that doing so would cause Taryn more harm than good. To rid her of the stain would tear the fabric of her being. Whatever the phantom had done to her, it was as much a part of her as the blood that pumped through her veins.

They placed several wards on her to prevent future attacks, hoping the sheer force of their love for her would be enough to strengthen their protective walls.

Rhoane, Fae's gentle voice whispered in his mind, *this is beyond my skill. If only my father were here.*

Rhoane nodded his agreement. Brandt's healing powers were legendary, his wards unbreakable. Except by Ohlin's sword. *I wish Myrddin were here. We could use his power.*

But Myrddin wasn't in Talaith. In fact, he'd been gone since before Harvest and no one seemed to know where except Lliandra, and she wasn't telling. Rhoane entertained the idea of asking for Lliandra's help, but he wasn't at all certain she wasn't behind either the Shadow Assassin attacks or the phantom.

I agree.

Rhoane glanced at Faelara in surprise. He hadn't meant to let the thought go out to her.

Faelara's weak smile did little to lift his spirits. Whatever haunted Taryn, it affected all of them. Their healing as complete as they could make it, Rhoane released Taryn's head, and Faelara bent to kiss the girl's temple.

"Would you like to be alone?"

A flicker of panic pinched her brows. "I don't think so. Please stay."

Rhoane caught Hayden turning away but not before he saw a glint of tears in the man's eyes. He understood. To watch Taryn suffer and know there was nothing you could do to ease her pain was the worst kind of torment.

Chapter 5

TARYN drank a second shot of dreem and set the glass on the table. It wasn't going as well as she'd hoped. After everyone had left the night before, she brooded in her sitting room, staring out the window at the raging storm. Despite Faelara's misgivings, she knew what she saw. It was real. Even if her body was unmarked, her belly was tender where the blade had entered. She pressed against the taut skin of her abdomen, wincing. Raising her tunic higher, she traced a finger along the vorlock scar, feeling the burn of poison that simmered beneath the surface.

The dreem settled her nerves but did nothing to settle her mind.

Whether the vision was real, she'd uncovered the secret of the assassin and was determined to duplicate his disappearing act. Her ShantiMari fluttered around her in expectant anticipation. Taking a deep breath, she pulled the shadows to her, wrapping them from head to toe like a mummy. After a few seconds, she coughed beneath the tight bonds and released her power.

"Okay, not a mummy." She wheezed against the musty smell of rotting cloth. "A cloak?" she asked Kaida, who meticulously cleaned her paws with long licks of fur. "Right. What does a grierbas know of shadows?" Kaida's golden gaze followed her as she once more pulled the shadows around her. "Can you see me?" she asked when she'd fully imagined a cloak covering her body, leaving room to breathe.

I see you. But then, I see the Shadow Demon as well.

"Good point. Let's see how it works on the girls."

Taryn stepped lightly through the doorway of her bedchamber to the sitting room where Ellie and Lorilee argued about the arrangement of flowers. When neither of them noticed her entrance, a thrill of encouragement raced through her. She intentionally bumped a chair and delighted in their surprised faces.

"Saeko?" Ellie called, "was that you?"

Lorilee searched around the chair, frowning. Kaida sat by the doorway, tongue lolling to the side. "Kaida, you naughty pup. Where is your mistress?"

Kaida barked and trotted to stand beside Taryn.

"Don't be coy, you mangy beast. You gave us a fright," Ellie scolded.

Unable to suppress her giggles any longer, Taryn released her shadows, causing them to scream and grab their chests.

"That wasn't nice!" Lorilee gasped. "My lady."

"Oh, stop. It was hilarious and you know it."

"For you, perhaps, but you've taken ten seasons from my life," Ellie argued.

"Where's Saeko?" Taryn ignored their dramatics. "I want to try this out on her, too."

Ellie pointed toward the office and Taryn arranged the shadows to cover her. Ellie and Lorilee's sharp intake of breath confirmed it worked. She padded to the other room, hearing Saeko's humming before she saw the girl. When she stepped through the doorway, Saeko paused in her tidying of Taryn's desk and sniffed the air. Kaida prodded her hand with her nose and Saeko dutifully petted the grierbas. Her eyes darted around the room and then focused back on the desk.

"Leave those where they are. I want to read them later," Taryn said.

Saeko's head jerked up, eyes scanning the empty room.

Taryn moved around the desk to stand beside the girl and blew on her neck. Saeko jumped back, stepping on Kaida's paw. Her yelp further confounded Saeko, and she ran from the room. Taryn released the shadows and doubled over in laughter.

Three irate faces glared at her from the doorway.

"What? It's funny, admit it."

"No, it's not. Scaring people just because you can is hurtful. You should be ashamed of yourself." Saeko's hands were planted on her hips, her jaw set, eyes narrowed. "And they call you the Eirielle. Great and powerful balance bringer of Aelinae? Phooey."

If Saeko weren't in Taryn's office, she was certain the girl would've spat on the ground. Her laughter died away and she held out her hands, pleading with her maids. "I'm sorry. You're absolutely right. I was caught up in the excitement of learning something new. Forgive me?" She pouted and looked pitifully remorseful until they relented.

Taryn swept them into a great hug and kissed each of their cheeks. "What would I do without you, my lovely, albeit humor-starved, girls?"

"This is not becoming behavior for a princess of the realm," Ellie said solemnly.

"Since when has she ever behaved according to her station?" Lorilee giggled.

"True point," Saeko agreed.

A knock on the door startled all of them, except Kaida, who was halfway to the door before Ellie went to receive the visitor. Rhoane strode in, his face set with grim determination. Being around her maids always made him a bit uncomfortable, but why, Taryn had no idea. She assumed it was because they spent so much time together and knew her more intimately than he did. Whatever his reasons, he didn't feel the need to share them with her. Therefore, she never asked. But watching him that morning, it was something other than her maids that had him on edge.

Her hand fluttered to her scar, an unconscious reminder of her stain. He'd been in her head the previous evening and although she tried to hide as much of her taint as she could, he might've touched that part of her. She hoped not.

"Ladies," Taryn started with false enthusiasm, "would you mind bringing the prince and me some tea and scones?" At her look, they took the hint and left the suite. Once alone, Taryn embraced her betrothed, inhaling his scent of forest. Her lips brushed his before she asked, "What brings you here this morning? I don't train with the sword master for another bell at least."

Rhoane held her against him and the erratic beating of his heart echoed in her ear. He was frightened for her, of that she was sure. When he left the previous evening, she'd assured him she was fine, but she saw the doubt in his eyes.

She'd not told him of Marissa's role in her vision, but somehow he'd guessed she was involved. The guilt from deceiving him cut, but she wasn't sure she could trust him. Not yet. At least not where her sister was concerned.

If he hadn't believed her when she told him Marissa was bedding Zakael, there was no way he'd believe her sister was involved with the phantom. Taryn had made the difficult decision to wait until she had proof. If there was one thing she'd learned in the past few months, it was that she needed solid evidence to back up her claims.

"What is it, my love? You are trembling." She spoke in Eleri, hoping it might calm him.

"Did you sleep well?" He gazed at her, frowning. "You smell of spirits. Have you been drinking at this early hour?"

She seesawed her head from side to side. "Maybe a little. For courage." She stepped away from him and said, "I have something to show you. Close your eyes."

He looked skeptically at her but did as told. When she'd arranged the shadows over her, she said, "You can look now."

He opened his eyes and scanned the room. "Are we to play children's games?"

Taryn stepped around him and bumped the chair with her hip, making it rock to the side. Rhoane righted the chair, one hand outstretched to the empty air. With deliberate concentration, she held herself aloft, not making a sound. She moved to hover just behind him and pushed aside his hair to kiss the back of his neck. He spun around, eyes wild.

"How is this possible?" He searched the room, worry creasing his forehead.

"I'm not sure." Her voice came from a few paces away. She released the shadows and was once again visible. "When I was fevered at Ravenwood, I saw Valterys pull shadows over himself and yesterday in the garden, I saw Ebus appear to disappear. I'm assuming the Shadow Assassin uses the same trick."

She didn't mention that she saw the phantom show Marissa how it was done. If she hadn't seen her sister do it, she would've thought it a trick of the Dark, but Marissa was of the Light. Which meant either Marissa was like Taryn and had both Light and Dark ShantiMari, or something else. Something Taryn wasn't yet ready to admit and buried deep within the secret recesses of her thoughts.

Rhoane sat across from her with his hands on his knees, a stern look on his face. "You go too far, Darennsai. Working with Dark Shanti without a mage is suicide."

"After what happened at the Stones, I thought we agreed I must push myself. My enemies are powerful, Rhoane. Much more so than I am. I had hoped I managed to hide this fact from them, but after last night, I am not so certain."

"I do not like it."

"Nor do I, but what choice do we have? I do not have a hundred seasons to perfect my craft as you and Fae have. I might have a week, or a season—I do not know and I must be prepared."

"I cannot protect you if you conceal the truth from me."

Taryn snapped her head up to look at him. The way he said it, the underlying tone of his voice, worried her. He could never know the phantom had touched a part of her soul with his Black ShantiMari.

She shivered and shook off the thought. Rhoane sat beside her and stroked her arms, warming her. "You cannot be so overly concerned with my protection when what you are really doing is preventing me from growing." She turned to face him, cringing at the fear hidden in the mossy depths of his eyes. Fear she shared. "You have to let me take risks or I will never become what I must."

They both knew what she wasn't saying. That had she not pushed herself, the phantom might have succeeded and Kaldaar would've been freed from his banishment, taking Sabina as his brood mare to spawn generations of followers. It was Taryn's strength that had kept Sabina alive, and with the power of her sword, cleansed the girl of the Black Brotherhood's taint.

And now the phantom wanted her as Kaldaar's vessel. Marissa had said he always gets what he wants.

Well, she thought with a bitterness that soured her stomach, he should prepare to be disappointed.

"I could not bear it if anything happened to you," Rhoane said, wrapping his arms around her, pulling her close to him. She breathed in the clean scent of the vier and laid her head on his chest, comforted by the feel of his arms around her.

"We cannot let anything change us. We have to stay

strong together. If I lost you, I do not know what I would do," Taryn murmured, not wanting to ever leave his embrace.

"You will never lose me, mi carae."

The spoken oath should have calmed her agitated thoughts. Should have prompted her to open up to him, to tell him all the secrets she kept from him. But it didn't. It only made her want to shove the truth of what had happened to her at the Stones farther away from her mind. She never wanted him to know the phantom had infected her with his vileness. Never wanted Rhoane to look at her in disgust.

Chapter 6

THE small group dodged busy shoppers rushing to complete their errands before the pregnant clouds released their charges. They walked with purpose toward a specific tent, heavy cloaks muffling the sound of their boots on the cobblestones, hoods covering their faces. Taryn shifted beneath her cloak, trying to peer out from under the brim of her hood and failing. She kept her head down and followed Baehlon's movements as best she could.

Anonymity was his idea and she'd gone along with it from sheer lack of energy to argue. At least this time she remembered to tell him she was going to the docks. He could've pretended to be happy. Instead, he'd lectured her for half a bell about the dangers of traveling with so few guards, especially to that part of town.

In the five days since her last visit, she'd heard no less than a dozen times how foolish she'd been. When he wasn't reminding her to take a guard everywhere she went, he was questioning her about the mysterious ailment that caused her to call out to all of her friends.

She'd listened without argument and accepted his reprimands for what they were—genuine concern for her well-being. If he didn't care, he would've ignored the entire situation.

Like her mother had done.

She was certain Lliandra knew about the encounter on the docks, but Taryn had received no royal command to visit—in fact, since the incident at the Stones, she'd only seen her mother on three occasions, all of them formal dinners.

The sting of tears surprised her and she hastily wiped them away. Lliandra was a conundrum, to be sure. A fanciful riddle wrapped up in a huge swath of crazy. Taryn snort-laughed, eliciting the attention of her travel mates.

Hayden raised an eyebrow at her while Rhoane simply smiled that devilish little half-smile he had that made her belly tighten and knees weaken. The thoughts that skittered through her mind when he gave her that smile sent heat flaming across her cheeks and she pulled her hood farther over her nose. They were not thoughts a lady should have, she was certain.

Good thing she wasn't raised a lady.

Rhoane slipped his hand in hers and she bit her cheek to keep from grinning like a foolish schoolgirl. Truth was she loved the attention he lavished on her. Loved that each morning when she woke, he was at her rooms within minutes. Loved that he trained with her and never let her give less than her best. Loved that each night he would stay with her until she fell asleep.

She knew he would gladly stay the night, but she held back. For no other reason than she was afraid. Afraid he might see into her soul and realize she wasn't the Eirielle, but just a freak of nature who happened to have both Light and Dark powers.

"Never going to happen," Rhoane whispered to her.

She jerked in his direction, her hood blocking her sight. "Seriously, how do you see anything wearing this?" She pushed the offending material from her head and shook out her braids. Several heads turned to stare in her direction and

Rhoane gently replaced her hood.

"You will get used to it." He squeezed her hand and hurried his steps, putting distance between them and the curious onlookers.

They reached Adesh's tent a few minutes later and went inside, the eight of them crowding the small space. Carina and Timor slipped out to keep watch. The fragrance of spices filled the warm space and Sabina pushed her hood away from her face, inhaling as she did. The young boy Taryn met on her previous visit entered through the back of the tent and froze when he saw the group.

His wary gaze traveled over each of them, taking in Sabina with a slight widening of his eyes. When he saw Taryn, a broad smile broke the tension of his face.

"Princess, it is good to see you again." He pressed his hands together at his chest and bowed to her. "I'm sorry. Adesh is out of town at present, but I can help you with tea or spices." He gestured expansively to the many jars and bottles lined on shelves around the tent.

"I would love to sample some of your teas," Sabina said, a sultriness to her voice. Not since Paderau had she been near products from her homeland and Taryn knew the familiar scents made her homesick.

"I am Bornu, Adesh's apprentice," the young boy said with no small amount of pride in his voice. He stood taller than Taryn remembered, and spoke perfect Elennish.

Their visit lasted near on a bell, and by the time they left, Taryn's belly sloshed with too much tea. Sabina spent a fortune on spices that she had sent to the palace. She and Faelara delighted in every sample Bornu brought to them, comparing notes of bergamot and cinnamon with each other. Taryn had no idea teas had so many nuances, but after an impromptu lesson from the ladies, she considered herself an eager student on her way to becoming an aficionado.

"Do you have any grhom, Bornu?" Taryn asked as she perused the jars.

The lad blinked at her, uncomprehending.

Rhoane chuckled. "It is a spiced drink enjoyed by the Eleri," he explained. "Most other kingdoms prefer tea or spirits. Only the Eleri know the exact ingredients and how to prepare the drink."

Bornu's eyes brightened and Taryn suspected Rhoane had issued a silent challenge to the boy.

After tea, they made a hasty stop at Sulein's shop. Taryn asked the others to wait outside, only allowing Timor and Carina to accompany her to pick up Rhoane's gift. A beautifully made dagger caught her attention and she lingered over the display case while she waited for Sulein to return with Rhoane's pendant.

The *cynfar* was even more elaborately detailed than she'd envisioned. A diamond glittered in the center of the piece, a perfect stone without a single flaw. Tiny spider-webbed veins of silver crossed the crystal. Upon closer inspection, she saw they were roots, all emanating from the diamond. A laurel wreath enclosed the pendant, its leaves fluttering at her touch. Sulein had infused ancient Artagh ShantiMari into the charm.

"It's remarkable. Thank you, Sulein." She took him in and noticed he'd recently bathed and attempted to comb his matted hair. She fished a gold crown from her pocket and handed it to him, but he waved her off.

"You've paid too much as it is. I can't accept your gold."

Taryn narrowed her eyes at the funny little man. "Then you still have my gratitude."

A smile teased the outer edges of his lips. "Don't need none of that, either. Just be careful with godsteel. It can turn on you if abused." He shuffled behind the counter, kicking straw with his toes. He'd even clipped his nails.

"I will." Her gaze drifted to the display case, and she decided to purchase the little dagger for Tessa. Her mother would most likely kill Taryn if she knew she'd bought the girl a weapon, but it was perfect for her sister. "I'll take that dagger. Can you wrap it and the pendant, please?"

Sulein eyed her appreciatively. "You have a good sense for quality metals. This was forged from ore from the deepest mines on Haversham. It will never miss its mark, nor will it allow any harm to its owner."

A dagger made with Artagh power. It was perfect for her adventurous sister.

Sulein left them for several minutes and Taryn used the time to study his other masterpieces. For that's what his work truly was. Each item, whether a weapon or stylized trifle, was exquisitely crafted. The image of a grierbas caught her attention and she reflexively reached to stroke Kaida, but she'd left her at the palace. Her hand felt strangely empty and a desperate darkness overcame her.

Sulein returned and she shook the somber feeling from her mind. He handed her two boxes. Rhoane's small and wrapped in oak leaves; Tessa's long and rectangular, with cornflower blue silk fastened with pearls. The fabric matched Tessa's eyes perfectly.

"Again, thank you." Taryn reached for him and he leaned closer. Instead of running her fingers along his cheek, she cupped his face in her hand and sent a thread of ShantiMari to him. His eyes widened and his mouth gaped at the violation, but he did not pull away. "If you ever need me, I will come to your aid," she said in Eleri.

He nodded mutely, a star-struck look on his face. If all Artagh were like Sulein, she'd have no problem winning them over. She smiled sadly at the thought. War wasn't something she wanted, but knew was always an option.

On impulse, she withdrew her sword and laid it on the

counter. The starry-eyed look disappeared and he stood straight.

"Can you read the words on this sword? Do you know who made it?"

He shook his head and growled low in his throat. "That sword was made for a goddess. Not for the likes of an Aelan." The old Sulein was back and Taryn sighed. So much for winning over the Artagh.

"Yes, I know. But I'm in possession of it now and would like to know what it says. Can you at least give me the name of someone who might know?"

The door opened and Baehlon stuck his head inside. "Those storm clouds don't look like they'll wait much longer. We should be going." With one glance, he took in the entire shop, his dark eyes resting on the Artagh. "Have you concluded your business?"

Sulein barked several curses at Baehlon and then stormed from the room, slamming the door behind him.

"What the hell was that about?" Taryn demanded of Baehlon.

"What was what about?" Baehlon grinned as if he'd stolen a fresh-baked pie and eaten the entire thing before being caught. She suspected the crime was worth the punishment.

"Never mind." Taryn stormed past him to the others who waited beneath a low overhang.

Baehlon hadn't been wrong and they made it safely to the palace mere minutes before the storm broke. They were shaking out their cloaks when Tessa's voice tickled Taryn's mind.

Dear sister, all is ready. We're in the petite salon.

Taryn patted the leather satchel she carried. The same one Rhoane had given her on her first day on Aelinae. It held Tessa's dagger and Rhoane's *cynfar*. Nothing more. She always carried it, even if it was empty.

We're on our way.

Taryn knew Rhoane hated surprises, but hoped the party would be a welcome distraction. They were leaving the next day for the Narthvier and preparations for their secret trip had been strained, to say the least. Taryn still had to tell her mother they were leaving, but had put it off. *After the party*, she promised herself for the hundredth time.

She smiled brightly to her friends. "If you'll follow me, I have something I'd like to show you."

Sabina gave her a sly smile, having been in on the planning of Rhoane's surprise, but the others looked at her with questioning glances.

The party, as it turned out, was a huge success. Taryn had invited not just their friends, but Rhoane's valet, Alasdair, as well as several of the soldiers Taryn and Rhoane trained with. Lliandra made an appearance and stayed a short while before saying her goodbyes. She gave the soldiers and servants an imperious glance before sweeping from the room. Even Marissa stopped in for a quarter bell, excusing herself shortly after Lliandra left.

Taryn didn't mind. She preferred they stay away, actually. Rhoane surprised everyone by drinking and laughing, thoroughly enjoying himself. It was rare to see him so relaxed and Taryn was grateful she was at least able to give him that for one day. Of her gift to him, he was speechless.

"I suspected you were up to something with the Artagh," he said, "but I never thought you would craft a *cynfar* for me. I am honored, *Darennsai*."

The fact she had surprised him not just with the party, but the pendant, was all the reward she needed.

At the end of the night, Taryn said her farewells to her friends, lingering over hugs until Faelara and Sabina began to question her dawdling. She slipped the wrapped dagger into Tessa's hands with a whispered, "Open this when alone in your rooms and don't let Mother find it. It's from the Artagh's shop." Tessa's eyes widened and she tucked the parcel into a pocket of her skirt.

With a wink to Tessa and a last embrace to her friends, Taryn left the salon with a heavy heart. Rhoane insisted they keep their trip north a secret, even from their friends. He feared the Shadow Assassin might stalk them on the road and the only way to ensure their safety was to keep the details of their journey between the two of them.

Except Taryn had to tell her mother.

She stood before Lliandra's doors, taking several deep breaths to calm her fractured nerves. Her mother's mercurial moods kept Taryn on edge. She never knew if, at any given moment, she would be smacked or soothed. When one of the guards cleared his throat and indicated the door, Taryn shot him a foul look, but grinned all the same. She'd come to like the guards stationed at Lliandra's doors. They were fierce fighters in the training ring, and treated her as another soldier, not a princess. She respected that.

"Fine, fine," she mumbled and knocked with more force than she'd meant.

The door opened immediately and she was ushered into her mother's sitting room. Marissa stood by the huge windows that overlooked the ocean, and Myrddin was seated across from Lliandra. His reddened face had the look of someone who lingered too long in the sun. When she entered, he stood and smiled as wide as his sunburn would allow.

"Taryn. It's good to see you again." Within two steps, he was grasping her arms and kissing her cheeks.

"I'm glad you've returned. I missed you." The admission surprised her, but it was true. Although he kept mostly to himself, only becoming animated after several pints of ale, she'd missed his quiet counsel.

"I heard what happened. Are you recovered?" His denim

blue eyes searched her face, scanned her body. "Dreadful, it was to hear. I'm sorry I wasn't here to assist you. I promise that won't ever happen again."

The concern that shone from his features touched her. "It was Sabina who was injured, not me. We're both fine now. Thank you for asking."

He patted her hand in a grandfatherly sort of way. "I'll be sure to speak with Sabina tomorrow. Was the party pleasant?"

The four of them made small talk for the next several minutes before Myrddin begged off, citing exhaustion from his travels. Marissa followed Myrddin from the room, leaving Taryn alone with her mother.

"I take it this isn't a social call," Lliandra said the moment her servants left the room.

Taryn raised her chin and took a deep breath. She'd as soon face the phantom again than tell her mother what she was about to say. But it had to be done.

Chapter 7

THE carriage pulled away from the back door of the house and Marissa watched until it rounded a corner out of sight. She knocked twice, followed by a third a moment later. A small window opened and the face of Nena's doorman appeared. He took in Marissa without a word and opened the door enough for her to squeeze through. It enraged her she had to play this silly game, but Nena's rules were absolute. Crown princess or no, she had to follow them.

A young boy dressed in short breeches and nothing else led her up the back stairs to Armando's room. He rapped on the door before sauntering away, leaving Marissa alone in the darkened hall. An agonizing moment passed and then Armando opened the door, inviting her in. She stifled the gasp that always came when she saw his immaculate body.

Burnished coppery skin with dark, almost black hair covering his well-muscled chest, becoming a tantalizing trail over rippled abs and disappearing beneath the thin pants he wore. The fabric left little to the imagination and Marissa thrilled at the sight of his excitement.

She pulled her gaze to his eyes, the only thing about him that wasn't exceptional. Dull brown without a trace of ShantiMari sparking in their depths. She swept past him into the handsomely decorated room. Although masculine, she never felt out of place there. In fact, his room was one of the few places she was truly comfortable.

Perhaps it was the rich fabric on the walls, burgundy in shade, which complemented the dark-stained furniture. Or the way candles flickered within crystal sconces, casting shadows across the huge bed. Marissa grinned and settled her glance on two ornately carved black screens. Hidden from view were the whips and toys she craved.

Armando reached out to unbutton her gown and her skin reacted to his touch, igniting little flames to dance over her bare shoulders. The whore needed no ShantiMari. His power was in the way he used his body.

His breath tickled the hairs on her flesh as he worked the buttons of her gown, his fingers skimming her hips as he slid it off her body. She stepped out of her dress and stilled her desire, waiting anxiously for him to hang the blasted thing and return to her. Within moments, his hot lips were on the back of her neck, warming her. He licked a figure eight, enflaming her desire even more, and then his tongue left her skin. She whimpered at the loss, only to moan a moment later when he blew cool air against her. The hot and cold sensation went straight to her core. Her nipples strained to be touched; her sex moistened in anticipation. Armando knew what she needed.

"What will it be tonight, my dove? The lash? Or that wicked little toy you acquired from Ulla?"

"None of those." His eyes sparkled with mischief. "Tonight, I show you what it is to be loved."

Marissa quirked a brow. "I don't pay you to make love to me. I pay for the special kind of pleasure only you know how to inflict."

"If you aren't satisfied, you don't have to pay. Now shhh, and let me love you, Princess."

His mouth commanded hers, taking in her lips and

tongue with a promise of future savagery that quelled her argument for the moment. If he didn't satisfy her, she'd do more than not pay. She'd have his balls for supper.

His hands roamed over her body, massaging her breasts in time to the movements of his mouth. Soon she rocked with him, swept up in the simplicity of his actions. He caught her beneath her knees and cradled her in his arms, nestled against his chest. She'd bedded him dozens of times, sharing every orifice of her body and his, but the way he held her, protectively, lovingly, was more intimate than anything they'd done together. His heart beat against his chest in a rapid staccato, giving away his apprehension.

The fact he was nervous didn't anger her—quite the opposite.

She gazed at him as he gently set her on the feather bed. His unremarkable brown eyes took in her body, a look of hunger dancing in their depths. A blush crept across her cheeks, and she looked away. The sudden shyness surprised her.

A lone finger trailed its way from her lips, down her chin to her breasts where it made lazy circles around her nipples and then continued over her abdomen. She tensed as his finger rounded on her most sensitive parts, but instead of stopping to tease her, he ran both of his hands down her legs, gripping her ankles and spreading her legs apart.

A tortured moan escaped her lips as she lay naked and vulnerable on the bed. His responding smile gave little comfort. In fact, it stoked the fire of need nestled between her legs.

With practiced seduction, he untied his breeches and let them slip to the ground. His erection sprang forward, released from the thin fabric at last. Marissa's sharp intake of air brought another smile to his lips, full of wicked promises.

Armando positioned himself between her legs, massaging

her thighs, his thumbs almost coming in contact with her before moving away far too quickly. Each time his fingers neared, she would thrust up to force contact, but he was too quick.

The smell of her desire filled the room, mixed with Armando's exotic scent of musky spiciness. His cock bounced inches from her, teasing her with its perfection.

"Please," she said, "please make love to me, Armando."

His hands roved over her thighs to her hips, then up to her breasts. He bent low, taking one nipple into his mouth, burning her with his heat, making her ache for his touch. His tongue traced circles around her areola before moving to her other breast. She squirmed beneath him, eager for the touch, but yearning for his cock, kept just out of reach. She had no doubt Armando knew exactly what he was doing to her.

He raised up, his gaze locked on hers, the intensity thrilling in an unsettling way. A whimper escaped her lips and he slid into her with calculated slowness. She clenched around his girth, fighting the powerful urge of release. The fact Armando had barely entered her and she almost came undone frightened her. No man had ever had that kind of power over her body.

He rocked in and out of her, almost fully pulling out before pressing in to the hilt. He was too big for her like this. She couldn't possibly take all of him, and yet her body stretched to accommodate him. His hands rested at the sides of her face, his thumbs stroking her cheeks, his eyes boring into hers.

It was too much. Too close, too intimate. Of all the lovers she'd had, Armando knew her darkest secrets, but this intimacy was a boundary she never wanted to cross. Yet she didn't look away.

Her hands snaked up his back and over the hardened muscles contracting with his movements. Slow, ever so slowly, he thrust in and out of her. Her hips acted of their own accord, tilting to match his movements. A dizzying sensation started at the corners of her mind, spreading over her body. Unfamiliar sensations, a lightheadedness she didn't recognize, followed by a comforting warmth, made her giddy.

Armando's breathing became labored; beads of sweat dotted his brow as he controlled his movements. With each downward stroke, his chest skimmed her nipples, teasing them to tight little buds. Every part of her body pulled in on itself, taut like the string of a bow. She gasped at the feeling, unsure what to do.

He shifted his position, tilting his cock upward to stroke that sensitive part of her and she lost all thought as stars burst in her mind. Stars and fire and ice and a weightlessness that couldn't be defined. She trembled from hairline to toes and grasped him with her hands. Her stuttered cries echoed in the room, joined by his grunts of completion.

This is love. Pure. Simple. Love.

A strange prickling of her heart filled her with peace. *This is what it must feel like for others.* She'd always wondered, and truth be told, was a bit jealous of people like Taryn and Rhoane. People who could find pleasure in someone's company simply because they shared a bond of love. She held Armando tighter, silently thanking him for showing her what it meant to be loved.

When at last their bodies stopped convulsing and he softened within her, Armando pressed his lips to hers. "Well, Princess?"

"Well what?"

"Did I earn my pay?"

She pushed him off her and scrambled from the bed, furious with him, and herself. How could she be so stupid to think a whore would love her?

"You think that was special?" She tossed her hair with a

haughty sniff. "It was boring. *You* were boring. Next time, I expect *my* wishes to be fulfilled, not what you want. Do you hear me?" She retrieved her gown and slid it over her still tingling skin.

"No," Armando said when she stood in front of his mirror, arranging her mussed curls.

"No?"

"I will not beat you, Princess. You can find someone else for your needs."

He reclined against the headboard, too beautiful by half with his dark hair covering part of his face, his long legs stretched before him. And his cock. That magnificent piece of art that brought her to the edge of delirium rested against his thigh, half erect, taunting her. He had to be joking.

"I'm serious," he said as if reading her mind. "No more. I don't enjoy whipping you. Nena has others who will be only too happy to take up the task."

Marissa tossed a silver feather onto the bed. It landed with a dull thud beside his hip. The amount was a fraction of what he was worth and from the dangerous dip of his lips, he saw the insult for what it was. He'd made a powerful enemy that night.

Chapter 8

RHOANE touched the *cynfar* Taryn gave him for his birthing day. He was neither accustomed to nor prepared for the constant singing from the pendant nor the influx of emotions it brought. Not only could he sense Taryn's feelings, he felt them as if they were his own. Even though Taryn had shown him how to mute his *cynfar*, every now and again a flash of sensation would burn his skin.

He tapped the pendant with a calming hush. Taryn's meeting with her mother had not gone well. The empress was livid Taryn and Rhoane would not be traveling with them to Celyn Eryri in preparation for the Light Celebrations, but instead would be accompanying Carga to the Narthvier. They'd kept it a secret from everyone, knowing Lliandra would not approve. Well, almost everyone.

After checking for the fifth time his plan was in order, he went to the stables to ready their horses. When Taryn arrived a short time later, it was with resigned melancholy. Her maids would give their friends the notes they'd written, explaining their delay in joining them at the winter palace. Taryn suppressed her guilt but not enough to keep it from creeping through his *cynfar*.

He tightened both girths once more and gave a last glance at the palace. Taryn wasn't the only one tamping down guilt.

He'd not told her of his secret plan and as they made their way out of the palace gates, he hoped it would work.

Stars blanketed the moonless sky, giving scant light by which to traverse the convoluted streets. Most of the lanterns had been snuffed and stillness cloaked the city. They kept a casual pace, not wanting to draw attention to themselves. Yet each step of their horses' hooves clanged on the paved streets, echoing down every alley they passed. Eventually, they rode through the city gates and raced up the hill north of Talaith, where they both took their first real breath since leaving the palace.

Rhoane folded time, making bells last but a minute. It was the only way he could be certain they weren't followed. None but Eleri could manipulate time and they needed to be far from Talaith before Baehlon and Faelara set out with the decoys.

Carina and Timor, Taryn's two most-trusted guards, would disguise themselves as Taryn and Rhoane. It had taken several tries before the guards perfected their looks by manipulating their ShantiMari. Not only was it difficult to achieve, but maintaining the effect took vast amounts of energy. With Faelara's help, Rhoane hoped they would manage over the next few weeks. Taryn's life depended on it.

As for Kaida, they'd found a large grey mutt only too happy for a warm meal twice a day. He hated that he had to plan such an elaborate ruse, but to keep anyone at court from guessing his and Taryn's true whereabouts, it was necessary. If the Shadow Assassin or his master were watching, Rhoane wanted their eyes on the decoys and not his beloved.

With the rising sun, Rhoane stopped them on the banks of Lake Oster. "We will stay here for a brief rest and then be on our way."

"This lake is a two-day ride from Talaith. How did we get here so quickly?" Taryn asked in a sleepy, confused voice.

"An Eleri skill. Someday, I will teach it to you."

"You can manipulate time?"

"It is more of folding time around us. The days pass normally for everyone else." He led Fayngaar to the lake, leaving the reins loose for him to drink.

"Can't we just camp here for the day? It's so pretty." Ashanni joined Fayngaar at the water's edge while Taryn slumped against a tree. Kaida nudged her hand and settled against her leg. The grierbas could easily keep up with the horses, but even she looked tired.

"I want to put many leagues between us and anyone who might wish to follow. Besides, I promised Carga we would be there tomorrow."

"Do you think we're being followed?"

"No, but I do not want to be surprised, either."

Taryn turned to the grierbas. "Kaida, you better go find some breakfast. It looks like it will be a long day."

As it turned out, the day was relatively short, as was the night. They managed several days of travel in little more than two. When they arrived unannounced in Paderau Palace's courtyard, Duke Anje waited.

"So, you thought you could just sneak in here without any warning?" The duke scowled to Rhoane, but his smile belied the harshness of his words. To Taryn, he said, "Come here, my lovely niece." He clasped her in a massive embrace. "I've missed you."

Rhoane stepped aside to allow them their reunion. Taryn made a face from within Anje's embrace before winking at Rhoane. His grin was response enough. Taryn pretended to be annoyed by Anje's affections, but he knew better.

"And I you, Uncle, but do you really need to crush the breath from me?"

Anje held her out, looking her over from head to toe. "Are you recovered from the ordeal with Kaldaar? You took ten seasons from my life with that scare. You and Hayden both. What were you thinking?"

Taryn opened her mouth to speak, but he shook his head. "No, don't tell me. You saved Sabina from that madman." Anje spit on the ground and crushed his heel hard against the pebbled dirt. "To Herbret's relations, I curse them to the depths of Dal Ferran, which is where I'm certain Celia and Herbret are at this moment."

"Uncle, please," Taryn said, touching Anje's face with her fingertips. "All is well. Hayden and I did exactly what you would've done in our situation. Celia and Herbret paid for their crimes and I'm exhausted from our travels. If we could put the past behind us?"

Chagrined, Anje clucked her on the chin. "Of course. I'm sorry, Taryn." He planted a kiss on her cheek before turning to Rhoane. "Always a pleasure to see you. How has Talaith been of late?"

Rhoane embraced the duke. "Talaith is as Talaith has always been."

"That bad, eh?"

"I am afraid your son is most vexing to some on the council." Rhoane hoped to turn the conversation away from Kaldaar. Anje didn't need to know about the assassin being in Talaith, or the nightmares Taryn continued to have. "Hayden's knowledge of the laws and customs of Aelinae is impressive."

"Yes, it is. That boy was always too clever by half." His gaze drifted to the gardens before snapping back to them. "Come inside. Taryn, I have a surprise for you, but in truth I did think I'd have more time, so you must forgive me that it isn't quite ready."

Anje had remodeled a suite of rooms exclusively for Taryn's use. The decor was understated yet elegant, like Taryn. Small couches and overstuffed chairs filled her sitting room and on every table was a vase of fresh cut flowers. A row of windows overlooked the gardens and river beyond.

In her sleeping chamber, a huge bed dominated the space. Velvet panels in midnight blue hung from the four posts with a matching canopy wrapped protectively around the bed. Woven throughout the velvet in silver thread were tiny suns and moons—Taryn's insignia. It was sleeping quarters worthy of an empress. Rhoane glanced at Taryn, who wiped at her eyes with the back of her hand, a look of awe on her face.

"Uncle, this is too much. Too fine."

"Nonsense, my dear. This is nothing more than what you deserve. But there's more."

Rhoane followed the pair into the next room, where the duke's next surprise was a mystery to him.

Taryn nearly broke her uncle's neck hugging him for the thing she called a shower.

"What does it do?" A curtain hid a tall box with several knobs in the wall.

Taryn stepped into the space and gazed dreamily at the decorative tiles, each with her insignia stamped in the center. "You bathe in here. You stand under this." She pointed to a funny-looking disc. "And water falls over you. It's heavenly, trust me."

He raised a doubtful eyebrow. "If you say so."

"I thought you would be pleased." Anje's expression showed his excitement, but an apologetic tone edged his next words. "I'm afraid the library and study won't be completed for several moonturns. I have my agents scouring all of Aelinae for books and scrolls."

"A library? For me?" Taryn threw her arms around her uncle again. Tears streamed down her cheeks. "I don't know how to thank you. You've given me so much already."

A wave of her ShantiMari washed over them and Rhoane lifted his face to absorb her love and gratitude. He'd sensed throughout the rooms Anje's protective wards and the combination of the two powers raised the hairs on his skin. He added his Eleri ShantiMari to the mix and Taryn raised her eyes to him. The room filled with warmth, a cocoon of security that Rhoane wrapped around his beloved and her uncle.

Thank you, Taryn whispered in his mind.

A soft knock brought them out of the moment. Carga stood in the doorway, wearing a long gown of beige silk. Her dark hair hung around her face in loose curls.

"Carga." Rhoane knelt before his sister, kissing his thumb and placing it over his heart. "It fills my heart with joy to see you once more."

"You look so beautiful." Taryn embraced her friend.

Carga held Taryn tightly for a moment. "I was so worried when I heard the news."

Taryn's features pinched and Carga continued, "I have searched the collective knowledge of the Eleri and cannot uncover who is working on Kaldaar's behalf. Be careful, sister."

Taryn's wry smile belied the apprehension she tamped down, but not before it coursed through Rhoane's *cynfar.*

"Always," Taryn said and Carga's stern look made her laugh. "Okay, almost always. I'll work on that."

"Please do." Carga turned to embrace Rhoane. "I am well pleased you will be joining us, brother."

He put his forehead to hers, holding her face in his hands. "I have long waited for the day when you will be full Eleri once more and standing at the side of Verdaine."

"I am afraid that is no longer my path."

"You do not know that for certain." She was their high priestess before Zakael took advantage of her and it was not only Rhoane's wish but his father's that she resume the honored position.

Carga touched his cheek with her fingertips before turning away, saying, "Shall we give these travelers a chance to freshen up and then have dinner together? I have made the most amazing roast you will ever taste."

"You're still cooking?" Taryn asked, surprise lifting her tone.

"What else would you have me do?" She bowed her head to Duke Anje. "His Grace has been kind enough to provide shelter and anonymity for this long—the least I could do was prepare him one final meal."

"I'm going to miss your cooking," the duke said. "And your sage advice."

"Yes, I imagine you will," Carga said without a hint of sarcasm.

After they had dined, Rhoane left Taryn with the duke, giving them a chance for private conversation. He donned a heavy coat and left the palace by a lesser used gate. He roamed the city of Paderau, staying as much in shadow as possible. The streets near the palace were quiet with most of the inhabitants abed for the night, but the closer he got to the northern port district, the louder it became.

Street by street, tavern by tavern, he searched for clues the assassin had followed them. When the last of the bells rang for the night, he made a final sweep of the Golden Feiche. A weathered-looking whore, hoping for one last customer before retiring, sidled close to him. The rank smell of her breath made him gag, but he smiled into her pockmarked face.

"What'll ya say, sweetie? How 'bout a romp upstairs afore

sunrise?"

"I would love nothing more, but I am in search of a friend." He gazed lovingly at her, as if she were the most desirable woman he'd ever met. "You have not seen a man dressed in black, hood worn low, most likely, hair of spun gold and eyes the color of frozen cliffs?"

"Aye, you be a poet, dontcha?" She reeked of cheap mead and piss. Her body odor assaulted his nostrils as she scratched absently at her armpit. "Naw, can't say that I have. Since 'e ain't here, love, how 'bout a toss?"

Rhoane clucked her on the chin. "Perhaps another time." He slipped a silver feather into her palm before turning away from her watery grey eyes.

An old crone sat alone at a corner table, watching him with a little too much interest. As he hoped, when he exited the tavern, she followed him into the night. Half a block from the dock where he had fought the assassin several moonturns earlier, he spun around, grabbing the crone's cloak. Her feet dangled above the ground as he held her close to his face.

"Speak," Rhoane commanded, using an ancient tongue of Elennish.

A hiss came from deep within her, a fetid snarl that escaped her lips in an inky haze.

"Who is your master? Tell me now or I will end his command over you." Her fragile bones would snap with just a touch of added pressure.

"No. I beg of you." Her hood slipped back, revealing a wrinkled forehead with short wisps of white hair. Her master's hold was the only thing keeping her bound to Aelinae.

"Does your master control the assassin who hunts my beloved?"

Her eyes clouded and then rolled to the back of her head. Another deeper, yet equally foul voice came from her. "The Dark One controls your assassin. None of my brethren can see them nor do we know where they are. They keep themselves hidden even from us."

"Why send your crone to me?"

"A warning. If the Dark One succeeds in destroying your beloved, all will be lost. Even now, the balance of ShantiMari weakens."

"Is this Dark One behind the efforts to free Kaldaar? I sensed much Black ShantiMari at Kaldaar's Stones and in the one called Celia."

"The Black Brotherhood has survived many ages without a new vessel. Whoever wished to use the Summerlands princess for this purpose did it without the consent of the brethren."

The Black Brotherhood were the sworn agents of Kaldaar, dating back as far as the Great War. If they didn't know who wanted Kaldaar freed, then who did? Who, or what, was behind Sabina's attempted rape? Rhoane tightened his grip on the crone.

"Are you telling me the Brotherhood does not wish for the release of your god?"

The crone gave a dangerous shake of her head. Rhoane loosened his grip, fearing her neck might snap. "Neither Kaldaar's nor Rykoto's freedom would benefit us."

Dammit. More riddles. Kaldaar was their source of power. "One last question. Why does the Brotherhood want Taryn to succeed? If the balance of Aelinae is weakening, is that not the perfect time for you to spread your Black teachings?"

"You asked two questions, Prince Rhoane of the Eleri. I will answer only one." Rhoane resented the smugness in the master's voice, but he was in no position to bicker. He needed whatever knowledge the Brotherhood had. "Without the Eirielle, Aelinae will fall into dangerous times. The Brotherhood cannot survive without the balance of power. The trinity does not reside within your beloved."

"She has the three strains of ShantiMari—she is the Eirielle," Rhoane insisted.

"It is a shame you feel you must limit her. Should our assistance be needed, my brethren and I offer it willingly." The crone slumped against his grip with the loss of the master's connection.

Not knowing where she lived, Rhoane found a secure alcove off the main road and gently placed the crone within the shadows. Hopefully, her master would protect her until she regained consciousness.

He stalked the streets, half looking for the assassin. His thoughts were a tumble of curses and riddles. If the Brotherhood were nervous about this mysterious "Dark One," they indeed had reason to be alarmed. But then, the master might be misleading him. Kaldaar could be the Dark One. After all, a god could hide himself easily enough. Assuming the master wasn't lying and the Dark One was not Kaldaar, then who? Someone far more powerful than Rhoane had originally guessed. Which meant Taryn needed to be even stronger.

He worried the master's words over and over in his mind. The trinity had to reside in Taryn, but he'd spoken otherwise. And if it didn't, how was Rhoane limiting her? He swore silently and kicked at the gravel path. The damned gods and their capricious games! Hopefully his father could help unravel the puzzle. Time was short and they needed answers.

The palace gate creaked as he pressed against the old wood, the sound echoing in the early morning quiet, disturbing a nesting owl who hooted his discomfort. Rhoane strode through the gardens to the large glass doors that led to the atrium.

He was almost fully across the room when Duke Anje's voice came from a darkened corner. "Was your search successful?" Anje lowered a book, his intense gaze visible to the Eleri prince despite the lack of light.

Caught, Rhoane took a seat beside the man and sighed. "It was enlightening and frustrating. The Black Brotherhood does not know who controls the assassin. I had hoped one of their own was behind the attacks, but now," he took a staggering breath and ran his hands through his hair, pulling free one of his braids, "I am just as ignorant."

"What happened at the Stones? Hayden is remiss and has yet to tell me everything. Did Taryn truly defeat the phantom?"

"As you know, it is difficult to fully vanquish a projection. The phantom's master was most likely injured after the attack, but I fear he is at this moment recovering still. There will be more attacks, and not just from the assassin or phantom."

"Do you think the two are linked?"

"I wish I knew. Kaldaar, Rykoto, the phantom, the assassin, Valterys, Zakael—Lliandra, even. There are too many unknowns. Too many who wish to use Taryn's power or destroy her."

"Tell me the truth, how concerned should we be?"

Rhoane leveled a look at the man. "If I were you, I would reacquaint myself with Dark ShantiMari. You will have need of it by the time this is over." Rhoane exhaled slowly. "Your time of living in the Light has come to an end, my friend."

Chapter 9

THEY stayed at Paderau only one day, much to Anje's dismay. He'd hoped to have more time with Taryn, to fully understand what had happened at Kaldaar's Stones. She assured him they would be together at the Light Celebrations—where they would have plenty of time to discuss the events of that horrible morning—but her immediate concern was delivering Carga to the Narthvier for her purification.

Anje couldn't fault Taryn for not wanting to discuss the event, but he suspected there was something she hid from him. Something important. Something that terrified her.

He stood alone in the courtyard, pulling his cloak around him to fend off the early morning chill, and waved as the three travelers slipped out of the palace gates. The feeling of dread that came over him lingered, embedding a chill deep within his bones.

The others would arrive in a few days and Anje needed to be there to greet them, but first he had to make an unplanned visit. It had been many seasons since he'd used the hidden chamber in his dressing room. For several long minutes he stared at the door, hoping he wasn't making a mistake. One wrong syllable and he'd end up with Kaldaar, banished to the edge of nothingness.

Gathering his courage, he blew out the breath he'd been

holding and touched the seal etched into the wood. His muffled words echoed in the tight space, warming the air. Dust motes swirled in a tempest until the chamber itself spun out of control. Anje continued chanting, despite the fear that gripped his heart. He'd been too long in the Light. It was suicide to attempt this after so much time away.

And yet…

And yet he continued to say the words, to infuse his power into the wood, to believe it was possible. For Taryn, he told himself. For her, it was worth revisiting the horrors.

The spinning stopped and the air settled.

Anje gathered his thoughts and smoothed his jacket before turning the door handle. When he stepped out of the chamber, he was no longer in his home, but in the room he'd used as a small boy in Caer Idris.

He'd done it. He'd crossed time and space. A wide smile broke out on his face and he danced a little jig. Dark curtains blocked the light, but Anje could see the room was not being used. It looked much the same as it had when he lived there, with a few changes. New bedding, different pictures, and of course, his personal items were nowhere to be seen. His hasty departure that fateful day meant he'd left much behind. Over the years, he'd often wondered what his uncle, Valterys's father, had done with his beloved items.

Anje shook himself. He'd not let the past derail his purpose.

He turned from the room and hurried to Valterys's apartment. At that early hour, his cousin would most likely be in his study or the dungeons. Bile churned in his gut at the memory of seeing his cousin, blood streaking his face and arms, a satisfied smile on his lips, taunting him.

Pushing the horrific image away, Anje quickened his pace. The sooner he saw Valterys, the sooner he could leave the vile place.

"Uncle?" Anje didn't recognize the voice of his nephew, but the figure who stepped out from the shadows was disturbingly familiar. He had the height and looks of his father.

"Zakael." Anje greeted the man, keeping his hands to his sides.

"I was unaware you would be visiting today." He tapped his lip with a long finger. "In fact, I can't recall you ever visiting. Which makes me wonder to what we owe this honor?"

"I'm here to see my cousin. If you'll excuse me." Anje didn't wait for an answer. He was being rude, but Zakael deserved no less. The boy was as twisted as his father.

Zakael followed Anje up the stairs to Valterys's rooms, standing quietly beside his uncle while Anje knocked on the door. After a moment, a servant answered. Seeing Zakael with the stranger, he allowed them in without saying a word.

As he'd hoped, Valterys was in his study, reading a scroll with a dozen others scattered across his desk. He waved a dismissive hand, not bothering to look up from his work. "I'm busy."

"Yes, aren't we all." Anje hid his smile when Valterys's head jerked up in surprise. "I'm here to discuss my niece."

Valterys took in Anje, then Zakael. A look passed between the two men that renewed the churning in his gut.

"What about my daughter? Is she in danger?"

"At the moment, no. I'm sure you heard about her altercation with one of Kaldaar's minions." Anje studied the placid expression on his cousin's face, his anxiety turning to anger. "You call yourself a father? Any sane man would've gone to his daughter and offered counsel after what she experienced. Unless..." Anje let the word hang between them, his misty eyes never leaving the steel gaze of Valterys. Their coloring might be the same, but Anje was nothing like his cousin, which was why he'd been cut off from the rest of the family after the death of his oldest son.

"What? Do you expect me to run after her every time she has a scuffle? Wasn't it in *your* city she was nearly murdered by an assassin?"

"Was that by your command, dear cousin? Are you in league with Kaldaar and wish your own daughter dead?"

Valterys barked a laugh and stretched his arms to the side before crossing them over his chest. His glare was meant to cut, but Anje had grown immune to his cousin's intimidation.

"Hardly. Aelinae needs Taryn, and I am doing my best to make certain she stays alive." He held something back; Anje could see it in the way Valterys's jaw clenched, but he dared not ask what. Not just yet.

"Good. Then we are not at cross-purposes." Anje forced himself to relax, for his shoulders to slump in docile countenance. "She needs you, Valterys, as a father and a mentor. Without the trinity, she is bound to fail."

Valterys stood then and nodded. "Of that we are agreed. Will you see to it that she comes to me of her own will? I'll not have her here under protest."

Up to that moment, Zakael had been silently observing the conversation, but at the last word, he held out his hand to silence the others. Anje's stomach tightened again.

"No. Send her to Gaarendahl, where I can help unlock her Dark powers."

Anje eyed him skeptically, but Zakael's grey eyes, so similar in shade and shape to his father's, held a promise of sincerity. Trusting him was the last thing Anje wanted to do and began to object, but Zakael cut him off.

"I guarantee you her safety. No harm shall come to my sister during her visit. Of this, you have my word." Zakael placed his hand over his heart and bowed his head.

Anje looked to Valterys, who was rubbing his chin

between thumb and forefinger, distance lingering in his gaze as if he was physically present, but mentally far away. Finally, he nodded and said, "Yes, she'll go to you first, son. Unlock her powers, instruct her as you can, and then send her to me. She must have the trinity to complete her tasks." His focus snapped to Anje and he added, "For Aelinae."

The three of them placed their hands over their hearts.

"If you'll indulge an old man," Anje said after the oath was made, "I'd like to reacquaint myself with my childhood home. It's many long seasons since I roamed these halls."

A tic pulled the corner of Valterys's lips, but he smiled through the irritation. "Of course. Take as long as you'd like. Your belongings are stored in the attic." The last was said almost as an afterthought.

Anje drifted in and out of rooms, most of which looked strangely the same as they had when he'd run through them as a lad. Memories crowded his thoughts. He'd lived happily at Caer Idris until Valterys told him he would marry the younger sister of the empress. Not that Anje didn't want to marry the beautiful princess; it was what Valterys expected of him once he was firmly ensconced in Lliandra's court.

But it hadn't happened as Valterys had planned. Lliandra, distrustful of Valterys and his brethren, had sent Gwyneira and Anje to live in Paderau, far from her court and the Light Throne. There, they made a good life for themselves and their children. Until—

The duke shook himself and shoved the dangerous thought to the darkness where it dwelled, eating away at him every moment of every day.

Without realizing it, he'd retraced his steps until he stood before a nondescript door. A visitor to the castle would never know that beyond the plain wooden planks and simply made iron hinges lay the dungeons. It was there Anje had discovered his cousin's peculiar interests.

He spun and hurried away from the darkened corridors and dank smelling cells. Several servants scuttled out of his way as he rushed toward a door he knew led outside. It banged open and Anje gulped in fresh sea air. The salty tang bit his throat.

It was a mistake to return to Caer Idris. He should've known better, but he had to see the place for himself, see Valterys. Had to know what his cousin planned for Taryn.

Anje walked through the gardens, breathing in the sweet scent of flowers that bloomed between Harvest and Wintertide. Their delicate fragrance, buttressed against the brine of the ocean, soothed his fractured nerves. It was in this very garden that Duke Anje had married the love of his life. It was there she'd promised to love him, even beyond death.

He bent and inhaled the essence of Gwyn's favorite rose, one she'd taken stalks from and carefully cultivated at both Ravenwood and Paderau. In every petal, he saw his beautiful bride.

The slamming of a door brought him out of his reverie and he looked up in time to see Valterys stride hastily away, a sack over his shoulder. Intrigued, Anje kept to the shadows and followed his cousin. When Valterys stopped suddenly and scanned the area, Anje froze, hoping the scant leaves of a ficus hid him from his cousin's view. It annoyed him he still felt the need to hide from Valterys. He was an adult, not the child he'd been when Valterys had practiced his various forms of torture on him. Old habits were hard to break.

Valterys gripped the bag tighter, his face turned up to the clear sky. A chill whipped around Anje's legs and up his trousers. The form of Valterys altered from that of a man to a sleek black feiche. With the beat of his strong wings, Valterys lifted into the sky.

Anje swore. It had been ages since he'd transformed. Ever since he turned his back on Valterys and shut himself off from his Dark ShantiMari. The desire to follow his cousin was too strong to deny. It was for Taryn, he told himself. Her safety was more important than his own fears.

Stepping around the ficus into the sunlight, Anje held his hands out to his side, imagining the form of a levon. If he wanted to follow Valterys, he'd need the speed of the smaller bird. With his parcel, Valterys required the bulk of the feiche, which worked to Anje's advantage.

He suppressed a shudder as his head morphed into a feathered crown and strong beak. His body followed, flowing smoothly into the bird's shape. That he could transform so easily after a long period of abstinence intrigued him, but it was the bird's desires that flooded through him. Hunt. Feed. Fly.

Anje beat his wings, catching an updraft that propelled him into the air and sent him spiraling to the right. He countered the warm rush beneath his wings and flew in a steady line, his vision locked on the speck in front of him.

Keeping his distance, he followed Valterys over the Spine of Ohlin. When Valterys banked north, Anje's nerves betrayed him. His cousin was heading toward the Temple of Ardyn. Many continued their devotion to the fallen god, but not Anje. When he left Caer Idris, he left behind everything his family held dear, including their alliance with the mad god.

He swooped around the back of the temple, transforming into the form of a man with slightly more effort than it had taken to become a bird. The bird's hold on him worried Anje, but he had neither the time nor the inclination to understand why. His focus was on Valterys and what he was doing at the temple.

By the time he reached the entrance, Valterys had laid a body on the altar and flames rose from the floor to the top of the domed building. Valterys spoke in a manic rush, apologizing to the god for being delayed. He didn't mention Anje by name but said an unscheduled visitor had prompted caution on his part.

Rykoto's visage shimmered in the flames, a forked tongue snaking out to taste the body.

"She is delightful, my son. Fresh. Virginal. Her blood will fulfill my desires for now."

A look of relief spread across Valterys's face. Anje crept farther into the temple, using the columns to hide himself. Twice the mad god's eyes roved over the room, settling where Anje hid, but he said nothing to Valterys.

"My lord," Valterys began, "Kaldaar remains exiled, the Eirielle grows stronger, and your queen awaits your command. All is in order."

Rykoto's gaze flicked once more to where Anje hid. A tendril of flame slithered up the altar to pluck a piece of flesh from the dead woman's thigh. Several more followed; with each one, Rykoto moaned his pleasure.

Sickness crept up Anje's throat and he swallowed hard against the urge to vomit. But he did not look away. He forced himself to watch until nothing but bones remained on the altar. Even when Rykoto held her heart in his fiery grip, taking pleasure in eating the organ, Anje kept his eyes locked on the horror. This was why he'd forsaken his god and family for the Light.

Satiated, Rykoto turned his attention to Valterys. "Have you uncovered who was behind Kaldaar's scheme?"

Anje glanced at his cousin. He'd suspected Valterys of not only orchestrating the events with Kaldaar's minions, but of manipulating the assassin as well.

"No, my lord. The two Aelans involved with the plot were given a traitor's burial. There has been no more from Kaldaar's agent. Most likely, he was vanquished at the Stones. The Eirielle's powers are greater than I was led to believe.

However, she has yet to unlock her Dark ShantiMari."

"There is still time." The air warmed within the temple, and then snowflakes drifted from the ceiling to dust the ground. "There is yet still time."

"Great Lord, what is your bidding?" Valterys knelt before the flames, his head bent in supplication.

"What of Julicta's daughter? Does she live?"

A frown crossed Valterys's features. "I know not of who you speak."

Anje breathed a sigh of relief. Valterys was a bold man, but not stupid enough to lie to their god. If he didn't know Sabina was the vessel, he couldn't have been involved with the Kaldaar scheme. Or, he *was* lying, and as Anje feared, the cause of all their problems. It was difficult to tell with Valterys. Lies slipped from his lips like the smoothest dreem.

Rykoto's voice broke through the air, laced with disappointment. "Be gone from here. I need rest after my feeding."

Valterys bowed to the floor and the flames dimmed to nothing. The temple darkened without Rykoto's light, the warmth turning frigid in the snap of a breath.

Anje waited several minutes after Valterys left before stepping from his hiding place. He'd reached the last set of columns near the door when the air warmed and a coil of fire slithered around his neck. He turned slowly, dreading the sight of Rykoto in the flames.

The god's head danced above the tiled floor. Unlike the image presented to Valterys, Rykoto's black hair hung in dirty lengths around his face. Purplish half-moons set off his dark eyes. His cracked lips opened to reveal yellow teeth in his rotting mouth.

"Have you returned to us, my son?" Rykoto asked in a rasping voice vastly different from the smooth tones that came from his handsome face with Valterys.

Rykoto's true self alarmed the duke. Either the god had used all his power to exert his dominance over Valterys, or he was trying to manipulate Anje by garnering sympathy. Either way, the duke stayed wary.

"No, Rykoto." A note of sadness touched his words. "I followed Valterys here to learn of his plans regarding my niece."

"The Eirielle."

"Yes, the destroyer and savior."

"She will be mine."

"Not if I can help it." Anje straightened his shoulders and awaited Rykoto's lash. The dark god didn't tolerate disobedience.

"You are tainted by Nadra, boy. Why have you forsaken the Dark?"

"I have forsaken nothing. Dark ShantiMari burns through my veins. Until this moment, I hated my heritage and tried to hide my Dark powers. I was ashamed of my family, believing I was as twisted as they. But that's not true and I think you know it. In fact, I think you fear the good I could do with my Dark ShantiMari. That is why you show your true self to me—you think to punish me, to make me feel responsible for your imprisonment. I didn't cause this, Rykoto."

"Not you, but your ancestors did."

"You deserved everything they gave you."

A hiss issued from the cracked lips, tearing them. Blood oozed down his chin. "You dare defy a god?"

"I do. Whatever you and Valterys are planning, I pledge, with every fiber of my being, to stop. You will never return to the lands of Aelinae."

Searing heat filled the space and Rykoto lashed out at Anje with a fire-tipped spear aimed at his heart. Too unaccustomed to not using his power, Anje fumbled to call forth his ShantiMari. A bright circle of light appeared in front of him, absorbing the spear and turning it to dust.

Rykoto roared a great plume of smoke, staining the ceiling of the temple.

"Sleep now, Rykoto," a small, feminine voice said. Tears sprang to Anje's eyes. He couldn't trust his hearing. A rainbow formed over the mad god, showering him with flecks of stardust and glitter. Slowly, much slower than Anje would have liked, the image of Rykoto weakened until there was nothing left of the god. Nothing but a smattering of shimmering dust on the floor. Even that disappeared within the space of a heartbeat.

Anje stood with his mouth open, shock and heartbreak immobilizing him.

The cluster of light floated near him and a tendril reached out to stroke his cheek. He leaned into the warmth of his wife's touch. Tears spilled over his cheeks.

"Be well, my love. I am with you, as ever I was in life."

The light faded and Anje searched the room, frantic to see a speck of his beloved Gwyneira, but she was gone. He stood alone in the temple with only his broken heart and shattered memories for company.

Chapter 10

LEADEN skies heavy with rain threatened them most of the way north. Even with Rhoane manipulating time, they arrived at the first veil with steam rising from their horses and Kaida little more than a mass of soggy fur.

Carga said little when they passed through the first few veils, her anxiety becoming more noticeable as they made their way farther into the forest. Taryn rested her hand on Carga's, wishing her peaceful thoughts. From what Rhoane shared of his experience, it was torture for an exiled Eleri to return to the Weirren. It felt akin to a thousand tiny cuts being inflicted over and over without reprieve.

Darennsai, Kaida said quietly in Taryn's mind, *I would very much like to see my sire and dam.*

Go to your family with my blessing. Find me at the Weirren when your visit is complete.

Kaida barked before running off into the woods, a streak of grey against the mist. At Rhoane's questioning look, she explained, "She wants to see her family."

Carga laughed nervously. "I know how she feels. It seems forever since I have been in these woods."

"The forest has missed you," Taryn told her. Rhoane and Carga exchanged a meaningful look and Taryn challenged, "What? You thought the trees only spoke to you?"

Carga suppressed a grin. "Not at all, sister. How wonderful you can hear it."

Leaves of gold, russet, and crimson rested like gems set in a sea of green. Moss and lichen-covered tree trunks stretched up to skeletal branches. Other trees remained bare-trunked but full of lush, verdant leaves, as if the vier couldn't commit to one season or another.

King Stephan waited for them atop the steps to the great Weirren, watching their arrival with a guarded smile. Although his daughter had returned, he could not officially acknowledge her until she was purified. Stephan greeted Rhoane in the Eleri custom and then turned to Taryn. His eyes searched hers for several moments and he sighed.

"You are so very nearly Eleri. No longer Aelan, but not quite full Eleri. These will tell us when you are complete." He tapped her ears before kissing her on the cheek. "Welcome, daughter."

She curtsied low, saying in Eleri, "My heart is at peace with you this day."

"Not only have you learned the Eleri language, you know our customs as well." He bowed to her. "Truly you are a blessing." Sadness clouded his eyes as he looked at his daughter. "Carga. I will save our greeting for after the ceremony."

Tears shone in Carga's eyes, but she nodded her acceptance.

King Stephan led Taryn not to the queen's chambers as before, but to rooms adjoining Rhoane's. After she bathed and changed into an Eleri gown, she went in search of Eoghan. She smiled when she found him in the library, sprawled on a chair with a book in his lap. He and Eliahnna were made for each other.

There would come a time when she would have to explain to King Stephan Eoghan was leaving the Weirren for an Aelan girl, but that day was far off still. For the time being, she would keep Eliahnna and Eoghan's secret. When he bade her give Eliahnna a gift after their first visit to the Weirren, Taryn had declined, citing her tenuous position with the court. But Eoghan was nothing if not persistent and Taryn finally agreed to take his gift to her sister when they returned to Talaith.

Nothing more than a small piece of bark from the great tree, Eoghan had sanded the pendant smooth and inscribed it with Eleri words of devotion. To an outsider, it looked like a trifle, but to Eliahnna it was priceless.

"Does the sight of me really cause you so much pain, sister?" Eoghan asked and Taryn jumped. It still surprised her when Rhoane's siblings referred to her as their sister, but to them, when King Stephan declared her *Darennsai*, she became part of their family.

"No, my sweet brother, it fills my heart with joy to see you." She embraced him with as much warmth as she could muster. "I have a message for you from Eliahnna."

Excitement danced in his eyes. "Did she enjoy my gift?"

"Very much so. She wears it around her neck on a leather cord. Of course, she has to hide it from Mother, but I think she feels the risk is worth it."

"And what is this message you have for me?"

Taryn presented him with a shell Eliahnna found in the cove near the palace. "Eliahnna said you need to put it to your ear." When Taryn had done so, nothing happened.

Eoghan beamed at Taryn. "Thank you, sister. This gift is wonderful."

"Did you hear the ocean?"

"No, something more musical. Eliahnna spoke to me in the shell."

"I do not want to know what she said. I am already in enough trouble if your father finds out I am playing messenger between you two."

They sat opposite each other in overstuffed chairs and Taryn sank into the soft cushions, exhaustion washing over her. "Have you thought about this, Eoghan? I mean seriously thought of what your father is going to do when he finds out you have given your heart to an Aelan? She cannot become Eleri. At least, all the information I have found makes it sound like I am the only one who can do that."

"I know. I have been searching for a way myself, but I do not think she is meant to become Eleri. I think I am meant to live amongst Aelans."

Taryn paused, choosing her words carefully. "Perhaps you should spend more time with her before you make an important decision like that. You cannot just meet someone once and know you are meant to be together forever."

"Was it not like that with you and Rhoane?"

A familiar tugging of her heart burned against her guilt. She hadn't fallen madly in love with him the first time she saw him. He'd been an image from a dream. Perhaps in her childish fantasies, she fancied herself in love with him. When she met him in the cavern, it wasn't fireworks and love sonnets. There was attraction, yes, but neither love nor trust.

Her love for him grew over time. She hoped it was the kind of love that would last to eternity. "I was raised far from these customs. It has taken me longer to adjust than I think some people would like. If Rhoane and I are to be together for the rest of our lives, then I would like to know I am making the right choice not just for me, but for him as well."

"Rhoane never once doubted his love for you or the commitment it took to take his oath."

"What oath?"

Eoghan hesitated and Taryn urged him to continue. If he knew something she should know, he had to tell her.

"When Rhoane was told of Verdaine's prophecy, he

invoked an ancient Eleri oath that bound him to you. He vowed to love and protect you, forsaking all others until his death."

The air stilled for a moment. Specks of dust hung suspended in rays of the afternoon sun and then drifted off when she breathed again. "What you are telling me is if I should decide not to choose Rhoane, he will never have a mate?"

Eoghan nodded and her insides melted. "Rhoane was able to make that kind of commitment without ever knowing me. Why does that scare the hell out of me?"

Eoghan leaned forward, saying softly, "Because you are looking at this with your mind and not your heart. You love my brother, I can see that, but you are trying to rationalize all that has happened to you. Why do you think you spend so much time with your scrolls? To answer all those questions you have in your head. You do not need words to tell you what to do. You already know." He put a hand over her racing heart. "In here."

Tears welled in her eyes. "I do not know how."

He tenderly wiped her tears with his thumb. "Stop thinking so much and just feel. Let it come to you. Do not force it or it will drift away like smoke from a flame. Just be still and listen." He put his forehead to hers, holding her face between his hands. They were warm with gentleness beneath their strength, like Rhoane's. "Everything you need is inside you already. You just have to trust yourself."

Fresh tears rolled down her cheeks. "I am afraid."

"Of what, Darennsai?"

"Failing."

"If you do nothing, that is failure. If you try and do not succeed, that is learning. Success is in the doing, in the being present for every moment."

She sniffed, choking on a laugh. "Just how old are you,

anyway?"

"I am only one hundred twenty-two."

"Only." She dried her tears with the handkerchief he handed her. "Thank you."

He patted the pocket where he placed the shell. "No, thank you. Would you like to walk in the garden before dinner?"

"There is someone I need to talk to first."

Eoghan was right. She had to stop living in fear, but how to stop the constant loop of anxiety was the one riddle she had yet to master. One thing she knew for sure—ignoring a situation meant certain failure.

She might've skipped to Rhoane's room, or sprinted, or simply strolled there, she couldn't remember, for the fresh wave of anxiety that crowded her thoughts. Happy anxiety. At least, she hoped Rhoane would think so, too. Palms sweating, she stood outside his door for several minutes before knocking.

"Taryn, this is a surprise. Would you like to come in?" He opened the door to her, but she shook her head.

"Are you busy? I thought we could go for a walk." Taryn's heart lodged itself in her throat and the words tumbled out a garbled mess.

"Where would you like to go?"

"To the bower, if you do not mind."

Rhoane's wicked, little half-smile said he didn't mind one bit, but there was a question in his glance and her insides trembled.

They said very little as they wound their way up the never-ending steps to the top of the Weirren. The sun huddled low in the sky to the east, the air crisp. Despite the cold, the leaves of their bower were lush and full. The Weirren never lost its foliage, even in the darkest days of Wintertide. It was how it had always been.

When she shivered, Rhoane produced a thick blanket, wrapping it around her shoulders. A wall of his ShantiMari domed over them. He pulled her hair out from under the blanket, running his fingers through to the tips.

Taryn swayed into his caress. "I have been unfair to you, Rhoane. Despite the wedge Marissa put between us, you never wavered in your feelings for me. Even after Harvest, I withheld myself from you. I am sorry."

She ran her hands up his clothing to his face, letting the blanket fall around them. A fire lit in his eyes and uncertainty gripped her. She had much better control of her powers than she did the morning in the orchard when her tempest nearly choked the life from them, but she was hesitant. Terrified, more like it. And not just of her power.

She shoved her apprehension to the back of her thoughts and focused on the man in front of her. Held onto the desire he reflected back to her. "Before we go any further, I need to know that you want to be with me because you love me, as a woman and not as the Darennsai or anything I am supposed to be. If you do not, then I have no choice but to release you from your oath."

The desire vanished from his eyes and he stepped away as if burned. "How do you know about my oath?"

"Eoghan told me this afternoon. Was I not to know?" Her legs trembled and she shivered at Rhoane's sudden coldness.

"This afternoon? No sooner?"

"Just before I found you. It is what convinced me to stop letting my fears control me."

A strange looked crossed his face. Not anger, but a quiet resignation as if a lingering question had finally been answered. He closed the distance between them and their lips met, tentative at first, but then she pressed her body against his, kissing him, tasting him, delighting in the sensations that ran through her.

Rhoane lifted a fraction, his eyes searching hers. "I cannot change who you are, Taryn. To me, you have always been the Darennsai. To say I love one without the other would be false. But know this—I would take the oath again this very night if you asked. I am yours, mi carae, forever. I must know, though. Is this what you truly want?"

All her doubts—of whether she was good enough for him, whether she was strong enough to be his partner, whether she would fail—taunted her, but she shut herself off from the constant disquiet. "This is what I want. Here with you now."

She kissed him again, roughly, feeling his stubble scratch against her and wanting more. Wanting all of him. She tangled her fingers in his hair and melded her body to his. Strong hands roamed down her back and then up to her hair, by turns grasping a handful before smoothing it straight. Heat filled the space. The forest sounds dimmed beneath the roar of blood pumping in her ears.

Rhoane kissed her neck just beneath her ear and a rush of desire flooded her, exquisite, maddening, all-consuming. Her toes curled with each touch of his lips trailing heat down her neck to her shoulder. His hands trembled as he fumbled with the bows securing her dress. With agonizing slowness, he slipped her gown to her waist.

Her breath came in shallow gasps as he admired her naked breasts, his eyes dark with desire. Calloused hands gently massaged the flesh, his thumbs tracing her nipples until they hardened to marble nubs. That damned half smile crooked up his lips, making her already weak knees jerk in response.

A dark brow arched and he lifted his gaze, "Shall I stop?"

"Dear god no."

He dipped his head and took a breast in his mouth. The warmth of his tongue and scrape of his teeth rocked her. A firm hand gripped her back and his ShantiMari wrapped around them, keeping her upright.

She moaned, arching into his power. The touch of his ShantiMari ignited sparks of pleasure all through her body. It, combined with what he was doing to her breasts, almost brought her to a climax she wasn't ready yet to have. The sustained torment of his mouth on her skin was too good, too raw. His power subsided, leaving her gasping.

With a last lick to her breast, he nipped gentle kisses across her abdomen. When his lips touched her scar, she flinched, but not from pain. A delicious warmth spread over her as he ran his thumb along the jagged welt. His lips lingered over the scar, his breath hot against the disfigurement. A soft tingling spread from his touch and he placed a final kiss before sliding her dress the rest of the way down her body until she stood naked before him, shy and unsure.

When his hands went to the buttons on his tunic, she stopped him. With as much care and attention as he'd shown her, she removed his clothing, starting with his outer jerkin. His muscled torso flexed beneath the soft cotton of his tunic. Something low in her contracted and her breathing slowed. The crisp scent of apples mingled with a dark spiciness, upping her arousal to dangerous levels.

She slid her hands under the tunic and pushed it over his abs, past his chest, and finally above his head. A smattering of hair covered a well-defined chest, but what caught her attention were the numerous scars. Some long and ragged, others clean lines, all of them ghost tattoos, evidence of a difficult life. She wanted to know the story behind each one, but not right then. There was time later to uncover their truths, right now she still had more exploring to do.

When she touched his skin, it warmed beneath her fingertips, causing a slight sheen to bloom beneath the surface. She leaned in, kissing the nearest scar to her, much as he'd done to her vorlock wound. The bloom deepened, spreading across his abdomen to disappear beneath his breeches.

A growl, low and wanting, came from the depths of his throat.

Her insides clenched at the sound. Sexy didn't even come close to describing it. A grin tickled the edges of her mouth and she glanced up to find him watching her, a dark intensity in his mossy eyes. That look, combined with the swell of his erection pressed against her midsection, rough leather on her naked skin, made her ache with need.

Holy hell, she was going to lose it before he was naked.

Her shaking fingers fumbled with the ties of his pants and, once unlaced, she skimmed her hands across his hips, pressing the fabric over his ass until it dropped to the branches of the bower.

Finally, he stood naked before her, his presence filling the space, his scent overwhelming her already deliriously heightened senses. Every moment he wasn't touching her was anguish. Every inch of her longed to be caressed by him.

With exquisite gentleness, he lifted her in his arms and placed her on the blanket. Her heart beat in her throat when he lay beside her. His erection pressed against her thigh, gorgeous and thick, and for fuck's sake, if he didn't make love to her soon she might have to kill him. He shifted his weight, capturing her mouth with his. Her fingertips explored his impossibly soft skin, resting over his heart and feeling there the same wild thumping as in her own chest.

Hesitation flickered in his eyes as he beheld her face. She tilted her hips up to encourage him, and kept her gaze locked to his as he entered. A satisfied sigh of desire escaped her throat and he responded in kind. Bloody hell, why had she waited so long?

They were a tangle of flesh, moving in unison, low cries and moans hovering momentarily before drifting away on the breeze. The interplay of passion on his face humbled her. She wanted to meld their bodies into one, to feel his pleasure as her own. A dizzying array of emotions overwhelmed her. For a single moment the world stilled and she floated amongst the stars, then every nerve in her body contracted and stars burst behind her closed eyes. She didn't know whether to laugh or cry as her body convulsed with spasms. It was fireworks and rainbows, Light and Dark, sunshine and moonbeams. It was warmth and love, and oh god, Rhoane inside of her was perfect, she never wanted him anywhere else but there, with her.

Rhoane cried out and shuddered, a look of surprised relief on his face.

He lay next to her, panting, his arm resting across her middle, a satisfied smile on his lips. Neither wanted to speak, to break the spell of their lovemaking. Taryn lazily ran her fingers up and down his torso. She would never tire of touching him, of feeling his skin against hers. She traced the top of his ears with her fingertip and a groan started from his sternum to pass between his lips.

"An Eleri's ears are very sensitive. Do not do that unless you are willing to suffer the consequences." His eyes were lidded, his words slurred.

"And what would those be?" She lightly pinched the pointed tips.

Rhoane pinned her beneath him. His hair fell forward, touching her nipples. She moaned again, arching her back, the flames of desire igniting in her once more. His mouth covered hers, his tongue searching for and finding hers. She shifted beneath him, wanting to feel him inside her, but he laughed and pulled away. "Patience, my love." He sat beside her, tracing a finger down her arm. "We have the whole night if you wish."

"Are we not expected at dinner?"

His brows pinched in mock hurt. "Would you rather spend the evening with the others?"

"What do you think?" No formal feast was planned for the night, nor would there be until Carga's purification. Although Taryn had a momentary stab of guilt she and Rhoane weren't with the Eleri, somehow it was right they were together. A sense of belonging filled her. Her connection went beyond Rhoane to the forest, and the creatures that dwelled there, encompassing all of the Eleri in its scope.

The sensation traveled past the vier, to the stars and oceans, to the inhabitants of every kingdom in Aelinae. She *was* Aelinae. No, she was more than that: a cosmic entity unfettered by the constraints of flesh. She hadn't been floating in the stars, she was a part of them and they, her. Overwhelmed by the awareness, she swooned, then panicked at the sudden feeling of falling through the sky, past the leaves, to the hard ground far below.

Her muffled scream and blind clutching startled Rhoane. He grabbed her, roughly pulling her to him, rocking her like a child. "Taryn, what is it? You are so pale."

The awareness faded, but the intensity of emotion lingered. Tears streaked down her face. "I love you, Rhoane. Do not ever doubt that I do." He held her until she relaxed against him. His eyes sought hers, looking for answers, but she had no words to explain what had happened. All she knew for certain was that her fate was tied to Rhoane. Their lovemaking was the element needed to complete their bonding.

Their runes empowered them on their paths, which was why they needed Verdaine's and Ohlin's blessings, but the runes weren't what truly bound them. Sharing their bodies had created a bond stronger than any rune or oath, but how could she explain all that to Rhoane without alarming him, without confessing she had communicated with the universe? She didn't understand it herself.

His hands shook as he held her face close to his. "You are

my life, Taryn Rose Galendrin. My everything. I will never doubt you." His runes sparked, flaring against her skin for only a moment before dimming to a soft shimmer.

They spent the rest of the night in the bower, exploring each other's bodies and finding new ways to pleasure each other. Taryn shocked herself with her boldness, but Rhoane didn't seem to mind. He was equally adventurous. By the end of the night, they knew every smell and taste of the other.

Dawn had not yet made its way to the Narthvier when they lay under the heavy blanket, talking quietly. A thrill ran through her and Rhoane asked with some surprise, "Again?"

"I was just thinking that we never used ShantiMari."

"We should remedy that."

"I do not think we need it." She rolled on top of him, grinning like a child given a special treat, recalling how his ShantiMari had enhanced her arousal. "But just to be sure, perhaps we should find out."

His Eleri Shanti—pale green, powerful, electric—covered her skin while her ShantiMari enveloped them both. Their bodies moved in rhythm, becoming one in a peculiar and frightening way. Taryn could feel her own body as it reacted to Rhoane's. At the same time, she felt his body as if it were hers. The intimacy she experienced, as if she were he making love to her, was exquisite. By the look on his face, he felt the same. She merged with him, taking him into her body, her mind, and then finally, her soul. Nothing else existed but Rhoane.

In the late afternoon, Taryn walked with the other Eleri to the great lake in the Narthvier. Her feet barely touched the ground as she walked beside Rhoane, her hand on his. The gown she wore glowed white against the dirt path and green of the forest. The elaborate, twisted silver crown caught the light, reflecting tiny rainbows of color against the faces of nearby Eleri. She did her best to appear regal and unaffected, but the flutter of ecstasy that remained from her night with Rhoane made it nearly impossible. Not even Bressal's frown could dampen her mood.

He was furious Rhoane had shared his body with her. Through Rhoane's *cynfar* she'd suffered Bressal's anger as if she were present. If she chose, she could demand he accept her as the *Darennsai* of his people, but she didn't wish to incite his anger further.

Not on Carga's special day.

When they reached the lake, the Eleri spread out along the shore, leaving a path to the water's edge. Carga stood before the Eleri priestess who would perform the purification, with Taryn a step behind. When the priestess held aloft a basin, chanting in the ancient tongue of Aelinae, a soft light filtered through the sky to the ground. Only Taryn saw Verdaine as she truly was: a discordant mass of colors contained in a ball of light. It took her a moment to adjust her vision before Verdaine became the woman others saw.

The goddess's long hair flowed around her in colors of gold, green, crimson, and rust, a stark contrast to the pale skin and blue eyes that sparkled in the setting sun. Her bare feet hovered above the ground as she stood beside Carga. Her robes, as green as the grass in spring, pooled around them. She was a fire flower blooming from the terrarae.

"My children," Verdaine addressed the Eleri, "our daughter has returned to us from the land beyond the veils." She took Carga's hand and kissed it. "We have missed you, dear daughter."

Carga curtseyed to Verdaine. "I have longed for the scent of the woods and the feel of loam under my feet."

"King Stephan, is there any reason this Eleri woman should be denied the purification ceremony?"

Stephan stepped forward. "Nay, great lady. She has served her sheanna and will be welcomed as a maiden of our clan once more."

Verdaine inclined her head to Taryn. "Darennsai, you honor us with your presence here today." She turned to Rhoane. "Surtentse." The ancient title was as old as Darennsai and as mysterious.

Rhoane bowed low to the goddess. "You honor me this day."

"Come, my children, to witness the purification of Princess Carga so that she may be your sister once more." Verdaine motioned and Carga's gown fell around her ankles, leaving her naked before the assembled Eleri.

Taryn suppressed a gasp, but the others remained unaffected. The high priestess held her bowl aloft, chanting, "Hear me, Great Spirit, that you might absolve this maiden of her taint. Purify her body and soul so that once more she will know what it is to be Eleri. Embrace her in your forgiveness as she has proved her merit to you during her sheanna."

She motioned for Taryn to pour her bowl over Carga's head. As the oil ran down Carga's pale skin, the priestess held aloft another bowl filled with ash. She emptied it over Carga, chanting under her breath.

The Eleri watched with quiet resolve as Carga tread slowly into the lake. The oil and ash floated off her naked body, making a halo around her on the water's surface. When she was completely submerged, Taryn heard in her mind the voices of the Eleri chanting a song of absolution. The onslaught of emotion overtook her and she swayed where she stood.

Verdaine took her hand, smiling down at her. "You will become accustomed to the ancients in time, my beloved.

This is what it is to be Eleri."

"It is a little more than I was prepared for." Taryn held firm to her hand for reassurance. After Carga had stayed underwater for several minutes, Taryn asked, "Should someone get her?"

"She will emerge when she is purified. Do not worry about her." Verdaine touched Taryn's temple. "Quiet yourself and listen."

Voices of the Eleri drifted through her mind. Their emotions flowed over her, their words filling her until she was one with all Eleri past, present, and future.

This is what it is to be Eleri, Carga whispered.

"You hold yourself back. Let go and be truly one with us," Rhoane told her.

"I thought I was. I can feel all of you in here." She tapped her temple and then her heart.

"That is not enough, my love. You must release yourself."

Taryn frowned. The previous night she'd felt at one with the universe, but it had happened spontaneously. She didn't know what he wanted or how to let go. Carga emerged from the lake and Verdaine glided away from Taryn to embrace her, enveloping her in a floor-length cape of shining gold. A great cheer rose up and King Stephan approached his daughter, holding in his hand a crown made of twisted silver with tiny leaves that fluttered when he placed it on Carga's head. Radiant, Carga accepted her father's embrace with tears in her eyes. Her power flowed from her in waves of jade.

Her Mari lingered on Taryn's skin, similar to Rhoane's, but softer and full of grace. Taryn embraced the girl she first knew only as a cook. "Welcome home, sister."

"I have long waited to hear those words from you, Darennsai." She curtseyed low to Rhoane. "Surtentse."

Rhoane wrapped her in a fierce hug, as did Eoghan and Bressal.

The procession followed a path through the forest to the Weirren with air faeries darting in front of them, lighting the way with drossfire. Multi-hued Glamour shimmered under the air faeries' magical glow.

"This was a good day." Taryn sighed as they entered the large area where tables had been set for Carga's celebratory feast.

"Aye, it was. Would that every day was like this." Rhoane held her hand to his lips, a secret smile hidden behind her fingertips.

"If you can fold time, can you not also stop it?"

"Alas, no. There are limitations and the balance of Aelinae must be respected."

Taryn expected that would be the answer but just once she wished Aelinae didn't come first.

Chapter 11

SABINA slept fitfully beside Hayden, her nightmare causing her to moan and flinch. He draped an arm around her naked midsection, pulling her closer to him. His lips nuzzled the back of her neck, the scent of vanilla teasing him. She smelled of summer.

"Rest now, Sabina. There is nothing to fear." The words were breathed into her ear, a calming mantra he'd said far too many times over the past few weeks. "I am here. I will protect you."

Once she'd recovered from the ordeal, and felt strong enough, Sabina had led Hayden to her bed, where she'd begged him to take her maidenhood. Doing so would rid her of the last of the Black taint that marked her as Kaldaar's chosen vessel. Or at least, that was what Sabina believed. Hayden had been only too happy to accommodate her request.

He'd loved her from the moment they met in Duke Anje's garden room. He cared not that she was a princess or that she had no ShantiMari. Her intelligence had captivated him. During those first heady days, Sabina had been jealous of his friendship with Taryn, and it had taken many heartfelt promises that he felt nothing more for the mysterious woman than he did for his cousins. When they learned the truth of

Taryn's identity, Sabina had once more worried that Hayden would be better suited for the princess.

What neither of them had known, but soon was made clear for the entire court and world to see, was that Taryn was bound to Rhoane not just by the oaths wrapped around their wrists, but by a love deeper than any Hayden had ever witnessed. Even his parents' devotion was not as strong as what his cousin and the Eleri prince shared.

Sabina whimpered and thrashed, calling out Kaldaar's name as she often did. He braced himself for the scream that was sure to follow, cringing when it finally came. His love's sobs broke his heart then as surely as they had the first time he'd heard them. Nothing he nor Faelara, Rhoane, or even Taryn had done helped with Sabina's night frights.

He gently rolled her until she lay prone on her back, and then he nudged open her legs with his own. A devilish smile broke the frown she wore. "Hayden," she murmured and moved her hips up to greet his waiting erection.

He hated taking her this way, but it eased her fears, abolished Kaldaar's presence for the remainder of the night.

Her slender hands roved over his back to his buttocks, massaging and scratching his skin as he entered her. A low groan came from her throat, husky and full of need. Her eyes fluttered open and he saw the last vestiges of the nightmare leaving her.

"Kiss me."

He obediently obliged. The pace was gentle, their lovemaking lasting until the sun broke over the Summer Seas. Hayden loved Sabina, loved being inside her, loved holding her naked body against his own. Yet he wasn't satisfied. Something was missing in their relationship and he had no idea what.

Once Sabina settled into a peaceful slumber, he slipped from the bed and stood on her balcony, breathing in the salt air with all the happiness of an executioner going to the gallows.

Taryn. He cast the thought outward like a fishing net. She'd been gone several weeks and he missed his cousin dreadfully. The pitiful note she'd left did little to explain her sudden departure, or where she'd gone. He didn't buy the story that she and Rhoane were surveying property before joining the others at Celyn Eryri. For her to leave without a proper goodbye meant she was doing something dangerous and trying to protect her friends.

He scowled at the sea, angry she'd not trusted him. Had he not proved he could keep her secrets? Wasn't he as true a friend as Sabina and Faelara?

A truer friend I could not dare hope for. Taryn's thought brushed against his mind. *Don't be angry with me, sweet cousin.*

His heart leapt at the sound of her voice. Ever since that day when he'd laid a carlix's whisker away from death and she'd saved him from Ohlin's sword and the vile poison Marissa had wrapped around it, he'd been in love with her. Of course, he'd not known who she was, or cared, for that matter. To him, she was a goddess sent from Dal Tara just for him.

The journey from Ravenwood to Paderau had almost broken his heart as he realized her love was meant for another. It was then he started to see the bizarre images of flying contraptions and crowded city streets with buildings reaching to the clouds. They were her memories and somehow he was connected to her, although neither of them knew it at the time. It had taken him several moonturns before he confessed his knowledge to her. She hadn't been angry; in fact, she'd been relieved that she could confide in Hayden. Someone she could trust.

I'm not angry. I just wish you'd told me the truth.
Something else bothers you. What is it?

She was becoming as adept at changing the conversation as Faelara. Hayden chuckled to himself and stood with his palms pressed against the banister, gazing far out to sea, to where Sabina's people lived.

Sabina continues to have nightmares.

There was silence in his mind for several seconds before she replied. *Have Faelara make a sleeping draught for her.*

Hayden's heart quickened. His thoughts tumbled without grasping anything constant. *Faelara is not with you? She and Baehlon left the same day as you. Two of your guards are gone as well. The empress claims you are traveling together.*

Huh. Well, then don't tell anyone anything different.

Will you tell me where you are?

An awkward silence stretched out between them. Finally, he heard a resigned sigh in his mind.

Rhoane and I are in the Narthvier. We accompanied Carga here for her purification. I don't know why my mother said I'm with the others, but there must be a reason for it. For now, pretend that I am. Rhoane worries for my safety and doesn't want anyone to know where we are.

Hayden breathed a large sigh of relief. At last, she showed that she trusted him.

I've always trusted you, Hayden. Keeping my whereabouts secret is to protect you, not me. Her tone shifted and he heard longing beneath her words. *I can hear the ocean in your thoughts. I miss you.*

And I, you.

Is it normal that we can speak to each other over such a large distance?

He'd been wondering the same thing. *Not as far as I know.*

Maybe we shouldn't share this with anyone just yet.

Agreed.

So, what's up with you and Sabina? This is more than just her nightmares, isn't it?

Hayden breathed deeply of the salty air, searching for the right words. *When she has a night fright, I console her as best I can, but it's not enough. Lately, the only thing that calms her enough to sleep afterward is to make love to her.*

That doesn't sound bad. What's the problem?

It's become a duty.

Ah. So, you want to have wild monkey sex and she's half passed out whenever you do the nasty, is that it?

You say the most curious things. But yes, I believe you've uncovered the reason for my melancholy.

Have you tried making love when it's not the middle of the night? If you're just doing it to soothe her, your needs aren't being met. Seduce her, plan a romantic night, show her what you need. You've been with other women, Hayden. She's never experienced another man. It's up to you to teach her how to pleasure you. Right?

Hayden was relieved Taryn couldn't see his face. Heat flamed up his neck, covering his cheeks with his embarrassment.

Since when did you become an expert on relations between men and women?

A slight giggle sounded in his mind. *Since Rhoane and I arrived at the Narthvier.*

Once again Hayden blushed furiously, this time for his cousin. A hazy form materialized near the balcony to his right and Taryn smiled at him. His mouth gaped, not just at her ability to project an image of herself, but at what she was wearing. Gone was her usual get-up of leather trousers and tunic; instead she wore a flowing gossamer skirt and tight, midriff-baring top that did little to hide her womanly assets.

"You like?" she teased.

"Um, wow."

"The Eleri are more comfortable with me this way. When I dress like an Aelan, they take it as a sign I'm differentiating myself from them. They're a very touchy race."

"How are you doing this?"

Her shoulders raised and lowered in a shrug. "I have no idea. I was thinking how much I'd like to see you, and there you were." The image dissolved and her thought brushed his mind, *Well, that sucks. I'll have to work out how to do it again. I have to go, but Hayden, go see Adesh. Perhaps he can help with Sabina's nightmares. And make love to her. Properly.*

Yes, Your Highness.

Shut up.

I love you.

Love you more.

The connection ended and he nodded to himself. She was right. He had to reclaim his relationship with Sabina. They both had let the horrors of the Stones invade every waking thought. Herbret was dead. Kaldaar remained banished, and the phantom hadn't been seen since. Sabina would always be the seventeenth vessel, but she was no longer unbroken. She couldn't bear the offspring of Kaldaar's minions. At least he hoped so.

They needed something to distract them. Perhaps Adesh could help with that, as well.

He used the hidden walkways and corridors to return to his apartment. Since they'd only recently received her mother's blessing to court her, Sabina didn't want anyone to know he shared her bed. She feared if the empress learned of her debauchery, she'd alert Queen Prateeni and Sabina would be married off to a minor noble in the Summerlands. Hayden had his doubts that would happen, but kept his opinion to himself.

As inconspicuously as possible, he emerged from the hidden passageway into the hallway leading to his apartment. A lone figure walked toward him, and Hayden nodded his greeting. Seeing the man's face, he stopped and called after him.

"Tarro, a moment if you will." The tailor's wary glance took in Hayden's disheveled state. "I'm Lord Valen, Taryn's cousin." He didn't know why he was explaining himself to the empress's servant.

"Yes, I know. We met at Paderau, although not officially."

"Right. You made the footballs for Taryn. I was, um, I was wondering if you could find me some peasant clothing. Nothing flashy, just something I can wear in the city and not be noticed." He was saying too much, but seeing the man had sparked an idea and he was anxious to see it through.

"I'm sure I have something. When do you need them?"

"As soon as possible?"

"I can have them delivered in two bells. Will that work for you, my lord?"

"Yes, thank you." Hayden pressed his pockets, looking for a coin, but had nothing on him. "If you'll come to my rooms, I can pay for your services."

"That won't be necessary." Shorter than Hayden by a head, Tarro's pretty face smiled up at him. There was a spark of mischief in the tailor's eyes. "How is the princess?"

"She's well. I know she's rather fond of you. Shall I tell her you asked after her?"

The grin broadened, showing small, perfectly white teeth. Hayden idly wondered how he achieved such brightness. "I would like that, thank you. Is there anything else?"

Hayden pulled his gaze from the stunning smile and shook his head. "Not at the moment. If I require anything else, may I call on you?"

"Of course. Anything to help the princess or her friends."

Encouraged by his conversation with Tarro, Hayden burst into his rooms, giving poor Oliver a fright that certainly should have stopped his heart. With a rushed apology thrown over his shoulder, Hayden strode to his dressing room where he called out for the valet to join him.

"I need to look average," he said. "Like a peasant, but not too poor."

Oliver's scolding look reminded Hayden of when he was a lad and had done something improper. "What is my lord planning? Nothing dangerous, I would hope."

"Not to worry. I'm just going to stroll around the docks for a bit, and then see a friend about a tonic."

Two bells later, Hayden slipped through the palace gates and headed toward the already bustling docks. The early hour meant nothing to the ships with cargo to load or unload. The sooner the job was done, the sooner they could be out to sea. Time was money to the ship merchants.

A slight figure moved in step beside Hayden, and he grinned at the thief. "You're up early, Ebus. What? Since Taryn's left you have no one to spy upon?"

A snicker was his answer. "The princess is not the only person of interest in Talaith. Therefore I am always of use."

"And why are you not out earning your keep?"

Ebus looked up at him, a dangerous smile pulling his lips tight. "I am."

Taken aback, Hayden slowed his pace. "You were sent to spy on me? By whom?"

The little man put out a cautioning hand. "It isn't like that. The princess asked that I keep you safe while she's away." A dark brow arched over his even darker eye. "She's quite fond of you, you know."

"Yes," Hayden said, choosing his words carefully, "as I am fond of her. As a cousin and friend."

"Don't get your small clothes twisted. I was just saying she thinks highly of you. I've only been charged with keeping watch on three people. You, among them."

Hayden knew better than to ask about the other two. Ebus wouldn't say their names even under torture, he was certain. Instead, he kept walking toward the marketplace. If Ebus wanted to tag along, he wouldn't stop him.

"I'm curious about the garments, my lord." Ebus put special emphasis on the last two words.

"I don't want to draw attention to myself. You are a master of blending in—you can be of use." Hayden explained his plan to wander around the docks, ostensibly looking for work on one of the Summerlands ships, but his true purpose was to ferret out information about the heavy taxes imposed on Summerlands goods.

As far as he knew, no one on the Privy Council was aware of the increased taxes, nor were they willing to cross their empress to investigate. If Lliandra wanted to fill Talaith's coffers with Summerlands gold, they were more than happy to turn a blind eye.

Hayden couldn't dislodge the feeling there was more behind the taxes. Much more, but he had yet to understand what. By imposing illegal taxes on Danuri and Summerlands goods, she was weakening their economies, which could mean she was hoping to bring them under Talaithian control. Either by force or without.

"Stop walking like a noble. Tuck your chin, slouch into your clothing. You must reflect your status in life, and at the moment it is not one of comfort and pampering." Ebus cut into his thoughts and Hayden did as told. He scuffed his worn boots along the cobblestone street, wincing when he caught his toe on a raised brick.

"Do you sense the Shadow Assassin?" Hayden whispered as they passed from an alley to the main port.

"No. Not since that day Taryn saw him. Let's see what they're unloading." Ebus motioned to the far end of the dock where several men carried boxes down a gangplank to a waiting wagon.

Hayden scanned the ship, looking for signs to distinguish

where it had come from. Several symbols graced the bow of the ship, but no words he could decipher.

"Ho, ho!" Ebus called out. "My friend and I are looking for a day's work." He spoke proper Elennish, but with a thick accent. Ullan, perhaps.

One of the men gave the two of them a casual glance, taking in their attire and countenance. "We ain't got no need fer more men. Try the ship two down. Jus' came in from Menurra. I hear they had problems at sea. Some men didn't make it." He took his hat off and bowed his head.

Ebus said nothing to the man, but Hayden whispered, "May Julieta find peace for them." The man nodded and returned to his work.

The ship he'd indicated was larger and bore the crest of Sabina's family next to the name, *Flightrider*. It was an odd name for a ship, but Hayden had little time to muse upon a more appropriate name. Ebus contracted them to work four bells unloading merchandise to a warehouse two streets north.

Within a quarter bell, Hayden hated the little man. His legs ached from walking up and down the gangplank and then to the warehouse. His arms, used to nothing more than sword work and holding his love, shook from the effort of carrying heavy boxes filled with fruits, spices, and colorful fabrics from Menurra, the capital city of the Summerlands. By the end of the second bell, he loved Ebus more than he thought possible.

As the day wore on, the tongues of the sailors loosened. The deaths at sea hadn't been natural and many suspected Black workings. None of the men knew or cared about illegal taxes, but with the supernatural, they were obsessed. Many swore it was the ghost of Julieta punishing the sailors for crimes they committed against women; others claimed it was Kaldaar himself, risen from the depths of the sea to torment

Julieta's believers. Still more believed it was the Sea King looking for Summerlands men to father his many daughters' offspring.

Of all the claims, the only one to make sense was an illness had spread among the men and women on board. Those too weak to fight off the disease perished while the stronger of the crew were inconvenienced a few days, nothing more.

"Bunch of numpties, if ye ask me," a pretty girl not much older than Hayden said. "Superstition does nothing for morale, but they can't see past their noses to the truth."

"So, you don't believe in the wrath of gods, I take it?"

"Bah!" She spat on the ground and wiped her mouth with the back of her hand. "Ferran's fires, what good would that do? The gods don't put food in my belly. They don't offer me work or pay me a decent wage. I've done fine without their meddling so far. I don't see why I should change anything now." A slight lilt to her voice intrigued Hayden. It reminded him of the Eleri and his thoughts wandered to Taryn.

The girl and his cousin were similar in many ways, but the sailor far coarser. "What about the Eirielle? What do you make of the rumors she's returned?"

"The savior? Ha! What kind of fool do ye take me for? If someone's got the Light and Dark roiling around inside, they have my sympathy, that's what I think of it. I ain't got no need for ShantiMari, gods, or some spoiled princess." Her green eyes blazed with indignation. "Don't tell me ye believe all those fairytales. What? Do ye have a sappy poet's heart beneath those shabby clothes?"

"Yeah, right. What good's riddles and words when you're hungry, right?"

She glanced over her shoulder and then back to Hayden. "The quartermaster's paying a little too much attention to us." She shoved her box at him, resting it precariously atop the one he struggled to carry. "Fuck ye? As if ye'd know how!"

She stormed away, leaving Hayden to stare, baffled, at her retreating form.

His glance drifted up to meet the quartermaster's and the gruff man grinned at him before he followed the girl toward the docks. Hayden turned with a sigh and continued to the warehouse to deposit his goods. The next two bells passed in relative misery. A few more workers spoke to him, but he garnered nothing of value from their conversations.

At the end of their shift, Ebus collected their wages, handing Hayden the paltry sum. "Is this all? We worked our asses off." His muscles rebelled at every movement, every flinch and shudder.

"You're too pampered. Perhaps you should train with the princess more." Ebus spoke barely above a whisper and Hayden had to lean down to hear. Even that made his back spasm.

"I think you're right."

Adesh welcomed them into his tent, saying nothing about Hayden's unusual attire. He fussed with jars and scales for a long time before handing Hayden several pouches of teas to help with Sabina's nightmares, the entire time telling him what herbs to use when, and how to counteract the episodes with conscious dreaming. Hayden nodded and smiled, not retaining a single thing the man said. Even his brain was exhausted.

As they were leaving the spice merchant's tent, a lithe figure bumped into Hayden, excusing herself before pressing a note into his palm. "Yer being followed." He caught the briefest peek into her startling green eyes before she was swallowed up in the crowd.

Chapter 12

THE note held only an address. Nothing more. No signature, no hint as to what she wanted to tell him. Ebus elbowed him and nodded toward two gruff-looking men ambling their way toward the pair. Hayden ducked inside the spice merchant's tent and Ebus followed.

Adesh looked up in surprise since they'd left him only moments before. "Have you forgotten something, my lord?"

"Is there a back way out of here?" A note of urgency spiked his words and he hoped Adesh wouldn't ask questions.

The man said nothing, just led them through several tents before holding open the flap to the last one. "Through here, you will be near the cobbler's tents. Keep low and you will not be seen."

Hayden held the man's arm in his hands. "Thank you, Adesh. For everything."

His exhaustion turned to agitated frustration as they dodged shoppers. Late afternoon crowds rushed to get their errands completed before going home for the night. Twice Hayden spotted men who looked more at home on a battlefield than in the market square and ducked behind the nearest building. His heart rammed in his chest each time he crossed the street, certain at every corner he would encounter a brigand.

At last they reached the street scrawled on the slip of paper. Ebus gave a quick knock and the door opened immediately. An attractive woman, twice Hayden's age at least, answered and ushered them into a cramped sitting room. The girl lay sprawled on a couch, her legs dangling off the side, a book held to her face. The image jarred Hayden.

"What? Ye took me for a numpty, eh? Thought a dock worker couldn't read?"

"No, I, uh…" Hayden shook the truth of her words from his thoughts. "Why did you warn me?"

She sat up and gestured to the chairs opposite. Once Hayden and Ebus were seated, she began, "I'm Amanda, by the way. Ye don't have to tell me yer names, since it's obvious yer trying to hide who ye really are."

Ebus's eyes bulged, but he remained quiet.

"Why would you say that?" Hayden inquired. He'd taken pains to make sure he looked the part.

"Yer fingernails are far too clean for a day worker." Her gaze settled on Ebus and she smiled. "And neither one of ye did well carrying those boxes. I'd say yer more accustomed to carrying a sword than cargo."

"I like her," Ebus grumbled to Hayden. "Although, I do want to kill her."

Amanda's eyes widened, and then she smiled that infuriating smile again. Like she knew exactly which secrets to use against her enemy, but would draw it out as long as possible.

"Okay, let's say for argument we're not day workers. Again, why warn me?"

"I don't know, really. I guess I like ye and the thought of ye getting killed bothered me. Ye do realize who those men are, don't ye?" Hayden and Ebus both shook their heads. For whatever reason, Ebus was playing the simpleton. Hayden was fairly certain he knew not only who the men were, but what Amanda was going to say next.

"They're mercenaries. The empress hired them to patrol the docks. All yer questions today caught their attention. After ye left, I heard them questioning the quartermaster and some of the other workers. When I saw them head off in the direction ye'd gone, I followed."

Hayden shared a look with Ebus, who kept silent. "Why would the empress hire mercenaries when she has an army at her call?"

"Perhaps that's a question ye should ask her. We're not exactly on friendly terms."

Despite himself, Hayden laughed. He liked the brash young woman. "Perhaps I will. I am Lord Valen, but my friends call me Hayden." He half bowed to her from his seated position. "I thank you for your concern and your warning."

The woman who'd let them in whistled and tossed her hair. "Nobility in me own home. I never."

"Ye'll speak of this to no one, Matilde." Amanda threw a devilish look at the woman.

"Who would believe me?" Matilde kissed two fingertips and pressed them to the empty air before her. "You have my word."

Hayden held out the few coins Ebus had given him. "Is this truly what you make for a day's labor?"

Amanda glanced at the coins and nodded. "Sometimes less. It's honest work for a day's pay."

"No, it's robbery. How do you stand for this?" Ebus elbowed him, but he ignored the thief. "There should be laws to protect you."

Amanda snorted a laugh. "Laws! For us? Now I know the sun got to yer head. Nobody cares about the peasants and workers. Not the empress, if that's what yer thinking." The more agitated she got, the thicker her accent became. "All she cares about is them mercenaries and her precious cargo." She spat a great, yellow gob into the fireplace and Hayden looked away, repulsed.

"What cargo?" Ebus said, his eyes bright, his posture leaning toward Amanda.

The girl sank into the sofa, the fire in her spirit dimmed. "I shouldn't ta said anything about that. I don't know nothing."

Matilde brought them tea in chipped cups, the tray rattling as she set it down. Bits of cookie covered a tarnished plate. Hayden surveyed the room, noting the shabby furnishings, the peeling paint on the walls. They'd done their best to make it homey, despite their poverty.

"I can help you, Amanda," Hayden offered, not quite knowing where his thoughts were leading him. Matilde sat next to Amanda and he saw the similarities in their features. "I need you to help me, in return."

Matilde's eyes narrowed and she placed a protective hand on Amanda's thigh. "What do ye have in mind?"

"To be honest, I'm not quite sure." He brought the tea to his lips and inhaled a familiar scent. Unease tensed his muscles. He knew the tea. Knew the merchant who sold that particular blend. "But first, I need you to tell me all you know about Adesh, the spice merchant."

It was dark before Hayden and Ebus left Matilde's home. At first, she claimed to only know Adesh as a merchant, but after prodding from not just Hayden, but Ebus as well, she confessed to being in his employ. Since the illegal taxation began, Adesh had hired several crews to sail to the Summerlands to purchase his goods without the knowledge of the empress. The illegal transactions couldn't be traced and often his ships were targets for pirate attacks, but the reward was worth it.

Adesh was able to keep his jars stocked, as well as his brother Tabul's in Paderau. Thus far, he'd not garnered the attention of the empress, but Hayden's questions had brought too much unwanted attention on Adesh. The fact he went to the merchant's tent after working would possibly bring about raids on the spice merchant, or intense scrutiny he couldn't afford.

Hayden and Ebus had listened patiently, hearing tales of Amanda's skill negotiating with the Summerlands merchants on Adesh's behalf. The major parties didn't know who was purchasing the goods or from whom they acquired. If the ship was stopped by Lliandra's guard, they were to dump the cargo.

Adesh disguised the ships as pleasure vessels, even going so far as to decorate the sleeping quarters like the most fashionable houses. Hayden had to admit, the complicated scheme was brilliant.

Before he left, he promised his assistance to the women and the spice merchant, but since he would be traveling to Celyn Eryri in a few days, there was little he could do in Talaith. Ebus agreed to stay behind and uncover what he could.

That night, Hayden gave Sabina the tea prepared by Adesh and no nightmares disrupted her sleep. He lay awake most of the night, holding her close, imagining a life without night terrors and capricious gods.

But that would mean a life without Taryn. His hand stilled over Sabina's soft skin. For one perfect moment, he saw what Ohlin had seen on Taryn's crowning day. She was more than just the Keeper of the Stars. She *was* the stars, the sun, the moon, the universe. She would one day become a goddess as exalted as Nadra.

He'd always known what she would become, but how did he see the vision?

"Are you well, my love?" Sabina rested on her elbow, watching him.

"I am now." Thoughts of Taryn dissipated as he gazed

into the adoring eyes of the woman who'd captured his heart the first time they met. She'd been jealous of Taryn, worried that Hayden loved his cousin more than her, but that could never happen. He did love Taryn. Would always love her, but not how he loved Sabina. Madly. Deeply. Eternally. She was his equal in all things.

He leaned forward, taking her lips with his own. She yielded to him automatically, lying against the soft mattress, but he stopped her. "Tonight, we will know what it is to truly make love. For both of us."

At her questioning smile, he took her hand and placed it over his growing erection.

Chapter 13

TIME in the Narthvier moved at its own pace, but when their stay lasted one Talaithian month, King Stephan held a feast in their honor, signaling an end to their visit. Before the entire court, he knelt in front of Taryn and Rhoane. He called her *Darennsai* and Rhoane *Surtentse,* promising he would give them his life, his crown, his kingdom, or his sword, if they would but ask. Should his assistance be required, he would be as a servant unto them.

The air stilled in the Great Hall. Even the drossfire halted its magical flickering while the Eleri took in what King Stephan had done. Taryn herself couldn't believe it, having come to the conclusion the Eleri would treat her with respect, but would always view her as an outsider, the *gyota*, or destroyer, of Verdaine's prophecy. When Stephan rose, after kissing their wrists where days earlier Verdaine added her blessings to their bonds, a collective inhale filled the night.

Bressal and Eoghan next gave their oaths, followed by Carga. After her, came Janeira and then to Taryn's astonishment, all of the Eleri nobles swore fealty to her and Rhoane. The magnitude of their actions, the responsibility for their lives, settled on her with a heaviness she desperately hoped she could bear.

The next morning, they said their goodbyes and although Kaida did not meet them at the Weirren as promised, Taryn tried not to worry. When they arrived at the final veil and Kaida had yet to appear, a physical pain cut her heart.

Rhoane took her hand in his, giving a little squeeze. "Perhaps it is for the best. She is a wild animal, after all."

Taryn blinked back tears. "I know, I just—" A streak of white flashed from the trees and Kaida came bounding toward them. "Kaida! I feared you'd decided to stay."

Our journey has only just begun, my friend.

"You've grown and look at your fur—it's gorgeous." Kaida was no longer the gangly puppy Taryn had brought into the vier, but muscular and sleek under her coat of thick white fur.

Of course, I am grierbas.

I've missed you, my friend. Taryn inhaled the scent of the forest on her fur and Kaida nuzzled against her in reply. Warmth filled her and spilled to the forest where small buds formed on several plants.

Rhoane cupped one of the buds in his palm and whispered a few words. The bloom flourished into a starburst of silver, white, and crystal, the likes of which Taryn had never seen. "You created this." Rhoane's voice cracked with emotion as he stared at her, wonder dancing in his eyes and around the half-smile he wore. "You always surprise me, Darennsai."

"I really hope that is a good thing." The flower smelled of jasmine and sea air—of home.

Outside the vier, snow covered the ground and the air was colder than Taryn had expected. She wore a thick wool cape over several layers of clothing, but still she felt chilled. At night, if they couldn't find an inn, they made a small camp, keeping the fire lit for warmth. Taryn snuggled close to Rhoane, and Kaida would curl around them for added comfort.

Rhoane didn't fold time as he had on their journey to the

Narthvier, giving a feeble excuse that too much manipulation of time would offset the balance of Aelinae. As convenient as it was to pull out the "balance" card, Rhoane was deliberately delaying their arrival in Celyn Eryri. She finally quit asking him to fold time, trusting he had a good reason for keeping them wet and miserable.

The rain lashed at Taryn, and she distracted herself with thoughts of what awaited them in Celyn Eryri. The Light Celebrations, as far as she could gather, were created as a means to offset the dreariness of Wintertide. A weeklong celebration of games, drinking, and feasting began on the shortest day of the year to celebrate the coming of longer days and, ostensibly, the Light. Taryn looked forward to the games with the excitement of a football fan going to the World Cup. From some of the names, she could guess at the competition, but others she had no idea what to expect. In a rare show of emotion, even Rhoane had a light of excitement in his eyes when she spoke of the celebrations.

But first, they had to trudge through the miserable wind and rain. She cast one last pleading look at Rhoane, who did his best to ignore her, and pointed to a copse of trees nestled beside a river. If he wouldn't fold time, at least they could find a place relatively dry and the trees would provide much-needed shelter for the night.

While Rhoane searched for dry firewood, Taryn led the horses to the river where they could graze on the soft grass while she collected water. She braced against the shock of cold and dipped the wineskin beneath the surface. Pain unlike any she'd experienced stabbed at her forehead, then suddenly a hand reached up from the freezing water, grabbing her wrist. A silent scream filled her mind, but no sound came from her lips. She sent a frantic thought to Rhoane but was met with a wall of darkness. Panicked, she pushed against the mud. Her boots slipped on the slick surface, dangerously closer to the water's edge.

Rykoto rose from the river, pulling her to him. His red-rimmed, fire-filled eyes searched her face as she struggled against his grip. A forked tongue licked at the blood-smeared lips before flicking at her, tasting the air between them. Taryn jerked back, losing her footing and falling, but Rykoto steadied her. He cocked his head to the left and then right, studying her.

A sick smile was the only warning she had before he pushed her head into the river. Water flooded her mouth and lungs, and she choked, taking in even more of the dangerous liquid. Panic seized her, but she fought against it even as Rykoto shoved her head deeper still. When she called forth her power, it, too, was blocked.

Her arms flailed out, trying to grab anything that could break his hold. From far away, she heard Kaida barking and she reached for the grierbas in her mind, meeting silence. Darkness edged her vision.

She would pass out soon unless she freed herself from Rykoto. Her lungs constricted again and again, wanting to force out the water, but Taryn kept her mouth tightly shut. If she opened her lips, she would surely die.

Rykoto spoke to her with a gentleness meant to soothe her fractured mind. "Come with me, my beloved."

He walked before her, his hand outstretched to show a land of lush greenery with trees that bore heavy fruit. The sweet scent of flowers filled the air. Birds perched on branches, singing the prettiest songs just for her. It was all for her. A promise of her own private world with everything she could ever desire. Rykoto beckoned, his long black hair shining like polished obsidian. His calm, unmarked face assured serenity. The garden of delights would be hers for all eternity. If only she took his hand.

Her lungs convulsed, seeking air denied them. She

clenched her mouth shut against the freezing water that would pull her into darkness.

Rykoto waited, his words inviting. She reached out to take his hand. The garden was warmth and sunlight, not the cold emptiness that pinched her skin. His lips opened to speak, but when he said her name, it was Rhoane's voice she heard. She faltered, her hand nearly touching Rykoto's.

Kaida barked, urging her to breathe.

Confusion clouded her thoughts. The lush garden swayed and Rykoto grabbed for her.

"You are mine, Eirielle. Only mine. My brother's stain blackens your heart. I can heal you, my beloved."

His eyes burned fire. His blood-smeared mouth gaped at her in a twisted grin. Flames licked around her wrist. He jerked her to him, his forked tongue snaking out. She screamed, letting in the air she'd denied herself.

"Taryn!" Rhoane rocked her against his taut muscles.

She gasped for breath, looking wildly around her. "Where am I?"

"You are safe," Rhoane said, kissing her forehead. "I am here. I have you." A slight tremor lingered in his grip.

Kaida crept up to lay her head in Taryn's lap and she absently stroked the grierbas' wet fur. She shivered from the rain that slapped at them.

Rhoane adjusted his cloak to cover her. "What happened?"

"I was in the river. Rykoto was trying to drown me." His marred face swirled in her mind and she swallowed hard against the bile that inched up her throat.

"It was an illusion, Taryn. You were here the whole time."

Taryn stared at him, uncomprehending. "It was real. I was drowning. I couldn't breathe."

Rhoane asked no more questions, holding her close until she was able to walk to their camp. Later that night, after they ate a hot meal and drank several cups of grhom, Taryn told Rhoane what had happened.

He held her hand in his, tracing the runes with his thumb. "Rykoto is becoming stronger, but how is the question. We must find a way to block his hold on you."

She snuggled into him, as if he could protect her from what she said next. "I couldn't access my power or thoughts. Only a small trickle of Dark Shanti and that wasn't enough to do anything against him. I still had free will, but only just. His control is tied to my dark powers, I'm sure of it. I must learn to control my Dark Shanti."

Since the night of Celia and Herbret's burial, they hadn't spoken of Taryn going to her father or Zakael, but with the heaviness of Rhoane's sigh, she knew what he was going to say.

"We can no longer avoid it. You will have to seek out your father."

Taryn pulled away, staring into his eyes. "Not Valterys." Something about the man's calculated coolness unnerved her. "I thought we agreed Zakael is powerful enough to teach me what I need. If there is more to learn from Valterys, I want to at least have Zakael's strength before I have to face my father." Her body trembled and Rhoane pulled her against him. Soothing warmth spread through her, making her sleepy all of a sudden.

"Let us not worry about that tonight. You need rest."

There was more to tell him, about Kaldaar and a stain, but her thoughts were fuzzy and the enchanted garden drifted from her memory as she snuggled against Kaida with Rhoane curled along her back.

When weak sunlight filtered through the trees the next morning, she avoided thinking about the attack. Periodically, vivid images would pop into her mind, always accompanied with a sour taste that she'd push away with all the force she could muster. Sometimes Rhoane would peer at her, worry etched across his features, but he didn't question her. Instead, they spoke of the coming Light Celebration games. Taryn held to memories of her friends and happier times. Too much darkness filtered through her days.

The strain she saw in the tightness of Rhoane's smile, or the way he constantly scanned the landscape told Taryn the attack had him far more concerned than he let on. When she thought of the compulsion she'd felt in Marissa's rooms the night she saw her sister with the phantom, she kept it to herself. Adding to Rhoane's burden wouldn't do either of them any good. Until they reached Celyn Eryri and the protection of her family, they were vulnerable.

Without her asking, Rhoane folded time, making the trees little more than a blur. Unfortunately, his trick could only make the day pass quicker. It couldn't prevent them from suffering the ill effects of the weather and by the time they reached the town a day's ride north of Celyn Eryri, they were soggy, sullen, and exhausted.

Street lamps cast pale light on the cobblestones and their horses' hooves echoed through the near-empty streets. When they reached an inn in the center of town, instead of sending Kaida out into the freezing night, Taryn told her to stay close and try to not look threatening. If a grierbas could chuckle, Taryn was certain that's what Kaida did in response.

Inside the common room, to Taryn's surprise and delight, sat Duke Anje, Baehlon, Faelara, and her guard, taking their evening meal. Several of the duke's soldiers were seated at other tables, drinking and dicing. When all the hugs and well-wishes had been given, they sat together in the corner and Taryn learned of Rhoane's secret plan to send Carina and Timor to Paderau disguised as Taryn and Rhoane.

Baehlon boasted that their ruse worked so well not even the palace staff knew they were not who they said they were. When Taryn expressed disbelief, Carina pulled her

ShantiMari around herself and became a perfect reflection of Taryn for the merest moment before appearing as Carina once more.

"That's remarkable. I don't know whether I would be able to tell if you were me or not," Taryn said.

Carina inclined her head, a faint blush touching her cheeks. "You honor me."

Taryn recalled the odd conversation she'd had with Hayden. This was why her mother insisted Taryn had left Talaith with Faelara and Baehlon. For once, Lliandra had made certain her daughter was safe. A tiny wave of gratitude washed over her. It wasn't much, but it was a start.

They stayed up late into the night, the soldiers singing and carousing with one another while Taryn and her friends caught up on events. When the others were immersed in their own affairs, Taryn took Faelara aside and in hushed tones told her of the attack by the river. Faelara held her close, her ShantiMari embracing Taryn, searching for any signs of a lingering stain.

"I'm afraid I don't know what Rykoto meant. I sense nothing different about you. There is the vorlock venom, same as always, but otherwise you are unchanged."

Taryn felt anything but unchanged. With each passing day, she became someone she was not the day before. Aelinae had altered her until she hardly resembled the innocent girl who stepped through the portal.

"After the Light Celebrations, I'm going to seek out Zakael. I must unlock my Dark Shanti."

Faelara's eyes filled with tears. "Then Baehlon and I will come with you."

"No, my sweet friend. You can't say anything to Baehlon just yet. He'll bellow and bluster and make my life a bloody hell. Promise me."

"If you insist, but I think we should accompany you."

"If you do, Zakael might sense a trap. Pissing him off is the last thing I want to do."

"I suppose you're right. I don't like it, but you can't avoid it any longer."

When Taryn lay in bed later that night, unease settled over her like a heavy mantle. She didn't trust Zakael or her father, but they were the key to Rykoto's hold on her. She was certain of it. As Rhoane lay beside her on the small bed, his arm protectively draped over her midsection, she ached for the sanctuary he sought to give her. But she drifted alone, unanchored in a shifting sea of uncertainty. Always listing to one side, about to capsize at any moment. The only constants in her life were the grasping tentacles of the Dark as they squelched their way toward her.

Chapter 14

CELYN Eryri stretched before them in the hazy afternoon light. A storm hovered in the distance, its rumbling urging them on to the city gates. Hundreds of tents in varying shapes, sizes, and colors dotted the land around the city walls. People from all over the East came to participate in the Light Celebration games, which made the streets difficult to traverse with their large party. Close-set houses with steep sloping roofs led the way to a large square with a circular building in the center.

Taryn's *cynfar* hummed against her skin and warmth spread over her at the same time Faelara made an odd gesture while inclining her head toward the building.

"What does that mean?" Taryn asked her friend, tracing a figure eight with her index finger as Faelara had done. She'd witnessed others making the gesture, sometimes to her, but never understood why it was used.

"It's to ward off evil spirits. We just passed the temple to Daknys, and I wished her well while casting off any ill will that might be aimed at her."

Taryn glanced back at the temple; it didn't look like much from the outside, but just to be sure, she made the sign to ward off evil. The dragon's wings on her sword handle fluttered and glinted in the light before settling in place.

Taryn caught Faelara's astonished look and returned it.

They continued up the high street, past businesses and more homes decorated with colorful doors with matching shutters and empty window boxes. The street opened and there, looming in front of them like a decorative crag carved out of the mountainside, was the castle. Taryn drew in a deep breath at the marvel. Towers and battlements flanked the stone structure, with soldiers moving along them like little toys.

Several servants came out to greet them, but the empress and princesses were nowhere to be seen. The castle steward apologized, explaining everyone was down at the skating rink, overseeing the last of the decorations.

Ancient compared with the modern conveniences at Talaith and Paderau, Celyn Eryri held far more charm. Rough stone floors echoed their footsteps on the walk through nearly deserted halls and down corridors lined with heavy tapestries. Sconces set at even intervals lit the way, with ShantiMari enhanced flames dancing along the faces of nymphs and noblemen embroidered in the wall hangings.

A page escorted them to Taryn's room first and then moved to take Rhoane's belongings to his room, but Rhoane waved him off. "Thank you, Darius. I am sure I can manage on my own."

"His Highness remembers me?"

"Of course. You were the only one to beat me at archery last Wintertide. You have grown, my lad. I hope your archery skills have not improved as well." Rhoane indicated Taryn. "This is my betrothed, Princess Taryn."

Darius bowed low to her. "It is an honor, Your Highness."

Taryn inclined her head, greeting him in return before asking after her maids. When she mentioned Ellie, a touch of pink spread across his cheeks and he offered to fetch them if she desired. Not wanting to spoil their afternoon, she insisted she would be fine. Kaida sat beside him, nudging his hand with her head, which intrigued Taryn.

"She is taken with you, Darius. It isn't like a grierbas to seek out affection."

His hand faltered an instant before he pet the beast. "Again, I am honored." After another few pets, he left them alone.

"Should we join the others?" Taryn asked with little enthusiasm.

"And pass up the opportunity for privacy and that remarkable bed?"

She ran to the room, tossing her sword on a chair before hastily removing her clothing. Rhoane was a step behind, unlacing his Eleri boots between many muttered curses. When finally they'd rid themselves of their layers of clothing, they tumbled onto the soft mattress. The sex was hard and fast and nothing like the languid lovemaking they'd had in the Narthvier. Taryn loved it. Loved the intensity of being present in that moment.

A short while later, her maids arrived amidst excited chatter. Lorilee squealed and burst into her bedchamber. Upon seeing Rhoane, she dropped to a low curtsey, apologizing over and over again for the intrusion. A bubble of laughter floated from Taryn's belly. The poor girl would be traumatized that she'd interrupted her mistress.

Rhoane kissed her on the nose. "I suppose we should dress for dinner."

Their time alone had at last come to an end. "I suppose we should."

He rose from her bed, gathering the sheet around his naked body, and walked with absolute grace and dignity through her rooms. She heard the embarrassed squeals of her maids and then Rhoane's soft voice. "Ladies, always a pleasure to see you." The click of the connecting doorway echoed in the silent space.

A flurry of giggles erupted and her three maids were upon her, questions flying from all directions.

"Run my bath, you lazy sods!" Taryn commanded imperially, trying not to burst out laughing and keeping the blanket pulled to her chin.

Their questions amused Taryn. During her bath, and while they prepared her for the evening's activities, they peppered her with inquiries about her mysterious trip. Taryn evaded as much as she could, only telling them enough to satisfy their thirst for gossip and to keep the ruse alive. Still, she felt guilty for lying to them. As far as they knew, she'd gone to Paderau with Faelara and Baehlon.

"I met a very nice young man today. Darius, I believe he's called. Will he be competing in the games?" Taryn asked when the subject changed to the celebrations and what event each girl would be competing in.

Ellie's blush at the mention of Darius drew Taryn's interest. There was something about the young man; he'd not only captivated Kaida, but Ellie as well.

Lorilee was adding several pins to her hair when she paused. "You look so beautiful, Your Highness."

Taryn had missed her maids more than she ever thought possible. "Only because of you, my precious girls."

"There is a glow about you—a sheen to your skin similar to Prince Rhoane's," Ellie added.

"It's the Eleri coming out in me."

The Glamour beneath her skin was only the start of her transformation. When she became full Eleri, her ears would come to delicate points and her vision would be enhanced enough she could see nearly a league away on a cloudy day. During her stay in the Narthvier, Rhoane and Carga had explained all the physical changes that would occur. Nothing was immediate except the fact she would not bear children until well into her seventh or eight-hundredth season. Eleri longevity was a concept she couldn't fully grasp.

A knock drew their attention to the doorway, where Tarro arrived with several dresses. At the sight of her friend, Taryn asked, "Did Lliandra bring the entire court?"

"Not everyone, but most." Tarro smiled and she embraced the tailor.

"It's good to see so many familiar faces."

When Rhoane arrived to escort her to dinner, little flutters of excitement filled her belly. They wore matching outfits of black velvet with silver trim. A silver coronet rested on his glossy brown hair. The transition from traveling wear to court fashion was startling. Based on the look he gave Taryn, he thought the same about her.

No formal feast was planned until the celebrations started, but the atmosphere in the great hall was festive, with boisterous singing and much pounding of the tables amongst competitors trying to prove their merit before the games began. Lliandra greeted them warmly, kissing them on both cheeks.

"I trust everything has been resolved?"

"It has. Thank you, Mother." Taryn hoped Lliandra understood the meaning behind her words.

Sabina pouted behind the empress and Taryn braced herself for an onslaught of reprimands. When Lliandra drifted off to greet another guest, Sabina tapped her foot and shook out her long curls. Taryn stifled a laugh. The glare the Summerlands princess cast her might wither the will of a courtesan, but Taryn knew far greater evils. For her friend's sake, she put on her best apologetic demeanor.

"I should be quite vexed with you, my so-called friend."

"But you're not?" Taryn teased.

"Oh, I am. Leaving with only a note of explanation? And a poor lie of a note it was." At Taryn's look of alarm, Sabina said, "Don't worry. I will tell no one. Did you seriously expect me to believe you'd toddle off to inspect property without me? I have more knowledge of commerce in my little finger than you do in your entire body. I assume it had something to do with Prince Rhoane?"

Unsure whether Hayden had said anything to her or not, Taryn hedged. "His sister, actually. But you must promise to tell no one. Rhoane insisted on the ruse to protect me."

"Please. I'm your fondest friend, remember? I would never risk your safety for my own pride." She gave Taryn a sly smile and led her to a corner away from the crowd. "Besides, I understand it is you I have to thank for Hayden's enthusiasm in our bedchamber."

Taken aback, Taryn stared at her friend, words forming on her lips, but silence ensuing.

"He said you encouraged him to educate me in how to bring him pleasure." A charming blush reddened her cheeks and her eyes sparkled. "I had no idea! Do you know, I've not had a single nightmare since."

"Sister!" Tessa's shout startled both Taryn and Sabina. "I should like a word with you." Her youngest sister stomped across the floor with a chagrined Eliahnna following. "Do you have any idea how irritating it is when you dash off without warning?" Tessa tilted her chin with an imperiousness Lliandra would admire. "If I were Mother, I would send you to your room without supper. But since I'm not, an apology will suffice."

Eliahnna grinned behind Tessa. "It really is tedious."

"I am very sorry I didn't tell you I was leaving. I promise, next time I will give you more than a note for explanation."

She'd mollified her friends for the moment, but in a matter of days, she would have to make good on her promise. She and Rhoane had already discussed plans to leave for Gaarendahl as soon as the celebrations ended. Assuming, of course, the empress would concede to her leaving again.

Taryn scanned the room. "Where is Marissa? Did she travel with you?"

Eliahnna rolled her eyes and looked off to a distant part of the cavernous room. "She is there, with a fresh lordling. She's positively scandalous, but Mother allows it. I really don't understand why."

"She's in training," Tessa blurted and clapped a hand over her mouth, terror spiking in her blue eyes.

Eliahnna and Sabina giggled while Taryn swept the room with a bored look, taking in Marissa's victim before bringing her attention back to the girls. "He's handsome, but when aren't they?"

"You obviously don't remember Herbret," Tessa scoffed. Then, remembering herself, she said in a quiet voice, "I'm so sorry, Sabina. I wasn't thinking."

"A habit you've fallen into quite a bit lately," Eliahnna reprimanded. "We need to work on your tact, dear sister." To Sabina, she said, "Please forgive her impertinence."

Sabina's dark eyes shone clear and bright, with a little giggle hidden in their depths. "You are more than forgiven, sister of my heart. I have left my melancholy behind and wish to think of that morning no more. Herbret was indeed repulsive, as was no secret." She glanced over to where Marissa was doing a poor job of hiding her amorousness with the handsome lord. "I wonder what he has that she needs. Marissa does not bed someone on a whim."

An image of the phantom and Marissa pushed to the forefront of Taryn's thoughts and she shivered. It was true. Marissa never gave without getting something in return.

Chapter 15

THE Light Celebrations began on the eve before the shortest day of the year, which Taryn learned was called the Feast of Winter Veil. All the residents of the castle dressed in their warmest clothing and walked through the town, holding a candle before them to ward off the approaching darkness. When they reached the castle gate, the townsfolk joined them, and as they strolled through the city, they sang songs that told the tale of the first Light Celebrations. It was a tradition dating back over a thousand seasons.

Taryn walked with her family, listening to the songs, more at peace than she'd been in too long. It was as if the dangers from the outside world could not affect her while she was ensconced in the solemnity of the celebration. Rhoane held her hand and glanced at her from the corner of his eye when he thought she wasn't aware.

Since the vision by the river, Taryn had scarcely been alone. Either one of the princesses, Hayden, Baehlon, Lady Faelara, or Rhoane himself had been with her around the clock. The excuses the princesses had for needing to sleep in her apartments were the most humorous to Taryn. She'd let them, of course, not wanting to be alone, but too afraid to admit it.

She squeezed Rhoane's hand and smiled up at him. "This

is beautiful." Rhoane's voice joined the others and Taryn listened to the words. They sang of the gods who first created Aelinae. Nadra made the stars in the sky and gave the world Light. Ohlin made the sun and gave the world Darkness. Together, they nurtured the first plants and animals. When they were satisfied with these gifts, they populated the Narthvier with the Eleri and after a time, produced the other races of Aelinae.

Ohlin created the Artagh and races of the West, and Nadra the sea people and races of the East. Lastly, they gave Aelinae their offspring: Daknys to rule the Light, Rykoto to oversee the Darkness, and Verdaine to command the life force of every creature who walked the terrarae.

Excitement buzzed through Taryn as she listened. Each of those gods was a part of her. She was larger than the shell of her Aelan existence. The words echoed through her mind as the song gave thanks to the gods for the plants and animals, the sea creatures, and all of the races of Aelinae, the Eleri, the sun and moons, and above all else, the stars that guided them.

Taryn looked up at the clear sky and the stars that twinkled against a velvety blue landscape. She hoped Brandt was watching as she walked with the others in the procession. Tears stung her eyes and she wiped them away with the sleeve of her coat.

"Something wrong?" Rhoane whispered in her ear.

"No, just thinking of Brandt."

"He is with you, always." He squeezed her hand and pointed to the sky. "Look, he is just there." She followed where he indicated and saw a star blinking at them. Rhoane always knew exactly where any constellation was at a given time.

"Dal Tara." A small sob caught in her throat. "Grandfather."

A tear ran down her cheek and Rhoane kissed it away. A fierce sense of love wrapped itself around her and she held onto Rhoane's hand to steady herself. Awe and wonder washed over her as she stared into the mossy depths of his eyes. So much had happened since that first day in the cavern when she'd looked to him for strength. He'd given her that and so much more. He'd given her purpose.

Their runes brightened and she glanced down at their entwined hands. Only Ohlin needed to add his blessings for the bonds to be complete. Even without them, Rhoane was hers forever. He would never leave her or cause her harm, of that she was certain. Just as she knew he would always be there to hold her hand and to fight her enemies. In the depths of her soul, she believed in his commitment and love for her. They knew no bounds. She was his forever and the thought did not frighten her in the least.

"I am yours, *mi carae*. Always." She whispered for his hearing alone, and he raised her hand to his lips, pressing their flesh together in a way that made her insides tremble. "Even if you are naughty."

A lopsided grin was his answer. Damn him and his sexiness. She looked away before she did something indecent, her heart tripping in her chest.

The procession continued through the city until they came to a large open square. Tables filled the space for the feast that would be enjoyed by the entire populace of the city. Rhoane led her to a table set upon a dais. From their seats, they could see the gathered crowd, and the people could see them. Taryn had yet to grow accustomed to being on display and felt exposed and suddenly shy, but the other princesses joined them and distracted her with their excited chatter.

Musicians walked between the tables and jugglers threw sticks glowing with fire in the air, catching them and spinning around to great applause. The townsfolk craned their necks to get a glimpse of the beautiful empress and her daughters. Many of them pointed to Taryn and whispered to one another. Taryn had to stop herself from eavesdropping on their thoughts. The desire to know what they thought of her was almost too great.

After the meal, a local band set up on a raised stage and after all the tables were pushed aside to create room, many joined in dancing and drinking. It was a night of frivolity and Lliandra let herself be led around the dance floor by several of the high-ranking men of the city. Taryn danced with Rhoane or her sisters, and even Marissa laughed as she spun around in Myrddin's arms. Her sister was more relaxed than Taryn could ever recall and once again, she had the sense something was different about her sister, but what, she couldn't say.

Taryn took the lead from Myrddin and smiled at Marissa. "You look happy tonight, sister," she said as they danced a two-step around the square.

"I could say the same about you. Has something happened? You are positively glowing."

"It must be the celebrations. It was very peaceful and beautiful in a haunting way."

"Yes, I feel the same about the procession." Marissa's voice came from far away. "Are you enjoying Celyn Eryri?"

"Very much so. It's a winter wonderland."

"I've always found the cold too bitter, but this year is more pleasant." A thread of Marissa's ShantiMari enveloped them. The calculated coolness was there but dulled, strained even. "Will you be participating in the games?" Marissa asked.

Taryn let her sister's power tickle her skin for a moment. There was something in her ShantiMari, something elusive Taryn tried to touch, but fell short. "I've been coerced into an event having to do with ice and racing. I'm not sure how I'll fare, but Tessa thinks it will be grand fun. Baehlon thinks I should participate in the hunt, but I don't know. Chasing an animal for sport doesn't sound like fun to me."

"Oh, but you must! The hunt is my favorite." Her hand fluttered above her belly. "You really should consider it." The dance ended and Marissa curtseyed to her. "You make a wonderful partner."

Taryn grinned. "Thanks, I think." She walked beside Marissa to a table, neither speaking. Before her sister sat down, Taryn touched her arm. "I've sent a letter to Zakael, requesting a visit."

"Why are you telling me?"

"It was your suggestion. I just thought you'd like to know."

Marissa regarded her for a moment before replying. "I'm sure your visit will be exactly what you hope it to be."

The tone unnerved Taryn, but she kept her features blank. Changing the subject, Taryn said, "It is you who is radiant this evening, not me. You have an aura about you that I've never seen before."

Marissa shrugged. "It must be the wine. I see your betrothed is looking for you." She indicated to Taryn's left. "Perhaps you should dance with him and leave me to rest."

"Can I get you anything first?"

She shook her head. "Go. Dance with your betrothed. I'll be fine. See? Here comes Tessa to take your place."

Taryn kissed Tessa on the forehead as she passed, promising another dance soon. Rhoane took her hand and led her into the group of dancers. A lightness, freeing and full of promise, settled over Taryn as he spun her around the dance floor.

"It delights me to see you so happy, my love," Rhoane whispered.

"If only every night could be like this." She laughed as he lifted her high and twirled them, bringing her down gently, close to his body. "Kiss me and tell me you'll love me forever."

"Forever, my love." His lips touched hers and a jolt of electricity ran through them. His body stiffened, then relaxed as the kiss continued. Taryn held him tight to her, suddenly afraid to let him go. The feeling of lightness edged away, replaced with a biting joylessness that spread like ice crystals across her skin.

The games started the next day with trumpets and fanfare. Taryn sat in the royal box, wincing with each blast of the horns. Even Kaida curled deeper under her feet to avoid the dreaded sound. Baehlon in particular looked a bit green and she joked with him about not being able to handle his drink. He scowled at her as he made his way from the box to the participants' tent. He was scheduled for three of the five events that day and hadn't had the foresight, as many of the other participants had, to leave the festivities early for a good night's sleep.

Several men and four women took their places at posts erected in the ground. Taryn scanned the competitors, her gaze settling on one in particular. He wore his black hair short, with a goatee that stretched toward his chest with small bells woven through the braids. Too far away for most to see his features clearly, Taryn could make out the almond shape of his eyes against his burnished skin. The man gave a disgusted grunt in Baehlon's direction and Taryn sat straighter.

"Rhoane, that man over there." She pointed to the one she watched. "Who is he?"

Rhoane chuckled beneath his breath. "Denzil de Monteferron."

"You're kidding." Taryn stared at Baehlon's brother as he hurled taunts to the other man. "They don't seem to get along too well." Baehlon, for his part, was making lewd gestures to the other man.

"Denzil is a mercenary. Baehlon never forgave him for leaving the family trade of becoming a knight."

"A mercenary." Taryn cringed when a loud siren trilled, indicating the start of competition.

Screams and catcalls came from the gathered crowd as the men and women, all stripped of their shirts and slathered with goose fat, tried to climb the wooden poles. The first to reach the top would earn a gold crown.

The games had few rules, with only one being absolute: no use of ShantiMari was permitted. Since using one's power couldn't be proved, if it was even suggested that someone cheated, they were immediately evicted from the games and banned from participation for life.

Taryn cheered with the others, urging Baehlon to reach the top. His fingertips touched the ribbon a split second behind a spry woman twice his age. He cursed to the sky and then flung himself from the pole to land gracefully on the ground. His brother settled a pace to his right and they glared at each other before Baehlon stalked away.

Denzil's heated glance met Taryn's and for a moment she saw the hurt Baehlon's action had caused. Denzil blinked hard and looked away, only to return his glance a second later. She inclined her head in recognition of his efforts, a begrudging smile on her lips.

The rest of the day's events also required the participants to be half dressed and greased with goose fat. Taryn began to suspect Lliandra had devised the games as a way to choose her next lover. The empress watched with keen interest as the men and women wrestled with each other.

The young lordling Taryn saw with Marissa her first night in Celyn Eryri strutted to the center of the ring, taking his place before the trumpet flared. Marissa sat back in her chair, a bored expression on her face, but her gaze tracked the handsome man until the match ended. A look of relief spread over her beautiful features when he lost.

Over the course of the day, Lliandra would motion to Myrddin regarding one or the other competitors. After each event, the competitors were paraded before the royal box and given a kiss by the empress. Of the few men Lliandra had indicated, those who won were pulled aside.

Taryn grinned when the young lordling brushed his lips across Lliandra's, and up to her ear, apparently to whisper an impertinence. Instead of anger, Lliandra's eyes flashed excitement. The young man was escorted with the others the empress had chosen. Marissa hid her emotions well, but the narrowing of her eyes and tightness of her lips told Taryn she was not happy with the outcome. Score one for the assertive young lord, score zero for the crown princess.

Far in the distance, a spark of lightning lit up the dark sky. Lliandra cast a sharp look at the crown princess, who sat slouched in her seat, a bored expression on her face. Taryn observed the interplay, noting each woman's reaction to the other. They were allies, yes, but the petty jealousies they displayed bespoke of a hidden rivalry. If left unchecked, they would soon be adversaries.

Taryn studied her sister's profile as Marissa spoke with Tessa. Her sister was heir to the Light Throne and spying for Zakael. Marissa laughed at something Tessa said and turned to meet Taryn's stare. As if she knew what treacherous thoughts drifted in Taryn's mind, Marissa winked. Lliandra had no idea her daughter was her greatest enemy. Marissa raised an eyebrow and left the royal box, Tessa in her wake.

That night at the feast, the crown princess entertained herself with several lords and ladies, far from where the empress sat at a special table with the victors she'd chosen. Each man wore handsome clothes fit for a prince and filled their plates with rich foods, their goblets never more than half-full. Lliandra dressed in pale-blue velvet, her neckline dipping scandalously close to revealing her nipples. Her mother's appetite for pleasure was legendary and the chosen men strutted as if they'd won a prize far better than gold. Studs for a brood mare.

Taryn pushed her disapproval aside. If her mother chose to have many lovers, it was not her concern. She had Rhoane and needed none other but him.

Chapter 16

SCANT light from his drossfire lit the way as Rhoane strode from the battlements through the deserted hallways to his room. Most of the castle inhabitants slept, but he knew there would be one awake at that early hour and he wanted to freshen up before calling on her.

For the past few nights, he'd searched for ways to keep Rykoto far from his beloved's dreams. In his absence, he sent their friends to stay with her with the hope their presence would bring her calm.

Since the attack by the river, Rykoto had left Taryn in peace, but she slept fitfully at best. How the god managed to invade her mind, he didn't know. He'd consulted his father about the situation and he was at a loss as to how they could stop him. Myrddin was little help as well. Two of Aelinae's greatest thinkers were equally puzzled, each offering to search for answers.

Rhoane was determined to find a solution, even if it meant traveling the length of Aelinae and hunting down every Black or Dark master he could find. Someone had to know something to help her. He refused to let the desperate panic creep into his thoughts, but their time was drawing short. She had to release all of her powers to be complete. Without completing the trinity, she could not defend herself against Rykoto.

The trinity does not lie within your beloved. The crone's words taunted him. What had the master meant and how did it affect Rykoto's hold on Taryn? Rhoane needed answers, some of which could only come from Taryn.

Sabina slipped from Taryn's rooms, nearly colliding with him. She curtseyed a greeting, still sleepy from her night's vigil. "How is she?" Rhoane asked.

"She slept well, which is more than I can say." She stretched her back, turning her head from side to side. "Kaida insisted on sleeping with us like she did when she was a pup. I don't think she knows how big she's gotten."

"Thank you for being a true friend."

A spark of irritation lit in her velvety brown eyes. "A true friend wouldn't leave with only a note as explanation."

Rhoane took the reprimand in stride. He knew Sabina had forgiven Taryn. "If you must blame someone, let it be me. Taryn wished to tell you, but I prevented her."

"She is the most unusual person I've ever met, but I love her almost as much as you do." Sabina placed her hand on his cheek, frowning. "You should get some sleep. These long nights will demand a toll. Don't you have a competition coming up?"

"There is plenty of time for rest. This morning, I am taking Taryn ice skating before the hunt. Perhaps this afternoon you could keep her busy?"

"I'll show her *kalaith*, the art of communicating with a fan. It's about time she learned to be a respectable princess and not always running off with you to gods know where."

"I am sure Taryn enjoys her princess lessons. Remember, she was raised far from the court and does not see being a princess as a responsibility. It is up to us to educate her."

Sabina stood taller, tossing her long hair as she did with Hayden when she wanted something from him. "And where again was she raised?"

Rhoane clucked her under the chin. "Nice try. Someday we will tell you, but for now it must remain a mystery." They often played this game, but it was one he did not enjoy.

"Yes, I suppose it will. As is often the case with you and Taryn, I fear." She leaned close to whisper, "Have you spoken with Hayden regarding the situation in Talaith?"

With the danger Rykoto presented, it had completely slipped his mind. From Sabina's expression, he guessed Hayden had uncovered some interesting information regarding Lliandra's illegal taxes. "I have not. Today, I promise."

"I'll tell him to expect you. For now, you need to wash up and I need more sleep. Good day, Prince Rhoane." She dipped a shallow curtsey before yawning and slouching toward her room.

"Good night, Princess," he said to her retreating back.

In the long seasons Taryn had been away from Aelinae, he'd often wondered where she was hiding. Truth was, he wasn't sure he, even now, understood where Taryn came from. Why Nadra had chosen to put Taryn where she did was a question he wanted to ask the goddess, and yet Rhoane knew she would say it was part of his path to decipher. Sometimes he longed for a world without gods and their damned riddles.

After a quick nap and change of attire, he knocked on Taryn's door, only to be welcomed by her giggling maids. It seemed Darius had arrived to take Kaida for a walk, but Taryn insisted he stay to break his fast. Somehow, Taryn had discerned her maid Ellie had an affection for the lad. From what Rhoane could tell, it was reciprocated. One thing was certain: if Taryn wanted them together, they might as well sign the betrothal warrant that moment.

Blustery skies greeted them when they left the castle, making their way through the town to the frozen pond. Taryn shivered from the cold, leaning into Rhoane for warmth. She wore a handsome blue velvet cape trimmed with white fur over a heavy sweater and woolen leggings, but the cold managed to find its way through the fabric to her skin.

She turned her face to the grey sky. "It looks like it might snow. Will the hunt go on?"

There was little chance the weather would dampen Lliandra's favorite event. She would most certainly detour the storm, sending it off to the west. As the Lady of Light, she was able to control the weather in much the same way he could manipulate time. "The hunt has never been canceled or postponed."

"I think it's barbaric to chase an animal for sport."

"I completely agree." He kissed the top of her head, thanking Verdaine Taryn was more Eleri than Aelan. The Eleri hunted for food, not entertainment.

Kaida ran ahead of them, her white fur making her almost indistinguishable from the thick snow that blanketed the ground. She'd become such an integral part of Taryn's life Rhoane scarcely remembered a time when she wasn't at Taryn's side.

The day they found the grierbas, he'd fought against her decision to keep the pup, but could see now that she was as much a part of Taryn's path as he was. He knew Taryn could communicate with the beast and, truth be told, he was a little jealous he could not. There wasn't a creature in the Narthvier he couldn't speak to, except the grierbas.

Kaida loped around the pond, barking every now and again or dashing off to chase a rabbit while Rhoane helped Taryn become accustomed to the bone blades. She swore loudly each time she landed on her backside, cursing the animal the blades came from and the pond itself, which made Rhoane double over in laughter. He often assumed Taryn would excel at everything she did. To see her struggle with a simple task like ice skating only made her more endearing.

"This is ridiculous. These blades are less than useless." Taryn pulled herself to a sitting position after another bad spill. "Is this made of ice?" she asked, regarding the ornate border that ran along the perimeter of the pond. Her fingers traced the delicately carved roses, gasping when one drew blood. "It's bespelled." She sucked on her finger, frowning. "Who's responsible for this?"

Rhoane offered her his hand, pulling her up into his arms. "The winner of last year's ice competition. A blacksmith, I believe."

"Will you take me to him?" She had a spark in her eye that made him wary.

"Do I dare ask why you wish to see a blacksmith?"

"For proper ice skates, what else?" Her quick smile and flash of mischief tugged at his heart.

Iselt, the blacksmith, was a robust man. Stocky, with a bald pate and serious demeanor, he wore a leather apron over equally thick leather trousers, leaving his chest and arms bare against the heat of his forge. When they approached, he acknowledged Rhoane, giving Kaida a quick glance before looking at Taryn with far too much interest.

"This is Princess Taryn, Empress Lliandra's daughter," Rhoane said by way of introduction.

Iselt spit out a hunk of black goo and wiped his hands on his apron. "Heard there was another one, but didn't expect her to be a full-grown woman." His gaze roamed over Taryn's body with an appreciative nod.

"My betrothed," Rhoane added.

"Lucky you. What can I do for you, Your Highnesses?"

After a lengthy reprimand about bespelled roses, Taryn described what she required. Iselt brushed off her recriminations with a warning she needed to be more careful. Rhoane leaned against a counter, watching the two of them bicker and haggle over not just the roses, but Taryn's skates.

"What you propose, steel blades thin like a dagger, is too dangerous," the blacksmith argued.

"Perhaps I should look elsewhere. I was told you're the best smith in the area, but obviously my information was wrong."

Iselt took the bait. "It's your neck to break. I can have the blades ready in a week."

"Two days."

"Impossible."

"Then our conversation is at an end. Good day, Iselt." Taryn turned her back on the man and strode from the shop. Rhoane stayed where he was, an eyebrow quirked at the smith.

"Blasted woman! Fine, two days."

The price he charged was outrageous, but Taryn paid it without argument. She knew when to hold her tongue. Iselt watched her leave with an admiring smile until he met Rhoane's amused stare. He cleared his throat and took up a hammer. Rhoane tilted his chin in farewell, chuckling to himself. Taryn had no idea how her beauty dazzled those she met.

Taryn skipped up the road toward the cobbler, her mood carefree. It wasn't often he saw her with a genuine smile that touched her eyes.

"We'll need boots, of course. Do you suppose he'll know Tessa's size? I want to order her a pair of skates as well."

The cobbler did indeed have Tessa's measurements as he'd recently made her a pair of slippers. Once the cobbler had Rhoane's and Taryn's measurements as well, Taryn paid the man and they left his shop to wander through the streets of Celyn Eryri.

"Look at those mountains. They're perfect for *skiing*." She slipped her hand into his. "That's a sport where you strap lengths of wood to your boots and glide down the mountain."

"It sounds dangerous."

"Only if you do it wrong."

"You should tell Lliandra about this skiing. Perhaps she will allow it for next season's games."

"Maybe. She'd really like *hockey*, I think. A bunch of guys chasing a puck around the ice. Knowing her, she'd make them compete naked." A giggle escaped her lips and Rhoane bent to kiss it away.

"It sounds perfect for the empress."

"It's sort of like the football game I taught you in Paderau, but on ice with sticks that you use to hit a disk. I'm not describing it very well."

"I would be keen to play this ice game."

Taryn peered at him from the corner of her eye. "If you do, you have to promise to stay clothed. I don't need my mother gawking at you the way she does most men."

By the grace of Verdaine, Rhoane was spared the horrors of Lliandra's bed. He was certain if Taryn weren't promised to him, she would've tried to bed him already. A shudder of revulsion rippled through him and Taryn stifled another giggle.

He stopped to press her back against a wall, his lips capturing hers. She softened immediately, her hands wrapping up his back to the base of his neck. Since their first night in the bower, he couldn't get enough of her. Most of his waking thoughts were of her, naked, her limbs entwined with his own. His sleeping thoughts were even more vivid.

A swell of desire rushed through him, and his erection strained against his leather pants.

"Here? But Prince Rhoane, that's so wicked of you," Taryn teased, straddling his leg, pushing her hips against his. "God, I want you." The low growl of her voice excited him further. "Let's go back to the castle and spend an afternoon in my bed." She nipped his ear and slid out from his embrace, tugging on his hand.

The skies were no longer an ominous grey but not quite a friendly blue, either. Townspeople crowded the streets and Rhoane had to keep himself from throwing a protective barrier over the three of them. If Taryn noticed the looks of apprehension or the quick signs to ward off evil, she didn't show it. She walked beside him, one hand in his, the other on Kaida.

Midday bells rang out and Rhoane swore under his breath. "The hunt will start soon and we must be there to see off the riders. Then we can languish in your bed." He glanced at her clothes. "Your mother will not approve."

"If she doesn't like what I'm wearing, she doesn't have to look at me." Her voice trembled slightly despite her words of bravado.

The riders for the hunt were already making their way to the south gate. When the hounds saw Kaida, they went berserk, pulling at their leads and baying with such frenzy the horses shied away from them. For her part, Kaida watched with detached interest, but Taryn sent her to the castle as a precaution. It wouldn't do for the hounds to linger on Kaida's scent, throwing off the hunt. Taryn had a hard enough time persuading her mother to let Kaida stay with her as it was; she didn't need to give Lliandra reason to ban her outright.

Nobles and peasants alike jockeyed for position to get the best start. Hayden and the duke looked resplendent astride their black geldings, wearing matching capes with their House insignia embroidered on the left breast. Anje bent low to receive a favor from Sabina.

She tied the scarf around his wrist and then stepped to Hayden. He whispered something in her ear, making her laugh and blush prettily. She joined her friends with a smile lingering on her lips.

"You don't hunt?" Taryn asked her friend.

"I don't ride well enough yet. Perhaps next season."

Faelara joined them just as Baehlon maneuvered his giant horse through the throng to join Hayden and Anje. On his wrist was tied a dark green ribbon, the exact color of Faelara's gown.

"Why do they find such pleasure in chasing a giant, tusked pig?" Faelara asked no one in particular. "Although, they are delicious, I will admit."

"Where's Marissa?" Sabina asked, scanning the crowd. "She never misses the hunt."

"I hear she is abed with a stomach ailment," Faelara offered.

"She said Mother won't let her ride this year because she's the heir. Something about being too old," Taryn said.

"Most likely she's upset the empress claimed her lordling." Sabina indicated the young man riding beside Lliandra. It was the handsome man they'd seen with Marissa. His velvet brocade jacket matched Lliandra's, and around his neck, he wore a satin scarf of the same icy hue.

"Oh look, she's given him a collar. How sweet for her pet." Sabina's tone held an edge Rhoane had never heard and Taryn glanced at her friend.

"Surely you're not jealous?" Taryn asked.

"Of him? Hardly. He's a minor noble from some backwater town west of Haversham. His parents are importers of gems from the Artagh, which is why, I'm certain, Lliandra is smitten with him. No, what irritates me is the way your mother and sister compete for flesh as if the owner of said body has no say in the matter."

"It looked to me like he volunteered for the position."

"They always do," Sabina said sadly.

Taryn looked questioningly at Rhoane.

"It is a great honor to be the empress's concubine. Even

more so if you can produce an heir with her. If he is successful, his family will be well rewarded. If he fails, he will most likely never return home."

Sabina snorted and Faelara wrapped an arm around the girl.

"Lliandra tried to seduce my brother once, but he declined. She never forgave him." Sabina stomped the ground with her slipper and turned away with a twitch to her lips.

"Do you think that is why she's placing the taxes on her country's products?" Taryn queried.

"It is possible," Rhoane mused. He'd forgotten about the incident with Sabina's family, but that had been ten seasons past. Surely Lliandra had moved beyond her petty anger. The empress placed a possessive hand on the young lord while speaking to another noble. In truth, Rhoane wouldn't put it past the empress to hold a grudge, waiting for the perfect moment to inflict her punishment.

Trumpets blared and Lliandra rode down the road surrounded by the victors she'd chosen, the young man close to her side. Rhoane felt a momentary sadness for them. Lliandra's love was nothing if not fickle, and while one of the men might sire a child for their empress, he would find cold comfort when she no longer had a use for him.

He gripped Taryn's hand, once more thanking Verdaine for giving him the greatest gift possible. Let Lliandra have her many lovers; he needed no one but Taryn.

Chapter 17

RAIN slashed at the windows of Caer Idris, disturbing Valterys's thoughts as he paced the floor of his study. The foul weather was certain to detain Marissa, if she came at all. His messages to her went unanswered—not unusual, but concerning nonetheless. Of course, she spied on him for Lliandra but the crown princess had her own agenda as well. The business with Kaldaar brought them closer in unexpected ways Valterys wasn't ready to examine. Marissa had yet to tell him the exact nature of her part in the scheme with Kaldaar's minion. He had to be careful. More importantly, he needed to stay focused and discern the truth in her carefully constructed lies.

It amused the Lord of the Dark she was so very like him. All the long seasons he spent with Lliandra at the Crystal Court weren't solely to produce an heir. He'd taken the time to foster a relationship with Marissa that had continued after his affair with the empress ended. He was the father she never had, she the daughter Lliandra forbade him from having. He spoiled Marissa not with coin, but attention. Their relationship benefitted them both.

Until recently, Valterys thought, his pulse racing at the memory of Marissa's creamy skin beneath his the last time he saw her in Talaith. She'd been frantic over the loss of her beloved Celia. They both were. Neither had expected Taryn to defeat the phantom at the Stones. For her own reasons, Marissa hadn't warned Valterys that morning when Lliandra and her guard rushed out of the palace to save the Summerlands princess. Although, even if she had, he couldn't have followed. There was no way he would've been able to explain his presence. It was difficult enough to sneak into her rooms that night to console her. She'd lain in her bed sobbing while he cradled her in his arms.

Of course later, when she'd finally drifted to sleep, he'd snuck away and spied his daughter with her betrothed on the battlements. They were discussing, of all things, a visit to him—or Zakael. Which fit his plans perfectly.

A crack of lightning startled Valterys and he swore at the dismal sky. Wintertide at Caer Idris was miserable. Courtiers and hangers-on kept the palace a hive of activity, but he missed the heady celebrations at Celyn Eryri. Long ago, there were similar games held at mid-summer, but his grandfather's grandfather did away with the tradition and no one had seen fit to revive the Dark Celebrations.

When he and Lliandra were coupled, Valterys would spend two moonturns with her at the snow palace, drinking until the wee hours and singing songs of Light and Dark. Since then, Wintertide was nothing more than a time of contempt for the Overlord of the West. There could be no Light without Dark and no darkness without light. Valterys scoffed at the ancient saying. Life was indeed dark without his Lliandra.

A knock at the door disturbed him from his thoughts. When he turned toward his visitor, his pulse quickened to see the crown princess enter the room. She flung her damp cloak over a chair before curtseying demurely.

"My dear lord, I'm terribly sorry it has taken me this long to get away. Mother had a feast planned every night and I only just slipped past her guards."

Warmth from her lips lingered on his cheek. Her musky scent filled his nostrils. "You look lovely tonight. I trust the weather wasn't too ghastly." He poured her wine, enjoying the way she held her glass, touching her lips to the rim before taking a sip. Her pale throat contracted and released once and then twice before she spoke.

"What is so urgent you needed to see me?"

Valterys pulled his gaze away from the delicateness of her skin. The closeness and intimacy they'd shared since the ordeal with Kaldaar had to stop. Things were different now and he didn't like the effect she had on him.

"I'll be visiting with our lord and want to be apprised of anything he may need to know. The girl? Has she mastered ShantiMari?"

A slight toss of her hair revealed her irritation at the mention of Taryn. Marissa detested the girl and it was intriguing to see her composure crack the slightest bit.

"My spies tell me she is adequate. You know I wasn't at the Stones when she vanquished the phantom and even she insists it was her sword's power, and not her own that managed to banish it. Which only proves what I've been saying all along. Her strength is not what it should be."

"If you were the Eirielle, you mean."

A flash lit her violet eyes before they softened. With a flirty swish to her hips, she moved in front of him, a look of challenge on her face. "If I were the Eirielle, we wouldn't have to play these ridiculous games." Her fingertips scratched down his tunic until they rested between his legs. With an expert touch, she caressed him, all the while tracking his response. "My offer still stands, Valterys. Light and Dark—we can make our own future."

With effort, he kept his face placid and removed her hand. "There is but one Eirielle. I have already created her with Lliandra. Despite your hopes the child you carry will be another anomaly, all signs contradict this."

Her confidence faltered but only for a moment. "I was unaware Zakael had told you."

"What of the empress? Have you shared your news with her?" He bit back his bitter disappointment it was true. He'd hoped Zakael was wrong. He'd hoped he might be the one to father Marissa's child. And yes, he'd hoped they might create yet another Eirielle. The prophecies be damned.

A slight pinch to her mouth gave away her irritation. "We want to wait until it is born before we make any decisions. If it's a girl, she will be raised in Talaith and if a boy, he will be raised at Gaarendahl."

"Not here? So my son does not plan to usurp me when the child is born?"

"Of course not."

"And Rykoto? You've promised yourself to him as his queen."

"When the Eirielle is destroyed and I sit on my throne beside Rykoto, it won't matter where my child is raised. Zakael can have him or my mother—it matters not to me."

"You are so beautifully devious, my sweet girl." His loins flamed and he cursed himself. Why did his match for cruelty have to be Lliandra's daughter?

"It's a gift." She moved her hand to the top of his trousers, giving a slight tug. "Why won't you share my bed? We could bring each other exquisite pleasure."

"I've no doubt of that, but you carry my grandchild and are promised to my god. Despite your gifts, as you say, I'm not a foolish man." He ran a thumb down her cheek, pulling at her lip. If not for Rykoto, he'd take her then, but he valued his life far more than a tryst with her. "I find, my darling, my needs are met in other ways, but I thank you for the compliment."

"I do hope someday you will change your mind." She took his thumb in her hot mouth and he struggled to keep himself in check. After several agonizing moments, she released him.

"As for news, tell Rykoto everything is moving according to plan. Mother has Taryn's complete trust. I've convinced her to come to Gaarendahl where Zakael can help her control her Dark Shanti."

Valterys nodded for her to continue; he knew all this.

"It seems Rykoto has access to Taryn's mind and this terrifies her. He nearly drowned her."

"Did he now?" Valterys kept his tone light. What was the god thinking?

"The beast that travels with her is quite canny at sniffing out harm aimed at Taryn. If you should ever encounter them, make certain you separate her from the hound." She tapped her chin. "I think that's all."

"What of the Shadow Assassin? Have there been any more attacks?"

Marissa's eyes narrowed. "He has not been seen for many moonturns. The rumors persist that you or Zakael are behind the attacks."

"I would be surprised if they didn't." Nor did he doubt for a moment she was behind most of them. If nothing else, she delighted in causing chaos in Lliandra's court. "Thank you, Princess, for coming to see me. Would you like to stay for the night, or must you return to your mother?"

She cocked her head to the side. "If I stay, can I watch you work?"

A delicious thrill ran through him. "It would be my honor."

Valterys stood on his balcony until Marissa was little more than a speck in the predawn sky. Her interest in his work and her insight into improving his little games was addicting. Her enthusiasm for torture exceeded even Zakael's lust for pain. Valterys shoved aside an image of his son with Marissa. The gods only knew what they did in the privacy of their bedchamber, and he chose to leave it that way. It was far safer if he didn't think of her as anything other than an accomplice to his own plans.

Yet she made it near impossible not to think of her without wanting to touch the fragile skin of her wrist. To feel the blood rush through her veins, the beat of her heart when it grew excited. The first stirrings of need unsettled him and he checked the position of the sun before returning to his room to splash cold water on his face. His relationship with Marissa had been much simpler when all they'd wanted was to destroy Lliandra and use Taryn to do it.

If he hurried, he could reach Rykoto before the sun was too high over the horizon. He'd wasted precious time with the girl as it was—he didn't need to further incite his god's anger.

When all was in order, Valterys left Caer Idris for the frozen north. As he circled above the temple, he forced out all other thoughts, but what needed to be done. Rykoto was a demanding master. He had to be vigilant in his efforts to please the god. After he had laid the feast on the table, Valterys said to the empty air, "Great Lord, it is I, your humble servant, here to do your bidding."

Flames rose from the floor, inching their way up the giant slab of marble, stained red from seasons of sacrifices.

He forced himself to watch as the flames touched the naked flesh, recoiling with a hiss. Rykoto liked his meals fresh, but Marissa's visit had hampered his preparations. A tentative thread reached out to pick off a piece of skin from the dead man's leg. On and on it went until the bones were bare. Rykoto always left the heart for last. The flames rose, a moan of delight echoing throughout the dark temple.

Blood oozed from the purple organ as it sizzled beneath Rykoto's flames. A peculiar warmth, not unlike the feeling of euphoria from making love, spread through Valterys when his god devoured the last of the sacrifice. His thoughts wandered to Marissa and he tamped down the traitorous image. Rykoto's face appeared before him in the firewall and Valterys bent on one knee.

"My hunger grows. This lad was but a babe."

The man was in his fortieth season and nearly too heavy for Valterys to bear during the flight. "Yes, my lord." He would have to come twice as often to satisfy his strengthening lord. Damn.

"I do not favor the taste of rotting flesh."

The man was twelve bells dead, if that. "Yes, my lord." Valterys tensed against the expected punishment, but it did not come.

"What news have you? When will I be released from my prison?"

"The Eirielle has not yet mastered her Dark powers. She is leaving to train with my son in less than a fortnight. Once she bears the trinity, she will be ready."

"And the other matter?"

It was always the same. "She is eager to sit at your side as your queen."

The flames sparked once, then showed Marissa enter her rooms at Celyn Eryri. She tossed her gown aside and stood naked before a mirror, admiring herself, keeping a protective hand over her abdomen.

"She is with child. What folly is this?" The flames rose to the top of the temple, scorching the marble roof.

"If I may, my lord, the heir to the Light Throne is no stranger to men's beds. I thought you valued this in her. As for the child, he is my grandson and will be of no concern to you or your queen."

Marissa's image danced in the flames. From the depths of the temple came Rykoto's ghastly chuckle. "There is only one anomaly. You are fools to think otherwise. Do you try to subvert me?"

"No, Great Lord. The whims of the crown princess are her own. This child was not planned nor wanted by his mother. He will be raised at Caer Idris as my son's heir."

The flames subsided and Marissa disappeared from view. "I want the blood of her firstborn. Alive."

Valterys fought the urge to vomit. He couldn't conceive of letting Rykoto pick clean his grandson before eating his heart. "Of course, my lord."

"Leave me. I have need of respite after my feeding."

Valterys wavered, but his chance to ask Rykoto about the visions was gone. Flames licked at his boots and he sped from the temple to the sound of Rykoto's mad laughter. His demands were getting out of control, but surely the lives of his two children were worth immortality.

Chapter 18

HAYDEN raced ahead of Taryn, calling her name and encouraging her to move faster. Her poor mare wasn't made for racing and she soon fell behind. Hayden reined in his gelding, noting the snuffling he made. His mount wasn't much better than Ashanni. He could remember when his father had purchased both of them, and he had to admit the season had long since passed when they were yearlings. A touch of heartache seized him at the memory. His brother had just celebrated his twelfth summer. The gelding was a gift for him.

That was long before he ever heard about the Eirielle or knew about Valterys. They were days filled with sunshine and innocence.

"Come on!" Hayden urged, shoving his memories to the far reaches of his thoughts, where they dwelled with restrained misery. "We'll be late, and I'd like to show you the rig before the race."

They rode toward the field where Hayden's race would be held. It was a perfect day for it too, with cloudless blue skies and crisp Wintertide air. Taryn urged Ashanni forward and the mare lunged ahead of Hayden.

"Hurry up, cousin! We're going to be late," she called after him. He kicked his horse and nearly overtook her before they came to the track. Taryn slid from the saddle. "I hope you fare better than that on the course today."

"You cheated!" Hayden laughed and took her by the arm to escort her to the makeshift stables where he had a surprise for her. The empress had personally selected the horses for the day's event. All Ullan beasts of fine stock.

As they walked among them, Taryn whistled. "Mother wasn't kidding when she said only the finest would do. These are beautiful horses." Taryn stroked the muzzle of a tall stallion, his cream body offset by a long, black wavy mane and tail. "I don't recall seeing them at the palace. Are they kept here all year?"

"These were recently purchased from a desert tribe in the East while you were away on your secret mission." He winked at her.

"Don't tease. I'll tell you all the boring details someday, but right now I'd like to hear more about these desert people who breed such gorgeous creatures."

"Nope, not right now. First, I want to take you for a ride over the course." He motioned to a stable hand and led her out to the freshly laid track. "You see here? They've run a sledge over the snow so the riders know where to go and there," he pointed off into the distance, "see the flags? That's how we know where to turn in case the path isn't visible."

The stable hand approached them, leading a large grey gelding harnessed to a camion on wooden skids. Taryn walked around the contraption, shaking her head. "You're going to race in this?"

"Of course."

"You're braver than I thought." She kicked one of the skids. "It's a freaking chariot on skis. This is suicide."

"If I'm not mistaken, it was you who said I should compete in the games," Hayden protested.

"Yes, in an event that wouldn't end in your death. How

fast can you go in this?"

"I don't know. Why don't you let me show you?" He held his hand out to her and beckoned her get in the chariot.

"You're kidding, right?" She backed away.

"Don't tell me there is something that frightens the all-powerful Eirielle? I never thought I'd see the day," Hayden teased.

"I'm not afraid of riding in it. I just like my body parts better when they're attached to the rest of me."

"Suit yourself, but I'm going to take a twirl around the track to get a feel for the ground. Nothing fast, mind you." Hayden climbed into the camion and flicked the reins.

The grey started off at a gentle trot and he smiled to Taryn and waved as he rode off. The wind in his face exhilarated him. The gelding begged to step up the pace, but he held back. After one circuit of the track, he returned to where Taryn stood watching him intently. "You see? Nothing so nefarious as bodily injury here."

Taryn bit her lip. Indecision and excitement roiled in the depths of her blue eyes. "Well, it did look a little fun. Why not?" She stepped in beside him and he snapped the reins.

The grey took off at a trot but soon sped up to a full gallop. Taryn held the side of the chariot with a vise-like grip. Hayden laughed and flicked the reins once more. The grey leapt ahead even faster. Taryn screamed at Hayden to slow down, but his laughter drowned out her cries.

They rounded a turn and Taryn braced herself against Hayden, offsetting his balance. He shifted his weight to counter her.

"You're going to kill us, you bloody idiot! You're going too fast. We'll fall."

The aforementioned fall never came. Instead, they took the turn with Hayden leaning his body out of the camion and swinging them farther into the curve. Again and again, he did this until on the final turn Taryn leaned with him. They were beginning to rise up when one of the skids hit a rock, throwing Taryn against the side of the chariot. She grunted out a curse and held her midsection.

Hayden pulled in the grey. "Are you hurt? Blood and ashes, I'm sorry."

"I'm fine, you dolt. Let's do that again!" Taryn took the reins and snapped them. Immediately the gelding lunged forward and they raced around the track with Taryn keeping a firm hold on the reins. Her face shone with excitement and when they pulled into the stable, she didn't stop grinning. "That was awesome."

Hayden took the reins from her and handed them to the stable boy. "You should enter in the race today." A flush warmed his cheeks. He hadn't expected Taryn to enjoy it so much but was glad she did.

Taryn shook her head. "Mother would never allow it. If she knew I was here with you now..." She shuddered. "Let's not think about what she'd say."

Hayden held her hand as they walked along the row of Ullan beasts. Her power encircled his wrist, and he looked at her in surprise. "Are you doing that?" Her ShantiMari warmed his skin, with a reassuring protectiveness.

A sly grin quirked up her lips. "Doing what?"

"You're infuriating, you know that?"

"So I've been told. I do like these horses." She smoothly changed the subject, her power still wrapped around their hands. "Not that I don't appreciate Ashanni, but she's getting old and I worry about all the hard riding we do." Taryn looked over her shoulder at the old mare as if worried she'd heard. "She's a good horse, though."

"You should ask Lliandra if you can have one of these. She'll be taking them all back to Talaith at the end of our stay here."

Taryn's face lit up. "Do you think she'd let me?"

"If she doesn't, you can go to Ulla and get one of your own."

"I could, couldn't I?" she said in a mysterious voice.

"Oh, no. What monster have I created now?" Hayden laughed. "If you do decide to visit the desert, you must take me with you."

"It's a deal." She hugged him fiercely and her body trembled against him. Whether from the race or the thought of owning one of the Ullan horses, he wasn't sure. For the merest of moments, her ShantiMari embraced them fully and he experienced the enormity of her powers.

Eyes wide, he shuddered. To have that much power contained within one body was terrifying to comprehend. "I wish I could help," he murmured against her ear.

"You do, my sweet cousin. In more ways than you'll ever know." She pulled back and nudged his ribs. "So, Rhoane tells me you found a spy in Talaith. Now who's keeping secrets?"

Cold filled the space where her power had been and he longed for the warmth of her ShantiMari.

"I meant to tell you, but you're never alone." Two figures approached and Hayden bit back the words he was about to say. "And now I suppose it will have to wait further. Who is that man with Baehlon?"

Taryn glanced past the stables and squinted into the sunlight. "His brother, Denzil."

"Brother?" Hayden searched his memory for any mention of the man, drawing a blank. Baehlon's family was not one he'd researched thoroughly—a fact he would soon rectify. He prided himself on knowing every House in Aelinae. "They don't look to be getting along."

"He's a mercenary and that pisses off Baehlon."

"I think I saw him once before." Hayden thought back to the day he met Amanda at the docks. "He was following me.

Amanda, the spy you just mentioned, warned me that he was working for your mother."

Taryn squinted again, her face moving forward several inches as if that small distance would bring clarity. "If he's one of the mercenaries she hired to patrol the docks, what's he doing here?"

"Competing in the games?"

"Besides that. Mother wouldn't let him leave Talaith unless she had a good reason."

Hidden by the shadows of the stables, they observed the two men for several minutes. Baehlon's hands gesticulated wildly while Denzil remained calm.

"You should get to know him better," Hayden suggested to Taryn.

She looked at him as if he'd lost his mind.

"I'm serious. He's Baehlon's brother; Baehlon is sworn to your House. He has to at least acknowledge you as the daughter of his empress."

"He's Danuri and Geigan. His loyalty should be to my father, not mother."

"All the better. You can worm out of him why he's working for the enemy, so to speak. But wait." Hayden realized a flaw in his thinking. "If Baehlon is also Danuri and Geigan, why is he honor bound to you?"

She ruffled his hair. "For being so smart, you can be such an imbecile."

"What?" He had no idea what she meant.

Trumpets signaled the call of riders to the race. "That's you." Taryn touched his cheek with her fingertips, trailing them along his jaw. "Be safe out there. If anything happens, I can't use my power."

"Don't you dare. I'll win this race of my own accord, thank you very much."

Taryn surveyed him with an impish smile. "All for a kiss

from the empress." Dreamy laughter trailed after her as she drifted away to join the others in the royal box.

Sabina leaned close to speak with her and and Taryn pointed to where Hayden stood. She waved and Hayden raised his hand in greeting. A slight shake to his fingers gave away his nerves. Fortunately, the women were too far away to notice.

The riders lined up to take the reins of their horse and Hayden was relieved to see he was given a sturdy black stallion. The horses were drawn at random by the stable master and Hayden had secretly been hoping to receive either this stallion or the one Taryn had admired.

They took their places at the starting line and Hayden breathed in calm as Taryn had taught him to do. The other riders fidgeted and stomped the floor of their camions, but Hayden ignored them.

When the trumpets flared, he snapped the reins and flew away from the others. He and the stallion were as one as they raced around the track. On the first pass, he took a turn a little too sharp, his shoulder mere inches from the ground, but the stallion adjusted his speed to keep Hayden from tipping into the snow. With a quick body alignment, he righted the chariot and sped off.

The crowd roared their approval, although Hayden guessed a few of the onlookers had hoped he would crash. Each time one of the racers fell or smashed into another racer, the crowd erupted in cheers and jeers. The horses pounded past the stands, the noise of the crowd drowning out all other sound. Hayden kept calm, focused on each turn of the course. The racers needed to complete three circuits of the track and by the time they sped past for the final lap, only six remained of the fourteen who started.

Hayden held his own against a wily little man with arms of steel. His horse was a mammoth beast with hooves the size of a man's head. They thundered past and just as Hayden was catching up, a skid caught on a rock and he was thrown backward, pulling up on the reins.

The onlookers screamed taunts at Hayden as he recovered and snapped the reins, but it was too late. He came in second, a mere length behind the other man. He guided his stallion to the stables and hopped out of the camion. After a pat on the stallion's neck and a murmured apology for losing the race, he dusted off his cape and started for the stands.

Sabina stormed past the crowd and skidded to a stop a pace from him. "Don't you ever frighten me like that again, Lord Valen." Her hands flailed about, a look of aggrieved consternation marring her pretty features.

Before he could answer, she smothered his face with kisses, nearly suffocating him. The polite clearing of a throat drew Sabina's attention away and a flush bloomed across her cheeks.

"Well done, son." Worry danced in Duke Anje's eyes.

His father had tried to talk him out of racing, but Hayden was determined.

"It was a good race," Taryn said, giving him a shaky hug.

"No one was killed," his father said dryly.

"Not this season, at least," Sabina retorted.

Taryn shuddered. "People have died racing?"

"Several in fact, but this is a popular event and the participants know the risk."

Sabina's lips tightened with disapproval. What he wouldn't give to loosen those lips right then. Right there, in front of everyone. But there was protocol to uphold. Damn it all.

"Oh come now, the empress adores the race. She used to partake of the camion, didn't you know?" Hayden's gaze remained on Sabina's pout.

"She used to race? And yet they're not naked and greased

up? Amazing."

"It would make it rather hard to hold your balance, don't you think?" Sabina asked.

Hayden chuckled. "Taryn was making a jest, dearest."

"I never know when she's serious."

Hayden wrapped an arm around Sabina and pulled her against him, delighting in the warmth of her body. "That's the treasure of my cousin—none of us do."

His father motioned to the horses. "Do you like her latest additions to the royal stable?"

"They're gorgeous. Hayden and I were looking them over before the race."

"Do you have a favorite?" Anje asked and Hayden grinned at his father's subtle manipulation of the subject.

The stable boy led the handsome black and tan to a stall with Taryn's gaze following his every step. "That one caught my eye. He's gentle, but with a fierce heart."

"He did not win."

Taryn snorted and with a dismissive wave of her hand said, "Due to his rider's skill, not his. The man driving the chariot was an idiot and if he'd only trusted his horse, he could have won."

His father nodded with a knowing smile. "You've learned much since that morning so long ago when I gave you Ashanni." Pride underscored his words. "I should like you to have the horse."

Taryn cocked her head and half-smiled. "I thought these were Mother's horses."

"Not entirely. She purchased them on condition of their prowess. Since your horse barely finished, she will overlook him and therefore open the door for me to purchase him," his father explained.

Hayden suppressed an immense feeling of awe for the man.

"You don't have to buy me a horse. I owe you so much already." Taryn's cheeks blossomed pink. It was a delight to see his too often of late stern cousin blush.

"My darling, when will you stop saying this? You owe me nothing. Allow me my entertainments and let me spoil you a little."

Sabina snickered and they all laughed. Everyone knew how much the duke lavished on his nieces, Taryn especially.

"All right, you can buy me a horse." She sighed and looked back to the stables. "He is a very fine horse and Ashanni wasn't built for the type of riding I've been putting her through. Do you think she'll be upset that I'm replacing her?" Taryn asked, concern edging her voice.

His father's expression was a mixture of delight and consternation. "You really do care about the horse's feelings, don't you? You are a remarkable girl."

Taryn shrugged. "We've been through a lot together and I don't want her thinking I'm abandoning her."

"Tell you what. I'll take Ashanni to Paderau with me, where she'll be with all her other horse friends and when you come to visit, you can ride her out in the countryside."

Hayden observed the interplay between his father and cousin, noting the way Taryn studied the duke from the corner of her eye. Finally she said, "I can't tell if you're mocking me or not."

Anje answered with a laugh.

"Is he mocking me, Hayden?"

Hayden snaked his free arm around her. "It doesn't matter. You get a new horse, I get a silver crown for my efforts today, and tonight, we celebrate being alive."

Rhoane and Baehlon approached, tossing compliments and congratulations his way. Beyond them, Baehlon's brother stood to the side of the royal box, his focus on Hayden's group of friends. He glanced at the knight and Eleri prince before turning back to Denzil, but the man was no longer there. A chill swept over Hayden. The man couldn't possibly disappear like the Shadow Assassin. Or could he? If so, then Hayden had to find out whom he really worked for.

Chapter 19

TARYN lounged on an overstuffed chair in the great room of the castle, flipping her fan open and closed with suppressed irritation. On the next couch, Hayden was once more regaling the court with his near-victory in the chariot race. Taryn could almost recite the story in its entirety. She silently mouthed the words, matching Hayden's cadence perfectly. Sabina slapped her hand with a stern look at the fan and an arched eyebrow, daring Taryn to disobey.

She didn't begrudge him the second-place finish, nor was she jealous of the reward he received from her mother—his choice of the magnificent Ullan horses. Unsurprisingly, he chose the black he'd raced with. Taryn might've been upset had he chosen the black and tan, but even then, she was excited for her cousin.

She shared in his happiness, often sneaking away to bring sugar cubes and carrots to the stables, always making certain to have a little something for Ashanni as well. Despite Anje's teasing, Taryn didn't want to hurt the mare's feelings by showing too much enthusiasm for the black and tan.

Inactivity had soured her mood. The morning's training was canceled due to bad weather and she was restless waiting for the day's events to commence. Between listening with rapt attention to Hayden's tale, Sabina corrected Taryn's fan manipulations. Her friend insisted she learn the art, but Taryn played coy, often making mistakes just to annoy Sabina. Which wasn't very kind of her, but she couldn't see how snapping a fan closed at just the right speed and with the exact flick of her wrist would do her any good.

As she flicked and fluttered her fan, she was fairly certain she insulted half the court, but no one said anything to the contrary. When Sabina wasn't looking, she would bat her eyelashes and grin like a fool with the fan concealing half her face. If caught, she would act genuinely chagrined and be a perfect student until the next opportunity for mischief.

Darius passed with another page and she waved the fan at him.

"You just told him you will meet him by the stable in half a bell," Rhoane said, sitting on the arm of her chair.

"I did not." In truth, she might have.

"He tells me he has been training with you and your guard. Is there something I should know?"

"I'm thinking of taking Darius with me to Talaith. I can use good men like him."

"Have you asked your mother? Technically, Darius is her servant."

"Mother thinks everyone is her servant. But I checked and the residents, while they are employed by Her Majesty during the Light Celebrations, are not officially a part of her household. Still, I'm just kind of hoping I can ask and she'll say yes."

Rhoane kissed her nose, wished her luck, and then left to practice before his archery competition. Bored with the fan and restless, she decided to take a walk. Kaida, warm by the fire, stayed with the princesses. A chill blew up the hill and she pulled her cape tight against it before heading in the direction of the archery field. On impulse, she turned to visit the jeweler's to inquire about Sabina's gift.

The little shop off the high street was warm and Taryn loosened her grip, allowing her cape to flow loose around her. The cape had been a gift from Faelara upon her arrival at Celyn Eryri. Pale-blue velvet trimmed in white fur, it not only kept the chill from invading Taryn's body, but rendered her fashionable, which made her mother happy. Despite the lighter fabric, it was as warm as the heavy, utilitarian wool cloak she'd had Tarro make for her trip to the Narthvier. She saw his handiwork in the delicate stitch work of the cape and could only guess how thrilled he was to have her dressing more like a lady.

The jeweler popped his head through the doorway to his workroom and upon seeing her, smiled broadly. "Your Highness. I had not thought I'd see you today. Alas, the ring is not yet finished." He held his hands out, palms up. "Would you like to see it?"

Even unfinished, the ring was exquisite. Made from a stone Taryn had found in the Narthvier, its color an exact match to Hayden's green eyes, the jeweler had fashioned an elaborate setting that set off the inner glow of the gem.

"It's stunning. Thank you." She handed the ring to the jeweler and smiled at the slight blush to his aging cheeks. He reminded her of Brandt and her heart pinched.

"It will be ready by the morning. I close at midday bells for the afternoon competition."

Taryn thanked him and left, unsure where to explore next. As she exited his shop, she turned left, running smack into a passerby. She mumbled an apology and floundered to steady herself, groping the man's well-muscled chest in the process. Mortified, she ducked her head to avoid being recognized. It would not do to have the empress hear she'd molested someone on the street.

"Princess?"

Taryn's gut dipped at the title. She slowly raised her head, a flood of relief sweeping over her at the sight of Darius. "Oh, thank the gods it's you." At his puzzled expression, she added, "I was checking on Sabina's gift. What are you doing?"

"I thought I would practice before the event." He gestured to the bow slung over his shoulder. "I would really like to win today."

"Even if you don't, Ellie won't think less of you."

His head jerked up and his mouth worked, but no words came out.

"Please, don't try to tell me you aren't fond of her."

"It wouldn't be proper, Your Highness. She is a lady's maid. I'm but a page and only part-time at that."

She bit the inside of her cheek, contemplating. Darius shifted from one foot to the other, impatient to practice, but not daring to disobey a noble.

Finally, Taryn said, "If you worked for me, you'd be her equal in status." His eyes grew to the size of saucers, his pupils dark against a thin ring of emerald. She put a finger to her lips. "It has to be a secret right now, but I'd like you to come to Talaith as part of my personal guard. You'll be trained not only with a sword, but you'll continue the martial arts training we've started here."

"I, yes, I would love to. Can I? I mean, would the empress allow it?"

"You leave that to me. Just make sure this is something you really want to do. Talaith is very different from Celyn Eryri. Think about it and talk to your family before you decide."

Darius bowed low to her with a promise he would do as she said. He ran off in the direction of the archery field and Taryn hurried to the castle, nervous with excitement. She'd noticed something about Darius, something she'd not wanted to mention to Rhoane until she was certain. That day's event would either prove or disprove her theory.

Time moved with inexorable slowness. Taryn paced the great hall, then around the battlements, and finally ended at the stables. Ashanni nickered to her and she gave the mare several sugar treats before slipping a few to the black and tan. She was petting the stallion when a stable boy who'd been mucking stalls approached.

"Name's Nikosana."

"I'm Taryn." She indicated the horse. "What's his name?"

The boy grumbled a laugh. "Nikosana."

"Oh. I thought that was your name."

His grin warmed the chill in her heart. "I'm just a stable boy, my lady. My name doesn't matter." He turned to go and Taryn stopped him.

"Everyone matters."

He cocked an eyebrow, a frown pulling his lips dangerously low.

"Never think you're less than anyone." She pointed to the bucket in his hand. "You care for these noble creatures, making sure they are warm and safe. That makes you important." She quirked a smile. "If you think about it, it's not much different from what I do."

He bowed low, his hand over his heart. "I will endeavor to remember your wise words, my lady."

Before she could reply, the stable master called out and the boy rushed from the stall. Taryn returned her attention to Nikosana. "Everyone matters. Never forget that."

He snuffled and tossed his head. Taryn laughed under her breath and stroked his forelock before giving Ashanni several pets.

"My lady," a gravelly voice said from the shadows and Taryn tensed, her palm resting on her sword. "I mean you no harm, but cannot be seen speaking to you." A sultriness to his voice triggered familiarity and she faced the darkened corner where the stranger hid.

"What do you want?"

"A warning, nothing more." White teeth dazzled against his dark skin.

"You have a nice smile, Denzil de Monteferron. Like your brother."

A soft chuckle drifted toward her. "It is about the only similarity we possess."

"You said a warning, about what?"

"Be careful who you trust, Princess."

Taryn snorted a laugh, disturbing the dozing horses. "That's your big warning? Thanks, but you're a little late."

He shifted forward and his almond-shaped eyes shone bright in the dim light. "Adesh the merchant, he has ties to the Black Brotherhood. He claims his pleasure ships are for smuggling goods into Talaith, but there is more to those voyages. Your cousin is playing a dangerous game, trusting the Summerlands merchant."

"I'm assuming you're telling me this to keep his illegal goods from upsetting my mother's illegal taxation. Either way, my concerns are less with the economy of Aelinae and more for its safety."

"They are one and the same, Eirielle." He slunk back into the shadows at the approach of the stable boy, who methodically went to every stall, giving each occupant a flake of hay before exiting through a far door. When he'd gone, Denzil whispered, "Not everything is as it seems. I'm trying to unravel the reasoning for the empress's taxation, but being a hired sword, I can't get any information. If you are willing to trust me, I believe we could help each other."

Taryn chuckled her disbelief. "Did you seriously just say that? You want me to trust you and yet you just told me to be careful whom I trust. Um, isn't that a little hypocritical?"

Silence answered her. She scanned the area, looking for any sign of ShantiMari and finding none. After a minute, she poked a hoe into the corner, hitting the wooden wall. He'd managed to disappear without her sensing anything. A chill struggled up the back of her neck, fighting through the hairs that stood on end.

Trumpets blared and she jumped in response, her nerves scattering. She gave one last pat to both Ashanni and Nikosana before jogging to the field, joining her sisters along the way. Sabina linked an arm in hers and smiled up at Taryn with the goofy smile she constantly wore. Taryn wondered if she grinned like a loon every time she and Rhoane made love. Probably. She returned Sabina's ridiculous smirk and wrapped an arm around her friend. The familiar tug of twisted ShantiMari rested beneath the Summerlands princess's skin.

Denzil's words echoed in her mind. If Adesh had ties to the Black Brotherhood, that might account for the odd twist to his ShantiMari, and Sabina was tainted by the phantom, but surely Ebus was not involved with the Black Arts. Taryn held Sabina tighter. When she returned to Talaith, she'd have a long chat with both Ebus and Adesh.

They took their seats in the royal box and waited anxiously as sixteen men and women stood a pace apart with bows drawn, anticipating the signal from Lliandra. Taryn fidgeted, a knot of nerves stuck in her belly. The archers released their arrows and sixteen thumps were clearly heard. Each hit within a specified circle moved the archer to the next round, where the target was placed at a farther distance. A miss meant the archer was out of the competition until only two archers remained. Early on, it became evident the day's event was between Darius and Rhoane. Everyone else was just a distraction.

The other competitors fell away as the targets were moved farther and farther across the snowy field until they were little more than tiny dots. On Rhoane's final shot, Taryn held her breath as he drew back. He paused a moment to set his sight and then released the arrow with a hushed whoosh. It flew straight and steady, hitting the target in the exact center.

Darius closed his eyes and made a figure eight above his head before he nocked his last arrow. The silent crowd heard the arrow sing through the air, hitting the target with a dull thud. The judges took measurements, arguing for several minutes before declaring Rhoane the winner. Taryn let out a whoop, flushed with pride.

Seeing Darius compete with Rhoane had proved her instincts right. The only obstacle to his future was Lliandra. Ellie glanced at her with a shy smile and Taryn resisted the urge to tell her everything. After all, her future was going to be affected as well.

Once the empress had given the awards, Taryn went to Rhoane, congratulating the other competitors on the way. He spun her around, grinning like a schoolboy. "Congratulations," she whispered before kissing his lips. His tension drained away and his muscles relaxed as he held her close to his trembling body. "What's wrong?"

"Aftershock," he joked. "I was nervous Darius might win."

From the look of it, Darius was feeling the same way. "Come on, we need to get some food in you before you collapse." She reached out a hand to Darius. "You, too. I'm willing to bet you both stayed here all afternoon and haven't eaten since this morning."

The men wore sheepish grins and Taryn scolded them for not taking proper care of themselves. Darius sulked on the way to the castle, but by the time they entered the great hall for the night's feast, his mood had improved. After they ate too much—while drinking even more—Taryn snuck away to find her mother. When she approached, Lliandra dismissed her ladies-in-waiting, beckoning Taryn sit with her.

"Rhoane showed great prowess today."

"He did. I'm very proud of him and Darius." Taryn watched Lliandra's face, but the empress gave no indication the boy had caught her interest. "I was thinking of taking him with me to Talaith as part of my personal guard, if you approve, of course."

Lliandra's gaze shifted to where Darius sat with the other competitors. "He has remarkable skill with the bow, but I don't recall him having anything else to offer. Why him?"

"I trust him."

Lliandra's blue eyes regarded her for a long moment. "But you don't know him."

Taryn looked through the Mari to her mother's skin beneath the mask. The mountain air did her good. The sallow color was gone from her face. Even her cheeks had a faint blush. "I can't explain it, but there is something that tells me he'll be important in my journey. Just as something tells me all is not right with you."

"How long have you known?"

"Since arriving at Celyn Eryri," she lied. "Who else knows?"

"No one." Lliandra grabbed her hand. "Promise me you'll keep this between us. Not even Myrddin is aware that I am fading."

A lump caught in Taryn's throat. "Why haven't you told him?"

Lliandra pulled her close, a barrier surrounding them. "Once you start to fade, you can no longer produce heirs and your ShantiMari dwindles. I keep up this farce in the hopes that I might bear one more child to secure my throne, but I know it's pointless. My mother's fade lasted three seasons; her mother's only one. I have no idea how long I have and there is too much to be done before then."

"Can I help?"

Lliandra held Taryn's face between her cold hands. "Oh,

my daughter. How I wish you'd been raised at court. There is nothing anyone can do, not even Nadra. My time draws near." Tears stung Taryn's eyes, threatening to spill down her cheeks. "We'll have none of that. A princess of the realm does not cry in public." She kissed Taryn on the lips, a slow melding of young and old. Images spread through Taryn's mind, things she didn't comprehend, too quickly to grasp before they were gone as if they'd never been.

Lliandra pulled away, a single glistening tear resting near her eye. If Taryn didn't know better, she would've thought it was a jewel placed there for decoration. She wiped it off with her thumb and held her mother close, inhaling her heavy perfume.

"You should be celebrating with your friends. Not worrying about an old lady."

"You're my mother. I'll always worry about you."

"Isn't that what I'm supposed to say to you?" Lliandra joked and then her tone became serious again. "I've seen the way you look at the black and tan and I want you to have him. Ashanni is a good horse, but too gentle for the hard riding you put her through. Nikosana has a stout disposition and will see you through your travels."

Taryn stuttered a thanks, shocked her mother had noticed something so insignificant. Lliandra smiled in that way a person does when they know they've done something good and it warms them. She didn't have the heart to tell her Anje had already offered to buy the horse. That would only cause irritation and resentment. Instead, she hugged her mother, grateful she'd at least offered.

"Now go. Enjoy yourself, my daughter. You may take Darius for your guard if you so desire."

Taryn drifted to her table in a state of mixed emotions, elated Lliandra would allow Darius to serve her and devastated her mother was dying. Each time her thoughts circled back to the fact Lliandra had given her two gifts in one night, guilt cut her core, because it meant her mother wanted something. And she'd use Taryn to get it.

Chapter 20

THE ice skates Taryn ordered were delivered early the next day. She held up the skate and inspected Iselt's craftsmanship. Somehow he managed to make the blades solid and yet delicate at the same time, even working a flourish into the design, which Taryn admired. Not to be outdone, the cobbler crafted the soft leather boots with the right amount of stability and comfort. In all, the skates were a work of art. She replaced the leather shields over the sharp blades and slipped her feet into the boots.

She walked around her room a few times, getting a feel for the skates. An urgent excitement rushed through her as she removed the skates. If they hurried, she and Rhoane would have time before the day's events to take a few laps around the frozen pond.

Rhoane? She sent the thought to her betrothed, hoping he wasn't busy.

Yes, my love?

The skates have arrived. Want to try them out?

I would like nothing more. I will see you in half a bell.

Her pulse quickened as it did every time she heard his melodic voice. She hoped she never tired of being in his presence.

As she devoured a piece of toast and guzzled her tea,

the girls quickly arranged her hair in a complicated series of braids that culminated in a single loop down her back. When they finished, she admired their work in the mirror and complimented them on their skill, but insisted it was too impractical.

Ellie sulked at the reprimand. "You look so pretty with your hair done properly. You should let us arrange your hair every day." Most days Taryn tied her platinum locks in a loose bun atop her head, much to her maids' horror.

"I'll make you a deal. I'll let you do my hair if you wear pants for a day."

Ellie blushed and Lorilee squealed in laughter. "Oh, Ellie, you must!"

Taryn went to her wardrobe and returned with several pairs of her trousers. "Pick your poison."

Saeko touched the fabric but said nothing. Ellie held up a pair of woolen breeches and sighed. "Her Majesty will not approve."

"I pay your salary, not my mother. Try them on," Taryn urged. "You too, Saeko. I see you eyeing them. See how they feel and then tell me they aren't more comfortable than a skirt."

The girls tugged the pants up under their skirts, giggling the whole time. "It's quite strange to have so much fabric on my legs." Ellie laughed.

Saeko held her skirt and looked down at the leather trousers she'd tried on. "I feel as though I could run a thousand races in these."

"I told you. What about you, Lorilee?" Taryn asked the fair-haired maid.

"No, thank you. A woman should be properly covered." Her cheeks glowed crimson with her blush.

Ellie shimmied out of her skirt and tied her chemise around her waist before stomping through the room, mimicking Taryn, and they all laughed.

"You need to make it more authentic." Taryn selected several blouses and tunics from her armoire. "These will give you the full effect."

Saeko changed without any provocation and admired herself in the mirror.

Ellie tugged her chemise over her head and replaced it with the garments Taryn offered. "How do I look?" She turned to the side and back.

"Like a boy." Lorilee giggled.

"Are you saying I look like a boy when I'm dressed like this?" Taryn pouted.

"Not in the least, Your Highness!" Lorilee's blush deepened. "Ellie doesn't have the chest to fill out the blouse like you."

"Good save. I think you look amazing, Ellie. How do you feel?"

Ellie threw her hands to the side. "Free!" She skipped and pranced about the room and all the girls danced with her, laughing.

A knock on the door made them all stop and stare at one another before breaking into fits of giggles. Lorilee let Darius into the room and he looked from one to the other, frowning.

"Am I interrupting?" he asked.

"Not at all. We were just having some girl time," Taryn said.

He bowed to her then. "Forgive me, Princess, but you asked me to escort you to retrieve Princess Sabina's gift."

"Bloody hell, I totally forgot." She paced the room for a moment. "I told Rhoane we'd skate this morning. Could we go this afternoon?"

Darius shook his head. "The jeweler is slated to compete today and will close his shop early."

Taryn looked to the other girls for an answer to her dilemma. They stared back, in silence. "Ellie, you go with Darius to get Sabina's gift. I'll give you money to pay for it. Make sure you tell him how grateful I am and that I'll come later to thank him myself."

"Yes, Your Highness." She curtseyed, but her look was uncertain.

"It will be fine. Won't it, Darius?" she asked innocently of the squire.

He choked out his answer, covering his discomfort with a cough. "Yes, I'm sure it will be."

Ellie indicated her clothing. "I need to change and fetch a proper coat."

"Nonsense, just wear what you have on and here, take my cloak to keep you warm." Taryn handed her the blue velvet cloak Faelara had given her. "I insist."

Ellie's face turned ashen. "Princess, this is too fine for a maid." She held out the garment to Taryn. "I'll get mine."

"It's just a cloak. Take it and be gone."

Still, she hesitated. "If you are sure you won't need me this morning?"

Taryn handed her several coins. "Go, have fun. Darius, you can show her the city if you'd like. Just make sure you get to the jewelers before he closes. Tonight is Princess Sabina's party."

"Yes, ma'am." He bowed again, a huge grin belying his stern tone.

"Now, go before I change my mind." Taryn waved them out the door and turned back to her maids. "Why is it so hard to get two people who like each other to spend time together? Sheesh."

Saeko regarded her with open wonder. "You truly are unlike any mistress I've had before."

"I'll take that as a compliment. Now, help me get dressed

for ice skating."

When Rhoane arrived a few minutes later, she was finishing the laces on her Eleri boots. He surveyed the dressing room and asked, "What happened here?"

It looked like her wardrobe had exploded, with clothes scattered haphazardly on the floor and furniture. "I was trying to assure my maids that wearing pants isn't such a bad thing." She motioned to Saeko. "What do you think, Saeko? They're comfortable, right?"

"Yes, much more so than I would have thought."

Rhoane raised an eyebrow toward Lorilee. "Not a convert, huh?"

"No, sir. I prefer my legs covered properly. It isn't womanly to wear men's trousers."

Taryn laughed at the sheer nonsense of her remark. She should've been offended, but wasn't. "Oh, my sweet Lorilee, someday I will convince you otherwise." She gave Rhoane a knowing look as she stood up. "I not only persuaded Ellie to try them, but sent her on an errand wearing my pants."

Rhoane whistled between his teeth. "You should hope Lliandra doesn't see her."

Taryn sniffed. "She's a part of my household, and Mother doesn't have a say in how my maids dress."

All the same, Taryn hoped Ellie was able to avoid the empress. She called Kaida and the three of them strolled the short distance to the frozen pond where the skating competition would be held. Before Taryn could say anything, Kaida raced off to chase rabbits, her white fur blending into the snow, making her nearly invisible. Taryn sat with a huff and jerked her boots from her feet before shoving them into the new skates.

Rhoane inspected the blades as Taryn had and gave a brief nod. He thumbed the serrated tip. "What is this for?"

"To help you stop. Just put them on and give 'em a try."

Rhoane did, taking his time to lace the boots properly before walking a few steps on the thin strip of steel. "The balance is off."

"That's because you're used to fat bone blades. Just wait until you see how fast you can move with these."

In a complete reversal from their previous tries, Taryn glided across the ice. Now it was Rhoane who struggled to keep upright. They circled a few times at a timid pace, breaking in the leather boots and getting a feel for the ice. Rhoane pushed ahead of Taryn and she raced after him, moving them faster and faster around the ice until Rhoane caught his skate and went spiraling across the pond. When she reached him, he lay on his back, laughing.

"You gave me a heart attack, you terrible man." She knelt beside him, running her hands over his head and length of his body, checking for broken bones. Finding none, she slapped him on his gut and stood, offering him a hand up.

"What did you say those serrations were for?"

"Stopping," Taryn said, shaking her head. "At least now you know they work."

They were gliding slowly around the pond when a soldier ran up to them, waving frantically.

"Your Highnesses, come quick! There's been an accident."

They skated to the soldier, Taryn's mind spiraling with imagined horrors. "What's happened?"

"I don't know details, just that you are needed."

In a rush, they removed the skates and laced their boots without the usual care and intricacy. Taryn called to Kaida and sprinted toward the town center, following the soldier's lead. A crowd had gathered outside a shop and as they neared, her footsteps faltered.

"That's the jewelers where I sent Ellie this morning." Stark fear took hold of her. Her pendant hummed a consoling tune, warmth spreading across her chest.

"Do not jump to any conclusions. It could be anything."

Through the doorway of the jeweler's shop, Taryn glimpsed pale-blue velvet lined with white fur. A red stain ran the length of the fabric.

Chapter 21

TARYN swallowed a scream and rushed through the villagers who'd gathered on the high street. Ellie lay on the floor with Darius hovering over her, whispering calming words. A blood-soaked rag covered her face and she whimpered softly. Kaida ran into the shop, curling herself along Ellie's side, licking her hand in comforting strokes. Taryn's vision blurred and she swayed against a rush of anguish.

From far away, Rhoane asked, "What happened?"

An elderly voice, the jeweler's, answered, "I'm so sorry, m'lord. They were picking up Her Highness's gift when all of a sudden this man appears from nowhere and slashes at the girl. If it wasn't for the bravery of this 'un, she'd be dead."

Darius turned away, a haunted look in his eyes. Rhoane questioned the jeweler further, but Taryn hardly heard his words. She knelt next to Ellie, saying in a soothing voice, "I'm here, Ellie. I'll take care of you." She gently took the cloth from her face, stifling a gasp at the deep gash that ran from Ellie's chin to her left eye. "Someone give me a clean cloth." When no one moved, she screamed, "Now!"

Three cloths were thrust at her. "Ellie, you are such a brave girl. I'm going to do what I can for your pain and to heal your wound. Be strong, my sweet." She struggled to blink back the tears that stung her eyes. Rhoane knelt opposite her, holding the wound closed, his ShantiMari flowing into Ellie. Taryn's power entwined with his. Together, they worked through the hundreds of nerves and blood vessels in her face. She imagined each reconnecting while the skin knit back together. In her mind, she envisioned Ellie's face as it was before, perfect and smooth. She hoped it would be enough.

Sweat beaded her forehead by the time they were able to stop the bleeding. Even with their combined healing, an uneven track ran down Ellie's face. "We need Faelara and Myrddin's help," Rhoane said, frustration clipping his words.

Rhoane ordered a cart brought to the shop and they carefully lifted Ellie into the back. Taryn sat beside her, holding her hand and speaking softly while sending calming thoughts to Ellie's mind with suggestions to sleep. When they reached the castle, Taryn ordered that Ellie be taken to her rooms before heading in the opposite direction.

"Where are you going?" Rhoane asked.

"I need to find Myrddin. At this hour, he'll be in his tower. Stay with her and send someone for Faelara," Taryn said over her shoulder as she dashed off toward Myrddin's tower.

The door stood slightly ajar and she called out to him, but heard no answer. She pushed it open, calling again. Entering his rooms without his permission gave her pause, but Ellie's life was more important than social etiquette. She strode to the open door that led to the stairs and yelled into the heights of the tower.

Again, silence met her. She took the stairs two at a time, stopping on each floor in her frantic search for Myrddin. Either he wasn't there or he was deaf. Her caterwauling could wake the dead. At the final flight of stairs, she held her breath, willing him there. Ellie needed him.

She entered the room at the top of the tower, pausing a moment to take in the sights before her. Bottles and scrolls were scattered everywhere. Taxidermy animals perched precariously beside bits of rock or half-eaten meals. An acrid stench fought for dominance over the smell of rotting food and Taryn covered her nose with her cloak. On one table, a scrap of black velvet covered a domed shape.

Myrddin obviously wasn't there and etiquette dictated she leave, but curiosity got the better of her. She lifted the fabric to reveal a looking glass the size of a child's head. An image flared in the ball and she stared, transfixed, as several soldiers carried Ellie into her sitting room. It took her a moment to realize what she was seeing. Not just seeing, but she could hear the conversations taking place.

The image flickered to Marissa's rooms. The princess sat at her desk, writing a letter while chatting to one of her maids. Taryn struggled to process the information, but the shock of Ellie's attack dominated her attention.

What she saw in Myrddin's spying glass bewildered her. It made no sense.

A step on the stairs alarmed her and she quickly covered the looking glass before moving to the other side of the room, studying a dead owl. When Myrddin entered, she rushed to him. "Oh, thank the gods! There's been a terrible accident and I came here to find you. We need your skill at healing. I tried, but it's beyond me." She was talking much too fast.

When Myrddin's eyes glanced at the looking glass, a stab of guilt hit her, but she continued, "Please, there's no time to lose. My maid was attacked in the market." She tugged on his sleeve, practically dragging him from the room down the stairs.

"In the market, did you say?"

His distractedness sparked her anger and she snapped at him. "Yes, just a short while ago. We don't have much time. She's lost a lot of blood. I'm afraid she'll be scarred for life. We need you."

She propelled them faster down the last few flights of stairs and ran full-out through the castle, with Myrddin easily keeping pace.

When they entered her rooms, Faelara sat beside Ellie, holding her hand. "I gave her a sleeping draught."

"Can you help her?" Taryn asked Myrddin.

He ran a finger over the wound, his ShantiMari covering Ellie's face. "She'll have a scar as you said, but we can try to make it less ghastly."

Taryn cringed at the word. "If it wasn't for Darius, she'd be dead." Darius stood apart from the others, his eyes rimmed red, wide with shock.

For several long minutes, no one spoke while Myrddin worked on healing Ellie's wound. Taryn held her breath while pleading silently with every god she'd ever heard of to please help her friend.

Myrddin whispered archaic words and placed his hand fully over Ellie's face. "Your healing was quite good, Taryn. There's not much more I needed to do." He glanced at Darius before giving them instructions on Ellie's care. "Rhoane, I think a paste of durnock root will suffice."

Rhoane spoke with one of the soldiers, who raced from the room to find the root. Myrddin consulted briefly with Faelara and Rhoane before leaving. When he'd gone, Faelara addressed the two maids. "Keep the wound covered with a fresh cloth and do not let her look in a mirror until the swelling goes down." They gripped each other's hands, holding back their tears.

Ellie was like a sister to all of them. The horror of her attack left them shattered. "Darius, are you all right?"

He nodded slowly, as if in a daze. "She will live, won't she?"

"With proper care and rest, yes," Faelara said.

Darius cleared his throat. "With your permission, Your

Highness, I would like to tend to her."

"You aren't responsible for this, Darius," Taryn said softly.

"I should have stopped him. He came out of nowhere and was so fast."

Rhoane put his hand on the lad's shoulder; a thin thread of his ShantiMari flowed into Darius and he visibly relaxed. "If not for you, Ellie would surely have perished. You are to be commended, Darius."

"Please, I would like to see to her recovery."

Taryn glanced at Rhoane. "If you've no objections, I would like that."

Baehlon burst into the room, ordering everyone out except Taryn, Faelara, and Rhoane. When the room was clear, he nodded to Faelara, who covered them with a barrier. From the corner of her eye, Taryn saw her looking glass and said, "Perhaps we should move this discussion away from Ellie." Taryn added another ward to Faelara's as an added measure of privacy.

When the group was settled, Rhoane asked, "What news?"

"It was most certainly the Shadow Assassin," Baehlon said in a near whisper.

"How do you know?" Taryn's legs trembled and she leaned against the wall for support. "And why would he attack Ellie?"

A look of profound sadness clouded Baehlon's eyes. "Taryn, I'm fairly certain he meant to kill you, not your maid."

Taryn swallowed a wave of nausea. "I wasn't there." Nothing made sense to her. Ellie. The Shadow Assassin. The horrific gash on the girl's face. Her mind groped for answers.

"The jeweler." Baehlon touched her chin so she'd look at him. "He blames himself, Taryn. Last evening, he was boasting down at the pub about the ring he made for the

Eirielle. So pleased were you with his creation that you visited his shop in person and said you'd be collecting it in the morning."

"The assassin thought Ellie was me. She was wearing my cloak," Taryn said, a sick, sinking feeling in her gut. "He overheard the jeweler and lay in wait." Her knees gave way and she sagged into Baehlon.

Faelara gripped her shoulders, her fingers digging into Taryn's skin. "I know this is difficult, but you must be strong. Not only for that poor girl lying over there—but for the rest of the court. They cannot see you appear weak."

"Fuck the court." Taryn directed her rage at the gods and their cruelty, for certainly they had allowed this to happen. They'd allowed every horrible thing that had happened to her and it wasn't fair. She'd never asked to be the Eirielle and now her maid, her sweet Ellie, who was only doing what she, Taryn, had told her to do, lay maimed and disfigured because of her. Ellie wasn't trained to counter an attack. If not for Darius, she would be dead. Taryn took a deep breath to calm her nerves and swallowed her bitter anger. "Where is he?"

Baehlon shook his head. "In the wind once more, I'm afraid."

"No, he's still here. Once he learns he got the wrong girl, he'll try again." Kaida stretched along Ellie's body, whimpering softly. "He should've known it wasn't me. Ellie didn't have Kaida with her."

"Most likely he thought he got lucky," Rhoane said.

Cold waves cascaded over her, giving her clarity, bolstering her resolve. "We'll go through the city and find him. If he's here, he cannot hide for long."

"You'll stay in the castle under guard," Baehlon insisted.

"Like hell I will. He tried to kill me today. That makes at least two times now. I won't cower and hide from him while my friend suffers. I owe it to her to find this bastard. You can either come with me or not, but I'm going." She stared at him with her chin lifted, jaw set.

"She is right, my friend." Rhoane put his hand on Baehlon's sleeve. "I do not like it, but we must find this fiend. She and Kaida can sense him when we cannot."

"I will help as well," Faelara offered.

Baehlon's jaw twitched. "This is too dangerous. Fae, you and Taryn will stay here while I take the soldiers out to search the city."

"If you start a full-blown search, he'll disappear again. I'll take Kaida with me while you, Fae, and Rhoane search alone. The less conspicuous we are, the better our chances of finding him. I can't believe I'm saying this, but I really wish Ebus were here."

"Aye, as do I, Princess. He can sniff out that shadow menace like no other," Baehlon said.

"Well, at least we have Kaida." Taryn grabbed her coat and sword. "Let's go. Darius will keep watch over Ellie."

Once in the city square, they made plans to check with one another every few minutes. Rhoane held her close for a moment before storming away. Faelara moved in the opposite direction from him, and Taryn took the path in the middle. After a few paces, she realized Baehlon was walking beside her.

"You didn't think I would let you wander off alone with the assassin so near, did you?"

"Truth be told, I'm glad of your company." The ball of nerves in her gut relaxed a fraction.

With most of the townsfolk up by the castle, the streets were nearly deserted as they made their way toward the city gates. Kaida ran ahead and then back to them, sniffing at doorways and the air. Rhoane and Faelara sent regular updates that they found nothing amiss in their search.

"Where could he be? It's as if we're looking for a ghost.

How can we possibly protect ourselves from someone who can fly around and be invisible?" Raw anger seeped into her veins. "I hate it when someone plays dirty. All the more reason that I must go to Zakael to learn his Dark Shanti."

Baehlon stared at her. "Don't talk like that. Zakael would rather steal your power than help you."

Taryn bit back a curse. She'd not meant to tell Baehlon until absolutely necessary. "It's the only way I can get strong enough to defeat this Shadow Assassin, along with everyone else who wants to kill me." She put her hand on his sleeve. "I'm sorry, Baehlon, but I must go. It's clear to me now it should be sooner rather than later."

"You've discussed this with Rhoane?"

"And my mother. It is agreed I will go to Gaarendahl after the Light Celebrations. Rhoane will accompany me."

"How am I to protect you when you keep running off? I swore before the entire court that I would do all in my power to keep you safe and now this? Ohlin's beard, but you vex me so."

"It's easier traveling with a smaller group and I just thought…" She paused, not knowing how to say what was in her heart.

"Thought what? That you'd trot off to the one person who just might benefit most from your death? Did it ever occur to you Zakael might be behind this assassin we're tracking?"

"I don't think he's controlling the assassin. It's just a feeling I have. I know that doesn't count for much, but I don't think Zakael will harm me."

"Taryn, you don't know him. You don't know what he's capable of."

"Right now he needs me as much as I need him. Whatever secrets I can get from him will help me with whatever is coming. I'm not stupid, Baehlon. I know Zakael is power mad and I do know what he's capable of. He killed Brandt right in front of me, remember?"

"Then why weren't you going to tell me?" Baehlon's gruff voice sounded hurt.

"I was trying to protect you. If you don't know where I am, then no one can force the information from you," she said quietly.

His voice dropped to a thunderous whisper. "You were trying to protect me? Do you think I'm such a simpleton that I can't withstand a bit of torture? Did you think one slip of ShantiMari into my thoughts and I'd spill everything I know about you? God's truth, girl! You should trust me more than that." He stormed away, his braids jangling with each angry step.

She stared at him, her thoughts a whirlwind of quiet indignation. He had reached the end of the block before she ran to catch up. "Baehlon, wait. It isn't like that. You saw what happened to Ellie. That's what I'm trying to avoid. I don't doubt you would fight to the end to protect me, but I couldn't bear it if something happened to you.

"I know enough of the world to know that if someone wants to get close to me, they'll go after my friends. Today a girl was nearly killed because someone thought she was me. We're dealing with people that I can't even imagine being. I can't wrap my head around this type of violence. As much as I try to be stoic, the truth is I love you all too much. If you died, a part of my soul would die as well."

He stood still for several moments before speaking. When he did, his voice was soft and full of concern. "Whether you want this or not, it is your burden and responsibility. In life, there is not always an easy solution. You must accept that people will die. Some by your hand and others because they are close to you. It's unavoidable. It will never be easy, but it will happen nonetheless."

His big hands cupped her shoulders with a harsh squeeze.

"I made a vow before the empress and her court to protect you. Die for you, if need be. It was an oath I made freely—of my own choice. Every one of your friends, even your maids, understand the risks involved in knowing you. They all accept the danger."

She stared at him, stunned. "Why?"

"Because they love you just as much as you love them. More important, they believe in you, Taryn."

Instead of lifting her, his words clung to her like an anchor pulling her beneath the waves. Kaida nudged Taryn's hand and then ran to a doorway near where they stood. She scratched at the door and sat, waiting for them. Taryn shoved her conflicted emotions down, tamping them out to focus on the task at hand.

They unsheathed their swords and stood on opposite sides of the door, listening. Her ShantiMari probed through the house, touching the memories of the family who lived there, nothing more. "I sense no one inside, but be cautious all the same."

When they entered the home, Kaida slipped past them, running upstairs without making a sound. A chill flowed from her pendant across her skin. She signaled to Baehlon, nodding up at the landing. They took each step with care, attentive to any sound or movement in the silent home.

Kaida sat in front of a closed door at the end of a short hallway. Taryn sent a thread of her ShantiMari into the room. A shock of heat snapped back at her.

Baehlon, something is there. I can't say what, but it isn't friendly.

With deliberate slowness, he turned the knob. As the door opened, she caught a glimpse of the Shadow Assassin's startled face before Baehlon rushed forward. The villain snarled at him and then rushed to the open window. In a heartbeat, he changed into a feiche and flew out, but not before Baehlon swiped his sword at the bird, cutting several feathers off his tail.

Taryn threw her ShantiMari into the air like a net, catching the screaming feiche in her trap. The assailant's power pushed against hers with a force that knocked her back. Kaida barked with a savage wildness, her sharp claws digging into the window frame. Every screech the feiche made was like an ice pick stabbing her inner ear. Added to the pain were Kaida's incessant yelps and the thrumming of the assassin's power hitting her in clumsy waves. The melee made it difficult to focus her thoughts.

"He's fighting me. Call Rhoane and Faelara," Taryn shouted to Baehlon as she channeled all her strength into holding the net that ensnared Ellie's attacker.

The feiche stopped struggling and hung limp, suspended above the street. Taryn held her net firm, waiting. One moment he was a bird, the next a man with a dagger, cutting against her net with vicious cruelty. Every precise cut sent his ShantiMari slamming against her. She added more threads to the net, but he hacked through them more quickly than she could wrap them around him. With a sickening feeling, she realized he could see her threads of ShantiMari as surely as she couldn't see his.

One more slice and he'd be free.

"Oh, the hell you will," Taryn yelled and leapt out of the window after him.

They tumbled to the ground, landing with a hard thud. She lay on top of him, adrenaline rushing through her from the madness of the capture. When she forced her thoughts into his, he should have screamed at her brutality, but there was nothing. No sound. No thought. Nothing.

He pushed against her to roll out from under her, but she pinned his arms behind his back, her knee pressed against him. "Who are you? Who sent you here?"

Baehlon crashed out of the house with Kaida a step behind. Rhoane raced up the street, the color drained from his face. "Taryn! Are you all right?" He looked from her to the man struggling on the ground.

"I'm fine." She pulled the assassin's arms tighter, wrapping her ShantiMari around them with a vicious twist.

Faelara arrived, out of breath from running. Together, they bound him with their power, pulling him to his feet. Blood trickled from his mouth and he had a gash on his ass from Baehlon's sword, but other than that, there were no injuries she could see. His dead eyes, as pale as ice in the northern sea, glared at her. She recoiled from the hatred she saw in them.

His dagger lay on the ground at her feet, along with a star-shaped weapon that fell out of his belt. Taryn recognized it immediately. A hira shuriken—a throwing weapon favored by skilled ninja. She slipped them both into her boot before catching up with Rhoane.

Baehlon held back to wait for the guard to search the house for clues, but they would find nothing. The man was a ghost. Not a ghost—a cipher. It chilled her to watch him walk beside Rhoane. He might be bleeding, but she sensed nothing inside that would indicate life. It was as if he existed solely to kill her.

Chapter 22

THE prisoner hung from thick cords of ShantiMari, his blond head limp between his shoulders. Half a dozen guards, all skilled in the power, surrounded him. He'd been rushed through the hidden passageways and corridors to the dungeon, where he was questioned by Rhoane and Lliandra's captain of the guard. As yet, the prisoner had said nothing.

Kaida sniffed at the assassin, growling low in her throat. *He smells of rotting food and debris, nothing like man.*

Taryn paced the open area outside the cell. She'd listened to the two men question him, her frustration rising at his silence. Only once did he look up. When their eyes met, an electric shock burned through her veins but she refused to look away. The assassin lowered his glare to the ground, but not before Taryn caught the smallest of grins marring his face. A vicious desire to hurt him rushed through her. The ferocity of emotion, the need to make him suffer, terrified her.

When Rhoane asked her to leave, she didn't hesitate. The time for talk had ended. As much as she wished him dead, she had no desire to see him tortured. They could do what they wanted to him; he'd neither feel pain nor give them any information. Of that, Taryn was certain.

She walked aimlessly through the castle with Kaida padding beside her. Courtiers and servants bowed out of her way, some making the sign to ward off evil. Taryn ignored them and their misplaced fear. Nothing she did would convince her detractors she wasn't to blame. She couldn't even convince herself.

Let them whisper. When the time came, they would clamor for her help, their mistrust put aside in the hope she could save them. A litany of her failures ran on an endless loop through her mind, banqueting on her faltering confidence. She wasn't what they wanted her to be—villain or heroine, she was just a woman. Scared, scarred, and alone.

Kaida nudged her hand and she attempted a smile for the grierbas. *Okay fine, not totally alone.*

You do yourself and your friends a dishonor, Darennsai. Be grateful for what you have been given.

Kaida was right. She had failed, yes, but she'd also succeeded many more times. Still, the threat of the assassin, or any other enemies for that matter, wouldn't lessen just because he was locked up. Her anxiety ratcheted to dangerous levels. She already existed in survival mode, on constant alert to an attack, either mental or physical. There had to be a way to live without fear.

There is. Kaida nudged her hand again, her wet nose warm against Taryn's chilled skin. *You will find your way. Believe, Darennsai.*

"I wish I knew how," Taryn whispered. She braced herself before opening the door to her rooms.

Darkness shrouded her sitting room, the stench of blood heavy in the air. Taryn flinched at the sight of Ellie lying on the bed they'd brought in for her. She apologized for not returning to the girl sooner, but Darius assured her Ellie had been sleeping the entire time she was gone. He motioned to a chair, saying quietly, "The jeweler found those in his shop and thought they belonged to you."

Two pairs of ice skates rested on the cushions. How pitiful

it seemed that only a few bells earlier she'd been enjoying her morning with Rhoane. A lifetime had passed since then. "Remind me to thank him tomorrow."

"He also brought this." He handed her an ornate wooden box.

Taryn opened it and stifled a sob. Inside the box, on a bed of green silk, sat the ring Taryn had the jeweler make for Sabina. The stone glistened and winked in the dim light. She set the box on her writing table. Ellie's eyes shifted behind closed lids with her dreaming. A whimper escaped her lips. "Who made the paste?"

"I did, Your Highness," Saeko answered from the corner. "Before coming to the palace, I worked for a noblewoman gifted in the art of healing. She knew of many ointments and tinctures to allay any ailment. It was a simple thing, really."

Taryn ran a finger over the hardened substance. "Thank you, Saeko."

Lorilee sat beside Taryn, smoothing Ellie's hair. "Did you find the man who did this to her?"

Taryn gave her maid a sidelong glance. They had decided to keep the assassin's identity a secret as long as they could to prevent panic during the celebrations. "We did."

Lorilee breathed a deep sigh of relief. "Why did he attack poor Ellie?"

Taryn caught Darius's eye and frowned. He knew, but how? "We will know more when the captain is done interrogating him."

They jumped when the door to her apartment banged open. A frantic-looking Hayden darted into the room, his wild glance scanning their faces.

"Taryn, thank the gods. I heard there was…" His gaze went to the figure on the bed. "So it is true. There was an attack this morning." He sank into the chair opposite Taryn and ran a ragged hand through his hair. "When I didn't see you at the arena, I feared the worst." Hayden rubbed his eyes and indicated the prone figure of Ellie. "Why?"

Lorilee began to cry and Taryn put her arm around the girl. "We must be strong for Ellie. She won't thank us for our pity when she wakes."

Lorilee snuffled and wiped her eyes with her sleeve. "Yes, ma'am. I'm sorry."

Taryn stood suddenly, grimacing at the state of the room. "Why is it so stuffy and dark in here? Get some candles lit and open a window."

The maids busied themselves making the room less daunting and Darius stood. "If you'll excuse me, Your Highness, I would like to get my supper. I'll return before you leave."

"Yes, of course." Taryn stopped him. "Where am I going?"

Hayden answered for Darius. "It's Sabina's birthing day. We were going to celebrate it in the garden because the weather is so fair." His voice sounded leaden and far away. "But now we'll have to postpone."

"No. We'll celebrate with Sabina as planned. I want no more moping. Ellie is going to make a full recovery," Taryn said. "Darius, get some rest, you need it. Saeko and Lorilee, go with Darius. I'll stay here with Ellie."

"But, miss, we need to dress you for the party," Lorilee argued.

"Until I met you, I was doing a pretty good job of dressing myself." She touched the braids they'd arranged that morning. "We can figure out what to do with this mess later. For now, I insist you take a break and get some fresh air. It smells like a morgue in here."

Hayden smiled at her when the others left. "You are remarkable, do you know that?"

"Why? Because I sent my maids to eat? That sounds sensible to me."

He chuckled and let the question stand. "Tell me—was it the same Shadow Assassin from Paderau?"

"Why would you say that?"

"I've been coming to this city my entire life. I can't recall a single time there was violence during the celebrations. This is a friendly place with good people who aren't accustomed to attacks in broad daylight. Who else could it be?"

"Yes, it was the same man. He's being questioned now." She scowled at her cousin. "You have to promise you won't breathe a word of this to anyone."

"I will promise, but believe me, half the city knows by now. Would you like me to stay with you until your maids return?"

"Thank you, but I'd like to be alone for a while."

"I'll have some tea and cakes sent up. I'm sure you've not eaten all day." He kissed her forehead and left her alone with Ellie.

Taryn gently wiped the dried blood from Ellie's neck and hair. She removed her stained clothes before dressing her in a nightgown. As she was finishing, Ellie woke from her drugged sleep, moaning in pain.

"Princess," Ellie said in a sleepy voice. "Where am I?" She tried to lift up, but Taryn put a hand on her shoulder.

"You're in my rooms. Don't try to move."

"My head hurts." Ellie prodded the paste on her cheek. "Oh." She gave a little sob. "It wasn't a dream?" Tears filled her eyes and she squeezed them shut.

"I'm sorry, my darling girl. You need to rest, so you'll get better." Taryn sent a silent thought to Darius to bring food for Ellie and another to Faelara asking for more of the sleeping draught. "You're going to stay with me until you're healed."

Ellie's fingertips fluttered above the paste on her cheek. "Will I be scarred?"

Taryn took a deep breath before saying, "Most likely, but Rhoane and I did our best to leave you unmarked."

Tears slid down her cheek into her hair. "Why, Princess? Why me?"

There it was. The one question she'd been dreading. "The man who attacked you today..." Tears stung Taryn's eyes. "He thought you were me." She struggled to hold herself together, but Ellie deserved to know the truth. "I'm so sorry. I hope you can forgive me."

"Forgive you? Why, Your Highness?" Ellie asked in a quiet voice.

"It was I who insisted you go with Darius." Taryn searched her eyes. "If I hadn't made you wear my cloak... oh, God, Ellie, I'm so sorry." Tears flowed over her cheeks to drip on their clasped hands. Her runes shimmered beneath the liquid and then flared for an instant before settling into her skin, too quick for Ellie to see, but one rune in particular caught Taryn's attention.

"If what you say is true, then the attack on me saved your life today. For that, I will be forever grateful."

"How can you say such a thing?" She lifted her gaze from her wrist to search Ellie's eyes, seeing there a strength she'd never noticed. Fierce. Noble.

"I am but a maid in your household, my lady. You are invaluable to the realm."

Taryn kissed Ellie on the lips, holding her face between her hands. "I'm lucky to have you with me."

"No, Your Highness, it is I who am blessed." She squeezed Taryn's hand. "What of Darius? Is he...?"

"He is unharmed. In fact, he is the reason you are with us now."

"What do you mean?"

Taryn told Ellie a condensed version of events at the shop, omitting the more gruesome details.

"Do you think he will shun me now that I am marked?" Her fingertips again fluttered above the paste, a deep furrow creasing her brow.

Anger swelled in Taryn, followed by a cut of pity. Ellie wasn't a soldier who wore her scars with honor, but a simple girl who was caught up in something larger than she was.

"I doubt very much that Darius is shallow enough to worry about something so trivial. And if he does, then I'll just have to kick his ass, won't I?"

"You wouldn't!" Excitement danced in her eyes. "I'm sorry for the way I treated you when you first arrived in Talaith. It was unfair of me to judge you. I am grateful you chose me to stay with you."

"I am blessed to have you in my life, my sweet Ellie." Taryn wrapped her in a powerful hug, her ShantiMari swirling like a vortex.

Ellie's muffled voice wheezed, "I can't breathe."

Taryn reluctantly let her go. She would make it up to Ellie, somehow. "Darius should be here soon with your dinner. Let's tidy you up before he arrives."

She helped Ellie to a sofa and brushed out her hair, much to Ellie's dismay. She was tucking several pillows and a blanket around the girl when Darius entered, followed closely by Lorilee and Saeko. By the time Faelara arrived with the sleeping draught, Ellie looked tired. Only after she dozed off did Taryn allow the other two girls to help with her attire for the evening.

At Sabina's party, Taryn did her best to appear carefree in the company of her friends. She smiled too much and drank spiced cider to dull the pain. As Hayden predicted, news of the attack spread through the court faster than vorlock venom through veins, but no one wanted to ruin Sabina's night. Eventually, Taryn's sisters pulled her aside to ask after her welfare and that of her maid. Eliahnna and Tessa's concern for Ellie touched Taryn.

Sabina hugged her friend, whispering in her ear, "Thank you. For coming tonight and for my lovely ring. I love you, my friend."

Taryn held her tightly, trembling. "I love you, too." Tears stung her eyes and she looked away before Sabina could see them. Every person gathered there that evening was a potential target to her enemies. She couldn't help but worry the next attack would be against them. The thought filled her heart with dread. With a determined effort, she forced a smile and laughed at Hayden's ludicrous jokes.

She had to be brave for them. To not show the fear that lingered in her every thought. It was nothing to pretend for the evening, but that night in Taryn's bed, Rhoane held her close as she cried in his arms. His protective embrace couldn't shield her from the realities she faced, but for a little while, he soothed her fractured nerves.

The next morning as the sun was cresting over the mountains, Taryn strode silently to the dungeons. She'd barely slept for the nightmares that chased through her mind. She wanted answers that only the assassin could provide. Rhoane walked beside her, his face set in a grim reminder he didn't agree with her and thought she should stay away from the prisoner.

She stood before the assassin in the cramped cell, following the threads of ShantiMari that held him taut. She recognized most of them, but several were new, probably from the soldiers guarding him. No one wanted anything to happen to the prisoner on their watch.

For a long time, days perhaps or merely a bell—she couldn't tell in the dim dankness beneath the castle—she studied him. He kept his head lowered, his eyes trained on the floor. Golden strands of hair obscured most of his face, but what she could see might have been handsome on a living soul.

An aquiline nose and strong jaw, dark brows that bent toward each other in a frown. Pale lips stretched to a thin line against even paler skin. Not quite white, but not cream, either. Eggshells. His skin was the color of a fresh egg. She peered closer, beyond his flesh to where his veins, an odd hue of blue-grey, crisscrossed beneath his skin.

Shadow Assassins were born of death. They had no worldly appetites or functions, but this one bled. The tiniest of flutters indicated a heartbeat, but she heard nothing to indicate life inside his corpse.

"Who are you?" she asked in a near whisper, forcing him to strain to hear. A thread of her ShantiMari wrapped around him, probing his skin and bones. Her fingers twitched to touch his flesh, but she instinctively knew Rhoane would never allow it. "I said, who are you?" She tightened her power and he flinched. So. He *could* feel.

The assassin lifted his head, glaring at her with his hollow eyes. "I am you." Laughter, low and manic, came from his sternum.

A sharp pain cut at her heart and blackness crept along the edge of her vision. Her ShantiMari trembled in her veins, unsettling her. "Who sent you?" Taryn labored to stay calm, in control.

He dipped his head between his shoulders. The laughter stopped. A sneer crossed his face as he glanced at Rhoane, then back to Taryn. "*Ceadach lambeth.*"

"No!" Rhoane slammed his hand over the assassin's mouth. "Taryn, get out of here."

"What did he say?" She squeezed her power against the assassin and he moaned in pain.

"Taryn, please," Rhoane insisted, his voice steel, unyielding. "I will explain everything, but you must leave at once."

She tied off her power, securing it around the man before backing out of the cell. Rhoane spoke rapidly in Eleri, his ShantiMari flooding the room. Her pendant blazed against her skin and she ran up the steps, bursting through the door to the outside world. She bent double, gasping for breath.

"Taryn, is everything all right?" Myrddin's voice came from beside her.

"I just need some fresh air." She stood upright, wiping her brow with the back of her hand. The ice pick of pain continued, spreading from her heart outward to her extremities.

"You've been visiting the prisoner, I see." He glanced at the door behind them. "Nasty business, that. Has Rhoane been able to extract any useful information?"

"Not yet. Perhaps you should try."

Myrddin stroked his beard. "I'm sure the captain can handle it. If you've recovered, I've been sent to fetch you. It seems your mother is quite keen to see you race today. I've been told to make certain you arrive in time for the event."

She glared at him, confused. "Are you serious? She expects me to race with that…that thing down there?"

"The assassin is well guarded. There is no threat to you, my dear, so why shouldn't you compete as planned?"

Taryn bit back several choice words. A soothing warmth enveloped her with gentle suggestions of calm. She'd never experienced Myrddin's power, nor did she expect it to be as comforting as it was. There was a strength to the threads unlike any she'd ever known. Myrddin would never give an exact age, but rumors said he was over four thousand seasons. With his ShantiMari cloaking her with gentle caresses, she guessed he was even older. She wrapped a tendril of her own power through his, tucking a strand of his care away for later.

"You're right, of course."

He placed her hand in the crook of his arm and ambled

toward the castle proper. "I know this is difficult, Taryn, but you can't let the assassin or anything else deter you from living a life worth having." His blue eyes sparkled in the sunlight, full of mirth as usual. "You are the Eirielle, yes, but you are also a young woman. You should be enjoying yourself, not constantly under pressure."

"Easier said than done, my friend."

His arm slid around her shoulders and he held her close. The scent of his tower filled her nostrils. Musty, like old books, but in a comforting way. "You've forgotten how to relax and laugh. The girl I met on the road to Ravenwood laughed easily and often. I'd like to see her again sometime."

She returned his hug, at once reassured and protected.

"And you shall." They continued in comfortable silence until Taryn broached a subject she'd often wondered about. "Myrddin, you keep saying your power is too old to help me unlock my Dark Shanti, but I don't think it is. Are you sure there's nothing you can do to help?"

"With your powers, no. I'm afraid I speak true. My ShantiMari is of an age very different from now. What I can do is help to instruct and reinforce what the others have already shown you."

"I suppose that's better than nothing." They passed a terrace that overlooked a river far below and Taryn stopped to admire the view. "When we return to Talaith, can we at least resume our studies? Perhaps you can search other libraries and oracles for clues that might help in my path?"

"I would be honored." He leaned over a sturdy wall, his face hidden in shadow. "I have a confession to make. When you first arrived, I kept myself aloof. Not because of anything you'd done, but from petty jealousy." He straightened and faced her, taking her hands in his. "You see, Taryn, I always wished you'd been my daughter with Lliandra."

At her shocked expression, he continued, "Yes, your

mother and I have been lovers for quite some time. Even through Valterys and Zakael, I was by her side. I've loved Lliandra since before I can remember. When she conceived you with Valterys, my heart broke a tiny bit. But then, when she sent you away with Brandt, well, I took my anger out on you, I suppose. Can you forgive me?"

Myrddin had been Brandt's oldest friend, like brothers. Walking beside him under the glow of a Wintertide sun, she shared a little of what they'd had. "There's nothing to forgive. You're here now and that's all that matters."

He escorted her to her apartments, chatting all the while about his and Brandt's escapades. She listened to the stories with a newfound fondness for the mage. He would never replace Brandt, but it was nice to have someone who knew her grandfather. No matter what Lliandra or anyone said, to Taryn, Brandt would always be her grandfather. He gave up his mortal life to protect her; he deserved much more than the honorific.

Rhoane entered her rooms just as she was gathering her skates and cloak. "Will you still race, then?"

"I've been given a royal command, so yes."

"Then I will accompany you."

"You can tell me what the assassin said on the way."

"We are lucky. The assassin attempted to place an ancient curse on you, but his power is weak."

"What kind of curse?" She ducked around several courtiers dressed in their winter finery, chittering excitedly about the assassin. When they saw Taryn, their faces froze in a moment of horror before they recovered themselves. "That's not obvious or anything." Taryn indicated the horde.

"Ignore them. They will make up stories to entertain their half-witted minds." Anger laced every syllable, giving his words a bite.

Taryn reached for his hand, taking it in her own and

squeezing. "Thank you. For protecting me, for believing in me, and for loving me even though I'm a super freak."

He pressed her fingers to his lips and winked. Once they passed through the gates, Rhoane said low enough only she could hear, "The assassin used a curse favored by the Black Brotherhood. It is meant to stun your powers long enough for another to take control."

The night she saw Marissa with the phantom, she'd been compelled to do whatever her sister asked. "Can someone do that? I mean, I know Rykoto blocked my powers, but can someone else, not a god, take control of another?"

"It is possible, but unlikely. The person being controlled needs to be extremely susceptible to suggestion. We are lucky you are not such a person."

Taryn wasn't as sure as her beloved. Something had weakened her in Marissa's rooms and made her believe she was stabbed.

"I am most vexed by the archaic language he used. It has not been in fashion for many millennia."

"The person controlling him must have access to ancient wisdom and curses. Which means we need to know what he knows. Oh joy, more studying."

Rhoane squinted at her from the corner of his eye. "I do not know if this makes you happy or not. I thought you enjoyed your time in the library."

"I do. When I'm reading for pleasure and not for survival."

The midday bells began their lengthy melody just as they approached the skating rink. Taryn's stomach pinched when she saw the gathered crowd. She slipped on the bone blades and then made a few laps to loosen her tense muscles.

Tessa skated gracefully to them. "I was afraid you'd back out. Are you well, my sister? You look pale."

"I'm well enough to beat you." Taryn forced a smile.

"Nice try, but I can see through you. The assassin is locked in a cell. You are safe now." Her words echoed Myrddin's in a chilling way.

"I know, but his presence unnerves me. Let's not dwell on that. I have a surprise for you after the race."

"But I haven't won yet," Tessa argued.

"It isn't a prize for winning, dear sister. Besides, who's to say you will win? I've been practicing all week with Rhoane."

"She is quite good, Princess. You have some competition this year," Rhoane teased.

The announcer called the skaters to their post and Taryn gave Rhoane a quick kiss before she skated off to take her mark. When the race started, she lunged, skating as fast as she could. The transition from steel blades back to bone was awful. She fought against the ice for speed. Thoughts of the assassin and Ellie were replaced with staying upright. Not making an ass of herself became her new focus. Tessa passed on her left and Taryn dug deep to catch up to the spry little thing.

As they rounded the first corner, one skater passed Taryn and then another. Soon she found herself competing for last place. Eventually, she managed to catch up to the lead pack, but Tessa was too fast. When she skated past the royal box for the last time, Tessa waved to her family, blowing kisses. The race was complete. Taryn neither won nor lost.

"Well done, sister. I had money placed you wouldn't even finish. You lost me two silver crowns," Tessa confessed after the race.

"You bet against me? How could you?" Taryn wanted to be hurt, but found it delightful in a sardonic way.

"I've seen you skate, and you aren't that good," Tessa said matter-of-factly.

"Yeah, well, let this be a lesson to never bet against me."

Tessa glided to the royal box to receive her prize from Lliandra while Taryn held back to clap for the winners. She was removing the blades from her boots when a shadow fell across the snow.

Lliandra stood in front of her, a vision in a deep-green velvet cape and hat. "Do you think me terrible for making you race today?"

"I did earlier, but you did the right thing. I feel better now—lighter, I guess."

They walked arm-in-arm toward the castle. "I do not like to think of you anywhere near Valterys or Zakael, but with the events of the past few days, we have no other choice. Promise me you will be safe."

"Now that the assassin is no longer a threat, we can travel in safety."

Lliandra bent her head toward Taryn's. "My darling daughter, never think you are out of danger. You must live each moment as if the assassin were hunting you still. That is what will keep you alive."

Her mother confirmed what Taryn already knew. Even with the assassin locked up, other threats waited in the shadows. Her anxiety spiked another notch.

Lliandra lifted her face to the sun, inhaling the crisp air. "I do so love this city. It's unfortunate what happened, but you must not let your heart derail you from your tasks. People will die—it's that simple. The less concerned you are for their well-being, the less painful it will be for you."

"How can you say such a thing?"

Lliandra's eyes filled with sadness and a longing that almost broke Taryn's heart. "Darling, I am nearly three hundred seasons. Those without ShantiMari live to be half that. I have seen my share of death. It never gets easy and it never ends. It is a fact of life. One you must accept." Lliandra looked away but not before Taryn saw a tear slide down her face under the mask of Mari.

Kaida nudged the empress's hand until Lliandra stroked

her head. "Kaida seems rather fond of you, and I think the feeling is reciprocated," Taryn teased.

"Your grierbas is quite remarkable, as are you. You have a pure heart, my daughter. Never lose that. Never let anyone take that love and goodness from you. I see in you a greatness that defies the gods and an immense sorrow.

"I don't know what I would've done had that been you the other day." She held Taryn tightly against her. "My time draws close, but there is much we must do before then. You must learn to control all three powers and quickly." She let go of Taryn, shaking her head. "I never should have let Brandt take you so far away. There is too much to carry out and not enough time. I fear you will not be ready when the day arrives."

"What's going to happen? Do you know?" Her gut lurched at imagined scenarios.

"I don't know the future, I'm afraid. Just bits and pieces of images that flash into my thoughts."

"I'll learn, Mother. I'll go to Zakael and get stronger in all my powers."

"Go to your half-brother. Take from him all you can. He is nearly as powerful as your father. When you've finished with him, return to Talaith." Lliandra touched her cheek. "Together, we will make Aelinae balanced once more."

Chapter 23

A LIGHT snow fell as Taryn and Baehlon walked through the square toward the temple. A few townsfolk rushed past, but no one paid her any mind. They were too busy with their final preparations for the end of the Light Celebrations. Taryn skipped up the few steps to the temple and entered into the darkness. Baehlon lit several sconces while Taryn wandered to the center of the space. Kaida circled the room, sniffing the air before returning to sit beside Baehlon near the door.

She wasn't sure why she'd come. For a long time, she simply stood, staring at the marble pillars that ringed the temple's interior. A few benches were tucked into alcoves along the wall, but otherwise it was an empty space. Taryn walked in a slow circle, touching each column. Her pendant buzzed with contentment as she moved from one to the next. Baehlon kept to the shadows, but she knew he was there.

A set of colored tiles on the floor caught her attention and she followed the stones in a labyrinthine path until the tiles ended abruptly. Taryn stared at the floor and then at the wall a few steps away. Nothing indicated why the colored tiles ceased and she shrugged.

A bright light descended from the ceiling, coalescing into a beautiful woman surrounded by hair as black as onyx, her skin the color of melted chocolate. She held out her hands to

Taryn. "Welcome, my daughter."

Taryn curtseyed low to the ground. "Are you Daknys?"

"I am. I have long wanted to meet you." She glided to a bench and sat. Taryn shifted her sword to the side before taking her seat beside the goddess. "Ah, you have my father's gift with you. May I see it?"

Taryn pulled the blade from the scabbard, handing it to her. It began to pulsate and glow. "What's happening?" Taryn asked, tempted to take the sword from Daknys.

"It is remembering me." She held the sword out before her, squinting down the blade. "You've taken good care of Ynyd Eirathnacht."

"Who?" Taryn was certain she didn't know anyone by that name.

"The sword. There is much power in a name—you should know this." Daknys blew on the blade. It turned a soft pink, followed by blue and then violet. "You are troubled, young Taryn." Her fingers danced along the edge of the sword. "Ynyd Eirathnacht has accepted you as the Eirielle. This has awakened my lover and betrayer." Daknys handed the sword back to Taryn. "He hunts you in your thoughts."

Taryn carefully replaced the sword in the scabbard. "You learned all this from blowing on it?"

"No, my dear, from you. Your heart told me what your mind could not." She tilted her head, smiling at Taryn. "Rykoto knows you hold the key to his freedom."

Taryn glanced over her shoulder at Baehlon and whispered, "You mean the seal?"

Daknys laughed, a rich, hearty sound that filled the temple. "No, but you will need it soon enough. What Rykoto seeks is much more valuable than the seal."

"What then?" Taryn asked. "I don't have anything else, unless you mean the crown Nadra gave me or this sword."

"It is none of those things and all of them. You will have

to discover what he seeks on your own, little one. It is part of your path."

"I hate riddles." Taryn sighed. "Can you at least tell me how to stop him from entering my mind?"

Kaida padded to where they sat and curled herself at Daknys's feet. The goddess petted the grierbas, whispering something only the two of them heard. Kaida glanced at Taryn knowingly, sending a chill of dread down her back.

"I cannot. I will say this. You must never let Rykoto have what he seeks and to succeed, you must know what you need from him."

"That doesn't make sense. Why do I want anything from him?"

"This path has been laid before you. I cannot intervene."

"Bloody hell, then why come here to see me if all you're going to do is tell me what you cannot do?"

"In life, there is always suffering and pain, but there is also love." She traced the runes on Taryn's hand. "You must protect that love with your entire being."

"Is something going to happen to Rhoane?"

"I know much of what is to come, but life is malleable." She touched Taryn's cheek. "For me to tell you could possibly bring about that which might otherwise be averted. Either way, it would only make you suffer all the more." Her shoulders lifted in a shrug and her hair fanned out around them. "Until you believe in who you are, nothing I say will matter."

"I know who I am," Taryn said defensively.

"Yes, but you do not believe in yourself. That is why Kaldaar was almost released from his banishment. That is why Rykoto haunts your thoughts. You have no belief, which gives them power. You must become stronger, Taryn. Kaldaar is close to being released. That can never happen." Her face held the sadness of a dozen generations. "What he did to

Julieta is nothing compared to what he will do to Aelinae if he is freed."

"Do you know who is behind the phantom? Who wishes Kaldaar to return?"

"I do not. They are powerful, of that we are certain. They can hide themselves from us."

Taryn assumed Daknys meant the other gods and a sliver of anxiety cut through her. If they couldn't see the phantom, how would she ever defeat him for good?

"You will grow in your power and your belief. Use the gift the phantom has given you. Embrace it. Nurture it." Daknys lifted from the bench, her gown and hair floating on the air. "I must go now, little one. I hope I have eased your sorrows a little." Daknys inclined her head to Kaida. "You would do well to learn what you can from the little hunter."

"Wait. The Shadow Assassin. Do you know who controls him?"

"You have the answer within you already. Believe in yourself. Trust in what you cannot see." The light surrounding her brightened, then rose to the ceiling before winking out with a spark.

Taryn's thoughts whirled in a tempest timed to her racing heart. She kicked at the marble floor. "Fuck!" She yelled up to the darkness where Daknys disappeared. "Fuck, fuck, and fuck. I fucking hate riddles!"

"The meeting did not go as well as you'd hoped?" Baehlon asked in a quiet voice.

Taryn pushed past him, out of the temple and into the cold. "She said I knew who was controlling the Shadow Assassin. Well, she said the answer is within me. That I just need to believe. What does that mean?"

Baehlon fell into step beside her and Kaida kept close to her thigh. "I think it's all the free time they have. They've nothing better to do but make up tasks for us mortals to complete at their whim."

"I hate riddles," Taryn said.

"It seems Daknys set you up for a good one. Perhaps Rhoane can help us decipher it."

A sinking feeling slowed her pace. "Maybe." Instead of returning to the castle, Taryn turned them toward Southside Gate. She stopped on a bridge to gather her thoughts, idly watching the water flow downstream. "Ever since the attack at the Stones, I've had this sense of dread. It lifted when we arrived here, but now, it's even worse."

"Are you sure you don't want me to come with you to Gaarendahl? Another sword could be useful," Baehlon offered.

"I doubt swords will be necessary where we're going. I need you to stay with the empress. Be my eyes and ears. Something she said to me the other day has got me thinking. She said when I'm done learning what I can from Zakael to return to Talaith. That together we would bring balance back to Aelinae."

"Aye, that's what she's been saying from the beginning."

Taryn dragged her gaze from the river to glance up at the big man. "It was the way she said it. I don't know…as if she needs me to have my Dark powers to accomplish something. I need you to find out what she's up to besides the illegal taxes. Be my spy, Baehlon. Talk to the servants—they know everything that happens in the palace. Find out everything you can about Lliandra and Marissa. If they are planning something, I need to know. Especially if they think I'll help. Mother or no, I won't be anybody's puppet." She surveyed the area, orienting her location. "Come on, there's something I need to do."

They hurried through the city streets until they neared her destination. When they were several shops away, Taryn pulled Baehlon into a pub, taking a table near the window.

She told him to keep watch over the area, marking who came and went and then she slipped out the back door, pulling the shadows around her.

Iselt dropped his tools when he saw her standing in the middle of his workroom. It took only a fraction of a second for him to compose himself before he bent at the waist in the most pathetic bow she'd ever seen.

"Your Highness. I did not know we had an appointment today." He retrieved his tools from the floor before gently removing the blade she was inspecting. "What can I do for you?"

Taryn tapped her nails on a tabletop and regarded him for several moments before taking a risk she hoped she wouldn't regret. "I have need of your skill, Iselt." With care, she extracted the throwing star and dagger from a pocket, holding them out to him. "I need to know where these were made and for whom."

Iselt drew back. "They reek of Black ShantiMari. You should not have touched them." He withdrew a rag from his apron and took them from her, inspecting the insignia on each. "I don't recognize the marks. I'm sorry, but I can't help you." He held the bundle out to her, but she ignored it.

Instead, she raised a hand to his face. He looked at her with wild eyes but did not pull away when she ran the back of her fingertips over his cheek up to his ear. She pinched the rounded tip of his ear and smiled when he swayed into her touch. "I saw the Artagh in you, but half Eleri as well? Now that is a surprise."

Anger flashed in his eyes. "My whole life, no one has ever guessed. How is it you know?"

"Because," Taryn said softly, "I am *Darennsai*."

"I'll not swear fealty to you."

"I'm not asking you to."

An internal debate raged across his features. Finally, he

said, "If you keep my secret, I will do as you ask."

"I have no intention of telling anyone about you or what transpires here today. Do you understand?"

He nodded miserably, still not trusting her.

"What I ask of you will come with no small amount of danger should it be found that you are helping me. In return, I will ease your suffering. If you ever need my assistance, you will have it."

The play of emotion across his face intrigued her. Something made him seek anonymity to the point of disguising himself with what little ShantiMari he possessed.

"Are these from the man who attacked your maid?" He waved the bundle in his hand.

Taryn wasn't surprised he'd heard. There was no such thing as a secret at the Light Court. She told him about the Shadow Assassin, his previous attempts on her life, and finally, about his capture. He listened carefully, asking only a few questions, periodically nodding his head while making notes in a journal.

"It will take some time to find the maker. I have to use alternative methods, but I will do as you ask."

Taryn fulfilled her end of the bargain by removing the remnants of Glamour that shimmered under his skin. By the time she'd finished, his ears were rounded and his skin as dull as an ordinary man's. She tied off her power to make the effect permanent.

"Thank you." Islet pinched the skin on his forearm again and again to make certain no Glamour bloomed beneath his touch. The mistrust didn't completely leave his features, but it was enough.

She said in a quiet voice, "Darius will be joining my household in Talaith. If you should feel the need to relocate, I can make the necessary arrangements."

His face paled. "I don't know what you're talking about,

Your Highness."

"Darius doesn't know, does he?"

Iselt shook his head hard, refusing to face her. "I'd like it to stay that way. He's had a good life here. What was between me and his mother is past. She never told her husband, and I thought it would be best for the lad if I let him go."

Taryn wasn't happy she'd been right. This was another thing she couldn't share with Rhoane. Not yet, anyway.

She gave Iselt several gold coins with as many reminders to watch for his safety. He promised to send word when he had information. The heavy clang of metal rang out as she pulled the shadows around her and slipped from his shop. She took a risk in trusting a complete stranger, but she'd made certain his fate was tied to hers. If for no other reason than the love of his son, he'd help her. Daknys said she needed to believe in herself, but at that moment, she needed to believe in others even more.

Chapter 24

IN COMPLETE contrast to the solemnity of the first night of the Light Celebrations, the final night was a raucous welcoming of the new season. Gone were the haunting songs and candlelight procession through the town. Instead, the townsfolk gathered around a huge bonfire in the town square, drinking and feasting with the rest of the court. Taryn made a brief appearance to toast the participants of each event and then slipped away before her mother could command her to stay.

Throughout the day, she and Rhoane had said their goodbyes to their friends, each time hearing their recriminations and doing their best to explain why Taryn needed to go to Zakael. None of them favored the trip—including Taryn and Rhoane.

Duke Anje caught up to her as she and Kaida hurried back to Ellie's bedside. They didn't speak, but Taryn knew what he was thinking. He'd tried to talk her out of going to Gaarendahl, promising he could help her with Dark Shanti, but they both knew his power wasn't nearly the equal of Zakael's. In the end, he had relented, but there was a strained apprehension in her uncle she'd not previously noticed.

When Anje followed her into her rooms, Taryn stopped him with a touch on his sleeve. "Please, Uncle, no more about

Gaarendahl. Ellie needs calm and rest. It would do no good to argue in front of her. I've said my reasons for going and you have yours for my staying. Let's be done with arguing and move forward."

"Of course, my darling. We will speak no more of your trip. Tonight, we are here for your maid."

She regarded him skeptically, unsure if he really meant it. He was not usually so easily swayed from a good debate. As if to prove her wrong, he took a seat beside Ellie, speaking softly to her about the wonders of Talaith, reminding her of all she had to look forward to on their return.

Darius slumped in a chair, his eyelids drooping, and Taryn feared if he didn't get some rest, he would collapse. During Ellie's convalescence, he had hardly left her side.

"Darius, you need food. Go get something to eat. In fact…" Taryn took in Saeko and Lorilee. "All of you get out of here. Celebrate with the rest of the city and enjoy yourselves. I don't want to see any of you until tomorrow." They blinked at her, uncomprehending. "I mean it. Go!"

When they left, she curled up on the couch with Kaida resting her head in her lap. Together, they listened to her uncle's outrageous stories of his courtship to Gwyneira. Every so often Ellie would laugh, followed by a low moan of pain. When the duke stopped, Ellie would beg him to continue.

Later, after Anje said goodbye with words of advice and admonitions to be careful, Ellie helped Taryn pack by approving which outfits she would take on her trip. In that small bit of usefulness, Taryn saw the first hint of recovery. Ellie still woke every night screaming, hiding her face with her hands, but Faelara was working with her to ease her through the trauma. Even Sabina had visited the maid, encouraging Ellie to trust that with time, it would get better.

With so many invested in her health, Taryn hoped Ellie would see their efforts for what they were—an outpouring of love and a true desire for her to be whole again.

Taryn held up a dress for her maid to approve, but the girl struggled to keep her eyes open, her head nodding with sleep. She tucked her in bed with a kiss on the forehead, hating herself for leaving the others to continue Ellie's rehabilitation, but the trip to Gaarendahl couldn't be delayed.

Rhoane entered her rooms just as she finished packing. She suppressed a gasp at his appearance. Deep bags puffed under his eyes and his hair straggled from half-formed braids. Even though he was exhausted from interrogating the assassin, he greeted her with a smile, asking after Ellie. She gave him a brief update and then they talked quietly about the prisoner and Rhoane's frustration that he'd said nothing more than the few words he spat at Taryn. Their only hope was to seek help from a master of Black Arts in Talaith.

Even if the assassin never said anything, as long as he was locked in the dungeons, unable to harm anyone, she was at peace.

Before first light, she and Rhoane slipped from the castle to the stables and saddled their horses. Nikosana snorted and huffed at Kaida, who snarled in return. Frustrated with their behavior, Taryn demanded quiet, her voice rattling the rafters. Niko glared at her with his large, chocolate-brown eyes, and she met his glare with her own.

"I will not tolerate either of you acting up, is that understood?" He pawed the ground, his coat twitching in agitation. Despite her daily treats, she'd not had a chance to ride him and unease crept into her voice. "Nikosana, Kaida won't harm you." She held out her hand to Kaida and instructed her to come forward to sniff Niko's muzzle. The stallion reared up, but Taryn held the reins firm.

"She is a hunter. He is her natural prey. Did you expect he would be as docile as Ashanni?"

"What I expect and what actually happens is rarely the

same thing," Taryn grumped. She tried one more time to introduce the two and Nikosana allowed the grierbas to sniff his muzzle before tossing his head. "That's good enough for now. You two better get along on the road, or I'll find new companions."

Kaida barked at her and loped from the stables, her bushel-brushed tail held high.

They left the castle and the city behind them, riding at an easy pace, relishing the break from court life. Fair weather followed them for the trip and unlike their journey to Celyn Eryri, Taryn begged Rhoane to slow time, postponing what was to come. Each day, at the first sign of nightfall, they found an inn and bedded in comfort for the night. Sometimes they would sit in the common room, listening to the other patrons. Other times they would linger in their bed, enjoying each other's company. Around midday on their fifth day of travel, Gaarendahl's shadowy silhouette loomed against the backdrop of a stormy sky and Taryn pulled Nikosana to a stop. Rhoane reined in Fayngaar, giving her a curious look.

"Are we making a mistake?"

"Only you know the answer."

"Tell me what you feel." She tapped her belly. "In here."

"Zakael holds the key to many unanswered questions. You have set yourself upon this quest to find those answers," Rhoane told her.

"I suppose, but that doesn't make it any easier. I guess there's no more delaying the inevitable."

Taryn's heart thumped in her chest as they crossed the long bridge that led to Zakael's home. The castle was made of rough-cut stones, similar to Celyn Eryri. Whereas her mother's winter home looked like something out of a fairytale, Gaarendahl hunched like a grotesque fortress on a peninsula with jagged rocks forming a deadly moat. A siege here could last months with the inhabitants of the castle snug in the protective embrace of the sea. No beaches softened the fall, only sharp reefs.

A servant in Zakael's livery greeted them while several young boys rushed out to take their bags. Taryn slipped one hand into Rhoane's, keeping the other on Kaida for assurance as they made their way into the dark castle. To their surprise, Marissa was waiting for them in Zakael's study. She wore a loose-fitting gown that did little to hide her voluptuous figure. Taryn was accustomed to her sister's provocative attire at court, but to see her dressed so informally was a shock. More than her clothing, it was her manner that suggested she was a frequent visitor to Gaarendahl—her ease at directing the servants, her familiarity with even the smallest detail.

"Princess," Rhoane said, his voice tight. "We were not aware you would be joining us."

"Zakael thought having a friendly face around might make you more comfortable." She kissed Taryn on each cheek. "I'm honored he wished me to be here."

Zakael hovered beside her and she beamed at him from under her lashes. "Lord Zakael has been so gracious to welcome us to his home."

"Prince Rhoane, I trust your journey was pleasant?" Zakael said in a friendly tone.

"It was. If you would not mind, however, we have been on the road for several days and could use a change of clothes."

"Where are my manners?" Zakael rang a bell and two servants appeared in the doorway. "We'll see one another at dinner, where we can discuss the purpose of your visit."

Once away from the study, Taryn said to Rhoane, "Was that weird to you as well?"

He nodded, putting a finger to his lips, his gaze directed at their guides.

They were led to separate rooms at opposite ends of the hall from each other. Rhoane accompanied Taryn to her room and made certain she was settled before following a servant to his quarters. The candle glow became smaller and smaller the farther he walked before disappearing with a final, echoing click of his door.

That night, Zakael starred as the host and Marissa as hostess in a macabre performance. Whether meant for their benefit or not, Taryn couldn't say, but it was clear from their intimate interactions they were much more than just acquaintances. Rhoane held her hand all evening and through her *cynfar* she sensed his sorrow. Even now, he wanted to trust Marissa.

I am sorry.

It is best I see this for myself. I confess I would not have believed it possible.

For the next two days, Zakael played coy with her. What he taught her of Dark Shanti was little more than she'd learned on her own. Occasionally, he tossed out a command she hadn't thought of, but those tidbits were rare. He constantly tested the strength of her powers, probing her mind and body with his ShantiMari as if trying to find a weakness to exploit. She tolerated the subtle nudges and kept her powers muted in an attempt to play off his ego.

To taunt her, he devised lessons meant to make her supposed paltry skills look even more pathetic. Taryn went along with the game, making mistakes often enough he would underestimate her abilities. While he tested her, she studied every nuance and inflection of his actions, but it was when he thought himself alone she learned the most from her half-brother. When he fully flexed his ShantiMari, she saw how he bent shadows, warping and binding them to do his bidding.

It hurt her to watch. Every command he made, every thread of power he used, he infused with a sadistic twist. She forced herself to stay hidden in corners to learn what he withheld from her. The sheer amount of power he wielded humbled her. It swirled around him in a constant frenzy to be unleashed. Zakael rarely let his guard down, making her surveillance difficult at best. Only once did she almost get caught when Marissa entered Zakael's study unannounced, wearing only a silk robe. Her ShantiMari whirled around the room in a fury of emotion and Taryn slipped out the door a moment before it would've collided with her own power.

On their third night in the gloomy castle, Taryn awoke to the sound of Kaida snarling at the door. Taryn crept from her bed, sword in hand, and yanked the door open. A surprised Zakael stared, dumbfounded, before finding his voice.

"Taryn, I thought perhaps you would like a tour of the castle grounds. They are far more beautiful at night."

"I'm sure they are, but no, thank you."

A devilish glint lit his eyes. Behind him, two huge hounds sat on their haunches and Kaida lay on her belly, her paws outstretched, relaxed.

"You were meant to be mine, Taryn Galendrin. Verdaine's prophecy is an Eleri folly, nothing more. We are meant to rule Aelinae together. That is what's meant by bringing balance to the world. Surely you can see this is the only way."

She'd heard his ramblings on the topic enough over the past few days she could recite them in her sleep. "You're a sick bastard, Zakael. Let's not even think about the fact that you're fucking my sister and then you show up expecting me to fall into your arms. Marissa I get. You're not blood related to her, but we share the same father. That's just gross." She closed the door, but he blocked her.

"It's what the gods desire. I've seen our future. We shall be exalted above all others."

"Blah, blah, blah. I get it. We're to be gods. Nice fantasy, Zakael. It's late—I'm tired. Can we play this game another time? How about maybe never? Now move your fucking foot before I slam this door on it." For once, he did as told.

She shut the door and locked it with her power. Not even the exalted Zakael could get through her wards. Just to be safe, she slept with Kaida in her bed, her sword beneath her fingertips.

The next morning, Taryn wrestled with telling Rhoane about the incident. They strolled the gardens at the far end of the grounds where Taryn hoped they had a modicum of privacy. Despite the ugliness of the castle proper, the gardens were lovely. Winter blooms of white and blue wove between deep green shrubs. Vines covered the walls and archways, dripping crimson flowers that tickled her head.

"How is your training going?" Rhoane asked as he did every day. Zakael refused to allow the Eleri near them when he worked with Taryn, but she knew Rhoane stayed close. Even without her pendant, she sensed his presence. He never used his power, but it was always nearby, a constant protection available if needed.

"It's not. I mean, Zakael's showing me simple things, but I doubt he's ever going to truly help. I think—" A flicker of shadow caught her attention and she slid her gaze to where she could discern the outline of a person not more than three paces from where she stood. "I think he's trying to figure out how to best use me."

We need to leave this place. It is not safe here. Taryn layered the thought atop her spoken words. Kaida explored the outer gardens, sniffing the air, her gaze settling on the shadowed form. Taryn cautioned patience.

"That was always a possibility. If you do not feel Zakael can be of help, perhaps we are better suited elsewhere." *What is it? You are unsettled.* His eyes widened and then narrowed. *There is something just beyond your right shoulder. I know not what, but I sense something unpleasant.*

"You're right. I had hoped this meeting with my brother

would be beneficial to both of us. It's a shame, really."

Zakael? Is he hidden in shadow? Taryn resisted the urge to confront her brother.

Yes. He is right behind you. Be careful, my love. "Perhaps you should give him a few more days. Talk to him. Let him know what you desire."

"I will. Maybe I'm expecting too much from myself, too." She shivered dramatically. "It's cold. We should be inside by the fire. Kaida, come!"

Zakael followed them all the way to the door of the great room. After they were seated and Marissa brought them refreshments, he arrived, apologizing for keeping them waiting. They played a genial game of cards; the whole while Taryn and Rhoane made plans for their departure. They agreed it would be best if they left without notice early the next morning. That night, Taryn would stay in Rhoane's rooms. She'd not given a reason why she wanted to leave, but she suspected he could guess. Zakael wasn't exactly discreet in his behavior toward her.

After lunch, Taryn and Zakael excused themselves to his study, where they were to have the day's lesson. She loathed being alone with him but went along with the ruse to keep him from suspecting they'd made other plans. For two bells, they pretended he taught and she learned until finally Zakael lounged behind his desk, a mug of ale held in his hand. Two huge beasts rested at his feet, chewing on several bones.

He could've been handsome if not for his cruelty.

Zakael glanced up as if he'd heard her unspoken words. A glint in his ashen eyes set her on edge. "My beautiful sister," he drawled, taking a long swig of his ale and licking his lips. "How many times will you deny me?"

"As many times as you ask. Are we finished here?"

Zakael rose, his movement so swift she hardly saw him until he stood a hair's breadth before her. His fingers cupped her face, pinching her a little too hard. "We'll never be finished, will we? Not until you give yourself to me as you're meant to do." The intensity of his gaze rocked her core. She hated this part of their conversation.

"Zakael, I've told you. We will never rule together. I am promised to Rhoane. My duty is to Aelinae, and the welfare of this world is what I care about more than a throne."

His laughter, hollow and cruel, careened through the room. "The good of Aelinae? It dwells in our union, but you are blind yet to see the truth."

"And you're delirious. Seriously, this conversation is getting old. Either teach me how to use my Dark Shanti or fuck off." She turned to leave, but he gripped her tighter, his hand roving to her throat. She sucked in air and glared at him. "Release me this instant." Her ShantiMari swirled in rage, begging to be unloosed, but she tempered the frenzy. It was just like Zakael to abuse her to test her powers. She wouldn't give in to his need.

"You and I both know you didn't come to Gaarendahl to control your ShantiMari. You're perfectly capable in that regard." His words slurred slightly and Taryn smelled ale on his breath. He always had a mug when she was around, but that day he'd been drinking more than usual.

His misty-grey eyes were like the overcast sky outside, dark and moody. His attempt to restrain her was clumsy and out of character for the usually controlled man. "You don't want to do this, Zakael. Release me before this gets out of hand."

He snorted a laugh. "You have no idea what I want, you stupid cunt. Go! Go back to your pathetic prince. Let's see how long you last before you return, begging." He shoved her backward and she stumbled over a throw rug. "You need me, Taryn. Need what I can give you. Need the knowledge that only I possess. You'll be back, mark my words you will, on your knees begging for it."

His sickening laughter followed her as she fled his study.

Chapter 25

TARYN raced down the hallway, rubbing her neck where Zakael had choked a little too hard. He'd not only frightened her, but his advances were getting more brazen, more forceful. His ShantiMari was too strong to fight off alone. They had to leave Gaarendahl now, before Zakael made real on his threats.

By the time she reached Rhoane's room, she shook from head to toe—from nerves, from fright, from too much anxiety for far too long. All she wanted was to grab her belongings and get the hell out of her demented brother's home.

With a shaky hand and even shakier breathing, she entered Rhoane's bedchamber and froze at the sight before her. Rhoane, back arched and naked, was making love to—Taryn.

The scene made no sense. Was she not in her body? Did Zakael not just try to assault her? Rhoane's gaze slid toward her, confusion too slow in crossing his face. He looked down at the other Taryn and frowned. His sluggish movements were that of a man entirely too drunk, or drugged.

The other woman's face shifted, cruelly morphing into that of Marissa. Her sister's violet eyes shone with a sick triumph.

Her lips curled into a snarl as she snaked her arms to embrace Rhoane. "You truly do love to watch, don't you?"

Bile splashed against the roof of Taryn's mouth as a low scream started deep within. Biting back sickness, she turned and fled, a tangle of anger and repulsion crowding her thoughts.

Rhoane's anguished cry slammed into her as she ran down the hallway. His anger blazed through her *cynfar* to their bonds. His ire was directed at Marissa, but she cowered from it all the same. She stumbled into her room, tripping over Kaida before crashing to the balcony and vomiting over the edge.

When nothing remained in her stomach, she gulped in salty air, burning her fragile throat. She welcomed the pain. It was a necessary distraction from the vision that wouldn't leave her thoughts. Revenge, horrific in its beauty, thrust to the forefront of her mind.

With a flick of her wrist, she tossed the mattress against the wall. Buried deep in the feathers was her sword. A dark melody played in her mind and she stilled for a moment, letting it wash over her. Kaida sat on her haunches, waiting. Taryn took a deep, shuddering breath.

"Marissa raped Rhoane."

Hearing herself say it out loud made it all the more terrible, all the more real. "She's my sister. Why would she do this?" Tears stung her eyes and she bit her cheek to keep from crying. She couldn't—wouldn't—think it possible Rhoane had wanted what she saw in his bedchamber.

You know why. Kaida pawed at the bed, growling. *You are Darennsai. You do not let her determine your fate. Think long on your actions. What you do this night affects all of Aelinae.*

Her heart beat wildly with a ferocity that frightened her. Uncontrollable rage sped through her veins, equaled in strength by her ShantiMari's desire to be unleashed.

Damn it, but Kaida was right.

What she did this night wasn't about her. Wasn't about

her hurt, her anger, or even Rhoane's rape. But she refused to let Marissa go unpunished. "Are you suggesting I take Marissa to my mother? I have no proof. It will be her word against mine. Zakael won't be any help. Hell, he probably encouraged her. Can't I just kill her?"

You are asking the wrong questions.

"You can be annoying at times, you know." Kaida's tongue lolled to the side of her mouth. "Stop laughing, you mangy beast. Come on." Before Kaida stopped her, she sprinted from the room.

By the time she reached Marissa's rooms, she'd shoved her pain aside and replaced it with calculated calm. At her sister's open door, she covered herself with shadow and stepped lightly to where Marissa reclined on her bed, humming to herself.

It amused her that Marissa thought so little of Taryn's skill with ShantiMari that she didn't expect retaliation. She took advantage of her sister's self-assuredness to sift through her thoughts. A black stain, much like the one she bore, wove through Marissa's being. Unlike Taryn's, the stain found welcome refuge in her sister's thoughts and power. When she'd had enough of the detritus found there, Taryn placed her sword on Marissa's neck. Kaida stayed in the corner, her golden eyes fixed on the crown princess.

"Make one sound and it will be your last," Taryn said, letting the shadows slip away.

Marissa's lids flew open, and she glared at Taryn. She opened her mouth to speak and seeing the blade at her throat, closed it.

"I should kill you for what you've done. The gods know I want to." Taryn held the sword tighter, delighting in the fear she saw in Marissa's eyes. "But I won't. Not tonight, at least."

Her ShantiMari burned through her. She fought to keep her focus, to not give in to her rage. "My blade wants your blood." She moved it to above Marissa's heart, pressing it down to make a small cut in the pale skin.

Marissa gasped, sinking into the bed, away from the sharp tip, but there was no escape.

"Afraid you might be poisoned? Ynyd Eirathnacht knows you well and wants revenge." Taryn sent a thread of her Dark ShantiMari down the blade into Marissa's body. "Shall I let her have it? She relishes the taste of your fear." Taryn bent to swipe the cut with a fingertip, tasting the blood in her mouth. "I know it was you who placed this sword over Hayden's heart."

Marissa shook her head, a look of pleading in her beautiful eyes. "I don't know what you're talking about."

Taryn laughed, a cold, mirthless sound. "I'm the Sword Bearer of Ynyd Eirathnacht. I am the one who saved Hayden and was poisoned by your spell. The sword sings to me of your fears and darkest secrets. I know your father wanted this for you."

Taryn flicked the sword at her sister. "He longed for you to be the Eirielle. When that didn't happen, he planned Lliandra's murder. It was you who poured the poison into your own mother's drink. But she survived your treason, never knowing it was her daughter who sought her death. For a crown, Marissa? Or was it for more?" Taryn looked deep into Marissa's violet eyes; there was no triumph, only cunning and a small bit of fear.

Taryn stepped back, removing the sword from Marissa's heart. "I know what it is you desire, sister." She held out her hand and a vision played as if on a screen. It showed Marissa, clothed in rich fabrics covered in jewels, wearing a crown studded with diamonds the size of a child's hand, sitting at Rykoto's side as his immortal queen.

"I also know what it is you fear." A new image danced on Taryn's hand. It showed Rykoto tearing tiny bits of flesh from

Marissa in a prolonged orgy. Taryn fought the urge to recoil from the image and the grotesque pleasure Rykoto received from eating her heart; instead, she kept her hand steady, watching the horror that played across Marissa's pale face.

"You wouldn't." Marissa stared at Taryn's hand. "Please, kill me before that."

"Give you mercy when you've shown me none?" Taryn let the image fade.

False tears slid over Marissa's cheeks. Behind the ruse, Taryn saw hatred in her steady gaze. "Please don't hurt me." Her voice held just the right amount of remorse.

Marissa's ShantiMari flared around her, and Taryn raised her sword higher until the point was level with her sister's eyes. "Don't, Marissa. Just because you've never seen me use my power, don't assume I have none."

The lavender threads faltered and then receded. Taryn lowered her sword and pressed her hand against the shallow cut on Marissa's chest. Blood oozed beneath her fingers through Marissa's robe. "This will heal. Mostly. Every time you think of this night, I expect it won't be pleasant."

"We're more alike than you think," Marissa said, her voice flat, detached.

"We're nothing alike—you're selfish and cruel."

Marissa's eyes held a shred of sadness for a moment and then filled once more with animosity. "You can't see it right now, but someday you will."

"I know you detest me, but how could you do that to Rhoane? He trusted you."

"Who's to say it was all me? It wasn't as if Rhoane stopped once he saw you. I'd say that makes him culpable, wouldn't you?" A cruel smile spread across her face.

Taryn slammed Marissa against the wall with her ShantiMari. Her sister gasped and groped at the invisible hand that choked the life from her.

"You drugged him, you fucking bitch. You had to make him think you were me to even get him to touch you. What we have, Rhoane and I, you'll never know and for that, I am sorry for you."

Taryn threw her on the bed, releasing her throat with a twinge of regret. She finally understood the cause of Marissa's muted ShantiMari. As much as she wanted to kill her sister, she couldn't destroy the innocent life inside her. The child was, after all, her nephew.

Through her gasps, Marissa glared at Taryn. "I don't need your pity. You're an ignorant Offlander pig and will never be my equal." Marissa raised her chin, drawing in a deep breath. "Mother will never love you as she loves me. Never."

The words stung, but Taryn couldn't let her sister know how much they hurt. "I'm going to leave you now before I do something I might not regret, like cut your fucking head off. Stay away from Rhoane."

"You might think you can erase me from his life, but you'll find that harder to accomplish than you think. I suppose now you'll take him home and have him purified. Oh, yes, I know all about the Eleri customs. You might be able to cleanse his body, dear sister, but in his mind, he'll always know what he did." She ran a hand over her body in a suggestive manner. "I think he quite liked the change."

A roar of blood rushed through her, clouding her hearing for a moment. Taryn struggled to steady herself. Her grip tightened on the sword. She imagined Marissa's head bobbing off her shoulders to the floor. Taryn fought with her emotions. It would be too easy to kill Marissa. For one brief moment, Taryn saw into Marissa's mind and knew that Rhoane had frightened her. He pounded his anger into her. He'd hurt her.

Taryn bound her sister to keep her from moving or speaking and then set several wards around her rooms to prevent her from leaving. Many long days would pass before they wore off and Taryn expected to be far from Gaarendahl by then. Just before she left, Taryn turned to Marissa, saying only one word.

"Pain."

Marissa's face contorted with silent anguish and the wound bled anew.

"You've chosen your path. Now I choose mine. If you ever fuck with me or my loved ones again, I will kill you."

A soulful melody from her sword and pendant swirled around the room, echoing Taryn's words into an unbreakable oath. Kaida howled, adding an eerie end to the song. Marissa visibly shook against the headboard and Taryn turned away before compassion made her do something stupid.

Marissa deserved whatever she got. Her sister played too many dangerous games and one day her duplicitousness would catch up to her. Kaida was right; the night wasn't just about Taryn's revenge on her sister. She had to think of the good of Aelinae.

Taryn strode down the silent hallway to Rhoane's room, sword in hand, alert to any danger. Thus far, Zakael had yet to appear, but he had a nasty habit of being where she least expected to see him. She knocked on the wooden door, the sound echoing off the stone walls with a horrendous clanging. When no one answered, she entered cautiously, calling out Rhoane's name. He came around a corner, sword drawn, eyes wild.

"Rhoane, it's me."

He paused, incomprehension shadowing his face.

Taryn gently lowered his blade. "It's okay, Rhoane. I'm here."

He blinked and took a step back. "Is it really you?" Then he held the sword to her throat. "What have you done to Taryn?"

She held out her hand to show him the runes glittering in the dim light. In Eleri she said, "Rhoane, it is me, the Darennsai. It is Taryn." At the sound of her name, he dropped the sword and fell to his knees, tears streaming down his face.

"I have failed you, my beloved." His words came out slurred from the remnants of the drug.

She knelt before him and reached to embrace him, but he backed away. "No! Do not touch me. I am tainted."

Tears spilled over her cheeks. "Rhoane, we have to leave right now. I am going to take you to the vier, where you will be purified."

"Yes, purification." He put a hand on his head. "She drugged me."

"I know." She stood and waited for him to rise on unsteady legs. "Can you ride?"

"Well enough." Her ShantiMari wrapped around him, lifting him up, supporting much of his weight. He sagged into her power, pulling it around him like a comforting blanket.

What few belongings they had she threw into their bags, the whole time keeping an eye on Rhoane. His unsteady gait made their escape difficult, but they raced from the castle to the stables, where they hurriedly saddled the horses.

Once they were across the long bridge and outside the gates, Taryn allowed herself to look back. Gaarendahl loomed large against the cliff, its windows dark and foreboding. Zakael's gaze blazed at her, but he didn't try to stop them. A sick feeling nestled in her thoughts that he'd gotten from them exactly what he wanted.

Chapter 26

TARYN watched Rhoane that evening and for the next several days as he slipped deeper into himself. On good nights, several morsels of food would pass his lips before he waved her off. If their skin came within a hair's distance of touching, he jerked away as if scalded. Each day brought new challenges and she accepted them with composed serenity. Inside she roiled with hatred for her sister and questioned her decision to let her live. The baby. She'd spared Marissa's life for the unborn child she carried. For that, she would endure Rhoane's pain, taking as much as he'd allow as her own. She'd take it all if she could, if it meant he'd return to her. Her Rhoane.

They rode hard for the first few days, stopping at night to sleep for a few hours before they saddled up again. Rain battered them relentlessly, slanting from the north or blowing gusts from the east. Their horses and clothes were soaked through, but Taryn pushed them on with a merciless desire to get them home.

After a week of relentless riding, a village appeared on the horizon like a beacon of warmth and it took Taryn all of a second to make the decision to stay there for the night. When they reached the stables, Rhoane slid off his horse, regarding her, uncomprehending.

"We need rest and provisions." Her ShantiMari folded itself around him, warming his cold skin, keeping him upright. Kaida waited until they were inside the inn before she ran off to hunt. She'd not left Rhoane's side since Gaarendahl and considered it her duty to protect the *Surtentse*. Kaida's presence allowed Taryn to rest, but the grierbas was just as exhausted as she.

After a silent meal in the common room, the innkeeper led them to their room. When they were alone, Taryn went to Rhoane. He reflexively jerked away when she put a hand on either side of his face. "Look at me."

He raised his eyes to hers. In them, she saw his pain and shame. A searing heat coursed through her pendant and bonds, overwhelming her. It would've knocked her backward, but Rhoane held her steady, knowing what she hadn't. This was the torture Rhoane had felt every moment of every day since his betrayal. Her touch only amplified it. The pain he'd allowed her to take, it was nothing compared to the torment he suffered. Bitter tears stung her eyes.

"Kiss me."

"I am tainted." He tried to pull away, but she held him close.

"Please let me in, Rhoane, or this will destroy us." She put her lips to his and he stiffened, but didn't pull away. Encouraged, she pressed her body against his, welcoming the warmth of him, melting into their kiss. Despite his objections, his body responded to hers. She stripped his jerkin over his head, quickly followed by his shirt, and pushed him onto the bed.

She kissed his eyes and nose, then his lips before moving down his chest and across his abdomen. When she untied his breeches, he shook his head. "No, you will be tainted."

Taryn tugged on his pants, pulling them off. Rhoane lay on the bed naked, his face a torment of fear, anguish, and desire. She stripped off her clothes and stood before him, robed only in her shining hair. The pulse in his throat quickened as she lay next to him, kissing the heartbeat on his neck. "We will be purified together, my love." She rolled on top of him, kissing his lips, tasting ale on his tongue. His eyes were wild, and he put up his hands to stop her.

"Do not do this, Taryn. You should not touch me."

"I am yours, Rhoane. For all ages. Your trials are mine. We will suffer together and be healed as one." She slid him inside her; he closed his eyes, arching his back to meet her. A small, agonized moan escaped his lips and she kissed it away. Her ShantiMari enveloped him in its healing power. Physically he held back, but mentally he left himself exposed, vulnerable.

Taryn entered his thoughts with trepidation, but he coaxed her further into his mind, inviting her to understand the struggle he battled. She witnessed Marissa's seduction, then rape, and Rhoane's subsequent reaction. How naive of her to think she could take his pain as her own. To relieve him of the burden when doing so would never alleviate the memory? He blamed himself for everything that had happened. He could've stopped himself and didn't.

Tears coursed angry streaks down her cheeks and she shrieked at the heavens for what Marissa had done to him. How easily she'd been manipulated! She'd been far too trusting. Going to Gaarendahl had nothing to do with Taryn learning to use her Dark powers. Zakael never intended to help her. In fact, Taryn could see now how the whole affair had been carefully planned so Marissa could rape Rhoane. To destroy their bonds. To weaken Taryn.

Rhoane was studying her, a look of surprise on his face. He'd opened his mind to her in the hopes she would hate him, but she couldn't hate Rhoane for what he did. She understood. He was used by her half-sister and half-brother in the most vile, disgusting way imaginable and Taryn would never forgive either of them, but of Rhoane? He needn't ask for forgiveness. He did nothing wrong. They'd not weakened her. They'd strengthened her love for Rhoane.

His ShantiMari enveloped them, comforting in its strength. Finally, he gave himself to her completely. When she arched her back, he exploded inside her, whispering her name over and over again.

Far away, in a castle overlooking the stormy sea, Taryn knew Marissa felt their union and cried out in bitter pain. The wound above her heart bled anew.

Taryn lay next to Rhoane, their naked bodies tangled together, their powers coalesced into one. "You are tainted now." Sadness tinged his words.

"I know." Taryn stroked his smooth chest. "And in a little while I am going to be tainted again." She propped on her elbow to kiss him.

"You mock me."

"Never, my love."

His eyes flinched for the merest of moments.

"What is it?" She traced his forehead with her fingertip.

"We should not have done this. Father will never allow the purification. I will be sheanna once more."

Taryn shushed him, letting her hair fall over his chest. "You leave that to me."

He absently stroked her hair as she hoped he would.

"If only for tonight, let there be just the two of us in this world. Only our happiness matters. Tomorrow, in the harsh glare of the sun, we will once more know our sadness."

"When did you become so wise?" He entwined his fingers around a handful of her hair, gently pulling her to him. He rolled her over, entering her so tenderly Taryn held her breath. He moved as if she were made of the finest Danuri glass and the slightest pressure might shatter her.

Rhoane held her arms above her head, stroking the soft undersides down to her torso and farther still to her hips. He raised himself up, watching as he entered her again and again in such a way like he wished to memorize every detail of their lovemaking as if it was the first time.

Or the last.

Taryn shuddered at the thought and Rhoane bent his head back in delirious rapture. They came together, faster and stronger than either expected. His eyes became wild again, this time with desire. He fell on her, pulsing deep into her body. She wrapped her hands in his long Eleri hair, pulling it ever so slightly and then scratching down his back.

She cradled him in her arms until they both fell into a deep sleep. When she woke the next morning, he was sleeping beside her, a small smile on his lips. She lay with him until his eyelashes fluttered and his eyes opened.

"Good morning, my love," she said, kissing his lips.

"You are too good for me. I do not deserve you."

"We deserve each other."

He held her close, breathing in the scent of her hair. "You are selfless in your devotion and I betrayed you. I am not worthy."

"Do not talk like that. It does no good." Taryn searched his eyes, but he held back from her; he'd retreated into the dark place once more. "We must continue to the vier."

They rode on, stopping at night and riding hard by day. When they neared the vier, Kaida bounded ahead of them, oblivious of the veils and wards set to protect the Narthvier. She was just as excited as Taryn to be home again. "Kaida, go see your family. Come to the Weirren when you're ready."

Kaida bowed her head. *I have done what I can for the Surtentse. Now it is up to the tree-things to heal him.*

She ran off before Taryn had a chance to thank her. With Kaida gone, she felt more alone than ever since arriving on

Aelinae. She looked at Rhoane, at the distance in his eyes and the dirt on his face. He wasn't her Rhoane anymore. She didn't know the stranger who rode beside her.

When King Stephan saw Rhoane, the sadness in his eyes almost crushed her spirit. It wasn't just the king who grieved for his son, but the entire court, their prince. The Eleri regarded Taryn with new fears and doubts, placing the blame of Rhoane's malaise upon her, she was certain.

After she settled Rhoane in his room, Taryn met first with Carga to explain all that happened and then went to see King Stephan, with Rhoane's sister for support. Bressal demanded Rhoane be *sheanna,* but Taryn argued against such a drastic measure. When he insisted, Taryn showed him the rune representing his oath to follow her, to be her servant if need be.

King Stephan stepped between them. "Rhoane will be purified."

"I must be purified with him." Stephan looked at her in surprise and Taryn confessed that she'd taken Rhoane into her body as a means to heal him.

"You are not all-powerful, Taryn. Your touch can heal, but this is beyond you. Only the collective Eleri can heal the soul of one who is tainted," Stephan explained.

"Tomorrow, I will perform the ceremony for Rhoane and you as well. It will not be easy and you will not like what you discover about yourself, but it must be done," Carga said.

Taryn was suddenly afraid. "Will it hurt him?"

"Still you think of him before yourself?" A note of sadness tinged Carga's words.

"He is a part of me and when he hurts, I feel it. I need him, Carga. I cannot be Darennsai without him."

"Of that, you are wrong, Taryn," Stephan interjected. "Rhoane is broken. Only he can bring himself from the dark place where he resides. His love for you kept him strong until now. We can only hope it will be enough."

"Broken?" Taryn asked, confused. Tainted she understood; broken was new.

"When the crown princess took him into her body, she split his spirit in two. Purification will ease his suffering, but only Rhoane can heal that which has been torn asunder," Carga explained.

"I do not understand. When Carga and Zakael were together, she was not harmed."

"That was mutual, Taryn. I wanted to share my body. Marissa stole something from Rhoane he was not willing to give." Carga wrapped her arms around Taryn. "You will both be purified, but you must brace yourself for the possibility you will be alone in the end."

Restful sleep eluded Taryn that night. Instead, she dreamt of a dark castle where an ominous shadow crept from the corner and whispered ancient words to her. She tossed against the covers, her hands reaching for Rhoane and finding cold, empty blankets. The nightmare shifted to her beautiful sister. Her black curls glistened in the moonlight; her lavender eyes flashed with gaiety. In an instant, her visage changed.

Rhoane knelt at her side, a collar around his neck, a golden chain dangling from Marissa's fingers. "He is mine, dear sister."

"No." Taryn wheezed in her sleep. "No."

Marissa yanked on the chain and Rhoane's head snapped back until Taryn saw the thin line beneath the leather collar. Her sister bent low, taking her time to reach Rhoane's lips. An ephemeral light passed between them and Taryn woke screaming.

Carga burst through the door, followed closely by Illanr and Carld, and then Eoghan.

Drenched in sweat and shaking, Taryn did her best to calm her rattled nerves. "It was a nightmare. Nothing more.

Please, go back to bed. I am fine, really."

Carga checked her forehead while the faerie maids fussed with her nightclothes and bed linens. Eoghan, completely out of sorts in her bedchamber, excused himself. Rhoane stumbled in a moment later, looking ruffled and dazed.

"She is well, brother. Return to your slumber."

"Let me see for myself." Rhoane pushed past Carga to Taryn's bedside. He stood for several moments without speaking before saying at last, "Can I get you anything?"

Snappy retorts bubbled to her lips and she bit them against her tongue. "No, my love. I had a nightmare, nothing new." Her wistful smile did not diminish the worry in his eyes. "Tomorrow is a big day. You need your rest." Her fingertips trailed along his as he turned away from the bed. The sound of his footsteps shuffling against the wood floor echoed his retreat.

When the others left her rooms, she curled tight against herself and sobbed into her pillow, muffling the sound. Taryn feared her nightmare had become real. That Marissa had stolen Rhoane's soul so completely there was nothing left of the man she loved.

The next morning, Taryn shivered beside the lake, naked except for her unbound hair and a tiny circlet Carga had placed upon her head. The purification ceremony was performed at sunrise, when the last of the night's stars were making their descent below the horizon to the west. Rhoane flinched when she reached for his hand, but did not pull away. Carga stood with Verdaine, Nadra, and Ohlin chanting the ancient words of absolution. A haze of discordant voices and sounds joined the chanting and Taryn tapped her foot, impatient for the ceremony to be complete, for Rhoane to be healed. The chanting continued; the tapping became more pronounced. Oil and then ash was poured over their heads in a greasy, sticky mess that Taryn endured. She would endure anything for Rhoane. If only they could hurry the ceremony along.

Carga's gentle voice said, "Open yourself, Taryn. Allow their healing into your soul, your spirit, your body." This irritated Taryn. Rhoane needed healing, not her.

The icy water of the lake numbed her legs and then her torso as she stepped farther and farther into its depths until she was totally submerged. She waited beneath the surface with Rhoane, their hair floating around them in a tangled mass of silver and brown. He kept his gaze rooted to her, a look of concern on his pale face. As he stood with her in their watery purgation, she hoped with every fiber of her being he would recover. A slow shimmering started in her solar plexus, then spread through her body into Rhoane's, illuminating the water around them. Rhoane's eyes grew wide and she shook her head by way of saying she didn't know what was happening.

A loud cacophony sounded in her mind—ancient generations of Eleri adding their voice and power to the ceremony. Their ShantiMari pierced and pinched every inch of her body. The song Carga chanted rose in cadence and the ancients joined their sister in joyful harmony. Visions dating to the making of Aelinae danced through her mind.

The Eleri were a people of many planets, not just this one. The revelation shocked Taryn.

Her stomach cramped violently and she doubled over in pain. Rhoane tightened his grip on her, a look of panic creasing his features. The urge to vomit overwhelmed her, but she refused to open her mouth to the freezing water for fear Rykoto would drown her again.

The black stain Rykoto said Kaldaar had given her throbbed, threatening to constrict her heart. She fought against it, writhing in the depths of the lake. Fear settled in Rhoane's eyes and he motioned for them to rise to the surface, but she shook her head.

Nadra's voice whispered in her mind. *Daughter of Aelinae, do not fight against the Blackness in your heart. Embrace it. Become one with that power as you do the trinity. You will not be whole without it. Settle your mind and hear the voice of your people. Let them heal that which is broken inside you.*

Taryn frowned, not understanding. Rhoane was broken, not her.

She and Rhoane opened their minds to the ancients. Their thoughts were as one with all Eleri. She witnessed his entire life. From his birth and Verdaine's prophecy to what brought them there that day. Again she experienced his fury at Marissa for stealing his purity. The sheer amount of ire he kept suppressed washed over her. The hell he'd been through since Gaarendahl and torment of every moment devastated her all over again. She shared in his shame, as did all the Eleri. They did not recoil from Rhoane's brutality, but took his anguish into their hearts to cleanse him of his taint. To heal what was broken.

When Rhoane finished, she shared her past with the Eleri. They saw the small flat above the pub where she and Brandt lived for many years, all the places they hid until they could return to Aelinae, her first faltering steps in the cavern when she was bewildered and amazed there was such a thing as another world. She shared her doubts and fears about who Lliandra said she was. Finally, she understood what Nadra meant. She existed in a schism of beliefs, clinging to the girl who was unimportant on Earth, not trusting her importance to Aelinae.

How long they stayed submerged, she didn't know. When she had nothing left to give, Rhoane whispered, *It is time*, and they emerged from the water to stand before her people. In their faces, she saw compassion, not condemnation as she'd expected.

Rhoane. Her sweet Rhoane.

His face, above all, stayed in her mind as she opened herself and accepted she was the *Darennsai*. She was not just Taryn, but the Eirielle, the Child of Light and Dark. The *gyota* of Verdaine's prophecy. And she knew what all of it meant. She was not afraid. She allowed herself to finally believe.

The voices and the chanting stopped.

All of the world stalled for one solitary moment. Then came a long sigh, as if the universe welcomed her. She reached for the heavens and sought Brandt in the clouds. She cried out to him that she understood.

Everything he'd ever taught her, she knew. Kaida wailed in the distance and she howled with her friend. They were one, the grierbas and Taryn. Far away, beyond the wall, there was a great flapping of wings Taryn found very curious. She nodded to Aislinn, understanding that now was not the time. She missed the Eleri queen so very much.

Someone held her. Warm, strong, loving arms rocked her. She looked up into the face of Verdaine. Her tricolored eyes were full of laughter and mirth. The colors of a fall leaf—golden and auburn with touches of green—swirled together as her long hair danced on the breeze.

"Welcome, my daughter. Long have I waited for you," Verdaine said in a voice like the rustling of trees on a windy summer's day.

"And I you," Taryn said, reaching up to stroke her face. "You are so beautiful."

"As are you, my daughter."

Weightless, Taryn's body sunk into the goddess. Before she fell asleep, she murmured against Verdaine's neck, "Please help Rhoane. He needs you more than I right now." And her world went dark.

Chapter 27

THE crown princess paced her room, throwing items at random, and spewing curses that would make a pirate blush. Her agitation upset Valterys in ways he didn't like to dwell upon. Since learning of her pregnancy, his opinion of her had altered, and a protectiveness swelled inside his intentionally cold heart. He waited until the tirade abated before stepping into her bedchamber, startling her.

"What are you doing here? Shouldn't you be tending to Rykoto or torturing someone? You're as sick as your son, do you know that?" Her hand fluttered over her belly and tears glistened in her eyes. "He refused me. Me! After what I did for him, he refuses to bed me." She broke down, sobbing uncontrollably, her hands covering her face.

Valterys took her in his arms, comforting her. "Shhh, you don't want to upset the baby. It's okay, dear one. Tell me what happened."

Through choked sobs she told him of the events at Gaarendahl, from Zakael's tedious games to seduce Taryn, which the stupid girl had refused to play, to her rape of Rhoane.

"It was his idea, the cunning bastard. Now he says I'm tainted like the Eleri and won't touch me."

Valterys filled in the missing information with what he

knew of his son. Most likely, Zakael was looking for a reason to dismiss Marissa and concocted the scheme for exactly that reason. Being with child, he couldn't abuse her as he'd like, which meant she had no value to him. He'd raised his son to be cruel, but in his refusal to bed Marissa, he was showing kindness. Unfortunately, the princess would never see it that way.

"I'll speak to Zakael. I'm certain this is just a misunderstanding." Surely there was a way Zakael could satisfy her needs without endangering the baby. Thinking of Marissa's needs made his groin grow warm, his desire to heighten.

Marissa fluttered her eyelashes. "My lord?" Her heavy breaths pressed her bosom against his chest and he drew in a shaky breath.

"You know I can't. Rykoto would kill us both." His words lacked conviction. Most likely Rykoto would care piss-all if he bedded Marissa. At least, that's what his traitorous mind told him, and he desperately wanted to believe the lie.

"Please."

The whispered word dissolved the last of his reserve. He took her mouth with his, savagely claiming her. He tasted blood where he'd cut her lips, but continued raking his tongue against hers.

She tore at his shirt, loosening it and pulling it over his head, breaking their connection. Before he could stop her, she had his breeches unfastened and around his ankles, her hot little mouth on his swollen member. He moaned and grasped a handful of her hair. *Rykoto must never know.* The thought dampened his lust, but Marissa stoked his flames until Rykoto was nothing more than an irritation he'd deal with later. Much later.

He knew what Marissa craved, had always known, and provided just the right amount of pain. She needed a man like him. Someone who gave her exactly what she needed and yet treated her with respect. Zakael was young, but he was also impetuous and headstrong. He didn't know how to treat a woman of Marissa's stature. Didn't know how to treat a woman of any stature, truth be told. Zakael used men and women as playthings, nothing more. He took from them what he could, then discarded them like dolls from an errant child.

Zakael was a fool for throwing aside the crown princess and Valterys knew exactly how to take her mind off the heartbreak his son had caused. Her moans and cries echoed through the room each time he touched her sensitive breasts or placed his mouth over her delicious mound.

Her squirms and pants excited him further until he couldn't contain his desire and pounded into her, releasing his charge to her shuddering cries. Afterward, he lay beside her, languidly stroking her creamy skin, wondering why he'd denied them this pleasure for so long. Marissa slipped a hand over his cock and rubbed until he grew hard again.

"More?" Valterys asked, surprised he'd not satisfied her.

"Much more." She stretched a leg over him and straddled his erection. And for the next week, that's what he gave her.

Her appetite was not easily satiated, but Valterys did his best, finding new ways to entertain them or playing with some of Marissa's more exotic toys. Several times she allowed one of her maids to join in, a buxom lass with burnished curls and skin to match. Valterys might've stayed in Talaith for the rest of his days, but Marissa had let slip the Shadow Assassin had been imprisoned in Celyn Eryri.

With a kiss to Marissa's sleeping form, Valterys slipped from her room and transformed into a levon. He took flight from her balcony, heading toward the northwest. If Lliandra had the assassin in chains, Valterys needed to see the man for himself.

Needed to know Zakael was not controlling the demon.

The castle stood as it had all those long seasons ago when he was the Lord of the Court and competed in the games. He shook the thought from his mind. It would do no good remembering. Sadness clung to him like an unwanted tether. There was too much of his life he'd relegated to the far reaches of his memories.

He perched atop a steeple, observing the comings and goings of the court. The games had ended nearly a moonturn earlier, but Lliandra stayed on at the castle until just before Frost End. It's what had always happened, and far be it for the empress to alter tradition.

His beak clicked with his smile. After checking the position of the sun, he surmised at that very moment Lliandra would be in her rooms, resting. Which meant she was being thoroughly pleasured by one of her young studs. He idly wondered which of the victors had caught her attention at this season's competitions. Even when Valterys was her lover, Lliandra had invited the winners to her bedchamber. It was all he could do to tolerate that part of the Light Celebrations, but there had been many opportunities for him to fulfill his desires as well.

The levon's beady, black eyes drifted toward the dungeons and a heady warmth spread through the bird's chest. He knew those dungeons well and could guess at which cell they kept the prisoner. There would be time for that later. He lifted off the iron bar and coasted toward Lliandra's rooms. The heavy glass windows were sealed shut, but he landed on an empty planter box outside the one that gave the best view.

As expected, the empress writhed on the bed with a man a tenth her age, if that. Her golden hair fanned around her, creating a halo for her angelic features. Everything about Lliandra was staged for maximum effect and he was certain she kept herself from moving too much and mussing her glorious tresses. The man, or boy rather, pumping furiously into her seemed to care little what the empress looked like. His focus was on her breasts, his breath coming in great gasps.

Lliandra was making him wait for her. *How cute.* She'd tried that with Valterys on several occasions, but he'd taught her the folly of her ways, denying her a release until she begged him. The levon ruffled its feathers at Valterys's memory. Since sampling Marissa's banquet of lust, his opinion of the empress had shifted. He no longer craved the satisfaction only she could give. Marissa had released him from his torment, had mended his shattered heart.

Valterys cursed and the levon pecked at the window with its hardened beak. Lliandra ignored the sound, but the young man turned his head. For an instant, his eyes met the levon's and Valterys saw the sheer desperation etched into his features. His rhythm slowed as he returned his gaze to Lliandra. She said something that made him freeze mid-stroke and then pump harder than before.

Unwilling to witness the stud's destruction, Valterys dove from the planter box to glide around the castle, aiming the levon for a window in the dungeon tower. It was little more than an arrow slit, but he tilted smoothly through the tight space. His claws scratched at the rock floor and he transformed into his manly form.

The image of the youth seared into his mind and anger welled inside his heart. Lliandra must be desperate to conceive another child. He'd heard the rumors at her court and seen it reflected in the stud's fear. He wondered how many she'd killed because they couldn't produce an heir. And she called him a monster.

Concealed in shadows, he took the stairs slowly, stopping often to listen for soldiers, but the dungeons were silent. When he reached the bottom floor, where he guessed they kept the Shadow Assassin, he crept along the wall, not wanting to stir the air. They would have him bound with ShantiMari and too much of the power would hamper his ability to maintain invisibility.

Voices from ahead echoed off the walls and he paused in his steps. The conversation was benign: two soldiers discussing the changing of their shift, expecting to be relieved any moment. One was impatient to be off-duty as he had a girl waiting for him. Valterys smirked beneath his shadows. Women could rule the world if they just figured out how much men were under their control.

Certainly Marissa had subtly manipulated him into doing what she wanted. But he never did anything that he truly didn't want to do. Perhaps that was her power. Knowing what it was men wanted, and then granting them their wish. His desire stirred and he forced his mind away from Marissa. The constant image of her, naked and calling his name, was dangerous. If he didn't block his thoughts, surely Rykoto would pick out the memory as if it were a ripe sargot.

The night guard arrived and after several minutes of jovial teasing, the day guard left the dungeons. Valterys edged closer to the cells, staying as close to the wall as possible. Six guardsmen surrounded the assassin, with another two patrolling the area outside the cell. When he was close enough to see the Shadow Assassin, but not disturb the patrol, he stopped to study the man's features.

Blond, dirty, thin, he hung from several shackles of ShantiMari. His black clothes, ripped in more than one place, were covered in dust. A dark spot on his left shoulder caught Valterys's attention. If he didn't know better, he'd think it was blood, but Shadow Spawn couldn't bleed. Neither alive nor dead, they had no need of bodily functions.

A scuffle just outside the doorway leading to the dungeon steps Valterys had come down drew the attention of the guard. Valterys stepped farther into the shadows, never taking his eyes from the assassin.

A muffled shout, followed by a heavy thud, caused two of the guard to falter in their positions. "Stand," another commanded. "Our charge is to guard the prisoner." The soldiers returned to their positions, their hands grasping swords and maces.

Another thump and they stirred once more, but none of them moved from their space.

The door banged shut and heavy footfalls sounded on the floor. The guard murmured amongst themselves, asking one another what action they should take. A hooded figure entered the area and with raised hands, knocked out each guard in succession.

Valterys drew in a deep breath. That much power was rarely seen.

The stranger unlocked the cell with a snap of his fingers and set about untying the many strands of ShantiMari that held the prisoner. For nearly a bell, the hooded figure worked in silence. The assassin sagged against him when the last of the shackles were unlocked.

Valterys pressed flat to the wall, willing himself to become one with the hard surface. A cold breeze brushed past as the hooded figure darted up the corridor with the assassin over his shoulder. Ice-blue eyes glanced up and met Valterys's gaze, looking right into his soul. The Lord of the Dark suppressed a shudder, but didn't look away.

The assassin dropped his head, his blond hair flowing down the stranger's cloak.

Valterys counted to one hundred before following. He took the stairs two at a time, struggling to keep his shadows intact while rushing to the top of the tower. At the door leading to the battlements, he paused. He'd have to open the door. Not knowing what awaited him caused a tremor of anxiety to ripple through him.

He gathered the shadows tighter and opened the door slowly. Two guards lay unconscious and slumped against the wall. He hurried past them to the far end of the battlements, where another pair of guards was splayed on the ground. Of the hooded man, there was no sign. He glanced to the other side of the castle, where he saw several men patrolling. *If the stranger did not go that way, then where?*

His gaze lifted to the sky where he spied a single speck disappearing into the distance.

Within the space of a heartbeat, Valterys shook off his shadows and took on the form of a levon. He lifted into the air, beating his wings hard to catch an updraft, focusing his sights on the barely visible dot and flew as fast as the bird would allow. Several times, he thought he'd lost his prey, but would catch sight of him once more. His wings ached with the brutal pace. His chest heaved with labored breathing, but he continued on until the evening sky turned a dusky shade of crimson and he lost the hooded man to darkness.

He screeched into the sky, the levon's cry echoing to the clouds.

Taking stock of his surroundings, he turned toward the west, but not Caer Idris. At the Spine of Ohlin, he banked north. His levon's eyes scanned the land for a suitable offering and Valterys dove with frightening speed toward a young maiden alone in a field. Without any warning, he transformed into a man and plunged a dagger into her heart. He covered her mouth with his, absorbing the scream. Her struggle lasted only a minute until she fell limp into his arms.

She would make his flight longer, but he dared not visit Rykoto without a proper meal.

He touched down on the snowy ground and shifted into a man, adjusting the dead girl as he did. Her blood stained his clothing in a long line of crimson. It reminded him of Rykoto's lips and he smiled. His god would be pleased with the offering.

Once Rykoto had feasted, he turned his fire eyes on Valterys. He held himself still, thinking of the hooded man and the assassin, not Marissa.

"You have something to say?" Rykoto drawled the words, pulling them from the air and Valterys shuddered. He wasn't sure exactly how far into his soul his god would delve.

"The Shadow Assassin—I have seen him. Do you know who controls him?"

A hiss came from the flames and Rykoto's image flickered to nothingness.

"My Lord?" Valterys begged, "Please. I need to know who hunts my daughter. If he is successful, it won't bode well for any of us. As you well know." Valterys regretted the last as soon as the words were said.

Heat seared his face and bare forearms. "Yes, as I well know. And, my son, there is much else I know. You share the bed of my queen. She carries a son in her womb. My brother seeks vengeance against me. My lover guides the one who is sent to destroy me. Is there no one I can trust? No one who will honor me as I am meant to be honored?"

The shaking in his legs reached Valterys's throat and his voice trembled. "I honor you, Great Lord. Yes, I have shared your queen's bed. That doesn't mean we do not honor you. Quite the opposite."

The image returned, Rykoto's weary eyes capturing Valterys in his lie.

"Our goal has only ever been your freedom. From this we will not waver. Allow us our comforts with each other until you claim your queen. She is yours, my lord, as ever she has been. What can I do to prove my honor?"

Rykoto sucked in a breath and a blast of cool air from outside the temple swirled around Valterys. "Bring me the blood and the blade of the one they call the Eirielle by mid-summer. Fail me, and I will devour not just you, but your son and my queen, leaving your throne without an heir."

"As you wish, it will be done."

Valterys fled the temple, cursing his lack of willpower. The tryst with Marissa had been foolish and had angered their god, forcing an impossible timeline. He flew blind, his thoughts whirling with plans. Rykoto needed Taryn by midsummer, four moonturns hence.

Impossible.

Somehow, he had to make it possible. His life depended on it.

Valterys blinked at the sight of moonlight glancing off the ocean. It wasn't the Western Sea before him, but the Summer Seas. He'd returned to Talaith.

Marissa.

The gods help him, but he loved her. Had probably loved her far longer than he'd ever realized. Marissa used people to get what she wanted, he knew, and her ultimate goal was immortality. If he could give her what Rykoto had promised, she'd be his for all time. To do that, he needed Taryn. Needed her powers to be fully realized. He'd give her the training Zakael had withheld, and in the process he would take from her as much as Rykoto would tolerate.

The god needed her blood and her blade to be restored. Valterys needed her power to overthrow the god.

It was a brilliant plan.

Chapter 28

HUSHED voices brought Taryn from the darkness. She recognized Carga's gentle tone and small hands massaged her limbs. When she tried to move, her leaden body resisted. Her mind drifted in and out of shadow, where there was no movement. The faces of those who came before her mingled with those who were yet to be. She drifted in a sea of in-between.

She stood on the edge of a great precipice. Beyond her toes lay a bright vastness of empty space. Above her, only darkness. The land was barren of all living things. Tears burned her cheeks. She had caused the destruction, she was certain of it. How and why she didn't know, only that the destruction was done by her hand.

An immense sadness fell upon her.

She leaned out into the nothingness and let herself fall. Down, down, she went until the ground rushed up to meet her. This would be the end of all her troubles. She welcomed death. She took it into her breast to nurture it. Death didn't frighten her—in it she would be free. The thick air choked her lungs until she couldn't open her mouth to breathe. Wind swept her hair and gown away from her, taut against her skin, tangling in the chaotic air above her rapidly descending form. Soon. It would be over soon. No more responsibility.

No more worry or cares. No fear. Of the darkness. Of the light. Of herself.

A thought.

A face, and eyes the color of summer moss. This wasn't how it was supposed to end.

"No," she said aloud.

Her fall stopped. Taryn hung in the air, shreds of her tattered gown spinning against a breeze. Her silver hair settled and then drifted again in every direction. In the harsh light, her Glamour glittered like tiny silver sequins against her skin.

A memory.

Long lost yet recovered in the depths of her soul. With a slight shake, she became a great beast with silver scales and long, sharp claws. Immense leathery wings beat hard against the hot air. She flew into the darkness, spewing flames from her fanged snout. An exquisite thrill ran through her, delighting her senses. Sights were sharper, sounds clearer. She'd found her freedom.

"*Darennsai, cara del tienden.* Come back to us, Taryn. You have much left to do." Carga's voice beckoned from beyond the veil of Taryn's weightless void.

She called out to her friend, "I am here!" But no sound came from her lips.

There is yet time. Dream, still. When you awaken, there is much to be done. For now, rest, little one. Daknys's soft voice echoed in Taryn's mind. *Dream, my beloved daughter.*

Taryn returned to the warmth and comfort of her living death. There was yet time. She need not hurry.

The touch of Kaida's fur brought her once more from the darkness.

"Hey, fur ball," she said to the grierbas, wincing at the burn in her throat. "What are you doing here?"

Your pack mates are concerned for you. Kaida snuggled beside Taryn's fevered body. *As am I.* She whimpered and laid her face next to Taryn's.

What happened to me?

The tree-things do not know. They feared you would move beyond the veils.

How long have I been asleep?

What is time to a grierbas? Kaida growled.

Taryn suppressed a laugh. The effort hurt, and she closed her eyes, wrapping her arms around Kaida.

Thank you for watching over me, my friend. Tell them I will return, but I need a little more rest.

The next time she woke, it was to complete darkness. Outside her curtained windows, trees howled from a fierce wind. She stared up at the ceiling for quite some time before finding the courage to pull herself to an upright position.

At her movement, Illanr jumped up excitedly. "Darennsai, you are awake!" She ran from the room, returning moments later with Carga. "Look, Great Lady." Illanr put a hand to Taryn's forehead. "Her fever is gone."

Several drossfire-filled sconces flared to life and Taryn blinked against their brightness. Carga pressed her fingertips to Taryn's temples, sending ShantiMari flowing through her body. "Welcome back, my sister." Her face was drawn, with a new tightness around her eyes.

"How long was I gone?" Taryn took small sips of the water Illanr handed her.

"Several weeks. I was afraid we were going to lose you."

Taryn rubbed her head. "I had the most peculiar dreams." Then, remembering, she asked, "Rhoane? Is he well?"

"He was only gone a few days." She pushed aside matted hair from Taryn's forehead. "He came to see you every day. He is very worried about you. As are we all."

"I think I would like to get up."

"In time. First, you need to eat. Your body will be weak from lack of nourishment."

"I need a bath." She ran a hand through her dingy hair.

"I will have Illanr and Carld prepare one for you after you eat." She stood to go. "I must inform His Majesty you have returned. He has been quite vexed with your situation."

"Really?" Taryn was surprised. "I did not think he liked me."

"We Eleri are reserved in our emotions, but do not mistake that for uncaring." She left the room and Taryn laid her head on the pillow. Tiny green shoots grew out of the four posters of her bed, each with a small leaf attached.

With the morning sun came a parade of visitors, all eager to see to her well-being. When King Stephan entered carrying a bouquet of wildflowers, he blushed when Taryn asked where they came from, confessing he'd picked them that morning. Tears stung her eyes at his simple kindness. Eoghan and Bressal stayed almost as long as the king until Carga shooed them out, and they finally left.

When the room was quiet, Taryn asked in a small voice, "Why has Rhoane not come to see me?"

"He had some business to attend to today." Carga would not meet Taryn's look.

"Do not lie to me." Taryn's anger pulsed in her throat. "What has happened to him?"

Carga took a long breath, and smoothed her hair from her face before giving Taryn and even stare. "Rhoane is purified, but he is still broken. There is a darkness in him that has taken hold. He either cannot or will not remove it." She sighed. "You were gone for so long. I am afraid he holds himself responsible."

"Did he really come to see me every day?"

"Yes, Taryn, he did." Carga pulled a chair next to the bed. "You must regain your strength, Darennsai. You need to think about yourself now and how you can complete your tasks alone."

Taryn searched her face. "You think he will not recover. The prophecy says—" she started, but Carga interrupted.

"Prophecies are there as guideposts, nothing more. They are not an exact plan. Only you can make your fortune or failure in this world."

"I will not leave him."

"You must. Aelinae is more important than just one man."

"Not to me."

"And that is why you will fail," Carga said with disgust and left the room.

"Do you think I'll fail?" Taryn asked Kaida.

The grierbas lifted her head to gaze at Taryn and yawned. *What do I know about the fortunes of man?*

"Apparently, about as much as me."

It took another week before Taryn had the strength to leave the Weirren. While she lay in-between, memories resurfaced from all those months ago, including her secret meeting with the Eleri queen. She rode a gentle mare to the wall, not trusting herself on Niko just yet, and dismounted carefully. Her muscles ached from the unaccustomed actions of riding, having atrophied over the past month, but she had to see Aislinn.

The wall shimmered before her, a great expanse of ShantiMari that tugged at Taryn with irritating urgency.

"I knew you would seek me out, but it is still not time, mi carae."

"Your First Son is broken and the purification has not healed him. Is there anything you can do to help?"

Aislinn was as lovely as the first time Taryn had met

her, yet the sorrow in her eyes had doubled. "Alas, I cannot. Sometimes the greatest gift we can give a loved one is to do nothing."

"That, I cannot do. He is my love, my life. I will not give up on him!"

"Trust in yourself, mi carae. Do what you need to strengthen your powers. Rhoane will benefit from this. Seek your father. You are ready." She slipped through the wall, leaving Taryn seething at the empty air.

A peculiar noise, like the shifting of leathery wings, came from just over her shoulder, but when she looked, the forest was as it had been. Leaves canopied beneath a blustery sky; emerald fronds crowded the forest floor, bedecked with buds of white, red, blue, and yellow that resembled gems set upon a velvety lawn. Nothing was out of place and yet a disquiet nudged at her. A sense of something important she was forgetting.

She rode away from the wall, frustrated with the Eleri. Not just them but everyone on Aelinae, including the gods. She peered through the branches, wishing Brandt were there to advise her. Never had she needed him more than she did right then. She took the moonstone from her pocket and kissed it. *Guide me, Grandfather, for I am lost.*

Silence answered.

Later that afternoon, Eoghan echoed Carga and Aislinn's advice. He traced the runes on her wrist, his tricolored eyes, so similar to Verdaine's, clouded with worry. "You must let him go," he said. "He will return to you, but you must release him so he may find his way back."

It took her several days to gather the courage to seek out Rhoane. She slipped into his room and found him sitting at his desk, staring out the window. "Hey," she said in a quiet voice.

He looked up, surprise clear on his features, and, dare

she hope, joy. But as quick as it came, it disappeared. Taryn stifled a gasp at his appearance. From his sunken cheeks and wild, frightened eyes, he looked to have been the one in a coma.

"Taryn." His voice, once so musical and full of life, scratched at her ears. He wavered for a moment before getting up to greet her. "You look well." He kissed her cheek and then turned away to avoid seeing the tears in her eyes.

"I have missed you." It tore at her heart to see him broken. "Look," she said, pulling her hair back. "I am full Eleri now."

He traced a finger over the delicate points of her ears and she shuddered. The gesture sent waves of wild lust pulsing through her. His lips were too close, his scent too fresh.

"No," Rhoane said, his voice coming from far away, "you are something much more." It sounded as if the effort to speak was too much. He ran his hand through her hair and the faintest of smiles lifted the corner of his lips.

"I will be leaving the Weirren soon." His eyes flicked to hers for only a moment, then back to her silken hair. "I need to go to my father and learn about his power."

"Yes, that is what you must do."

She held his face between her hands. "I know you are in there. Come back to the light, my love. I can not fix you. Only you can do what I failed to do. I can not save you, mi carae." Her voice caught on a sob. "When you find yourself, come back to me." She fought against her desire to hold him in her arms, to suffuse him with her power. To heal what was broken.

His hands cupped her face, a long thumb tracing her lips while his fingers caressed her as if he were a blind man committing her features to memory. "I remember you." Tears rolled down her cheeks, over his hands. He kissed his thumb and placed it on her lips, then put his forehead to hers and said, "When next we meet, may it be in sweetness and not sorrow."

"When next we meet," she completed the Eleri saying.

The next morning, Taryn left the Weirren early with only Kaida as her companion. She'd said her goodbyes the previous night and slipped out while everyone slept. As she lifted each veil, a part of her stayed behind. When she reached the glen and closed the final veil, she did not look back as she turned to the west and her father.

Chapter 29

RHOANE crouched in the shadows until Taryn left the vier. When he could no longer see her riding west, he stretched his cramped body and returned to where he'd left Fayngaar. His great stallion nickered as he approached and Rhoane pet his muzzle. A movement to his right caught his attention and Rhoane swung about, reaching for a sword that was not there.

"Bressal." Rhoane remained wary. "Come to tell me you were right?" He was exhausted and in no mood for his brother's gloating.

"Nay, my lord. Just the opposite, in fact."

Rhoane glanced at him, surprised. "Why the change of heart?" He pulled himself into the saddle and guided his horse in step with the other man.

"I was there, at the ceremony." His gaze drifted into the distance. "And afterward when she lay between this world and the next."

"As was I. Yet I cannot think of what you mean."

"I do not deny that I will never understand the workings of the female mind, nor shall I ever try. But this I know for sure. Taryn would gladly lay down her sword and her life for you." He chuckled sardonically. "In a way, she already has."

When Rhoane looked pointedly at him, Bressal

explained, "I saw her life before this one. She was happy there and would have remained so had Brandt not brought her back. She could very easily return to where she came from, but she stays. She has accepted every condition put upon her by you, her mother, our father, everyone, and why? For you." Bressal's tone took on a harshness Rhoane knew all too well, touched with a protectiveness he'd not heard in too many seasons. Not since their mother was living. "She deserves better than you, that is for certes."

"Would you take up the challenge, brother? Is my crown not enough for your ambitions?" The sting of his words cut too close to the truths he'd been denying.

"I never wanted your crown. Still do not, if the truth be told. But since you are incapable of sitting on the Weirren throne, it is my duty to fulfill the obligation.

"As for Taryn, she deserves the promise of who you once were. Before you were broken. You can sit around and feel sorry for yourself as long as you like, but there is a girl out there who is fighting for all that you used to believe in. She is fighting for a future she herself does not quite comprehend. And she is doing it alone."

"She has Kaida with her."

Bressal scoffed. "A grierbas pup cannot give her the support and comfort of her betrothed."

The air left him as if he'd been punched in the gut. It was the truth he'd been denying himself and could run from no longer. "At the ceremony you saw into my soul as well. You know what I did."

"Showed her mercy, to be sure. I would have killed her." Bressal's flat tone left little doubt he would have.

"If I had not known her since childhood, perhaps. We were friends, Bressal, practically like brother and sister, and she knew how best to destroy me. And Taryn. She used us and to what purpose? How could I have been so blind?"

"That is a good question, but what I would like to know is, why are you continuing this idiocy?"

"You go too far." Rhoane's voice held an edge to it, but Bressal ignored it.

"This did not destroy the Darennsai. Taryn survived and from what I am seeing beside me, it looks like you will too. It is your choice now."

"Choice?" Rhoane scoffed at the word. Had he or Taryn really ever had a choice?

"Think, man!" Bressal continued, ignoring Rhoane's cynicism. "You are a prince of Eleri blood. Will you stay here and fade, letting that Aelan woman control your destiny? Have you lost your will to fight for what is right? If you remain, surely those who sought to destroy everything you believe in will win and they will not stop at one Eleri prince."

Some of his old connection with his brother welled inside him, comforting, challenging. "I appreciate your advice. It has been too long since we have agreed on anything."

Bressal smirked. "I am just as surprised as you."

The great city of Talaith lay before him. Prince Rhoane of the Eleri, *Surtentse* and betrothed to the Child of Light and Dark, sat on his horse, looking across the vast city to the Crystal Palace. The afternoon sun sparkled on the tiles, giving truth to the name. That first glimpse of the palace never ceased to fill him with wonder. It truly was enchanted. He took a deep breath and moved Fayngaar into a gentle walk.

He'd ridden south the very day Taryn left the vier. The ride had been filled with silence and an overwhelming desire to be with the woman he'd let go. It took less than a fortnight to travel the great distance, with one night spent in Paderau, where he learned of the Shadow Assassin's escape from Lliandra's dungeons. The demon had disappeared without anyone suspecting he was gone and someone—a Master capable of knocking out several armed guards who themselves wielded considerable ShantiMari—had helped. Rhoane had demanded they set off to retrieve Taryn from Caer Idris, but Anje tempered caution.

If Rhoane raced across Aelinae to rescue the princess, he might draw the sort of attention Taryn wished to avoid. Anje hadn't come straight out and said the words, but his irritation was quite evident that Rhoane had allowed Taryn to travel alone, even going so far as to accuse the Eleri prince of abandoning her.

Rhoane hadn't argued with the duke. In a way, he had forsaken her, much to his eternal shame.

He shoved his feelings for Taryn to the far reaches of his thoughts, as he had many times on the ride south. It would do no good to think of what he'd put her through without any sort of recourse to make it right.

She was alive; his *cynfar* told him as much. Beyond that, he locked himself out of her emotions. He removed his glove to inspect the runes yet again. The pictures remained where they'd been that morning. At the very least, Taryn remained bound to him. Whether she would want to undo their oaths was another matter entirely and not one he wished to dwell upon.

He passed through the city gates and into the palace grounds without a glance from the citizens. To them, he was just another traveler from one far-flung land or another, unimportant in their lives.

He patted Fayngaar's neck with silent resolution. Whatever waited for him in the palace, he had to face it with the courage and dignity befitting an Eleri prince.

Baehlon found Rhoane in his rooms and was not surprised to learn Taryn had not accompanied him from the vier. Rhoane told him a brief version of their stay at Gaarendahl and of their time in the Narthvier. He told his friend what Marissa had done and Taryn's response.

The giant knight scratched at his chin for a long time. The bells in his braids chimed softly in time to the rough skritch-skritch of nail against stubble. Of all the Fadair Rhoane knew, Baehlon he'd known the longest. The man never gave the same age, but Rhoane met him sixty-two seasons past, when he was already a knight in Lliandra's guard. If he had to guess, he'd put Baehlon's age somewhere close to one hundred seasons, but the Danuri aged unlike other Fadair, so one could never tell.

"Will you spend all evening in the company of your beard, or would you like to continue the conversation?" Rhoane chided when the knight appeared lost in thought.

"It depends if you'd like to hear what I was thinking." The scratching stopped and Baehlon sat up straight, his hands splayed across his knees. "Daknys warned her something like this would happen."

Rhoane glared at his friend. "What are you saying? Taryn knew?"

"Not entirely. Daknys said only that Taryn would be betrayed and wish to die, but if she could survive it, then she would be stronger for it," Baehlon explained. "It was while we were in Celyn Eryri."

"Why did you not tell me?"

"Taryn bade me not. She didn't know whether the harm would be to you or someone else. This was after the attack on Ellie, and she was concerned for all she loved." Baehlon nodded, breathing heavily through his nose. "I think she knew it would be against you."

"I have failed her, Baehlon," Rhoane whispered.

"Did she say that?"

"Never. She took me into her body to share in my shame. She could have killed Marissa, but she did not. She could have left me behind, but she showed me compassion when I deserved none."

"She acts from the heart." It was not a compliment. "She is too innocent for her own good."

"Aye, that she is. And now she is with her father and probably Zakael. I was wrong to let her go to Gaarendahl and then did nothing to stop her from going to Caer Idris."

"Taryn needs to learn to make her own way. She will come out of this with the maturity and knowledge she needs to fulfill her destiny. If you'd gone, she would have been split in her desire to please you and to take what she can from her father. You have not failed her. You've allowed her the freedom she needs to grow." Baehlon put his big hand on Rhoane's shoulder. "Exactly how long do you plan to feel sorry for yourself?"

Rhoane's head snapped up. "You dare?"

"Aye, I do," Baehlon said. "Much has happened since last we met and I need you with all your faculties. If your brain's muddled with thoughts of despair, you're no good to me."

Rhoane twitched in annoyance. Damn it all, but the man was right. He had to put thoughts of Taryn aside and focus. "What has happened?"

"Once Carga alerted me to where Taryn had gone, I sent Ebus to watch over her." He looked pointedly at Rhoane. "At least your sister thought we might like to know how you fared."

Rhoane accepted the criticism. "And the Shadow Assassin? Has there been any news?"

"None. Whoever released him from Celyn Eryri's dungeons has substantial power. They knocked out a dozen guards and unraveled the bonds holding the prisoner. Before we even had an inkling the assassin had escaped, they were in the wind. Fortunately, he hasn't been seen since."

That gave Rhoane little comfort. His worst fears were the assassin followed Taryn to Caer Idris. His gut told him neither Valterys nor Zakael controlled the man, but he couldn't be certain.

"And the others? How is Taryn's maid, Ellie?"

Baehlon gave a brief account of Ellie's progress, and then caught Rhoane up on the business that transpired in his absence. Marissa had returned to Talaith before the rest of the court and kept to her rooms. She complained of a wound that would not heal. Even Faelara's skill couldn't keep the cut from weeping. Rhoane paid little attention to Marissa's concerns—she deserved whatever discomfort she suffered.

"Young Hayden's been busy with the spice merchant and that miscreant spy at the docks. You should meet with him regarding his plans. Fancies himself a bit of a spy, himself." A dark brow rose above an almond-shaped eye and Baehlon grinned. "Not half bad, but if he gets himself killed, Anje will be none too happy."

"I will speak with him." The pressures of court life settled around him like a Wintertide cloak: heavy, worn, not uncomfortable, but not quite welcome either.

The conversation drifted to Faelara and Baehlon's countenance altered. Barely perceptible, he sat straighter, his shoulders flexed as if ready to defend. Rhoane hid a smile. Something had shifted in their relationship. Finally.

Baehlon gave nothing away, but when he stood to leave, there was a softness in the knight's eyes when he said, "Seek out Taryn's guard, Carina. If Taryn is in the Northwest, let her be seen with you here, in Talaith. Never had I met a guard more loving or more loyal than that lass. Than all of Taryn's maids, to be sure. Visit with Ellie, too. She would like to know her mistress is safe. Even if you have to lie, give her hope. That's what they need right now."

Hope. Yes, they all needed hope. Taryn was his symbol of hope. All of theirs, really. He'd do as Baehlon suggested, but first he wished to see another old friend before seeking out the empress.

Myrddin was in his tower, tinkering with jars of goo and bits of fluff. To Rhoane's relief, they talked about Gaarendahl only briefly. Something stayed his tongue from confessing what Marissa had done, saying only there had been a disagreement between the sisters. Of their disappearance, Rhoane told Myrddin they went to the Narthvier to see how Carga fared after her purification and to search the Weirren's library for information. As to Taryn's location now, he told Myrddin the truth. She was on her way to Caer Idris to see her father.

The mage paused in his fiddling, his stern gaze boring into Rhoane. "Alone?"

"It is for the best." Another lie amongst the many he'd already told that day.

"Do you truly believe that?"

"You and I both know Taryn must become *Darennsai* without being fettered to me."

Myrddin's scowl softened into a fatherly sort of sad little smile. "Yes, I suppose you're right. She loves you far too much, young prince. She places that love above Aelinae and that might destroy her. Destroy Aelinae."

"I know." The words were little more than a whisper. It was his darkest fear. His greatest desire. His guilt. He craved that love even though he knew it was wrong.

"And the assassin? You've heard nothing? Seen nothing?" Anxiety rippled beneath Myrddin's tone. The man worried for Taryn. They all did, but the mage rarely showed his emotions.

"Nothing. I will search the city, but I doubt we will find

him here." Rhoane lifted his chin toward the north. "He is resting. Taryn's ShantiMari damaged him and he needs to recover. I do not doubt we will see him again, but not so soon. Our danger lies farther to the west, I am afraid."

"Valterys," Myrddin intoned.

"Aye. May the gods watch over Taryn while she is there."

"At least she'll have someone watching over her."

Rhoane left Myrddin's tower a short while later after several more not so subtle hints he disagreed with Rhoane leaving Taryn on her own.

To Lliandra, he repeated his story with little added information. The empress was livid to learn of Taryn's whereabouts. She held Rhoane personally responsible if anything happened to her daughter. Rhoane took the blame Lliandra thrust at him. He was the reason Taryn went off alone, but he couldn't tell her mother why.

Lliandra leaned close, saying in a low voice, "What happened at Gaarendahl? Marissa has not been the same since we returned from Celyn Eryri. She will not speak of anything having to do with Taryn or yourself. Was there a quarrel between my daughters?"

Rhoane breathed a sigh of relief. He wasn't sure how to explain to Lliandra Marissa had raped him while Taryn watched. If Marissa said nothing, then he would do the same. Instead, he told her a different truth. "I believe Zakael's intentions went beyond Marissa's tolerance. He refused to teach Taryn anything having to do with the power and on several occasions hinted of a different liaison, of which Taryn had no interest."

"You say Taryn denied Zakael?"

"Yes, completely."

"Then there is no harm done. Marissa needs to forgive her sister and get back to the business of Aelinae." She stood and Rhoane followed suit. "Thank you, Prince Rhoane, for coming to see me. I hope you will stay in Talaith for a while." She held out her hand for him to kiss.

The empress had not entirely confirmed she knew of Marissa's relationship with Zakael, but she left Rhoane with little doubt. Marissa was of keen intellect and strong in the power, but it was her body she used best as a weapon.

The memory of her beneath him, a sick, triumphant leer marring her features, flashed vivid in his mind and he reeled, his stomach clenching. She had once been like a sister to him but now—now he despised her. Despised the very thought of what she had done to him all in the name of power. Zakael as well. For if he hated Marissa, he had to hate Zakael equally for his part in the scheme. They were Taryn's half-siblings, yet blood meant nothing to them. Power and lust were what they honored above all.

Until Gaarendahl, Rhoane would never have thought Marissa capable of great cruelty, but he'd always known Zakael took perverse pleasure in being vicious.

Taryn's half-brother kept his proclivities well hidden, but Rhoane had been at court the day Lliandra miscarried Zakael's child. He witnessed firsthand Zakael, wild with grief and madness, almost kill the empress. Others in the palace blamed his action on the loss of his son, but there was a glee in his violence that chilled Rhoane.

Zakael vowed revenge on Lliandra's House that day and to Rhoane's mind, was making good on his promise. For many seasons, Zakael was warded from entering Talaith, but with Taryn's return, Lliandra lifted the restriction.

Rhoane would never understand the Fadair and their habit of mating with whomever they wished. There was no honor in bedding first the father, and then the son, but Rhoane suspected the empress cared less about honor and more about the bloodline of her children. If she could make the Eirielle with Valterys, then certainly her reasoning was she could do it again with Zakael. Most likely, she was using her daughter in much the same way.

And he'd let Taryn travel alone to Caer Idris where Valterys, and probably Zakael, waited. The idea burned through him that Lliandra meant to use Taryn as well, but Rhoane tamped it out. Lliandra was devious, but she'd not subject Taryn to the same abuses she and Marissa enjoyed.

Taryn was not like them. Rhoane held to that truth with every fiber of his being. Taryn was good and kind. She would never submit to the same level of vileness like others of her family.

After an exhausting evening of telling the same lies to each of Taryn's friends, Rhoane said his farewells, wanting nothing more than to lock himself in his study with a carafe of his favorite dreem.

Hayden, unfortunately, had other plans. "Rhoane, a word?" He beckoned to a tapestry and disappeared behind it. Rhoane followed with a grunt of disapproval.

"I spoke to the mercenary we met in Celyn Eryri, Baehlon's brother," Hayden began. "He is working for the empress, patrolling the docks, but he is not what he seems."

"Why are we in a cramped corridor for you to tell me this?"

"I don't want Baehlon to know we've been in contact. There is a family feud between the two, and I don't want him getting in the way of my investigation."

"You have my silence."

"As I said, I've been communicating with Denzil as well as Amanda, the girl I told you about. She and her mother work for Adesh." At Rhoane's prompt, he continued, "They are readying a shipment to sail within a fortnight and I thought I should go aboard, undercover."

"Impossible. You are a courtier, Hayden, not a spy. Why not send Ebus?" But of course they couldn't; he was in Caer

Idris protecting Taryn. Where Rhoane should be.

"He's not in Talaith. Didn't you know?"

"Yes, I forgot momentarily." The day had been too long and his thoughts were muddled with exhaustion.

"I just wanted you to know. In case…" He paused, a note of apprehension in his voice. "In case you need to tell my father."

"You will not be sailing on that ship, Hayden. I will go. Or Baehlon. Not you." Hayden opened his mouth to speak, but Rhoane silenced him with a hard glare. Before he could argue further, Rhoane left the small space and strode to his rooms, fuming at the idiocy of some people.

Hayden was just a lad. Barely able to take care of himself. Rhoane stopped short at his door, shaking his head. Hayden was the same age as Taryn. And yet she carried herself with the grace and wisdom of someone much older. The thought saddened him. When she first arrived on Aelinae, she'd been full of youth and carefree. Too often of late, he saw the misery in her eyes, the responsibility that dragged her down.

Much of that had come from him.

He stormed into his study and poured a glass of dreem. The honey-colored liquid burned the back of his throat. A warmth suffused his rattled nerves, loosened his tense muscles. Usually, he allowed himself only one small cup, but that evening he contemplated drinking the entire bottle. He'd just stretched out on a chair when Alasdair entered with an apology.

Marissa stood in his doorway with her hands clasped before her, eyes downcast. She looked younger than he remembered, with a frailty that shifted his heart a fraction.

"I'm sorry to disturb you, Rhoane, but I had to speak with you." She looked demurely at Alasdair. "Alone."

The last thing he wanted was to entertain Marissa. But between his exhaustion and the dreem, he didn't have the will to fight her. "Certainly, Princess." He beckoned his valet to close the door and leave them. When they were alone, Rhoane said in a neutral tone, "What do you want?"

She motioned to a wine goblet. "Would you mind? I find myself nervous all of a sudden." Her voice was small and unsure. Rhoane poured her a glass of wine and then sat on a chair, waiting for her to speak. "What happened at Gaarendahl," she began, a blush staining her cheeks, "was wrong of me. I'm sorry, Rhoane. I never should have done that to you."

"Or Taryn," he added.

Her eyes flashed toward him, then down again. "Of course. Or to my sister. It was Zakael's idea. I went along with it because I thought I loved him. I know now he was just using me to get what he wanted."

"I do not believe you, Marissa. Why would Zakael ask you to do that?"

Tears shimmered in her eyes. "He knew if I shared my body with you that you'd be tainted. He thought Taryn would leave you and become his lover if that happened."

"But she did not," Rhoane said quietly and Marissa flinched.

"No, she rejected Zakael to stay with you. He is not used to rejection. His anger when you left was frightening." Her hand fluttered toward her face.

"It is in the past, Marissa."

"You must know I've loved you since childhood. When Zakael told me what he needed me to do, I won't claim I didn't want that for myself as well. To lay with you, to make love to you—it's something I've long desired."

"You knew I was destined for another." His hands shook with suppressed anger as he downed another cup of dreem. He didn't want to hear what she had to say, didn't want to relive that terrible day.

"I knew it would hurt Taryn. I admit, a part of me wanted that, too. She had everything I ever desired. This was my one chance to experience just a moment of what she'll have for the rest of her life. I couldn't say no."

"Yes, you could have. You were selfish and cruel."

"I know what I did was wrong, but the gods have seen fit to bless me with your child, Rhoane." She put a hand on her abdomen, smiling at him with a sick grin that made him want to vomit.

The alcohol churned in his stomach, threatening. "I do not believe you, Marissa. How do you know this is not Zakael's child?" His vision darkened and his hands went numb.

"I haven't bedded Zakael in ages. Once he got it into his head he wanted Taryn, he wouldn't have anything to do with me." Elegant tears rolled down her cheeks. "I had hoped when she left with you that he would return to me, but he cast me out. I came here alone."

"You must be mistaken."

"It's true, my darling. We're going to have a child. From my despair comes my greatest happiness." She sank to the floor and kneeled before him. "I am yours, dearest. I've told no one of this child for fear they'd tell you before I had a chance."

"What will you tell your mother?" His voice was hollow. His thoughts drifted to Taryn and how her heart would break even further when she learned of Marissa's continued betrayal. No, his betrayal. He'd allowed Marissa to rape him. Instead of stopping himself when he had the chance, he gave her a child.

"I wanted to speak with you first. I know you are a man of honor and you must understand I would do nothing to besmirch your reputation. My only wish is that someday you will come to love our child as much as I do and will be a part of our life." She grasped his hand, pleading. "Rhoane, you must believe it is the will of the gods. When you decide the time is right, I will tell Mother. Until then, do you think we should keep this between the two of us?" She beamed at him and his stomach tightened with disgust. He withdrew his hand, never wanting to touch the vileness of her again.

"Of course. Whatever you wish, Marissa." The darkness threatened to overtake him. He gripped the chair to keep upright.

"I know I've given you quite a shock, my darling, but soon you'll realize how wonderful this is." When he didn't answer, she stood and smoothed her skirts. "I'll leave you now. If you ever wish to spend time with me, my door is always open for you." She gave a little cry and put a hand over her heart.

"What is it?" Rhoane asked.

"Nothing to concern you." She pulled her shawl tightly around her shoulders, clutching it against her chest.

He led her to the door and bade her farewell as if in a fog. Yet again, he had failed Taryn.

Chapter 30

SPRING had come to Aelinae while Taryn lay in-between. The meadows were alive with vibrant hues in every shade of the spectrum. Taryn noted every wildflower, every town, every stream or lake they passed as a way to keep her mind from Rhoane. With grim determination, she'd closed the connection between her *cynfar* and her beloved. His emotions were too complicated and overwhelming to her still-fragile state of mind.

With each step closer to Valterys, Taryn's dreams became increasingly disturbed with images of Rykoto. He didn't try to harm her again, but his power pressed upon her and she shuddered at his growing strength. A little more than a fortnight after leaving the vier, Taryn rode Nikosana up the cobblestoned causeway leading to Caer Idris. Her throat constricted against the bile that rose from her churning stomach. A lone figure sat on horseback near the castle gates.

"Sister," Zakael drawled when she moved closer, "welcome home." He gestured imperially and the gates opened.

Taryn slowed her horse. She'd not expected to find him there. "It seems I have many homes, but I will thank you for your kind greeting." She inclined her head to him as she passed through the large stone and wood structure into the courtyard proper. Multiple strands of ShantiMari tickled her skin and she fought the urge to shake them away. Zakael rode beside her in silence, a smile on his face. "Does something amuse you?"

"Yes, you." At her extended silence, he explained, "I was certain when I saw you leave Gaarendahl, it would be your last foray into the West. Yet here you are."

"I am here to see my father. Perhaps he can give me the training you so desperately avoided." She leveled a look at him. "Without the added drama."

A huge wooden door opened and Valterys stepped out to greet them. He looked older since she'd last seen him. Taryn sighed; they were all older, it seemed. Except Zakael. He still had a youthful glow about him.

"Princess Taryn, this is a surprise indeed," Valterys said. "I was unaware you would be coming." He aimed a pointed look at Zakael.

Taryn dismounted and Kaida sat beside her, ears perked forward, muzzle raised. "Father." She inclined her head in greeting. "It is my wish to learn the ways of my inheritance."

"Is that so?" Again he scowled at Zakael. "This day keeps getting more and more surprising." Zakael started to explain, but Valterys held up his hand. "We will discuss this matter later. Right now, I'm sure my daughter would like to freshen up and perhaps get a warm meal in her before we talk business."

He eyed her critically. "You've wasted to nothing since last I saw you. Do they not feed you at the Crystal Palace?"

"I've been traveling of late. I assure you, my health is good enough for the purpose I seek here."

Valterys's face softened. "Well, come inside and we'll see if we can't improve your situation all the same."

Conflicting emotions fought within her, and she struggled to keep her face blank. She hadn't expected him to be kind or to appear so—she tried to think of the word and all she came up with was—*ordinary*. Not imposing or frightening, but old and resigned to his life. When she passed through the doorway, her bonds stung deep in her skin. Carved into the wood was an elaborate design of scrollwork with runes interlaced throughout. Zakael pressed into her back, compelling her to hurry after her father.

Valterys led them through several corridors before finally stopping at a set of double doors. "I was not expecting you, so please forgive me if I do not have appropriate rooms for you, Your Highness." He opened the doors to a vast expanse of rooms that took up half the wing. "These would be the queen's apartments if there were one in residence. Alas, as there is not, I hope you will find them suitable."

The decor reminded her of Lliandra's suite in Talaith. Cream and blue fabric covered the furniture and long drapes of silk pooled on the floor in front of floor-to-ceiling windows. Beyond the glass, Taryn glimpsed the Western Sea. "They are lovely, thank you. Were these rooms meant for my mother?" She hadn't meant to ask the question, but there it was.

Valterys cleared his throat. "If you need anything, there is a bell by the window. Do you know how long you will be staying?"

"I hadn't really thought about it."

"You are welcome here for as long as you like. I'll send up some maids for your care and let the servants know you are my guest here. If you'd like to redo the rooms, I can arrange for someone to come in the morning."

His kindness unbalanced her and she faltered in her response. "They're perfect just as they are. Father," she started, choking on the word. "Thank you."

"It is I who am grateful to have you here. I have long wanted to know you. Your Highness." He bowed before he left her alone.

She drifted around the rooms, looking out the windows at the sea far below and the gardens on the other side. Valterys kept a tidy castle, which surprised her. She'd expected to find barren wastelands for miles around. Instead, she found something completely the opposite. Birds sang outside her window, warning of the dark storm clouds that threatened on the horizon. Taryn breathed the salty air of the sea. It reminded her of Talaith. Suddenly, she was homesick for her friends.

They dined in Valterys's private dining room, an intimate meal of just the three of them, with Kaida sleeping nearby on a cushion. Their conversation included idle gossip and little of why she was there. By the end of the evening, she could recite every dish they'd eaten, which wine they drank, and several charming anecdotes about her brother's childhood. It was a grim repeat of what Zakael had done at Gaarendahl, but Taryn held onto her hope that with the sunrise would come an opportunity to meet with her father alone.

When Zakael offered to escort her to her rooms, Taryn declined. When Valterys insisted, she relented. If she wanted his help, she couldn't start by upsetting him. Once they reached her suite, Zakael let himself in and poured another glass of wine. After a moment, he poured one for her as well, which she declined. The last thing she needed was to become befuddled with Zakael so near. Instead, she went to the balcony for some fresh air.

Zakael stepped behind her, pressing his body into hers. She froze, afraid that any movement might encourage him. "Tell me why you are really here, Your Highness," he whispered in her ear. "And don't try to tell me it is to learn Dark Shanti. I saw enough of your skill at Gaarendahl to know you possess everything you need to command the trinity. You are here for one reason and we both know what it is."

With more control than she thought possible, she

maneuvered her body until she faced him. They were close enough she could see the pores of his skin. "Please, enlighten me."

Grinning as if he'd won first prize at a fair, he pressed his hardness into her, pinning her against the balcony wall. "Oh, I intend to."

He bent to kiss her but she pushed against his chest to stop him.

"Don't fight me, Taryn. When we last spoke at Gaarendahl, you were hesitant to join with me, but now that you are here, we can be as one." He ground his hips against hers, a suggestive leer marring his handsome features. "In all ways. I have thought of nothing else but you since you left so abruptly. We have an attraction you cannot deny." He traced her breast with a fingertip before pinching it hard.

Panicked rage surged through her. She gripped his wrists and held his hands away from her body. "You're drunk, Zakael. Don't do something you might regret."

He breathed acrid fumes into her ear. "I already regret not bedding you sooner. I want you, Taryn, and you want me— that is why you are here." With lightning speed, he reversed their grip, pinning her hands behind her back, holding her captive against the wall.

A low growl came from Kaida's throat as she crouched behind Zakael. Taryn cautioned her to stay, a dangerous plan forming in her mind. Sickened by his close proximity, it was difficult to swallow her disgust.

Her heart thudded in her throat as she relaxed her body, sagging against him. Zakael released his grip, a warning in his cloudy eyes. With an inviting smile, she raked her nails over the soft velvet of his doublet, teasing him with little pinches that made him moan. When she reached the drawstring of his breeches, Zakael arched toward her with anticipation.

"You know why I'm really here?" Taryn whispered.

He nodded and she slid a hand beneath the fabric, running her fingers over the silky smoothness of his hardened cock. She pinched the tip and Zakael gasped, his eyes closed. Her fingers flinched when they met metal and then traced their way along the ring he wore around his balls and cock. Intrigued, she tickled her way under the ring, cupping his balls in her hand, massaging them until he swayed against her.

"I'm here to learn how to control my power." She gave his balls a sharp squeeze. Zakael's eyelids flew open. "Whatever other reason you think is a fabrication of your own imagination."

"You fucking bitch," he spat at her and tried to step back, but she tightened her grip.

"That's what you want me to be. I'm your sister, Zakael, which makes this all the more disgusting." She held her face a finger's span from his. "I came here to learn Dark Shanti, same as my reasons for going to Gaarendahl. If you aren't going to help me, then I have no use for you."

He sputtered curses at her until she placed a finger over his lips, silencing him.

"I'm only going to say this once, so please listen well. You are to leave my rooms and never, ever enter them again. I will not now, nor will I ever, join with you. I do not want you."

She sent a small amount of her ShantiMari into his genitals with the subtle idea that if Zakael should ever think of her while having sex, he would immediately go limp and not get hard again.

He glared at her, his eyes hard bits of concrete. "I could kill you for this."

She shrugged. "You probably could, but you won't. You see, I still have your balls in my hand." As a reminder, she massaged them, gagging at the lust that lit beneath the steel.

Zakael was too easily controlled by his lusts. Something

her sister probably knew all too well. Taryn gripped harder and he yelped, the lust turning to a kind of tempered mania.

"And even when I don't, you still won't kill me." She ran her tongue over his lips, pressing her breasts into his chest, rubbing her pelvis against his thigh.

His cock jerked in response.

"Will you?" She breathed the words into him.

She quashed his balls and he sagged against her, defeated. "No."

"That's more like it." She released his testicles, pushing him off her. "I told you before—we need each other, Zakael. We should not be enemies." She resisted the urge to wipe her hands and spit the taste of him from her tongue.

For a moment, he stood like a man who'd lost everything. He slowly tied his breeches, making adjustments as he did. "I need no one." Steel flecks of his ShantiMari sparked around him, and Taryn tensed. "Least of all, you."

"So be it, Zakael, but if you ever harm someone I love again, I will not show you mercy a second time." It was a macabre echo of what she'd said to Marissa, and Taryn pitied her siblings.

"Is that what you call this? Mercy?"

His lightning quick movement surprised her as he covered her mouth with his. Without thinking, she brought her knee to his groin. Zakael doubled over and she slammed her elbow into his face. She stepped back, ignoring his desperate grabs, and swung her leg around, landing a roundhouse kick squarely on the side of his head. He crashed against the balcony, eyes wide with fear and awe. Taryn bounced on the balls of her feet, ready for more.

Zakael staggered upright, blood oozing down his face. "You'll regret this." He spun on his heels, transforming into a great black bird and then flew off the balcony.

Taryn and Kaida stared, dumbfounded, as he rose into the

air and banked left before disappearing from view. "Damn, I wish I could do that. Don't you?" she asked the grierbas.

Kaida sat on her haunches. *What do I know about the ways of flying things?*

Taryn scratched Kaida's head and bent to kiss her nose. "I need to wash my hands and rinse my mouth. That was revolting."

Chapter 31

EARLY the next morning, Taryn awoke to the scent of fresh rain and damp earth. Kaida stretched beside her and lazily thumped her tail. After Zakael had left the previous night, Taryn placed wards around all her rooms, deterring any curious courtiers from entering, as well as blocking her brother's access, allowing only servants. None could enter her bedchamber, however, and she paid special attention to the balcony, setting alarms if Zakael should so much as set a talon on the stone banister.

She lay on her back, tracing a design on the painted ceiling. Words wound their way around the garden scene and a familiar prickling slithered up her neck. Taryn stood on the bed to better see the painting. Runes, like the ones carved into the massive wooden door, dotted the landscape. Hidden in the detail of a red rose petal was the rune for death; on a leaf of a white rose, life. All throughout, the same runes were repeated. Life. Death. Life. Death.

Her fingertips brushed against the plastered surface and her runes flared to life, lifting from her skin to hover above the painting. They rearranged themselves and Taryn gaped at what she saw illuminated above her. A message. A warning, really.

There is no Light without Dark and no darkness without

light. Life is death and death is life. Beware the one who walks between worlds.

A knock on the outer door startled her and the runes swirled before settling onto her wrist. The ceiling returned to nothing more than a pretty painting. Except for one corner. Hidden in the darkness behind an image of a runyon tree, its spiked trunk pale in the morning light, caught between the grooves, Taryn saw the slightest movement. She squinted to better see and there, squatting in the corner, was a hooded man with skeletal features. His empty eye sockets stared back at her.

A shudder rocked her from head to toes.

In the other room, servants clanged noisily with her morning meal. She hopped from the bed and prodded a sleeping Kaida to wake up.

Tell me, do you see a man in the corner of the ceiling? By the window with the runyon tree?

Kaida stretched her paws and turned a golden gaze toward the ceiling, scanning it entirely before answering. *I see no man, nor do I see a runyon tree.*

"I'm losing my mind," Taryn said aloud and Kaida thumped her tail in answer.

After their breakfast, Taryn explored the gardens, sorting through what she'd seen in the painting, and planning her next move.

Her boots squelched on the damp ground as she trod through the freshly budding roses to the orchard. At the farthest point of the garden, a lone runyon tree huddled beside a cliff, its branches thick with emerald leaves. The ashen trunk curved slightly to the left, toward the sea. Thorns, some as thick as a man's thumb, protruded from the trunk, from the ground to the tips of each branch.

She approached the tree with caution, unease settling in her gut. Runyon were scarce in the east, but she remembered

Hayden's warning that the barbs held a deadly poison within their hardened shells.

"A thing of beauty, is it not?"

Taryn jumped at the sound of her father's voice, having not heard him approach. "If you consider a tree that feeds off the flesh of man to be beautiful, then yes."

A twinkle lit his misty eyes. "Even death can be lovely, my daughter. But come, there is something I wish for you to see." He held his hand out to her and she was reminded of Rykoto by the river.

She ignored the offer and stepped beside him, wary. He wore a long coat over his dark tunic and walked with measured steps, his shoulders bent slightly, hands clasped behind his back. That morning, he looked more like a poet or philosopher than the dreaded Lord of the Dark.

"Did you sleep well?" He glanced at the still dark sky. "I hope the storms did not keep you awake."

"Not at all. I slept right through them." They walked side by side for a while, stopping every so often to smell a flower or for Valterys to point out improvements he had planned for the summer. Eventually, Valterys led them to an area off the path and close to the edge of the cliffs. Taryn stood on the precipice and gazed out at the darkened sea.

"I've often wondered what lies to the west of here. I thought perhaps you could tell me what exists beyond our borders. That is why they call you Offlander, is it not?"

A chill of warning crept down her back. "They call me many things for reasons I do not quite understand myself." She checked that her thoughts were properly guarded. She knew exactly what lie to the west of his kingdom, but she'd not share that or any other information with him. Not yet.

"I know what you mean." A sad little smile lifted his lips. "I suppose they say all manner of things about me at the Light Court. It's my wish we know each other better to perhaps make our own judgments."

"I would like that." She glanced past the ocean to the dark clouds crouching over the water. "Why don't you have a wall here or something to keep people from falling off?"

He shrugged. "It's been my experience that if someone is determined to slip, no barrier will stop them."

Her instinct was to step away from the edge, but she stood firm. "It would just detract from the view, anyway."

"Exactly. So, tell me, daughter, what have you been doing all these seasons?" He faced the water, but his gaze never left her.

"I traveled with Brandt. I never knew who I was until we reached Talaith."

He penetrated her with a soul-grazing stare that said he didn't believe a word she uttered. "So you've said."

"And you don't sound convinced. Perhaps after you've had a chance to know me, you'll see that I don't lie all that well."

He laughed, a bitter sound against the wind that blew up from the sea. "More's the pity for you, I'd say. Being honest will get you nothing but misery at the Light Court."

"You really don't like my mother, do you?"

"I love Lliandra more than should be possible." A ferocity crossed his features and he turned his face to the ocean. "She tells the story of how I duped her, used her to create the Eirielle, but how do you know it was not she who misled me? I was, after all, the one who arrived to find my son dead."

"Are you suggesting Mother killed your child, my twin brother?"

His shoulders twitched. "I only know that when I arrived, there was a dead baby where there should have been life."

Taryn's gut roiled at the image. By the time Valterys arrived, Taryn was halfway to Mount Nadrene and he never knew. "How did you find out about me?"

His eyes matched the stormy skies as they bore into her. "Does it really matter?"

Taryn held his gaze, not backing down despite the intimidating tone. "To me, yes. Was it Marissa who told you?"

A smile quirked at the corners of his mouth. "She never told me, no."

Taryn nodded. "She told Zakael. Yes, I suppose she would." The air in her chest exhaled. Marissa had hated her from the moment she was born. Had harbored all those seasons a resentment so fierce it would cause her to one day betray Taryn in the most intimate and cruel manner she could think of.

Valterys studied her a little too intently. "Now you know. What will you do?"

His Dark power swirled around him, vast in its scope. She longed to touch it, to feel the immensity of his ShantiMari. A subtle thought teased her mind—he wanted her to lash out at Marissa. To test her strength against her sister in a form of combat where the victor would be decided by who survived. He kept his face placid—kind, even—but she wasn't fooled. Beneath his demeanor dwelled the brutal truth of who her father really was.

"Nothing. What's done is done." His power sparked with irritation, disappointment tinging the air. "She is my sister, and I will forgive her."

"You are a fool, young Taryn. Marissa would kill you if she had the power or the cunning."

"Is that what you'd like me to do? Kill my sister because she hates me?"

"You should eliminate anyone who stands in the way of who you are to become." His words held no malice, just a simple philosophy.

"That's not how I do things."

"More's the pity for you." Sadness lurked in his eyes mixed with loneliness, and behind that, anger.

"Look, I'm sorry life didn't work out the way you wanted, and I know you're kind of pissed at my mother for hiding me, but I had nothing to do with any of that. All I know is that I'm here now and everyone tells me Aelinae is unbalanced. Without your help, it won't make fuck all difference, will it? Because I'll never become the Eirielle, and Aelinae will either cease to exist or Kaldaar will return and we can all kiss the Light and Dark goodbye. So, will you help me or not?"

"Yes, you must master your Dark powers." He muttered as if he hadn't heard half of what she'd said. He ambled away from the cliff and strolled through the gardens, once again the wise philosopher, no longer the scorned lover of Lliandra.

"I'm afraid that will have to wait a few days. Your unexpected arrival came at a bad time. I'll be leaving for Danuri in less than a bell to conduct some business. When I return, we'll see about your powers."

He patted her on the shoulder and gave her a warm smile. "We have some fine horses in the stable. Give your stallion a well-needed rest. I'm sure you'll find our city just as enchanting as Talaith. When I return, I promise, we'll see about bringing balance to Aelinae. Together." He drifted away from her then, his back bent low to examine the flowers he passed.

Feeling utterly dismissed and none too happy about it, Taryn stalked from the garden through the palace to her quarters. Kaida kept close to her side, almost tripping her several times. The grierbas' behavior was odd, even for Kaida, and Taryn paid special heed to her friend. If something were amiss, she didn't want to be caught unaware.

After pacing from one room to the next in her vast suite, wearing a path in the thick carpets without so much as a servant disturbing her, she decided to explore the palace.

If nothing else, Hayden had taught her that every royal residence had secrets worth finding.

Chapter 32

TARYN'S first attempts to tour the castle were thwarted by an overly friendly seneschal. She'd taken no more than ten steps from her room when he materialized from the shadows, scraping and bowing, asking after her comfort. She grumbled her displeasure until Kaida directed her attention to the man's spectacles and stained fingertips. The sure signs of a man who spent too many hours poring over texts, making notes.

"I've heard Caer Idris has a library to rival Talaith's. I'd love to see it."

A derisive snort started in his throat and ended in a wheeze. "Hardly. Perhaps when the empress was in residence, but no longer. All the great books are locked in the Overlord's rooms. I can show you the pitiful excuse we have for a library if you'd like."

Taryn pointed to his stained fingers. "Are those from the scrolls in my father's rooms?"

Taken aback, he surveyed his hands. "This? No. I've been copying recipes for the cook. Her eyes are getting bad and she needed fresh ink to better see." He fidgeted with his glasses, taking them off to clean the lenses before replacing them on the bridge of his nose.

She hoped he was better at transcription than he was at lying. "Well then, I guess it's the lesser library for me."

The seneschal wasn't kidding about it being pitiful. The space, more of a nook really, consisted of two overstuffed chairs and a single wall stuffed with scrolls. No bound books graced the shelves and the scrolls were mainly accounts of the castle, with a few family histories written in the margins. Taryn read through all of them during the long days she waited for Valterys to return. Thankfully, Zakael went with him, leaving Taryn alone in the dark castle.

Yet, she was never without company. Either the mousy seneschal or another servant would appear the moment she deviated from the common rooms. Always pleasant in manner, asking after her needs, directing her toward her room or the main hall. Her father must have made it clear to his staff she was not allowed to roam unattended in his absence.

After yet another attempt to lose her minders, she sat slumped in a chair of the pitiful library. Rain ran in lazy swizzles down the window as Taryn gazed through the thick pane, seeing neither the rain nor dark clouds dancing on the horizon. On her lap lay a twice-read account of the battle between Rykoto and Daknys written by a chronicler of the Lord of the Dark, which meant it heavily favored Rykoto. According to the tale, Rykoto was subdued through Daknys's trickery and then thrown into a dungeon of sorts beneath the Temple of Ardyn. His release could only come from the "Blood and Blade of the one who is and is not."

Rykoto would live in his eternal hell only if all thirteen seals remained intact. Should even one seal be removed, there was a possibility for him to reenter the world of Aelinae. One seal that she knew of was missing. It was hidden at Paderau Palace, but if there were more missing—a dread-filled shudder shook her to the core.

The scroll claimed Daknys set clues into the temple that would help the Chosen One keep Rykoto imprisoned.

Unfortunately, these clues could also help free him. According to the scroll, if the clues were deconstructed in the proper order, they would reveal instructions to undo the bonds that kept Rykoto imprisoned. The text ended abruptly and she searched the space where she'd found the scroll for a second parchment that held the rest of the tale. She scanned every scrap of paper on every shelf but found no other mention of Rykoto.

When certain no one was looking, she tucked the scroll inside her boot. Valterys had more wards and alarms set on his room than she ever placed on her own, which meant she would have to wait for his return to gain access to his private library, where she suspected the rest of the scroll resided. If she were Sabina, she'd bat her eyelashes or thrust her breasts under the seneschal's nose in an effort to flirt her way into Valterys's rooms, but she'd probably look like a fool. Perhaps she should've paid better attention to Sabina's princess lessons, she chided herself. Not that she ever would admit that to her friend.

Her fingertips tapped along the dragon's wings of her sword. ShantiMari flowed through the halls like liquid, flaring in spits, sometimes with spells embedded into the threads. Caer Idris was a place of Dark power where rules of ShantiMari were enforced, but there existed an undercurrent that made her queasy. Tracking her unease to a single thread would be futile. She placed a hand over her vorlock scar where the poison thrummed beneath her skin. There, hidden amid the venom, was the black stain the phantom had given her.

The constant throbbing had become a daily nuisance she no longer thought about, and she realized with a start that too much of the past season had been spent on pursuits not of her choosing. *At least the phantom wasn't among the courtiers spying upon her at Caer Idris*, she thought dryly. Or making her do things against her will.

The seneschal darted behind a column and Taryn suppressed a laugh. *What I wouldn't give for a pinch of the phantom's ability to compel right about now. I'd command the seneschal take us to my father's rooms at once,* she told Kaida, absently rubbing her scar, ignoring the rush of irritation.

To what end? If you so chose, you could enchant the entire castle into doing your bidding, but you are needed elsewhere. Let us explore.

Explore? Would you like to elaborate? Inside? Outside?

Kaida padded away from the nook into a crowded hallway where several courtiers shuffled past, avoiding eye contact with her. The seneschal followed at a discreet distance, but Kaida increased her pace and after several turns, lost him. Taryn jogged to catch up, curious why the grierbas suddenly wanted to lose their escort.

Are we looking for something or are you just bored?

Kaida ignored her.

At last they came to a door leading down a long flight of stairs. A few torches flickered in the semi-darkness and Taryn hesitated, but Kaida forged ahead. After several minutes, she debated turning back when they came to a locked door. Kaida pawed and scratched at the door, whining.

"What is it?" Taryn asked. Even though she whispered, the sound echoed off the stones and she flinched.

Something is beyond here. We must follow the scent.

Taryn paused for a moment. What could lie beyond a locked door at the end of a very long set of stairs? Nothing good, Taryn told herself.

Against her better judgment, she touched the lock and it snapped open, the door swinging wide to allow access into a hallway that stretched far into the darkness. Kaida skulked along the wall. Ahead of her, a few torches lit the way, but it was still quite dark. Taryn wanted to turn back, but Kaida insisted she follow.

With each step they took, Taryn began to realize they were in the castle dungeons. Unlike those of Celyn Eryri, these were often used, and more than once, they heard the whimper of a prisoner, or brushed past bony fingers that clutched the cell bars.

Where are you taking us?

Just ahead. Kaida padded to a cell and sat on her haunches. She whimpered into the blackness beyond.

The face of a boy appeared, looking first to Kaida and then to Taryn.

You must take him from this place, Kaida told Taryn.

Why this boy when there are dozens of other prisoners?

He is not a boy. He is a woodland faerie from the Narthvier and will die if you do not take him away now.

Taryn placed her fingers over the faerie's. "What is your name?" she whispered in Eleri. The boy shook his head, pointing to his mouth. "You cannot speak?" She reached out to touch his forehead and he jerked away. "I will not hurt you. Come here," she begged softly. He moved a fraction closer to her, his eyes wide with fear. She stretched her fingertips through the bars and touched them to his temple.

We are friends. We can help you.

His mouth gaped and he made small sounds like a mewing kitten. *Darennsai?*

I am Taryn ap Galendrin, Darennsai of the Eleri.

He prostrated himself, touching his head to the ground, making more of the strangled sounds against the dirt. Taryn carefully untied the strands of ShantiMari looped around the cell bars before clicking the lock open. The door creaked as she opened it, sounding like a gong through the dungeons.

After a moment, when nothing stirred in the darkness, she crept to the faerie, touching his back. Little more than bone existed beneath his tattered tunic. He looked up at her with eyes full of fear.

We are going to help. She lifted him into her arms, shocked by how light he was. *Do not make a sound. We will get you out of here.*

He nodded, stroking her long braid for comfort.

She stepped through the door, slowly closing it behind her before replacing the lock. Voices in the hallway made Taryn's heart stutter. She darted after Kaida down a dark corridor and waited for the voices to pass. As they approached, she realized they meant to pass where she stood holding the faerie.

Blindly, the little group inched deeper into the shadows, where they tucked into an alcove seconds before a bright light illuminated the corridor. Zakael and Valterys walked a few steps toward her, then through a door to their right. Her heart rammed against her chest, her mind whirling frantically.

They were supposed to be away from the castle. Valterys lied to her. She shouldn't have been surprised, but she was. And hurt. She set the faerie beside Kaida with an admonition to remain where he was and keep silent.

Keeping close to the wall, she crept to the door they entered. Lights flared inside a dank room with all manner of chains and torture devices hanging from the ceiling and walls. Valterys stood in front of a man suspended from his bound wrists.

Half-healed wounds oozed into dirt-smeared bruises on his naked body. Another man, naked like the first, was tied to a wooden contraption that caught Taryn's breath. Ropes looped around his legs, binding them into a crouch, with his arms pulled taut against a wooden board, his feet dangled above the floor. Zakael stepped into her view and slapped the man across his cheek with the back of his hand.

Blood oozed from the prisoner's lips and Zakael did something that made Taryn's stomach churn. He leaned in as if to kiss the man, but instead licked the blood in several long strokes, a look of bliss on his face. It took all her will to resist the urge to burst into the room, ShantiMari flaring.

Surely her father and brother would subdue her, leaving her no better off than the tortured men. As if hearing her thoughts, Zakael glanced toward the door and she ducked.

"I've told you, these men know nothing. They've been here three moonturns and their stories have yet to change," Zakael said.

She peered through the opening of the door, keeping a rein on her emotions.

"Get me the rod," Valterys commanded, pulling at a piece of flesh that flapped loose on the suspended man's bare chest. "I'm going to ask you once more and this time you will tell me what I want to hear." Valterys held up a long metal object that glowed red on one end. The prisoner's eyes filled with terror, raw and primal, and he whimpered into his shoulder, trying in vain to escape from the hot poker.

"I've told you, my lord. I don't know anything about an assassin."

Valterys placed the rod against his skin, searing flesh. His scream cut through her and she leaned against the wall, palms clammy, heart racing. "I was on patrol—nothing more, your lordship!"

"Are you not one of Empress Lliandra's guards? Were you not with them at Celyn Eryri?" Valterys held the rod close to his face.

"I was there, but I was sent to scout the mountains after the empress arrived."

Taryn fought to calm her shaking legs, settle her breathing. Her ShantiMari demanded to be unleashed, yearned for justice.

"So you saw no Shadow Assassin?"

The guard shook his head. "I only know of the attack at Paderau. I wasn't there, but others talked about it." He was frantic, his eyes wild as he pleaded with her father. "That's all

I know. I swear it."

Valterys touched the poker to the man's face. When his screams died down, he said, "You lie. You knew the assassin was caught and you know who released him. Was it one of your men? Who? You must know something."

Taryn gasped, clamping her mouth shut. *The assassin was free.*

"No! I swear it!" He sobbed while Valterys held the rod close to the burn he'd just made. "I was on patrol in the mountains when he was freed. I've told you this before, your lordship. I never saw the assassin or the Eirielle."

Valterys raked a blade on the man's chest, making deep cuts in his skin, and then ordered Zakael to clamp weights to his nipples.

Taryn gagged. The weights would pull the skin farther and farther down, essentially skinning him. Cries of pain echoed through the room, pounding her with their desperation.

"How long do you wish to keep these men here?" Boredom tinged Zakael's voice. "I believe they know nothing of the assassin."

"Perhaps, but whatever knowledge Lliandra possesses on this matter, I must have. Even the most trivial piece of information could be important." Valterys turned his attention to the man bound to the board. When he saw Valterys, he shook his head and groaned.

"To what end? You have the girl—isn't that all you need?" Zakael asked.

"This is where it gets interesting, my son. Rykoto keeps blathering about three things and the scroll says I need her sword, her blood, and—" He paused and Taryn held her breath, waiting for him to name the third item. "Nadra's tit, will you stop that?" Valterys chided his son. "When I'm finished, you may kill him or whatever you like."

Taryn thunked her forehead against the wall in

frustration. *Fucking Zakael.* She'd been *this* close to learning the third item. She slipped a finger inside her boot, sighing at the sound of paper crinkling. The scroll was safe.

"When will you take her to Rykoto?" Zakael asked as he flicked one of the weights on the hanging prisoner and then stroked his flaccid cock. The poor man groaned in agony while trying to turn away from Zakael.

"What did I just say?" Valterys warned, a dangerous, bitter edge to his voice. "As for Rykoto, the timing must be perfect. I believe the codices point to mid-summer." Valterys tapped the man in front of him. "I think he'll make an excellent sacrifice for our god, don't you?"

Zakael peered over his father's shoulder. "You've plenty of other prisoners for that purpose. Are you sure you want to sacrifice one of Lliandra's men?"

Valterys' laugh was cold, unaffected. "Why not? It would be a suitable end to him, don't you think? To be given to the one he's sworn to protect his empress against? Put him in the first cell and see that he's fed. Rykoto is getting stronger and demands more nourishment.

"Stay away from the girl. I need her to believe me to be a kindly, if not confused, old man and I won't have you interfering with my plans."

"If not for me, she wouldn't even be here," Zakael argued.

A vicious chill entered Valterys's tone. "If not for you, she'd have been here sooner. You've cost me dearly, and once again I must fix your mistake. Be certain those armies are at the border by mid-summer's night. I need Lliandra's eyes cast away from the north. You are not to engage Lliandra. This is only a distraction to buy me time with the girl."

His footsteps paused on the other side of the door. "Do not fail me again."

Taryn darted away just before he yanked open the door and stormed down the corridor.

She cradled the faerie close, wrapping him in her ShantiMari to soothe his uncontrollable shaking. When her father's footfalls faded to nothing, the trembling lessened, but did not abate. The cries of Lliandra's men drew her attention back to the room and she crouched against the door. The faerie buried his face in her tunic, a skeletal hand clutching her braid. She chanced a glimpse into the room and stifled a gasp.

Zakael, his breeches lowered to his ankles, stood in front of the man bound to the board. One hand gripped the prisoner's hair while he pumped his cock into the poor soul's mouth. His other hand, meanwhile, stroked the suspended man's erection. Her brother's moans mingled with the muffled cries of the captives, the sound disturbingly rapturous in the torture chamber. He threw his head back and pumped harder, cursing the men, calling them vulgar names with a devilish smile on his face.

Her impulse was to look away, to deny what she saw, but she could not. Those men deserved more than her cowardice.

The strangled gasps of the man bound in front of Zakael tore at her. He was pinned in that hell without hope of an escape. At least the man hanging by his wrists could turn his face to the side, away from his captor.

Kaida, I can't just leave them.

There is no time. We cannot save them all, Darennsai.

Taryn hesitated only a second before she sent a thread of ShantiMari to the prisoners with a gentle suggestion that their hearts stop beating. One of the men shrieked and she doubled her efforts with the fervent hope for a peaceful transition to the other side. It wasn't much, but it was all she could do for them.

The faerie curled closer to her, away from their anguished screams. She made as little sound as possible as she sprinted through the corridors. Zakael's grunts and the dying men's whimpers echoed in the darkness, mocking her. This was a side of her brother she wished she'd never witnessed. He was truly devoid of compassion, of goodness. She'd hoped, fervently so, there was a spark of kindness in her brother but he'd proved to her there wasn't. A small part of her died in that room alongside those men.

From the continued trembling of the faerie, she assumed he'd experienced Zakael's special kind of torture. For that reason, and for those innocent men who suffered at the hands of her brother's twisted needs, she vowed vengeance. The faerie touched her cheek and shook his head. His soft brown eyes filled with tears and spilled over, coursing fresh tracks down his filthy face. A bony finger pointed toward the dungeons and back to her and then to himself before he again shook his head.

She didn't have time for his riddles. She'd sort it out later after they'd escaped.

The heavy door leading to the upper castle stood slightly ajar and Taryn paused to probe the other side with her ShantiMari. Sensing nothing, she cast it open and hurried up, taking the stairs two at a time. Her breathing grew more labored with each step, until she thought her chest would collapse from fear. If Valterys returned, or Zakael left the dungeons, there was nowhere for her to hide.

When at last they reached the final step, Taryn dared hope they might make it to her rooms unnoticed. She glanced around the empty hallway and then ran in a near-blind sprint, with the faerie boy clinging to her.

It only took a few minutes to pack her leather satchel and saddlebags. Into them, she threw her clothes and anything they might need on the road. The faerie stood self-consciously in one of her old tunics, which hung off his slight body. She rolled up the sleeves with a promise they would find him proper clothes and shoes as soon as they could. When all was in order, she grabbed her traveling cloak and a blanket for him, and then covered them with shadow.

At that time in the afternoon, the stable was nearly deserted. A few stable boys diced against the back wall, far from Nikosana's stall. Taryn set the faerie in a darkened corner, placing a finger to her lips for silence. He nodded mutely, his eyes like saucers in his gaunt face. With great care, she saddled the stallion, pausing every so often to listen, but the stables remained quiet. Just as she lifted the faerie into the saddle, bells rang out and her veins froze with fear they'd been discovered missing.

The stable boys and several guards strolled casually past the open barn door, and she breathed warmth into her chilled body. It was only dinner bells calling the servants in to dine. She took advantage of the momentary chaos of the shift change and rode brazenly through the gate, even waving at the guard as she passed. Valterys had told her to tour the city and that's exactly the image she wished to portray. The faerie huddled in front of her, invisible to anyone who looked. Kaida loped beside them, her golden gaze scanning the streets for danger. When they reached the western gate, Taryn kicked Nikosana into a canter and left Caer Idris behind.

Chapter 33

THE room was decidedly feminine and made for pleasure. In the center of the room, dominating the space, sat an enormous circular bed. Around the room, alcoves housed odd-looking chairs and other accoutrements that brought a blush to many a client's cheeks. Expensive couches stuffed with feathers and covered in rich velvet were placed strategically for special viewing. Rhoane reclined on one of the comfortable settees, stretching his legs in front of him, absently tracing his runes. When the door opened, he assumed a look of compliant boredom. The look of surprise on Nena's face cracked his demeanor and he smiled like a caught child.

"Prince Rhoane. Always a naughty boy, always sneaking into my rooms unnoticed. We have a front door, you know." She tossed her auburn curls and pouted prettily as she moved toward him, her hips swinging out, her breasts bouncing in their scanty bits of lace.

"Nena, always a pleasure." Rhoane took the mistress of the house's fingers in his own, kissing them. "I need information. What do you know about any Black Masters who might have come into the city in the last season?"

Nena snatched her hand from his grip. "Always the same with you. Never any fun. No foreplay, just 'Nena, tell me what you know.' One day I would like to show you what I know instead of telling you." She sat at her dressing table and ran a brush through her luxurious curls.

"I can't help you with your query. Men of that persuasion don't seek out my boys and girls. They like their encounters more, shall we say, pure."

"I thought as much, but how could I pass up a chance to visit with you?"

She gave him a cold stare in her mirror. "If you want my opinion—and that is all you ever want from me, unfortunately—I think the answer to your riddle lies somewhere in the streets of this city. Someone must have seen this mysterious assassin of yours."

Rhoane shouldn't have been surprised she knew about the assassin, but he was. "I was not aware that is common knowledge."

"My darling prince, since when am I common?"

"Never, and that is why I adore you."

With a sly smile, she said, "And I, you. We could make very beautiful dreams together, Prince Rhoane."

"I am sure we could, but then what? The dream would end and we would be left with all our worldly faults." Rhoane stood, indicating the visit was at an end. "Better that I leave you with your dreams, my dear."

"I hope she is worth it," Nena said, catching Rhoane off guard. "Your mysterious beauty of the three powers."

"She is. Believe me, she is."

Nena regarded him for several heartbeats before lifting his marked hand and tracing a rune. "She is not in danger, at least not at the moment, but her heart yearns for her beloved." The madame's voice held a strange, tinny echo and Rhoane peered into her eyes, beyond the dark irises to the depths of her core.

"How do you know this?"

Her lips quirked and the voice replied, "We know all

about the Eirielle. You have wronged her, Prince Rhoane of the Eleri. Without her strength, you will fade. Without her love, you are ash. Restore her faith. Restore Aelinae."

Nena's eyes rolled back and she collapsed into her chair. Rhoane lifted her and gently placed her on the bed. He left the house more determined than ever to find answers to the ever-increasing riddles.

It took Rhoane the better part of a bell to find Iselt, the blacksmith, amidst all of Talaith's workmen's quarters. He finally found him, hidden behind a tanner in one of the poorer districts of the city. Baehlon hadn't known why the man relocated to Talaith; only that Taryn had given him instructions to help the man in any way necessary. From what Rhoane could see, Iselt needed more help than he was receiving.

The dark smithy was less than half the size of the one he had at Celyn Eryri. The stench of rotting corpses filled the air and the streets were dotted with pools of scum-topped water. The slum was no place for a man of Iselt's talent. Whatever brought him south must've been of great importance. Unfortunately, Iselt wasn't in a sharing mood. Not only did he refuse to discuss why he left Celyn Eryri, he pretended to know nothing of Baehlon. If Iselt were disagreeable before, he was outright rude to Rhoane now.

Of Taryn, he said nothing at all.

Frustrated and discouraged, Rhoane slammed his fist on the bench, making Iselt's tools jump. "Dammit, man, she is out there alone while the man who seeks her death roams free. She told Baehlon to help you so I know there is a connection to her, one you are not willing to divulge. If there is something you know that can help her, please share it with me."

Iselt shifted from one foot to the other, chewing the inside of his cheek. Finally, he went inside his workroom, leaving Rhoane standing alone by the forge. He was about to leave when Iselt returned with a leather pouch in his hand.

"Do I have your word as an Eleri that what we discuss here will go nowhere else?"

Rhoane kissed his thumb and put it first to his forehead and then his heart. "You have my word."

Iselt handed the pouch to Rhoane and turned away as if ashamed of what Rhoane would find.

Rhoane tentatively upturned the pouch, cautious of the contents. "What are these?" A silver star and small dagger untangled from a very fine cloth.

Iselt faced him."Those came from your assassin. The princess brought them to me in Celyn Eryri. She needed my help finding the maker." His hands shook as he took the pouch from Rhoane, tucking the items inside. "I gave her my oath I would tell no one."

Rhoane gripped the man's arm. "If you gave your oath to Taryn, then you just as soon gave one to me. Were you successful?"

"I was able to trace them to a blacksmith living in a small village on the banks of Lake Eion. Dagwin or something. Doesn't matter because he's dead. Seems he met with a terrible accident last Harvest. He had no heirs and his business was parceled out to anyone that cared. I did some snooping, but couldn't find more of these weapons and no one remembered who ordered them made."

It wasn't much, but it was a start. "Thank you, my friend." Rhoane surveyed the small stall. "How is business treating you?"

Iselt shrugged. "It's slow with so many forges in town, but I make my way."

"Those skates you crafted for us, they were a work of art. A man with your talent could do a whole lot better than this."

"I like to keep to myself."

"Of course you do. If you ever decide otherwise, we could use a man like you up at the palace."

Iselt stared hard at him. "I'll keep that in mind."

Despite his gruff exterior and surly countenance, Rhoane liked the man. He leaned against a counter, stroking his chin in thought.

"Will you be staying all day? I could order us some tea."

"It seems I will be traveling in the next few days. I was thinking of taking a pleasure cruise, but you would be better suited to take my place."

"I'm a land man, Your Highness."

"Of course you are." Rhoane pushed off from the counter and cracked his neck. "Join me for a little chat down by the docks and see if perhaps I cannot change your mind. The pay is better than you make here in a moonturn and you would be helping the princess."

Iselt eyed him skeptically. He'd hoped the mention of Taryn would help, but it only served to upset the blacksmith more. Rhoane stalled his departure by drawing a copy of the dagger and throwing star, making certain to get the marks just right. When he finished, he tucked the paper in a pocket.

"In a bell then?" he asked carefully, fully expecting Iselt to decline.

"Where is this meeting to take place? I can't just lumber around the docks, now can I?"

Relief swept over him. He gave Iselt the address with an admonition to be certain he wasn't followed and to tell no one.

Iselt gave his word, and to Rhoane's surprise, swore him to his oath once more, leaving Rhoane to wonder what exactly had transpired between the man and Taryn.

He hurried to the palace, alerting Hayden he'd found the perfect spy to board Adesh's ship. They only needed to connect him with Amanda, and to possibly let Denzil know of their plan. Hayden insisted on accompanying Rhoane to the docks in his ridiculous peasant attire. He suffered the fool for the benefit of his ego. Iselt arrived at the appointed location on time and the introductions were made.

Amanda scrunched up her nose at Hayden's appearance but evaluated Iselt like an Ullan buying a foal. When she finished assessing the man, she turned her attention to Rhoane.

"Why don't ye come with us? We could use another good man like ye aboard ship."

"Thank you, but my services are required elsewhere." He'd been debating all afternoon about postponing his trip north to sail with Iselt. Not just to uncover Lliandra's illegal dealings, but to learn more about the man. The fact was, finding the Shadow Assassin was far more important to him than taxes, but if Iselt was important to Taryn's future, that took precedence.

"If ye change yer mind, we sail on the tide two days hence."

Rhoane left Iselt with Amanda and her charming mother Matilde, who served them bitter tea in chipped Danuri cups, and returned to the palace with Hayden in tow. They discussed at length the role Denzil would play, agreeing for the moment to keep his involvement secret from Baehlon. The last time Rhoane tried to mention his brother's name, the giant knight had bellowed enough to frighten citizens in the neighboring kingdom.

Which was exactly what he did when Rhoane told him he'd be traveling north, undercover and alone.

"Taryn will return any day and you're taking off to lands unknown on a fool's errand. And for what? The possibility of finding a blacksmith who might've made some weapons ages ago."

"I cannot stay here and wait. I need to keep myself occupied or I will go mad with worry."

"It sounds to me like you're running away."

"I can get information that will help us. If I stay here, I will just be tormented by Marissa."

"The princess keeps to herself. I've yet to see her this past cycle of the moon. Not that I'm complaining, mind you."

Rhoane had kept Marissa's secret, but it was time to tell his friend the truth. "She is with child and says I am the father." Saying the words aloud did nothing to dispel the unpleasantness of them.

"And you believe her? She's got more lovers than hairs on a carlix. I hear even her maids are used in ways better left for Nena's house. She'll take any advantage to put a wedge between you and Taryn."

"And for that reason I must leave Talaith. It was not until Marissa told me the child was mine that I saw all of her actions have been calculated to her desires. I will not fail Taryn again."

"Now you're speaking like a true prince. Go on your adventure, but what do I tell Taryn when she returns? Lliandra seems to think she'll be back for her birthing day. I hope so; the empress is planning a grand event to celebrate."

"She is?" Rhoane asked, surprised. He'd heard nothing of the plans. "How do you know?"

Baehlon grinned. "The servants. Taryn was right. They know everything that happens in this palace."

"Truly?" Rhoane was impressed. "If Taryn returns before me, tell her I will be here for her birthing day. Do not tell her where I have gone. Knowing her, she will try to rescue me and with any luck, she will succeed."

Baehlon laughed out loud and clapped Rhoane on the shoulder. "That she would. It's good to have you back, my friend."

Rhoane gave him a sharp look. "Was I really that bad?"

"Worse, but let's not dwell upon it. We have plans to make and stories to concoct. I'll have to tell the empress something about your sudden departure." Baehlon poured himself some wine and another glass for Rhoane. "Now then, where are you going—let's start with the hard one first."

They spent the evening with their heads together, planning Rhoane's elaborate lie. Alasdair brought them dinner and Faelara stopped in to offer assistance. When they had his attire set and the ruse in order, Baehlon escorted Faelara out of Rhoane's rooms. He was settling in for the night when a knock on his door made him tense. Alasdair escorted Princess Marissa to his sitting room and Rhoane gave him a dark look.

Alasdair said by way of explanation, "I told Her Highness that you were retired for the evening, but she insisted." Rhoane nodded, dismissing his valet. He remained standing, not offering her a seat. "What do you want, Marissa?"

"Won't you at least offer me a glass of wine?"

"No. Tell me what it is and be gone."

"You wound me, Rhoane." Her brows knit very prettily. When he said nothing, she continued, "I came here tonight to share my news. The baby is moving. I thought you'd like to feel your son." She reached out to take his hand, but he snatched it away.

"You have given me no proof this is my child. I understand you have many lovers—some you used just like me."

"You listen to the gossip of servants and scorned suitors. I thought you a better man, Prince Rhoane of the Eleri." Marissa tossed her hair with a stamp of her foot.

"Yes, I am an Eleri prince and if this child is mine, then I will take him to the Narthvier to raise him as such." He watched her face carefully and almost smiled when a flicker of fear lit in her eyes.

"You'll do no such thing. Our son will be raised here as a prince of the realm, with both of his parents."

"A son cannot inherit the Light Throne, but he can be heir to the Weirren Throne. As I am next in line for my father's crown, my son will take my place if I so choose. Taryn and I will take him to his people and raise him as an Eleri."

Marissa's chuckle sounded more like Kaida's growl. "And you think your lovely betrothed will forgive you so easily? You assume she will accept this child? That she'll love him? Then you are a fool."

Rhoane's hand shot out to grab Marissa by the throat, slamming her against the wall. She cried out and clawed at his hand, but he held her firm. "You do not know the first thing about my Taryn. She would raise this child as her own. She would love him because she loves me. She possesses something you have never known. Kindness."

"You think she'll show you compassion when she returns and learns about our child?" Marissa pulled her dress away to show him a small cut above her heart, fresh and bleeding. "This is the kindness she gave me at Gaarendahl. Nothing I do will heal it. At times, the pain is so severe I must stay abed all day."

He sensed Taryn's ShantiMari in the wound, her rage and pain mingled with Marissa's blood, but there was grace as well. While keeping one hand on her throat, he reached his other toward her breast.

She arched toward him, moaning as if he'd stroked her.

"Stop it. I am not touching you for pleasure. She is kind, Marissa. If she had been anything else, you would be dead. The gods know I would have killed you given the chance." Marissa's face lost color, but her chin rose in defiance.

"You call this kindness? Wounding me for all time?"

"You deserved nothing less and you know it. What did you expect from her? Sympathy? She showed incredible bravery that night. She was angry and confused, hurt by your betrayal and mine. Tell me, what would you have done in her place?"

Marissa glared at him. "I would never have been so stupid as to be there to begin with. As far as I'm concerned, she deserved what she got."

"I cannot kill you, Marissa, because you carry an innocent life, but—" He pinched her skin, forcing his Shanti into her, mixing it with Taryn's. "If this child is not mine, every Eleri will know of your betrayal and deceit."

Her eyes widened and she trembled slightly.

"Past, present, and future Eleri will know Princess Marissa of the Light Throne sought to destroy me and the one I love. The one they know and revere as the *Darennsai*. They will know of her forgiveness and your betrayal. Forever more, you will be known as the Black Princess for your evil deeds and dark heart. You will become the monster mothers threaten their children with."

"You go too far." Delicate tears flowed down her face to his hand. "Don't do this. Please."

"If you are without fault, then these are nothing but empty words." He pressed down on her wound to finish the oath. "This I swear, as First Son and Eleri Prince Rhoane, *Surtentse* and betrothed to Taryn Rose of House Galendrin."

Marissa screamed and he released her.

"Get out of my room."

She bent over, gasping for air. When she rose, a fire lit her lavender eyes. "You'll regret this, Rhoane. When our child is born, it is you who will suffer." She turned to go and he grabbed her arm.

"If you tell a soul about this child before it is born, you will not live to give birth to it."

"I'm starting to show—certainly there will be suspicion." He could almost see her mind working frantically. "At least let me tell Mother."

"No one shall know of this child. If it is mine, I have this right." He stood to his full height and she cowered before him.

"I will tell no one," she said, her voice nothing more than a whisper.

A low gurgle started in his belly, working its way up to his chest, bubbling out of him in uncontrollable laughter. In that moment of madness, he let go of the anguish he'd held onto since Gaarendahl. What was broken inside him began to mend. For the first time since that terrible night, he wanted to be whole once more. He was Eleri and he belonged—mind, body, and soul—to Taryn. If she would still have him.

A few days later, he slipped out of the palace grounds before daybreak, heading north. Fayngaar managed to slouch as they trundled past the guards, pulling a cart laden with spices and exotic fruits from the Summerlands. Rhoane, his hair shorn to above his ears and wearing patched peasant's clothing, saluted the guards while whistling a happy tune. The going would be slow, but he needed to keep up the disguise if he were to track down the assassin.

The moonless sky glittered with the last remaining stars, and Rhoane gazed toward Dal Tara. He sent a silent prayer to his goddess for guidance and another to Nadra that she watch over Taryn and keep her safe.

Nena's words echoed in his mind. Taryn was not in danger. At least not at that moment. He slapped the reins and Fayngaar grunted his distaste for the disguise. They trundled north toward Lake Eoin, but Rhoane kept his gaze to the west and Caer Idris, where he hoped Taryn was safe.

Chapter 34

NO MOON guided their way as they traveled southeast toward the Dierlin Pass. The first night of their escape, Taryn found them shelter in an abandoned shepherd's cottage. Niko munched moldy hay and Kaida caught several rats in the loft while Taryn and the faerie ate what crumbs they could find in the cupboard. When she sank to the floor, exhausted, a wave of emotion washed over her but she held back her tears for fear if she let one fall, a dam would burst. Kaida and the faerie curled close, but it wasn't their warmth she craved.

The frigid darkness that teased her since the Stones lingered, sometimes giving her chills that wracked her body, other times being nothing more than a nuisance. On several occasions, Rykoto whispered entreaties to her, but he didn't attack as he had at the river. Still, Taryn was cautious. The constant wariness wore on her and twice she had almost allowed Rykoto to convince her to leave her companions. Always in the middle of the night the voice came, coaxing her awake, easing her into a false sense of confidence.

Both times Kaida had prevented her from leaving or harming herself. Each time Taryn had lain with her arms wrapped tightly around the grierbas, too afraid to let go. Rykoto was getting stronger and more bolder each day and she was no closer to understanding her Dark powers. She couldn't rely on her father or brother for help, which meant she'd have to find someone else. Hopefully her uncle would have an idea of where she could start, but that had to wait until Paderau and there was a lot of riding between them and the duke.

They rode hard, day and night. Only when she was faint from lack of food would they stop to set snares or fish in a stream. At first, the faerie snatched his food from her with greedy hands, taking gulping bites, afraid Taryn might take the food from him.

Very gently, as if she were speaking to a child, she would say, "You must eat slower or you will make yourself sick." When she put a hand on his, he snarled at her, baring his teeth. "I am not going to take your food. Slowly, that is it. Just a small bite." When she gave him another portion, he looked at her with apprehension. "You can trust me. I am going to take care of you."

Gradually she earned his trust and one night, under a blanket of stars, the faerie found the courage to speak. Not with his voice, but in her mind.

His name was Gian. He belonged to a clan on the western border of the Narthvier. They traded goods with several villages nearby and it was when he was out hunting for pelts that Zakael had come upon him. He bound Gian in his ShantiMari and took him to Caer Idris. Beyond that, Gian would say no more. When Taryn suggested she return him to the vier, he sobbed against her, his sounds muffled in his throat. He insisted over and over again he could never return to the Narthvier.

Whatever he suffered while imprisoned in Zakael's dungeons had scarred Gian physically and emotionally. Taryn held him close, promising she wouldn't let anything happen to him. She stretched her power, pulling the shadows over them like a thick cloak.

On the sixth day of their escape, Taryn noticed a sleek black bird flying overhead. When it circled above them, her pulse quickened. Niko must've sensed the bird's presence because he pawed at the ground, snorting with angry huffs. She led him off the road and slid from the saddle, taking Gian with her.

"Go hide over there behind those trees," she told him. "Do not come out no matter what you see. Do you understand?" He nodded mutely and ran to where she'd indicated. "Kaida, go with him. Zakael will be here any moment. You must keep Gian safe."

Taryn removed her sword from its scabbard and stood in the center of a small clearing. The bird circled once and then swooped down, dissolving into the form of Zakael when its claws touched the ground. Her brother shook out his cloak, cracking his neck and shoulders before turning to face her. A sword appeared in his hand, its black steel glinting in the sunlight.

"You aren't making a very good escape, sister. I found you too easily. Why did you run away? It was most vexing to Father. And myself."

"I didn't run away. You and Valterys disappeared. I got bored, so I left."

"That's twice now you've left my home on short notice. Is it something I said?"

"What do you want?" Taryn flexed her fingers around the hilt.

"For you to return with me, what else?"

"Why—so you can ignore me? No, thanks."

"You seem to think you have a choice, dear sister, when in fact, you don't." He threw a ball of power at her and she sliced through it.

"Yes, I do." She deflected another of his attacks before swinging her sword low to catch his thigh. He danced out of reach, then came at her hard and fast, but she was ready.

With each thrust, she parried and deflected, circling around to slice his knees, followed by a cut to his chest, deliberately trying to throw him off balance. The longer they fought, the more astonished his expression. He'd underestimated her skill in all things, especially with a sword.

The clash of metal rang out as they slashed and jabbed at each other. Sweat ran down Taryn's face as she leapt around Zakael. He, too, was dripping from the exertion. Their fight disrupted the calm of the forest, agitating the animals, disturbing nesting birds. The whisperings distracted her focus, and she missed the tip of Zakael's blade by a carlix's whisker. The same couldn't be said about his fist. It landed squarely on her right jaw and she staggered backward.

A devilish grin spread across his face and he advanced for another assault. She spun quickly, elbowing him in the gut, then crushing his foot with her heel before turning to knock him on the head with the hilt of her sword. He went down on his knees, breathing heavily. Dazed from the blow he'd given her, and the energy she expended, she paused a moment to gather her strength and he grabbed her with his power.

His ShantiMari whipped around her neck, lifting her from the ground. She thrashed, gasping for breath. A thread of silky black snatched her sword from her hand while another pulled her arms above her head. She cursed herself for giving him the opportunity to restrain her.

A sharp jab to her mind sent her thoughts scattering for a heartbeat before she closed it against him. When she reached for her ShantiMari, a barrier prevented her from touching it.

Zakael stood, one hand on his stomach, the other stretched toward her. A thread of his power ran from his fingertips to her head. Somehow he was blocking her from accessing her ShantiMari. To block another's power was strictly forbidden.

"You've no idea how much I've been looking forward to this moment." He took a step closer. "Father wants you alive, but he didn't say by how much." His fingers twitched and the power tightened around her throat, cutting off all air.

She stopped thrashing and hung limp. Thick cords of ShantiMari wrapped around her ankles, pulling her legs wide apart. A pain-filled gasp came out muffled and pitiful. The exertion spent the air in her lungs.

Darennsai, shall I attack him? Kaida asked, surprising Taryn that Zakael had not blocked her thoughts as well.

Not yet. Wait for my call. Until then, keep Gian safe.

"Don't fight me, my beautiful sister." Zakael held his sword at waist level, chuckling under his breath. "You could still join me willingly. Either way, I will have you." The hilt of his sword traveled from the top of her leather pants to between her legs, where he rubbed it cruelly against her. "We were meant to rule Aelinae together, you and I." He reached out suddenly, grabbing her side, sending his power into her vorlock scar.

Pain shot through her, sparking fire in her blood. Once more, she sought her ShantiMari, but found nothing. Again, she thrashed against the bonds, but they were too tight. "I will never rule with you," she managed between breaths.

He pressed against her ribs. Searing heat, followed by icy chills, sliced through her body.

She bit back a scream.

"So much pride. Even this close to death, you think you have a choice. You've never had a choice, Taryn. Your fate was decided a long time ago by the Eiriellean prophecy. It says 'Light and Dark will unite Aelinae.' My dove, that means you are meant to rule with me, don't you see?"

"You're a delusional idiot," she rasped.

"I assure you, I'm neither." He lifted her tunic, whistling at her scar. "That's really something. Marissa told me of your bravery that day and I'll confess—I did not quite believe her."

Taryn flinched when he reached out to touch it, but there was nowhere for her to hide from his grasping hands.

"Oh, my sweet, after a few days in my playroom, you'll think this scar is nothing. I do admire your strength. You'll make a fine queen for me. In fact," his granite eyes became glossy in thought, "I believe you are my equal in all things. Your sister was never able to satisfy my needs, but you, yes, you'll know how to fulfill my desires, to satiate my needs. And I in return will never leave you wanting. I can tell you crave this."

He slid his other hand between her legs, rubbing his fingers against her above the hilt of his sword, half impaling her upon it.

"You know nothing about me." The hoarse words hurt to expel, took too much energy.

"I will train you to please me. Together we will rule Aelinae and all will be as it should."

His eyes half-closed in dreamy expectation as he bent low, his hot tongue licking from one end of her scar to the other. A moan reminiscent of the sound he'd made in the dungeon escaped his lips. Pain-fueled ecstasy.

Something broke in Taryn. Rage like she'd never known coursed through her. Hate, raw and unfettered, rocked her core. Images flashed through her mind, cruel and vicious in their scope. She wanted to hurt Zakael, to maim him beyond recognition so that he could never inflict pain again. A low chuckle started in her belly, working its way up until she was laughing out loud so hard that the bonds at her neck constricted, cutting off what little air she had.

He screamed at her for silence, striking her across the face with his fist.

A flash of white streaked through the stars of pain. Suddenly Kaida was on him, snarling and snapping at his face. The unexpected attack was the break she needed to reach her power. Mari sped through her limbs, burning Zakael's bonds.

Taryn's jaw throbbed and she tasted blood, adding fuel to her fury. She threw a wave of power at Zakael, pinning him down. Gian ran forward to grab Zakael's sword and then ducked behind her, disappearing into the bushes. Kaida pounced on his chest, snarling and snapping, her fangs an inch from his face.

Kaida, stop. See to Gian.

The grierbas snarled at Zakael a final time and then loped away to guard the faerie.

Taryn ripped Zakael's power from around her neck and fell to the ground. Ynyd Eirathnacht flew to her outstretched hand, pulsing energy into her, renewing her strength. The pain in her scar thrummed, then faded. Her pendant rose in song, with the sword answering the melody. Her ShantiMari burned in her veins, igniting a fire within, and she savored the sensation. Freedom, release, pure infinite pleasure coursed through her body. Never again, she vowed, would she allow herself to be taken prisoner and cut off from her power.

Zakael scrambled to his feet, but Taryn was on him. She punched him in the nose, then the sternum in quick succession before smashing the side of his head with the hilt of her sword. A trickle of blood oozed down his temple.

She wrapped her ShantiMari around him, throwing him high in the air. During his fall, he began to transform into a bird but she tightened her power against him, stopping the transformation with him as half-man, half-bird.

He screamed against her bonds in a terrible cry that scattered the birds in nearby trees.

"Become Aelan," she commanded.

"Fuck off," he spat at her.

"Very well. I'll just leave you here." She stormed toward

Nikosana.

"Wait!"

He transformed into his Aelan form and she lowered the bubble until it touched the ground. His ShantiMari swirled within the confines of hers.

"Release me. I'll not harm you," he pleaded.

"I'm not that stupid, Zakael. As soon as I let the barrier down, you'll try to trap me again. I should leave you here in this prison, at least long enough for me to return to Talaith."

His eyes grew large. "I'll starve to death."

"And I should care, why? Weren't you just gloating about how close to death you could bring me?" Taryn asked, her voice cool.

"Taryn, you aren't like this. You are caring and good."

"You make me sick." Her mind screamed at her to kill him, but her bloodlust had passed.

"I'll return to Caer Idris and tell Father I couldn't find you. I swear—I won't harm you." He held up his hands, placatingly.

"Teach me to transform and I'll let you go."

He sputtered, shaking his head. "It isn't something you do immediately. It takes a season or more to master."

"You don't have that long. Teach me." When she put her sword at his throat, it sang a song of death, and from the look on his face, he heard it.

"Put that down. I can't think with your blade on me." His power strengthened.

"Don't do it, Zakael. I'll know whether you're trying to overpower me."

Indecision etched across his face, and then he relaxed, drawing in a deep breath. "First, you imagine the beast you wish to become. Bird, grierbas, horse, cat—anything. Think of the lines of the animal, the musculature, the fur or feathers. All of it. You must become the animal in your thoughts and heart."

"Show me. Slowly."

"Transformation is dangerous. If you get it wrong, you could stay as the animal forever. Or worse." He actually sounded concerned for her.

She touched his throat, her blade drawing blood. "I said show me and take your time. Move by move." His arms began to change from that of a man to the long wings of a levon. His head and torso were replaced by a feathered crown and body. Finally, his legs grew scales and he stood on long claws.

Taryn stared transfixed as he morphed into Zakael once more. "Are you ever anything other than a levon?" she asked.

"No more questions. I showed you how it's done. Release me."

"I need to make sure I can do it first."

"Not on your first try. No one ever gets it right the first time out. Practice when I'm not around."

Taryn tied off her ShantiMari to prevent him from moving and closed her eyes, thinking of a great beast, her silver scales shining in the afternoon light. Her wings flowed out from her arms, and her head and body convulsed into the form of a fanged dragon. She scratched her feet on the ground, feeling her talons rake through the grass.

The beast turned her azure gaze on Zakael. He glared at her in absolute panic.

What an odd thing it was to be first a woman, then a dragon. They were nothing alike and the balance was completely off. She flicked her tail and shuffled forward to compensate.

Taryn took a deep breath and settled her mind into the dragon's. Her crouch softened, her neck lengthened, and her tail curled around her body. Sitting was one thing, but dragons weren't meant to laze around like palace cats.

Great leathery wings beat hard and she tilted from side to

side, until she relaxed into the movements. Once she had the rhythm, she lifted into the air. Kaida crouched low, near the edge of the clearing, and she sent a thought to her grierbas friend to not be afraid. *Stay with Gian. I'll be back shortly.*

She reached out with a claw and picked up Zakael as if he were a doll. He fought against her firm grip as she beat her wings harder, rising up into the sky. Exhilaration and terror commingled within her.

Once airborne, she panicked and plummeted toward the ground.

Zakael screamed at her, "Be the dragon! Don't think like Taryn—link your mind to hers."

Taryn let her mind drift into the dragon's and gasped as everything came into sharp focus. She saw through the dragon's eyes, felt the wind across her long snout. They moved through the air at an alarming speed. Her dragon mind scanned the landscape below them and then dove into a small canyon. Zakael cried out for her to stop, but the dragon knew what she wanted.

She sent a thought to Zakael to sleep and when he hung limp, she gently lowered herself to the canyon floor, dropping him to the ground before shifting into a woman with ease.

Despite what Zakael said, the change wasn't difficult at all. As if she'd always been a part of the dragon. Or the dragon a part of her.

After she had tied several bonds around Zakael, making certain they would take most of the day to unravel, she spiraled into the air, snorting a burst of flame from sheer happiness. When she returned to the clearing and transformed back into Taryn once more, it was with great reluctance.

Kaida crept forward and lay before Taryn. *You are Darennsai.*

Gian came out from his hiding place to prostrate himself before her. *Great One, I am yours to command until my last dying breath. This I, Gian of the clan Brenbold, swear to you.*

Their response to her transformation unnerved her. "Get up, Gian. You cannot tell anyone of this—do you understand?" He nodded and kissed his thumb before placing it over his heart. "Good," she said as she went to find Nikosana. "Because if Rhoane knew what I just did, he'd never let me out of his sight again."

Her pendant sent a shock of heat over her skin and she jumped. She'd deliberately kept thoughts of Rhoane at bay to better focus on what she had to accomplish at Caer Idris. Now that she was headed to Talaith, she didn't know whether he'd be waiting for her there or if he remained in the Narthvier. What she did know was she couldn't let herself think the worst. Her fingertips fluttered over the pendant—the desire to touch his emotions too strong.

A sharp pain in her wrist stopped her from reaching out to Rhoane. A new rune in the clear shape of a dragon was etched into her skin. She traced the new rune, then the others. They glowed as they always had, which she hoped meant she was still bound to Rhoane. The thought came unbidden—did he still want her? She had, after all, abandoned him.

Chapter 35

SABINA awoke screaming and Hayden wrapped his arms around her, making shushing noises, his limbs trembling. She'd not had a night fright since before they left Talaith for Celyn Eryri—he didn't welcome Kaldaar's return to their lives.

She huddled against him, her muffled sobs breaking his heart. No matter how skilled he became with ShantiMari or the sword, he could not protect his love from the banished god. "Sabina, what is it?" he coaxed once her cries quieted.

"I saw Taryn surrounded by blackness, injured and frightened. I couldn't reach her. I couldn't reach her." Sabina dissolved to tears and he rocked her, stroking her hair.

On rare occasions, Sabina had flashes of future events. More sensations rather than full visions, but they nearly always came true. If she feared for Taryn, then his cousin was in danger.

Taryn. He cast the thought west, not knowing exactly where she was, but having a vague idea.

Silence answered him.

Taryn, please speak to me. Sabina and I are worried about you.

Silence.

"What if her father—" Sabina cut off her words, a shiver

slicing through her. Hayden rubbed her arms and back, warming her. "We must find her, Hayden."

"Rhoane left a few days ago. Perhaps he is searching for her."

Even Iselt was gone, having left on Adesh's ship the previous morning. He could ask Baehlon or Denzil to search for Taryn, but where would they look? Aelinae was too large to find one woman, a horse, and a grierbas.

Neither he nor Sabina slept the rest of the night—instead, they lay curled in each other's arms. When the morning light shone through her windows, Hayden threw off the covers, but she reached for him.

"Stay. I don't care what the empress or anyone else thinks." She patted the mattress and he resumed his place beside her, relieved they no longer had to hide this part of their relationship.

Later that day, they met with Faelara and the younger princesses. Sabina told the trio of her vision, elaborating with chilling details that set Hayden's hairs on end.

"A great beast tracks her, but there is a light protecting her. Not ShantiMari, but something else. Silver in color, with shimmering hues of the rainbow. I also sensed a presence with her, a gnarled affliction. Whether this is the beast or not, I cannot say. But it is close to Taryn."

"What about Kaida? Is she still with our sister?" Tears glistened in Tessa's pretty eyes.

"I can't say. My visions are flashes of nonsense that I must piece together. Kaida has never shown herself to me."

Baehlon joined them and they recapped their conversation for the knight. His usually stern expression pinched with suppressed rage; his lips tightened to a thin line, turning dangerously white.

"We'll send a note to Duke Anje and ask him to search along the less traveled roads from Paderau to the Dierlin Pass.

If she has left Caer Idris, we should find her there. If she's still with her father, Dal Ferran itself will befall the man if he has hurt his daughter."

"What of us? We can't stay here and pretend nothing is wrong. We must search for her. Someone needs to go to Caer Idris and confront Valterys."

"No, Faelara." Baehlon's voice lowered to a gentle baritone. "We stay here where we can watch the empress and Marissa. If they know of Taryn's whereabouts, we'll find a way to uncover it from them."

"Tessa and Eliahnna, visit with your sister. Take tea with her as often as she allows. She's secluded herself since the Light Celebrations and will appreciate the company, but don't bring up Taryn by name. In fact, if you can convince her you're upset with your sister, then perhaps she will share what she knows. It's doubtful, but we must try."

"Yes, Lady Faelara, we will." Eliahnna answered for both of them. "Are you yet in Mother's good graces?"

"As a matter of fact, I am. We are to stroll the gardens together this afternoon."

Plans made for the women, Hayden excused himself, with Baehlon following close behind. The knight's presence unnerved him. He'd wanted to slip out of the palace to speak with Adesh, with the hopes of meeting Denzil along the way. If Baehlon insisted on joining him, he'd have to alter his course.

When they reached the side door, Hayden asked innocently, "Will you be training this afternoon?"

Baehlon shook his head and tiny bells sounded. "There's a man I want to see." His gaze rested on Hayden. "It's not the sort of place a lord should be found."

"Then I shan't disturb your errand."

Hayden debated for only a moment before deciding his task could wait. When Baehlon reached the palace gates, he fell in step a good distance behind the man. He strolled along the cobbled walk, hands tucked in his pockets, whistling a soft tune. Instead of turning toward the docks, Baehlon circled up a tree-lined avenue in a modest neighborhood.

The well-kept houses boasted small gardens with a few hardy buds pushing through the soggy soil. A few horses clomped their way down the street, their riders clad in light cloaks to ward off the lingering chill. The dregs of Frost End clung to their days with surprising tenacity. Hayden welcomed summer's warm embrace, having been too long at Celyn Eryri and the bitter cold. He shoved his hands deeper in his pockets and tilted his head toward the ground lest he be recognized.

About midway along the lane, Baehlon ducked beneath an arbor and hastened his steps to the side of a handsome home. Hayden waited behind a tree for several minutes until certain it was safe to venture forth. He kept close to the wall, his cloak shushing against the wooden slats. Baehlon's voice sounded from a short distance above him and he stilled, listening for movement outside the house. Creaking floorboards and the hard stomp of the knight's boots were followed by lighter footsteps.

Hayden pressed himself closer to the window, grateful for the slight opening.

A third pair of footsteps joined the other two and Baehlon's baritone filled the space. "It's about time, Denzil. Do you mean to keep us waiting all day?"

Hayden's mind whirled. Baehlon and Denzil hated each other.

"Stop your bellowing. You've naught been here but a moment. I saw you approach and waited until it was safe."

"Would either of you like something to drink? Tea? Or perhaps something stronger? We have ale or trisp. Some wine?"

Hayden recognized Tarro's voice immediately. This must be his home, but why would he allow Baehlon and his brother to meet there? The questions were piling upon themselves with no answers coming forward.

"No, thank you, Tarro. I won't be long." That was Baehlon. "What news have you?"

Hasty whispers warned Hayden a moment too late. A brawny hand clasped his shoulder and he glanced upwards where three amused faces stared at him.

"Would you like some tea?" Tarro offered genially.

"I would, thank you." Hayden traipsed to the back door, where the tailor met him with a steaming cup in his hand. He hadn't been serious about the tea but took it from the man with a mumbled thanks. That he'd been discovered chafed.

"As I was telling Denzil here, the first rule of espionage is make certain no one else is following the person you're interested in. Right, brother?"

Denzil lifted his chin and the tiny bells in his sculpted beard jingled. Now that he saw them together, he could detect similarities in their features, namely their almond-shaped eyes, and the broad expanse of chest that led to muscled arms, but beyond that, they were as different as could be. Denzil didn't have Baehlon's height, nor his serious demeanor. The mercenary's eyes danced with inner mischief and a smile rarely left his face.

"Aye. But he's green, this one. Unschooled in the ways of the world."

Hayden opened his mouth to argue, but they were right. His books, not experience, taught him much of what he knew. "Then teach me to be a spy."

The brothers laughed, a hearty sound that shook the timbered walls of Tarro's home. "You are a scholar, young Hayden, not a warrior or spy. Perhaps it's best if it stay that way."

"No, I'm serious. The world is becoming more complex and I could benefit from anything you might impart to me."

Denzil stroked his goatee, lips pursed in thought. "You know, the boy might be onto something. The princess is rather fond of him. If he insists on sticking his nose where it doesn't belong, he will most likely get himself killed."

"I'm proficient with a sword and ShantiMari," Hayden argued. "I can protect myself."

"Yes, but the world is full of thieves and murderers who are skilled at avoiding both. I'll do what I can, as will Denzil, and when Ebus returns, we'll have him teach you a few tricks. But I tell you true, you are a lord, not a spy. Never think otherwise."

Hayden understood what he wasn't saying. If anything happened to Zakael, the duke was next in line to inherit the Obsidian Throne. His father had told him on several occasions he would decline, passing the title to Hayden.

"Gentlemen," Tarro interrupted, "our time grows short."

"Yes, of course." Baehlon glanced up the stairs before raising an eyebrow at the tailor. "Is he not at work?"

"He is, but others will be coming home and none of you should be seen here. Least of all you, my lord."

"Then let's get to it, shall we?" Denzil offered. "As for news, I have some to report." He withdrew a paper from inside his heavy coat and handed it to Baehlon. "Proof the empress is forcing the taxes upon the Summerlands and the Danuri. It appears she tried to bribe the Geigan, but they have little interest in her gold. Dealing mostly in leather goods and minerals, they work closely with the Artagh, who also refused the empress. Ulla, however, is under her protection. For what reason, we've yet to decipher."

"And the reason for the increased taxes?" Hayden asked. He had several working theories, but no way to corroborate any of them.

"It's simple, really. She wishes to weaken the other kingdom's economies."

"But why?" Tarro asked.

Two facts popped into Hayden's mind: Tarro worked for the empress, and his lover was from the Summerlands. Surely his loyalties were to his lover and not the empress. Otherwise Hayden doubted Baehlon would trust him enough to meet in his home.

He surveyed the room, noting the expensive trinkets scattered on tables and shelves. A tailor could not afford such luxuries, but one of the most popular whores in Talaith could. Or, they were gifts from clients. Hayden met Tarro's amused gaze, puzzled at exactly how it worked—being the lover of a whore.

"Quite well, actually," Tarro answered the unspoken question.

Embarrassed, Hayden blustered an apology, but Tarro smiled genially. "You are not the first to wonder, nor the last. Yes, it's tiresome at times, but mostly, I don't dwell on what he does for a living."

"If you're finished?" Baehlon interrupted. "I believe the question was why is Lliandra draining the Summerlands and Danuri economies. Any thoughts?"

"To fill her coffers, of course." Denzil grunted. "The gods know she doesn't pay for shite, and the money has to be going somewhere."

"Not only to make her kingdom wealthier," Hayden began, "but as you said, to weaken the other kingdoms. I have a theory, but it's treasonous to think."

"And our little tea party is what, exactly?"

"Good point, Baehlon. I believe the empress is fading. She is stocking her treasury with coin for Marissa's rule, yes, but she's weakening two of the largest economies. Why? When Marissa takes the throne, she will cast aside her mother's taxes, apologizing for the wicked deeds of her predecessor and make amends to the Summerlands and Danuri."

"Interesting theory, but what about Ulla?"

"My brother has a point, Hayden. Why protect the desert kingdom?" Baehlon insisted.

"I haven't sorted that out yet, but I believe it has something to do with Ulla's proximity to the Narthvier. Taryn is, after all, linked to the people of the great forest. If Lliandra thinks there's any way she can coerce her daughter to turn against the Eleri, she has an army at their doorstep."

"She wouldn't!"

"I believe she would, Tarro. Fortunately for us, I know my cousin better than her mother. Taryn would never betray Rhoane's people."

The thought of Taryn pinched his heart. He'd tried several more times to contact her, each receiving no reply.

They ended the meeting with promises to keep one another abreast of any developments. For his part, Tarro took pains to make certain his guests left the house undetected. His skill with ShantiMari was minimal, but his ability to distract passersby with his flamboyant personality more than made up for the lack of power.

Hayden left first, skirting the edge of the lane where trees provided ample shadows in the late evening light. When he reached the crossroad that led to the marketplace, he hesitated, deciding he'd visit with Adesh another day. The sun dipped close to the ocean when he reached the palace gates and he veered left toward the gardens instead of entering the massive building.

Sunset was his favorite time of the day. The setting of the sun and rising of the moon reminded him of lovers cast apart for all time. Only a few times per season were they permitted to share the same sky, their orbs close, but not touching. It was a sad tale of unrequited love, and yet he thought the sun and moon were not unhappy in the arrangement. If anything, they were hopeful. Every morning and every evening they rose with the hope they would be together at last.

You should write a story about the sun and moon, my poetic cousin.

Taryn! Hayden almost spun around to find her standing behind him. *Are you well? We've been so worried.*

I'm well and will be in Paderau soon.

Something happened. Sabina had a vision—you were surrounded by blackness and in pain.

Tell Sabina there is no need to worry.

When will you be home?

Silence stretched between them and Hayden feared he'd lost her.

Soon. There are a few things I need to do first. Is everyone...

Her voice caught and he detected a slight sob in her thoughts.

Is everyone well in Talaith?

We miss you, but yes, we are well. He concentrated hard on the next words he spoke silently. *You are loved and needed by all of your friends.*

Thank you, my sweet cousin. I miss you more than words can say.

Give Father my regards. I hope to see you before the twin moons.

I will. He sensed her drifting off, but then her laughter echoed in his mind.

What of the twin moons, eh? Does the sun romance them both?

Another voice distracted him, and he thought he heard her speaking Eleri before her laughter died away and the connection ended.

He stood resolute at the seawall until the last of the sun's rays winked out and the moon rose in the west. Two moons for one sun! What a ninny he was, waxing poetic on the celestial cycle. Perhaps Baehlon was right; he was not fit to be a spy. His weapon was intellect, of that he had no doubt.

Sabina's soft voice interrupted his thoughts and he wrapped an arm around her shoulder, not having heard her approach, but happy for the company. She would be well pleased to know Taryn was safe, but for the moment, he wanted to share the eventide with his love. Lights twinkled under the moon's steady gaze and the scent of night blooming flowers perfumed the air.

Hayden turned Sabina to face him and cupped her cheek in his palm. "I love you, Princess Sabina of the Summerlands. More than the sun loves the moon, more than the stars in the sky. Your intelligence, your smile, the way you toss your hair and stomp your pretty feet when you aren't getting your way: they are as dear to me as breath itself. I don't ever want to be without you. Please say you'll marry me."

Tears shimmered in her eyes and spilled over her lovely cheeks, wetting his hand. "I'm sorry, Hayden, but I cannot."

Chapter 36

THEY saw no more of Zakael through the Dierlin Pass nor on the road to Paderau. Kaida predicted they wouldn't see him again anytime soon. At least not alone. They rode only during the day and stayed at an inn or farmstead whenever possible. She avoided her manor house and Ravenwood, certain they would be watched for her arrival.

In addition to searching the skies for Zakael, Taryn kept alert to any sign of the Shadow Assassin. From the way Valterys questioned Lliandra's men, she suspected he wasn't the one behind the attacks. If he were, he knew where Taryn was headed and certainly would've sent the assassin after her. Still, she wasn't taking any chances.

Taryn had not sent word to anyone regarding her whereabouts for fear the message would be intercepted. Her communication with Hayden was a risk, but the worry she sensed in each of his calls alarmed her. She risked the one communication and hoped she'd not been discovered.

When they crested the ridge and Taryn saw Paderau beyond the city walls, she hugged Gian to her. He gestured them forward with agitated excitement.

"Eager for a warm meal and soft mattress, are you?" she joked. He nodded, pointing toward Paderau. "Patience, my friend. Niko's had a long ride." Encouraged by a warm stall and fresh oats, Nikosana quickened his pace, with Kaida loping alongside them.

Gian gaped in wide-eyed wonder as they passed through the new city and into the older section of Paderau. It wasn't so long ago she had the same expression on her face when she first entered the city walls. When they turned onto the boulevard leading to the palace, he twisted right and then left to look at the fine homes.

"Just wait until you see Talaith. Paderau is pretty, but the capital city is gorgeous," Taryn whispered in his ear.

Grander than this? His shock sounded in her mind.

"Much more. There is a large harbor where ships bring goods from all seven kingdoms. Have you ever swum in the ocean, Gian?" When he shook his head, she said, "Well, you shall. The weather is warming up and soon it will be nice enough to swim at the beach." Suddenly, she felt a longing for Talaith, a physical ache that wrenched her heart.

What is it, Darennsai? Gian asked.

I miss my home.

There was a moment of silence in her mind. *My home is with you now.*

Gian, why can you not return to the vier? When he'd showed her his maimed tongue where Zakael had burned him so severely he was unable to speak, she had touched his mind with her power to lessen the horrors her half-brother inflicted on him. Even though he trusted her, he'd not told her why he couldn't go home. *I was unaware of the woodland folk becoming sheanna.*

She heard a gasp in her mind. *Not sheanna, no. The tall man did things to me that would make Eleri sheanna, but that is not why I cannot return.*

Then why? I know when Eleri are away from the vier, they fade a little each day. Is it the same for faeries?

Perhaps. I have heard Prince Rhoane has a woodland faerie

as his servant.

Alasdair. He is Rhoane's valet. Hearing Gian say Rhoane's name so casually tore at Taryn. In a matter of days, she would see him again. The thought thrummed through her thoughts.

I am sorry, Darennsai. I did not mean to upset you.

Do you know Illanr or Carld? They are Alasdair's sisters. They live in the Weirren.

He shrugged. *My clan is not often found at court.*

They reached the gate and the guard smiled while greeting Taryn with a stiff salute. She left Nikosana with a groom and gave Ashanni a quick kiss on her muzzle before heading into the palace. Duke Anje grabbed her in a bear hug and spun her around.

"My darling niece has come home at last." He held her out, scrutinizing her. "You're positively whittled away to nothing. We'll have to fatten you up before we see your mother. She'll have my head for lunch if she thinks I'm to blame for this."

"I'm well, Uncle, thanks for asking," Taryn said dryly. "I'd like you to meet a friend of mine." She reached behind her and pulled the faerie to stand before her uncle. "Duke Anje, this is Gian. Gian, this is my uncle, the formidable and yet utterly lovable Duke Anje. This is his home."

"And yours as well, my darling." He bent to Gian and said, "It is an honor to have one of the woodland folk staying in my humble home. You are welcome, Gian."

He clasped Gian's arm and Taryn saw there were tears in his eyes. He wiped them away before saying to Kaida, "And you, dreadful beast that you are, I see you're still hanging about with my niece."

Kaida barked and he laughed.

"She says she hopes you still have that wonderful mutton you fed her last visit," Taryn said.

"Does she now? We'll just have to see what we can find

for the mongrel. Come inside. There are many who are eager to see you." Taryn's step faltered and Anje turned back to her. "What is it, dear?"

"Who?"

"Just the usual—servants, myself, Lords Tinsley and Aomori, other nobles from across the land." He stopped. "Prince Rhoane is not here, if that is what you are asking."

A flush spread across her cheeks. "How much do you know?"

"Nothing more than court gossip and speculation." He took her arm. "If you wish to confide in me, I am a wonderful listener. I will also respect your silence."

They found a room for Gian close to Taryn's and left him in the capable hands of several servants. He begged to stay with her, but she explained that here, she was a princess and she must follow certain protocols. Sleeping with a faerie in her room was frowned upon unless he was her betrothed.

He'd blushed when she said the last part and Taryn was reminded of his innocence. As he'd explained it to her, a faerie of sixty-four seasons was the equivalent of ten Aelan seasons, making him, in essence, a contemporary of Tessa's.

While Gian rested, Taryn dined alone with Duke Anje in his private room. As they ate, he told her about the escape of the Shadow Assassin. Less than a month after she and Rhoane left Celyn Eryri, someone had knocked out the guard and freed the assassin. By then, she and Rhoane had left Gaarendahl and since Lliandra didn't know where they were, she let them continue their journey with the hope they would be safe.

When Taryn told Anje of the conversation she overheard at Caer Idris, he scratched at his beard, which meant something troubled him. It was one of the little things Taryn loved about her uncle. "Because there were no attacks on my travels here, I believe Valterys is not the one controlling the Shadow Assassin. He made it very clear to Zakael that he needed me alive. He said something about taking me to Rykoto at mid-summer," Taryn explained.

"Do you know for what purpose?"

"No, but he said he needed my blood and my blade." She retrieved the scroll she'd smuggled from his library. "I found this when I was there. It mentions those two things. There must be another sheet, but I couldn't find it."

Anje took the paper from her and read it. "I know this scroll. I spent my childhood at Caer Idris and I, like you, read everything I could get my hands on. At the time, it was locked in my uncle's rooms. Passing strange that it was just lying around." Anje tapped his fingers on the parchment, frustration apparent on his face. "If I'd known, I would've looked for it when I visited Valterys."

Taryn was taken aback. "When did you go to my father?"

"Just after you and Rhoane left for the Narthvier and Carga's purification. I thought it was past time I rekindled my Dark Shanti."

"You did that for me, didn't you?" He could've been killed at Caer Idris, but he risked Valterys's wrath for her. Warmth spread from her heart to her pendant and through her veins, blooming into a well of gratitude. "Thank you."

"I would sacrifice myself a thousand times over for you, my darling."

"I hope you never have to. But, Uncle, there's another reason I need your strength." She told him of her travels to Gaarendahl, ending with her appearance at his door. She left out nothing and Anje listened without interruption as she spoke.

When she finished recounting the events, she said in a near whisper, "There's something else that you should know. It was Marissa who tried to kill Hayden at Ravenwood. When I confronted her about what she did to Rhoane, Ynyd

Eirathnacht sang to me of her betrayal. She tried to deny it, but I know it was her."

He rested his chin on steepled fingers, processing all that she'd told him. When finally he spoke, his voice sounded as tormented as she felt. "You should never have had to suffer this. Your sister will be punished for her crimes. As for your brother and father, they, too, will pay. We must tell your mother all that you've shared tonight and declare war on them immediately."

"No, Uncle, that is not the answer. If we go to war only because of what they did to me, then hundreds will die for my vanity. I cannot condone any action that will lead innocent men to their deaths. Furthermore, I told you this in confidence. You can't tell anyone.

"Lliandra is an empress first, a mother last. As for Marissa, I will deal with her when the time is right. What she did was inexcusable, but she can still be of use to us. She is, after all, Zakael's lover and spy. We now know exactly whose side she's on and can move to make Eliahnna the heir to the Light Throne."

He looked at her, surprised. "You are next in line for the throne."

"I don't want it. I could never rule Aelinae the way my sister would. Besides, I am also heir to the Obsidian and Weirren thrones—do I wear a crown for all three?"

"Perhaps that is what the gods have in store for you. Have you thought about that? You cannot hide from your destiny. The sooner you embrace it, the better. If it is your fate to wear the triple crown, you must be willing to accept it graciously."

"I don't think that's what the gods have in store for me. There's a reason Ohlin gave me the name Galendrin, and the Eleri call me *Darennsai*. One is the Keeper of the Stars; the other, Daughter of the Sky. I'm pretty sure they have a plan for me, even if they won't admit it. But enough of this. What else has happened in my absence?"

Her uncle took the hint and told her of Paderau business and then what was happening at the Crystal Palace. Her friends were well but missed her terribly. Ellie had recovered from her ordeal but refused to leave the palace. A stab of guilt twisted her gut as surely as would a savage blade. She'd been too focused on herself, with the belief she shouldn't burden them with her troubles. In a gentle voice, her uncle reminded her that just a word or two that she was well was all they needed.

He was right and no amount of clever excuses could deny it, but he hadn't told her the worst yet. "Rhoane stayed in Paderau for a night on his way to Talaith."

Taryn swallowed a lump in her throat and asked, "Was he okay?"

"He was as pale as you are, my dear, and he looked as if he could use a good meal, too. He was quiet, more than usual. I could sense in him a great discord." Her uncle looked away suddenly.

"What is it? If there's something I need to know, please tell me." She held his hand in hers, running her thumb over his soft skin.

"He stayed in your rooms. I hope you can forgive me, but it seemed very important to him, and I could not deny him this one courtesy." Anje's face was pained as he looked at her. "You aren't upset, are you?"

A small cry escaped her. "No, Uncle, you did the right thing. That means he still cares for me."

"Of course he does. What would make you think otherwise? It is his love for you that torments him. Do you know what it is to be broken when you are Eleri? He holds his shame in his soul and this splits him in two. Only he can heal the divide."

"That doesn't make it any easier to bear."

He pointed at her runes. "As long as you wear these bonds, never doubt. Rhoane is as committed in his love to you as ever he was or these would be unraveling. It's that love that will heal him in time. Have faith and the strength of patience to give him the time he needs."

Patience was not her best trait, but it wasn't as if she had any other choice.

Chapter 37

DUKE Anje's fireballs were getting fiercer, closer together. Taryn ducked to avoid one, tangling herself in a vine that trailed from the tree above her. It wasn't until she was upended, her silver hair hanging nearly to the ground, that she realized her uncle had set the vine on her. He chuckled smugly to himself, until Taryn grabbed him with a creeper. Then his smug smile turned upside down with the rest of him.

The vines gently lowered them to the ground, where they discussed her growing skill with Dark Shanti. Anje couldn't conceal how impressed he was with her abilities, nor could he disguise his disbelief at how quickly she learned each new element. Even so, Taryn was not immune to injury. More than once she attempted something before Anje thought her ready, with disastrous consequences.

Just that morning, she'd tried to re-create the fire and ice she made after her coronation. Instead of setting herself on fire, she'd demolished a wooden cart nearby. When she tried to bring water from the river to douse it, she flooded one of the storerooms. It was a difficult reminder that she was not all-powerful and her uncle's recriminations to learn slowly were to be heeded. Most of the time.

"You learn quickly, Taryn, but there is danger in having

great power. You could call forth all the gold in my coffers; however, your riches would be fleeting. You see, there is an attachment to things we have as individuals. If I take all of your gold, it will eventually wish to return to you, and I would suffer severe consequences for my theft."

"ShantiMari has an honesty policy?"

"In a sense. If you abuse it, you must be prepared to accept what the power gives back. There have been those throughout history who believe themselves exempt from such rules. They are the practitioners of the Black Arts. Men and women who corrupt their souls and twist their power to evil ends. Whoever controls your Shadow Assassin is a master in the Black Arts. It takes a great amount of ShantiMari to control another's soul."

"When I searched the assassin's thoughts, there was nothing. No memory, no thought, no pain or fear. It was like he didn't exist beyond hunting me."

"A Shadow Assassin is brought from the spirit world and not made of flesh, but Rhoane told me when he cut the assassin, he bled."

"What does that mean?"

"It could be the man who hunts you was barely alive when he was turned. I dare not try to understand the ways of Black Masters. Once you delve into the mysteries, your soul is lost for all time. Now," he said, changing the subject, "there are a few more lessons I have for this morning and then we'll go for a ride along the river. Ashanni misses you, and I have a pony for Gian that I think he'll enjoy. But first, see that bench over there? I want you to move it to here." He pointed in front of them.

The bench was made of solid concrete, granite possibly. "It's too heavy."

"Humor an old man."

Taryn focused her concentration on the bench, trying to

lift it using just her Dark Shanti. When that didn't work, she pulled in strands from Eleri and then Light. She struggled and fought against the bench. Sweat ran down her face, her neck muscles bulged with the effort.

"It's no use. It won't move," she said at last.

Anje twitched his finger and the bench jumped from where it had been to settle at their feet. "You see, Taryn, you were using your ShantiMari, yes, but incorrectly." A snap of his fingers and the bench returned to its place under the sargot tree. Anje explained how she needed to gather the energy around them to move the stone instead of relying on just her strength.

Taking a breath to center herself, she tried again. The bench stayed as solidly placed as ever. She cursed in frustration.

"You can practice this. It's good that you can't accomplish everything on your first try. Otherwise, you'll think you're invincible." He chuckled.

"I don't see how this is funny."

"My dear, if everything comes to you too easily, you will become complacent and sloppy. You must always strive for perfection when using ShantiMari or you might cause great harm to yourself or those around you, but many things take practice and seasons to perfect. I have one more thing to show you and then we'll be done for today." He took her hand and winked at her. "I think you'll like this."

One moment they were standing in the garden and the next, in Duke Anje's chambers. Taryn looked around, blinking. "How did you do that?"

"It's fairly simple once you understand the basics. It's a trick of the Dark and not many can accomplish it. For someone like Baehlon, this is impossible, but for a great mage like Myrddin, it would be as easy as lighting a torch." He returned them to the garden and Taryn gasped. He explained how to use shadows and darkness to propel them through space. Physics wasn't something Aelinae was concerned with, apparently. If she could get past that, the possibilities of what she could do would be limitless.

"If the Dark can manipulate space, and the Eleri time, it doesn't seem fair the Light can move a storm."

"Affecting the weather is only part of it, but your mother should be the one to explain it to you."

"Yeah, like that'll ever happen."

"I believe we've done all we can for today. Let's find your faerie and go for a ride." He put his arm around her shoulder and they walked together inside the palace, discussing their travel plans for the next morning. As much as she hated to leave the solace of her uncle's home and the glorious shower he'd installed just for her, they'd been in Paderau almost a fortnight and it was time. Time to face not just her future, but also her fears.

Taryn kept her voice neutral, but her excitement at returning to Talaith bubbled just under the surface. "You really shouldn't spoil him so much, Uncle."

Anje started to defend himself and laughed, a full-bellied chortle that captured Taryn in its gaiety. Everyone knew his spoiling wasn't so much about Gian's well-being as it was about making his niece happy.

Gian loved his pony, so much so he spent several bells grooming her until her hair shimmered in the sun. He plaited her mane and tail, adding colorful ribbons that twirled with each step. The transformation in Gian was startling. Gone was his shaggy, lice-ridden hair, replaced with shining copper curls cut short in the latest court fashion. With the abundance of food available, he gained enough weight that his bones didn't protrude at wicked angles. Lords Aomori and Tinsley had taken Gian as their pet project, dressing him in Hayden's childhood clothing and teaching him court manners.

They spoke in a kind of sign language they'd developed

with the faerie. Each time Taryn watched the three of them from afar, she was more and more grateful to the young lords who were kind to Gian, gentle with him, and coaxing his trust in small measures.

By the time they were to leave Paderau, the three had formed a bond Taryn didn't want broken. When she told the lords they would be accompanying them to Talaith, Gian's hands flew in a flurry of excitement, matched only by Aomori and Tinsley's elated replies.

The pace of their travels, with all the carts and carriages making the trip slow moving at best, chafed at Taryn. During the day, she distracted herself with lessons with the duke or riding beside Gian, learning his finger language. At night, she sat around the campfire, drinking with the other soldiers and listening to their songs and boastful tales, all the while missing her friends and betrothed.

By the time they crested the final hill before Talaith, Taryn was weary of the saddle and ready to stay in one place for more than a sennight. When she thought back, she realized with a shock she'd been either traveling or in a coma for much of the past six months. Her bed at the palace beckoned and she urged Nikosana forward.

The caravan wove its way through the city, with Taryn keeping an eye to the shadows. It wasn't the threat of the assassin that made her heart beat against her chest in rapid succession, but the thought of seeing Rhoane. At that moment, combatting the assassin would've been easier to bear. Gian's excited chatter in her mind didn't help matters. When they first saw the shining spires of the palace in the distance, he'd shuddered at the immensity of the city.

The smile on his face as they rode through the palace gates set Taryn at ease. Certainly his clan wouldn't recognize him now as he rode his pony proudly, looking every inch a lord. Gian gesticulated to the crowd awaiting their arrival in the courtyard. Taryn scanned the faces, smiling at her sisters and friends. Sabina bounced up and down, waving a scarf at her with Hayden standing tall beside her, inclining his head as she passed. Tessa ran alongside Nikosana, asking questions about the young boy who rode the pony.

She dismounted and kissed Tessa's hair, holding her tightly. "I've missed you. How have you been?"

"Bored." Her eyes drifted to Gian.

"If you must know, he is a woodland faerie I found on my adventures. He's going to live with us for some time. His name is Gian." Taryn called him over.

Tessa curtseyed low and introduced herself. Gian blushed crimson.

"He doesn't speak words, Tessa. Lords Aomori and Tinsley have taught him sign language. Perhaps you would like to learn as well?"

Tessa linked her arm in Gian's and Taryn nodded to him that it was okay. They were of a similar height, but Gian had none of the baby fat Tessa retained.

Her blonde curls bobbed as she nodded. "Of course, I will learn this language so that you and I can converse. You simply must tell me what it's like to be a faerie. I was in the Narthvier, you know, for several weeks last summer and I saw all manner of creatures that enchanted me." They strolled away and before Taryn knew it, she was enfolded in many sets of arms.

"We feared the worst when Prince Rhoane arrived without you. He told us you were in the Narthvier, but I sensed much darkness around you," Sabina said in a low voice.

"I'm home now. There is nothing to worry about," Taryn assured them. "It's been too long since I've seen your faces. Let me look at you all." She kissed each one and walked arm-in-arm with them toward the palace.

At the other end of the drive, the empress spoke with

Duke Anje. Protocol probably dictated she should greet her mother, but Taryn was in no mood. Nor was she ready to face Marissa, who stood close to Lliandra's side. A sneer slithered across her sister's lips when their eyes met, a hidden challenge in their lavender depths. Taryn met the glare, then returned her attention to her friends. A blast of her sister's ShantiMari pummeled against Taryn and she stumbled.

Hayden caught her. "You've been too long in the saddle, cousin. You've forgotten how to walk on solid ground."

"At least I have you to catch my fall," Taryn said, taking his hand in hers. A tightness to his smile upset her. When she turned to Sabina, the same constraint pinched her features. Something had happened between the pair, something upsetting enough to cause a divide. Tension rolled off them in waves, battering Taryn's fragile senses.

She scanned the area for Rhoane, not finding him among the crowd. Eliahnna, always a little too perceptive, said in her quiet voice, "Prince Rhoane is not here. I'm sure if he knew you were to return today, he would've come home."

"He's gone? Where?"

"No one knows. He left one morning and hasn't been heard from since."

"It must be something important. I'll see him when he returns." She kept her voice casual, but her knees weakened and she swayed against Hayden. Sabina gave her a sharp look.

"Too long in the saddle?"

"Sure, let's go with that," Taryn said without much enthusiasm. "I've been dreaming of my lovely bed for far too long. I could sleep for a week."

After settling Gian into his rooms a few floors below hers, she closed the door to her chamber and sighed with relief. She wanted nothing more than a few bells of rest before having to answer questions, explaining her absence. But first she braced herself for the onslaught of her maids.

They fussed over her while asking about her travels. When she avoided answering them, they took the hint. Taryn inspected Ellie's scar, relieved it wasn't as hideous as her nightmares had shown. A thin white crescent ran the length of her face from temple to chin, almost beautiful in its symmetry.

"I've heard you stay hidden away in my rooms. Is this true?" Taryn asked.

"I find my tasks are better completed here, Your Highness. The other girls enjoy the duties that take them outside and so I defer to them on these matters," Ellie answered.

"Yes, well, you can tell yourself that lie all you want, but you're hiding, Ellie. We talked about this before I left Celyn Eryri. Now that I'm home, I want to see you walk with your head held high. With pride in your step." She paused, thinking for a moment. "I have a friend I want you to meet. Until then, we'll talk of this no more. I've been on the road too long and have missed your wonderful baths. Once I'm rested, we'll resume our conversation."

Ellie's voice was tight, her curtsey stiff. "As you wish, Princess."

Taryn sank into the hot water, feeling her weariness slip away. She dipped below the surface and silently let her tears of disappointment flow. She'd longed to see her betrothed. His absence could only mean he had abandoned her. The runes on her hand still glowed with their bonds, but she was disconnected from him. It tore at her heart with a savagery that left her wanting to shriek to the heavens. Instead, she vowed to keep her true emotions hidden.

Her maids dressed her in a fine silk gown and then arranged a tiara in her curls, all the while trading off telling her what had happened in the palace since she'd been gone. It was the usual gossip and intrigues that came with court life.

She half-listened as she sat in her favorite chair awaiting

Gian, admiring the perfect stitches of her dress. Each had been placed with precision by Tarro's competent fingers, and she imagined the care he took in making the gown for her. They truly cared for her, Tarro and her maids. The realization stunned her in the solar plexus, robbing her of breath.

She blinked away fresh tears and took up her looking glass, passing it between her fingers with pent-up energy. On impulse, she whispered, "Show me Myrddin." It flared to life, showing the mage speaking quietly with Lliandra. "What are they saying?" The glass ball remained silent. Apparently, only Myrddin's glass could transmit sound. "Show me what is in Myrddin's ball," she commanded. The looking glass sparked and sputtered and then blinked out. Her heavy sigh frosted the glass.

"Show me any intruders besides my maids who have entered my rooms." It was a vast request, but she was curious how much the glass would show. Images of servants coming into her rooms to air out the closets or clean her gowns glowed in the ball. Once or twice Margaret Tan would take an outfit, bringing another in its place. Windows were opened and furniture moved, but otherwise there had been nothing to indicate danger.

"Show me whether Marissa entered my rooms," she whispered. The ball remained blank. That, at least, was good news. "Show me Prince Rhoane." The words were out before she could pull them back.

Rhoane's face glowed in the ball. A sob caught in her throat. His hair was short as if he were *sheanna* and she frowned. Rhoane would never cut his hair willingly. His pointed ears tipped forward, listening beyond what others could hear. Where he was, Taryn couldn't tell, but the focus of his eyes and set of his jaw told her he was not in danger. Yet, he wasn't relaxed, either. She sent him a silent wish wrapped in love for his safety and success in his endeavor.

She inspected the glass ball and said, "Never let Myrddin hear or see my actions." She didn't know if it would work, but figured what the hell, it was worth a shot. As an afterthought, she said, "Or anyone who views his great looking glass." Lights flashed within the ball and then suddenly stopped.

Gian entered the room, fidgeting with the hem of his silk tunic, not meeting the curious glances of her maids. Taryn patted the seat beside her. "Gian, these are my maids. This is Lorilee—you might remember her sister Mayla from Paderau." Gian nodded his head to her. "This is Saeko and over here is Ellie. They are very important to me, as are you. There is nothing you can't confide in them. They are beholden to me and have sworn to keep my secrets safe within their hearts."

Do they also have a life debt with you?

No, but do you see the pretty girl with the scar? She nearly lost her life for me.

Gian gaped at Ellie with a curious expression.

She explained to her maids that Gian spoke with his hands and she would like them to learn his language. When Gian objected, she gently told him it wasn't just a game he played with the young lords, but a great skill. He blushed slightly but nodded agreement.

"Why can't he speak?" Lorilee asked.

"He was tortured and has no tongue."

Ellie gasped, covering her face. Without provocation, Gian showed them the charred stump. "Who would do such a thing?" Ellie asked.

"Zakael."

Her maids stared at her with identical horrified expressions.

"My enemies are many. Some we know, others we do not. I need you all to be strong in the coming seasons. If you wish to stay in my service, I require you to begin weapons training and martial arts. I can't bear the thought of losing any of you, but I will understand if you wish to leave my employ."

Ellie trembled so violently Taryn feared she was having an attack. Gian sat with her, stroking her hair, mewing kind words she couldn't understand. Stuttering through her tears, Ellie said, "I'd like to stay."

Lorilee and Saeko readily agreed to the training and anything else she required. It did not warm her heart to demand it of them, but if she couldn't protect those she loved, she'd make damn sure they could protect themselves.

Chapter 38

FORTUNATELY for Taryn, the Crystal Palace always provided a new opportunity for entertainment. As far as the courtiers were concerned, Taryn's disappearance didn't warrant their time or attention. Her adventures were a momentary concern and then they moved on.

Gian became a curiosity for several days but because he refused to speak with anyone, his allure dimmed. He spent most of his time with either Tessa or Lord Aomori. If they were busy, Taryn often saw him with Eliahnna, tucked in a corner with a book. Wherever he went, he alerted her to his location, should she require his company.

Since returning to Talaith, she preferred solitude to the boisterous rooms of the palace, often begging off from invitations with her sisters and even Sabina. The princesses did their best to cheer her, but melancholy clung to her like a second skin. No matter how hard she tried to shake it off, it remained, growing stronger each day. She was sitting on the seawall, contemplating the dark skies and heavy clouds one afternoon, when Baehlon sat beside her.

"Looks like rain," she said.

"Aye, typical weather this time of year. It will be warm soon enough, to be sure," Baehlon offered and cleared his throat. "What happened with Gian? It isn't like the woodland folk to up and leave their home."

She rested her head on her knee and told him about Kaida leading her into Valterys's dungeons, where they found Gian close to death. Baehlon winced at her description of his torture, nodding when she said she'd tried to take him back to the vier, but Gian insisted he had to stay with her.

"A life debt for a faerie is serious, Taryn. I get the feeling it's more than just saving him from your father."

"He hasn't said why he owes me a life debt. When he's ready, he'll tell me." Tears stung her eyes and she looked away before he saw them. "Did Rhoane tell you what happened at Gaarendahl?"

"Aye. Nasty piece of work, that. You did right to take him to his family." Baehlon put his hand on her shoulder and she sagged into it. He moved closer, wrapping his big arm around her shoulders, holding her close.

"Is he lost to me, Baehlon?"

"He's in shadow, it's true, but you've naught to worry about where his heart is concerned."

"I've been in Talaith several days and he hasn't returned. Surely he knows I'm here." Taryn sniffed, wiping her nose on her sleeve.

"I doubt that. He's keeping a low profile, working undercover right now. He won't be speaking with anyone from the palace, lest he is found out," Baehlon said.

"What's he doing?"

"Nothing you need to know about. Not yet, at least. In truth, I don't know all that he's up to. Just a bit of information here and there to let me know he's alive. This is what Rhoane does. It's what makes him excellent at ferreting out what needs to be known."

More than likely it involved her. If Baehlon didn't want to share information, she'd not pester him, but it upset her Rhoane would send word to Baehlon and not her. She had a right to know he was well. But then, she hadn't sent word to him while on her travels.

"Did Iselt come to Talaith?" She changed the topic to something benign. She'd hoped the blacksmith would, but he was an interesting man and not easily swayed.

"He did. Set himself up with a smithy and everything."

"Oh, good. Will you take me there tomorrow? I'd like to see how he's getting on."

Baehlon fidgeted and she glanced up at his broad features. His scowl reached the tip of his chin. "He's not in Talaith at the moment."

"Where is he?"

"Off on some bloody fool's errand your prince set him upon."

Taryn straightened and faced the knight. "He what? How did Rhoane know Iselt was in Talaith? What exactly has been going on since I've been gone? Rhoane disappears, now you tell me Iselt is gone, Hayden and Sabina are barely speaking to each other. Next thing you'll tell me is you and Faelara—" She stopped herself, a blush creeping across her cheeks.

"Yes? Faelara and I have what?"

"Oh, shut it. You love each other, but are too stubborn to admit it." At his shocked expression, she said, "Please. The entire court knows about the death of your wife and son. As tragic as that was, it happened twelve seasons ago. You loved Faelara before their deaths. There is no dishonor in owning up to it now. No one cares, Baehlon. Trust me. Just tell her you love her and be done with all the foolishness."

"Is that a command, Your Highness?" Amusement and anger shaped his words.

"Does it need to be? You know I'll do it, so don't go there unless you're ready to pay the fee, my friend."

"That doesn't make sense."

"Whatever. So, tell me where Iselt is and I'll let you off

the hook for now." She wagged a finger close to his nose. "Only for now. I'll expect some courting before summer's end. Got it?"

"If you say so. As for Iselt, he's on a pleasure ship spying for us."

Taryn doubled over with laughter, holding her sides. "Are you kidding me? Iselt? On a ship? How the bloody hell did Rhoane convince him to do that?"

"He told the man it would help you."

She sobered immediately. "That was a lie. Rhoane used me to manipulate him?"

"Don't look at it like that. Rhoane needed someone he could trust and since you have some sort of oath from the man, who better? Iselt isn't known in Talaith, he can handle himself, and besides, his business was crap. He set himself up in one of the poorer districts amid the filth and death. It was a good opportunity for him. I believe Rhoane promised him a job at the palace upon his return."

Her eyes narrowed as she thought of all the complications and implications of Iselt working at the palace, finally determining it didn't matter. Either he would be a part of Darius's life or he wouldn't. It was up to Iselt, not her, to make that happen. "Do you think he's in any danger on the ship?"

"Less so than in the cesspool he was living here."

She didn't like it, but Iselt was a grown man. He could've said no if he didn't want to go. She snuggled into Baehlon, replacing his arm around her shoulders and stared out to sea, trying to pinpoint where the blacksmith might be.

Baehlon stayed with her, keeping silent company until the air became thick with moisture and lightning flashed in the sky. Reluctantly, Taryn rose, calling Kaida from the orchards where she'd been hunting.

"Rhoane will be back for your party. I know what is in his

heart and whatever troubles him, isn't because of you."

She nodded mutely, not trusting herself to speak. Of course, what troubled Rhoane was because of her. She'd failed him too many times to count.

The heavy door closed behind them just as the clouds opened up, unleashing a torrent on the palace grounds. "That was good timing." Baehlon released his hold on her shoulder and turned her to face him. "I pledged before the court to lay down my life for you, and I would without hesitation, but I can't sit here and watch you mourn. For that is what you're doing, whether you're willing to admit it or not. Spend time with your sisters and friends. Go riding on Nikosana. Be the woman I met all those moonturns ago. She had fire. She wouldn't mope around all day, worried about a man. She kicked arse and to be honest, I miss her."

Taryn stared at him. Not only was that the longest speech she'd ever heard him give, it was full of truths she didn't want to admit, let alone hear. "You dare?"

Baehlon's laughter echoed through the crowded room. Many faces lifted, eyes narrowed, lips pursed, but it didn't deter the knight. He continued chuckling up the wide staircase until they reached her floor. "Aye, lass," he finally wheezed, "I do. You're as bad as he was when he returned. Both of you need a good arse whipping, is what I think." His face sobered and he took her chin between thick fingers. "Remember who you are, Taryn. Not the Eirielle, not the *Darennsai*. Who is Taryn ap Galendrin the woman? Remember her."

Tears burned her eyes. Dammit, but he was right. She reached up to kiss his cheek, breathing in his spiced scent. Like cinnamon, sweet with a little burn. "I love you, Baehlon."

"And I you, lass."

When Taryn returned to her rooms, Darius was waiting for her. "Your Highness, I have a message from the empress. She wishes to dine alone with you tonight."

"Darius, you're a soldier now—you shouldn't be made to carry messages."

"Begging your pardon, the pages were all busy and I volunteered."

Suddenly Taryn understood. His missive had nothing to do with her. "Thank you, Darius. Please, have some tea and cakes while I get ready."

Ellie jumped to help, but Taryn ordered her to stay with Darius. Her other two maids rolled their eyes at Taryn's obviousness, but she ignored them. If Darius went to the trouble of finding a reason to enter her rooms, he at least should be rewarded.

"Yes, Your Highness," Ellie said with a shy smile. Kaida just lolled her tongue at all of them. What was romance to a grierbas?

Taryn stood alone in her mother's sitting room, fighting her nerves. Each time she'd been summoned to the lavish suite, it ended badly. Lliandra entered amidst a flurry of feathers and ruffles. Jewels sparkled at her throat and wrists, more than Taryn had ever seen her wear at one time. She kissed Taryn on both cheeks before directing her to the dining room. When they were seated, their plates filled, Lliandra said, "You've been home several days and yet you do not come to see me. Have I upset you?"

Taryn almost choked on her food. "I sent several messages requesting a visit. Didn't you get them?"

Lliandra frowned. "Apparently not. Never mind, we are here now. Tell me what happened with your father." While they ate, Taryn told her mother a highly edited account of her visit with Valterys. Lliandra listened intently, asking questions as Taryn spoke. "And this Gian, how did you come to bring him to my palace?"

"He was imprisoned in Valterys's dungeon and I rescued him. Because of his deformity, he wished to stay with me rather than return to the Narthvier. If his presence upsets you, we can stay at Paderau."

"Of course not. You will stay here with your woodland rat. I do not want him crawling around unsupervised, mind you." Lliandra stabbed at a piece of meat as if to underscore her irritation.

"I don't understand why you dislike him. He's a good man and very trustworthy."

Lliandra sniffed. "Until I am certain he is not a spy for King Stephan or Valterys, I want him leashed. Do you understand?"

"He isn't a spy, Mother, but I'll keep him close to me if that is your wish."

"I'm glad we could settle that. There is one other matter that concerns me. Your sister says you haven't been to see her since your return." Lliandra met Taryn's stare with an even gaze. "Why have you been avoiding Marissa?"

Taryn's wine burned clear to her stomach. "She told you I'm avoiding her?" She was more hurt than shocked to hear concern for her sister in her mother's voice. "Did she by any chance mention what happened at Gaarendahl?" Taryn asked, keeping her voice level.

"No. In fact, she was most insistent she did not want to discuss anything that occurred there. Would you like to enlighten me?" Lliandra's voice was like ice.

"Not really. I will tell you, though, that Marissa is giving Valterys far more information than you know. And, she was responsible for nearly killing Hayden at Ravenwood."

"She mentioned you would tell me this. She claims to be innocent of the attack. What is your proof?"

Taryn stared at her mother. "Nothing except what I saw and what Ohlin's sword told me. I have a feeling that won't be enough for you."

"Until you have clear proof, I wish to hear no more of this

slander against your sister. You will go to her and apologize for your behavior."

"I will do no such thing. You know, when you first told me who I was, I thought finally I'd have a mother who would love me. Someone I could look up to. I've done everything you asked—I've kept your secrets, put up with your tantrums and whims—but it was all for nothing. All I've ever been to you is," she paused, trying to find the right word, "a weapon."

"Yes, that's what I am to you, Mother. An incredibly powerful weapon to use against your enemies. But you've forgotten something. Underneath all the titles, the power, the Glamour—I'm just a girl. A scared and vulnerable girl who needs her mother to guide and nurture her. I see now that you're incapable of being the mother I've always dreamt of having. You're too selfish. Maybe you deserve to have Marissa use you and manipulate you as she does."

"Watch your words, daughter. I am still the empress here. You will respect that. Your sister does not manipulate me. No one does." Lliandra held her hands flat on the table, vibrations from her ShantiMari rattling the china. The mask she carefully constructed cracked at the edges.

"And you forget I am *Darennsai*. You will respect me. Leave me out of your intrigues, Mother. I don't play games with people's lives." She curtseyed low before saying, "I hope you will come to see that I have only ever had your best interests at heart. I would give my life to protect you and all that the Lady of Light stands for. I don't want your crown, if that's what you're thinking. I only want what's best for Aelinae. Good night, Mother."

"You have not been dismissed." Lliandra stood to block Taryn's path and the two women glared at each other in a stalemate. Lliandra's power swirled with a constrained vengeance, slipping around Taryn's body.

She waited until her mother's Mari wrapped her fully

and a look of triumph clouded her mother's eyes. The blue threads tightened about her, clammy and smelling of rot. Taryn blew gently on the strands and they crumpled into blackened snarls and fell to the floor.

Lliandra gasped in horror at the sight of her power, visible and defeated at her feet. "How?" She choked. "How is this possible?"

"You told me yourself, I am the Eirielle. Within me is the trinity of power, but that's not all I possess. The phantom touched my soul with his Black ShantiMari. Perhaps if you were young and robust, your skills would be enough to overpower me, but your fade weakens you, Mother."

She scooped up the pile of ash and blew it into the air, where it became glittering motes of dust. "You really should control your anger. It isn't becoming for an empress to be so disrespectful of her gifts." With that, she pivoted on her heel and strode across the sitting room. When she reached the wall of crystal, she stopped.

Lliandra stood in the doorway of the dining room, eyes wide with disbelief.

"Never again use your ShantiMari against me. Are we agreed?" Lliandra gave the slightest of nods and Taryn swept from the rooms, her legs trembling beneath her full skirt.

Her mother also had highly underestimated her.

Chapter 39

THE cavern was the same as when Taryn first entered through the portal. Time didn't affect the crystals or sparkling expanse of water. She meandered through the forest of crystals, lost in thought. At the place where she and Brandt had fallen through the void, desperation tugged at her. Kaldaar dwelled beyond the jagged rock wall, between the worlds where he yearned for his freedom. She continued past the wall, careful not to touch it.

At the lake's edge, she slipped off her boots, delighting in the warm water soothing her feet. The same crystals she'd been enamored of when Brandt opened her eyes to the new world glittered with powerful ShantiMari. All around her, multi-hued threads laced between the rocks and walls. She wondered if the power was what she'd felt on that first day. A lifetime ago, but in truth, it had been only one season.

Standing on the spot where Brandt died, she relived the pain of that moment. He'd not visited her in too long and she missed him. She sat on the ground with Ynyd Eirathnacht resting on her lap, while a season's worth of sadness fell around her. By turns, she recounted the twists her life had taken since her first steps in the cavern.

Some memories brought smiles while others, tears. She'd fled her mother's palace after their argument to find solitude, but also she sought answers. No, she'd come to remember who she was.

"The only problem with running away is, no matter where you run, there you are." Nadra stood beside the water's edge, her gown floating in a halo, stars blinking beneath her skin.

"I didn't see you arrive," Taryn said, rising to stand before the goddess.

"No, I do not suppose you did." Nadra held out her arms and wrapped Taryn in a warm embrace. "You were far away in your thoughts."

"Everything's a mess. I was hoping Grandfather would be here to help me sort through some things."

"He is always with you, young Taryn." Nadra smiled. "You only have to ask."

"I thought he'd gone for good."

Brandt materialized and she stifled a cry. "I never left you. I kept my distance so that you could discover some truths on your own. You needed a chance to grow and learn without my interference."

"But you've always been there to guide me. I feel so lost. I've missed you so much." When he put his arms around her, he was solid. She inhaled his scent of aftershave and tobacco, feeling at once safe.

"And I you, my beautiful Taryn. You've done remarkably well considering all you've had to endure." He gave her a sad little smile.

"I don't know what I'm doing anymore."

Nadra floated nearer, reaching out to touch her cheek. Taryn leaned into the light of Nadra's caress. "Life is rather complicated for you right now. Is there anything you need from us?"

Taryn looked at her, surprised. "Are you allowed to help?"

"We can advise, yes."

"Well, since you asked," Taryn started. "Do you know who is behind the Shadow Assassin?"

"I assure you, if I did, I would break all covenants and tell you straightaway." Brandt glanced at Nadra. "I raised her as my own—certainly that counts for something."

Nadra gave him a disapproving look. "We do not know who controls the shadow soul. Whoever it is, they are very strong in the Black Arts to conceal themselves from us."

"What are you saying? You don't know everything that happens?" Taryn asked, stunned.

"No, darling. When we created this world, we decided it would be best to stay out of your affairs as much as possible. The best I can tell you is that we have an idea of what might happen," Nadra explained.

"I can't believe this. I mean, you're a goddess. If anyone would know what the future holds, it would be you."

"You must understand. Everyone has free will. The choices you make, they are yours alone. It would be irresponsible for me to predict the outcome of every single event. Think of it this way—for every decision someone makes, there are multiple choices. Now add to that the response of those affected by the decision. Compound this by how many living beings are on Aelinae. Why is it you think I should control every one of those choices and responses?" Nadra asked.

"You shouldn't. It's just…I guess I've always assumed you know what's going to happen. Is that why Daknys was so cryptic with me? Because she doesn't know either?"

"No one knows. It is for you to make your own future," Brandt said softly.

"Good one, Baba. You and I both know that's not true. My future was decided the moment I set foot in this cavern."

"No, dear one, it wasn't. Would you return to Earth?" Nadra asked. "Because if you choose that path, the doorway works both ways."

Taryn gawked, openmouthed, at the goddess. "But Brandt made me promise. He said I could never go back."

"I was frightened and doing what I thought was best for your safety." He took her hand and led her to the unimposing wall. "The words you speak matter, my darling. Use intention. Know where it is you want to travel and command the void to do your bidding."

Unease traveled along her spine. "But isn't Kaldaar in there?"

"Kaldaar is elsewhere. What you sense in the void is his anguish," Nadra explained.

Taryn frowned, not quite understanding.

"Would you like to return to London?" Brandt pressed his fingers against the rocky surface and mumbled the words he'd said in the cellar of the pub. An orange glow emanated from him to the wall, creating a doorway.

"No. Stop, Baba." Taryn removed his hand from the stone. "Not yet. Someday, maybe, but there is too much left unfinished here." Just having the option to return relieved a chunk of her stress.

"You've chosen wisely, child. There is much more to Aelinae than the three kingdoms you've visited. For you to bring balance to this world, you must discover the strengths and weaknesses within not only yourself, but all of the seven kingdoms as well."

Taryn returned to the shore and sat heavily on the sand, sifting it through her fingers. "I don't think I can do that while at the Crystal Palace, but Mother..." Taryn sighed. "Let's just say, she wouldn't support an extended trip unless I was her trained monkey and reported everything to her."

Taryn glanced at Brandt. "She's a peach, that one. I've done everything she's asked and still she doesn't love me. It kind of sucks."

Nadra and Brandt settled on the sand near her. "Dearest,

your mother loves you very much. There is something you must understand about Lliandra," Nadra explained. "She was born to be an empress. It is all she knows. She had children as was her duty, but mothering does not come naturally to her."

"Yeah, no kidding. She ignores me and then expects me to bow and scrape to Marissa, who treats her terribly. My sister is evil. Beyond evil." Fresh rage welled inside her with an image of her smirking face beneath Rhoane's. She shoved the image to the darkest, blackest region of her mind.

"Lliandra's bond with Marissa is complex and one I do not wish to examine too closely. The only advice I can offer is that perhaps you ask too much of your mother. She cannot give you what she doesn't realize is missing in your life. If a mother's love is what you crave, you have but to look elsewhere and you will see you've had it all along," Brandt said.

His energy embraced her as his hand stroked her hair.

"You have surpassed all that I'd dreamed of for you."

"I'm glad you never told me who I was. I came here without any pretense or ego. I've learned as I grew. I think I'm better for it."

A tendril of Nadra's light touched Taryn's cheek. "Your heart is great and will be tested yet again. When you think there is no hope, remember there is no Light without Dark and no darkness without light." She gathered them in an embrace, lifting them above the cavern until Taryn looked down on the clear waters of the lake far below. Nadra's light filled her soul. "Farewell, daughter."

Brandt held her face close to his before the two of them drifted away, becoming nothing but a spark in the blackness beyond and then blinked out.

She lowered to the sand, sitting for a long time by the edge of the lake, letting their words flow over her until she felt weighed down by all the thoughts and emotions that roiled through her. On impulse, she stripped off her clothes and ran naked into the water. She dove beneath the surface, frightening the tiny creatures that dwelled there. Her long hair glowed with a pale iridescence and she felt a giddy weightlessness. The Glamour under her skin shimmered in every color of the rainbow as she stretched her limbs, swimming around the lake.

When she tired, she crawled on an island and made a fire with her ShantiMari. Her naked skin glistened in the firelight. She felt primal, one with the cavern and all the elements within it. Her hair fell around her in a damp mess, spreading on the soft sand when she lay back. With a fingertip, she traced the scar under her breast. When the poison inside her burned, she welcomed the pain as a reminder she was not omnipotent. The jagged welt was a caution to her frailty and humanity.

She pressed harder, to the core of her being where the phantom's stain coiled and hissed. Daknys had once told her to embrace the gift. To nurture it. Taryn closed her eyes and coaxed the stain to open. She imagined her favorite flower in Paderau's garden, a night blooming rose. Delicate petals of the purest white unfurled to reveal not what the phantom had given her, but what he'd known was inside of her all along and unlocked.

Black ShantiMari.

Taryn shrieked and slammed both hands over her scar. She visualized the rose, still beautiful, but encased in a diamond shell, impenetrable. Fresh sobs wracked her body and she shook against the sand. She didn't possess just the trinity, but all four powers. What did that mean for Aelinae? What did that mean for her?

Rhoane.

Did he know? Anger surged through the anguish. If any of them knew and didn't tell her, there would be hell to pay.

Her fingers dug into the sand as her breath blew out in huffs, making a little divot beneath her lips.

Embrace the phantom's gift. Nurture it.

Daknys knew. All of the gods must know. *Learn the words.* Taryn traced symbols in the sand with her fingertips. "Embrace the phantom's gift—yeah, right," she whispered to the silent cavern. "Have you seen what a spaz I am with Dark Shanti? Baby steps, people."

Flames from her fire cast shadows across her pale skin, its warmth lulling her to dream. She fell asleep, safe in the knowledge that the cavern would protect her. That night, she dreamt of flying in her dragon form, a great silver beast as weightless in the air as she'd been in the water.

She soared high above the mountains and out across the plains. A flutter of anxiety touched her dragon mind when she circled above the Temple of Ardyn. In its depths, she saw where Rykoto dwelled. He shrank from her when she roared a great flame into the air. She drifted above the Narthvier, her eyes drawn to the wall of ShantiMari. Her dragon heart raced as she neared it and for a moment the urge to break through overwhelmed her.

With great effort, she denied the impulse, gliding over the Weirren. She inclined her head to the great tree and sped over the treetops. In the desert far to the east, she saw the colorful tents and buildings of the horse people and felt a longing to visit their lands.

Beyond, the sea glittered in the moonlight like jewels from a king's treasure. Pirate ships anchored in hidden coves waited to attack unsuspecting travelers. A familiar presence brushed against her mind as she dipped her wing into the cold water. Another dragon joined her and flew beside her over the islands of Sabina's people.

To the south, on the farthest edge of Aelinae, several islands hovered above larger landmasses. The Sitari women danced naked to the thumping of drums, their blue-skinned bodies glistening under the full moon. On a smaller island, high above the others, the elder Sitari cast their ShantiMari like a net over the islands. The pre-mating ritual was a tradition dating back to before the Great War. Taryn's dragon heart beat in time to the drums.

The other dragon led her farther to the west, across an archipelago with one large island in the center. The great fires of Haversham burned in their caves where Artagh crafted weapons for the gods. She joined her sword in song, a bittersweet melody of loss and love. That her sword missed the ore in the mountains amused Taryn's dragon mind.

They banked west and flew up the coast, along the shore over Caer Danuri, the ancestral home of Taryn's friend Lord Aomori. When they neared Valterys's castle, Taryn balked and turned to the east, but the other dragon flew on, and Taryn followed.

They ghosted over Caer Idris, dark and silent in the night sky. Taryn's dragon eyes saw into the castle to where Valterys stood facing Zakael, as if in argument. If she wished, she could hear them, but she turned away, toward the mountains.

She glided over the tips of the highest peaks and into the valleys. She followed rivers between steep crags to where they emptied into mountain lakes. Finally, she saw the cavern deep within Mount Nadrene, and she longed to once more be among her family. The other dragon banked away from the cavern, his moss-colored scales shining in the moonlight.

Awaken, Taryn. Awaken and remember.

The cavern was still when Taryn opened her eyes. She lay naked and alone on the island, her mind grasping, trying to recall the dream she'd had. Fragments drifted through her thoughts but never settled enough that she could recall its entirety. Having no idea what time of day it was or how long she'd been away, she dressed with a sense of purpose and hurried through the tunnels.

As she stood on the cliff's edge, preparing to transform in the predawn light, something in the dirt stopped her breath. Like a jewel washed upon the shore, a small moss-green scale glittered against the sand.

Chapter 40

OVER the next several days, with Baehlon's urging, Taryn spent much of her time in clandestine meetings. From her friends, she learned all they knew of the hunt for the Shadow Assassin. Taryn was more than a little surprised they'd been conducting their own investigation of not only him, but what was happening between the East and the rest of Aelinae. They all had their own spies, who reported on everything from pirate raids in the Summer Seas to the placement of Valterys's army at Lliandra's borders.

Taryn knew of Iselt being aboard one of Adesh's ships, but Denzil's assistance surprised her. He and Baehlon put up a splendid performance of brotherly rivalry. She'd even believed they hated each other.

Since her trip to the cavern, she worked hard each day, training with the soldiers. The physical exertion kept her focus away from Rhoane's absence, and the time she spent with her sisters helped lift her mood. A dark depression had taken hold somewhere on the road from Caer Idris and she struggled to put herself back into good spirits. The only mar to her happiness was Sabina and Hayden's continued quarrel. Neither would tell her why they were at odds, each believing it to be the other's fault and not wanting to involve her in something trivial.

They remained civil to each other, but Hayden did not share Sabina's bed and when they met in Faelara's or Taryn's apartments for a meeting, they sat at opposite sides of the room. One early summer day, they met in her rooms to discuss a foray into the city to meet with Adesh. She'd not been to the docks or the marketplace since her return and she longed to visit both.

"I don't think you should go, Taryn," Hayden argued. "You are too easily recognized and thus far, we've managed to keep our activities from your mother."

"If Sabina and I go together, we're simply shopping. Surely no one can suspect us of wicked deeds then? We'll bring Eliahnna and Tessa. I promised my little sister she could meet Sulein. It'll be perfect."

"I don't like it." Hayden crossed his arms over his chest, his brows furrowed deep enough to be worrisome.

"Yes, well, it's a good thing for us you don't have the final say in what we do with our time," Sabina retorted hotly. Hayden's glare chilled the warm room.

"She's right. You're not the boss of me, so there." Taryn stuck her tongue out at Hayden.

"Nice, cousin. Very mature."

"Oh, and your behavior is?"

His cheeks reddened with the reprimand, but he kept silent.

"So anyway, I've asked Tarro to take me to see Armando. I'm pretty sure he thinks I want to visit in a professional way, which is just eww since he was Marissa's favorite whore, and I'm not dissuading him. We agreed I needed to know if Armando has information and this was the only way to see him. At least with Tarro there, it won't be totally awkward. Or it might. I don't know."

"You're babbling, dear sister." Eliahnna placed a hand over Taryn's. "He's just a man who uses his body for pleasure.

He won't harm you."

"Says the pretty girl who will have tons of lovers someday."

Eliahnna winked. "Or perhaps not."

Taryn bit her cheek to keep from giving away her sister's secret. She and Eoghan continued to correspond despite Taryn's warnings to the both of them. "Or perhaps not," she teased.

After the meeting had concluded, Taryn asked Hayden and Sabina to stay. Each looked at her as if she'd bitten them. "Oh for fuck's sake, stop acting like idiots. What happened? One day you're all swoony in love, the next you hate each other."

"We don't hate each other," Sabina insisted. "I love Hayden with all my heart, but he's being rather stubborn about something important to me."

"Because it's archaic!" Hayden breathed in and out with a heavy sigh. "I asked Sabina to marry me."

"You did? Finally! But why are you fighting?"

"Because she denied me."

"I did no such thing. I said I could not marry you until you ask my father for my hand."

"Um, okay, so besides that being a little old-fashioned, it's kind of sweet. What's the big deal?"

"Her father is the king of the Summerlands. You do not simply walk up to the man and ask permission. There is tradition to uphold. A ceremony." Hayden glanced away, his gaze settling on Gian, who sat silently in the corner stroking Kaida's fur. A blush covered Hayden's cheeks and he mumbled an apology to the faerie.

"Can someone explain what's going on? What ceremony? Why is Hayden freaked out?"

"The ceremony involves piercing a certain *intimate* part of the male body as well as being tattooed."

The blush darkened and Hayden refused to meet her eyes.

Taryn suddenly understood and broke out in laughter. "I'm so sorry," she hiccuped between fits. "That's a terrible thing to do to a man! But Hayden, surely you love Sabina enough to endure anything for her?"

"That's what I've been telling him! He won't listen. He says it's barbaric, which means my people are barbaric. He doesn't think I'm good enough for him."

Taryn's laughter subsided and she struggled to keep a straight face. Each time she looked at Hayden, his demeanor slipped even further into despair. "We'll figure something out. For now, can you two please go back to loving each other? I need to see a happy couple. Desperately." She batted her lashes at them with her best pout.

"We will, as long as you promise not to make that face ever again. You look horrendous."

"Thanks, Sabina. You're a real confidence booster."

After they left, Taryn and Gian spoke at length about their problem, coming no closer to a solution. The tattoos she understood, but the piercing? Why would anyone in their right mind do that to their body?

The next morning, she was almost finished with her yogic stretches when Ebus entered her rooms, hidden beneath a swath of shadows. She lay on her stomach and arched her torso up with a soothing stretch. Kaida sniffed the air and padded to where Ebus stood. Her whine earned a shush from the empty air.

"It isn't nice to sneak into my rooms, you know." Taryn stretched into another position, twisting her body first to the right, and then left. She'd never been a fan of yoga, but her constant riding and training made her muscles tense and cramp. Even her martial arts couldn't untie the knots that formed in her neck and back. Yoga did.

It also helped her calm her mind and regain her focus, something training used to do, but had become too much of a duty and was no longer enjoyable. She struggled to regain the joy she once felt each time she held Ynyd Eirathnacht.

Ebus moved and Taryn scanned the room for his dark outline. Finding it, she snapped a thread of ShantiMari against his ankle.

"Blast it, woman!" His chuckle belied his anger. The shadows faded from him and he shook out his hair. "I'd like to know how you do that."

"You have your secrets. I have mine." She stood, patting a cloth against her heated skin. "What brings you here today?"

"I've just returned from Caer Idris, where I've been for many moonturns." At her look of surprise, he added, "Aye, I was there when you stole away with the faerie boy. As well as long after. Your father was not pleased when Zakael returned without you. His rage is unequaled. No lady should ever have to see it. Your brother's punishment will not soon be forgotten, I'm afraid. As for you, Valterys is most keen for you to meet his god."

"I don't have any plans of going near Rykoto. Not yet, anyway." Taryn almost felt bad for her half-brother. She witnessed firsthand her father's punishments, something she wouldn't be too soon to forget.

Gian entered the room, startling them. He signed to Taryn, asking after her visitor and if he should return later.

"Stay, Gian. This is Ebus, a dear friend of mine and Prince Rhoane's. Ebus, this is Gian. He's the faerie I stole from my father." Gian grinned at her and bowed to the spy. A knock at the door meant the rest of the group would be joining them. "We're meeting to discuss Lliandra's taxes. Would you like to stay, Ebus?"

He pulled his shadows tight and whispered, "If you don't mind, I should like to observe only."

Gian's eyes widened and he looked from the empty air to Taryn. "I'll teach you someday. For now, say nothing of

Ebus." The faerie nodded and took a seat on the couch. Kaida sat beside him and his hand went to her soft fur.

The others trickled in and chatted together until everyone sat in Taryn's spacious room, drinking and eating. Listening to her friends and watching them deftly handle difficult situations made her realize she'd done to them what others had done to her—she underestimated them. Not only were they able to gather information without leaving palace grounds, they had a knowledge of court politics, which allowed them to subvert attacks.

That morning, she learned the courtiers only tired of Taryn's ordeals because Eliahnna or Tinsley would start another rumor, one more titillating than that of the Eirielle, something they confessed wasn't easy to do as Taryn was still the court's favorite topic.

When she and Baehlon left the meeting for their sword training, a weight had been lifted. For her sisters and friends to go to such extremes to protect her was humbling and she was grateful for them.

"Rhoane should be made aware of what we've discussed."

Baehlon grumbled that he'd not heard from the prince in too long.

"He is well, my friend," Taryn told Baehlon. "Of that, I am certain."

"You've been in contact with him?"

"Not exactly." She grinned. "I just know."

"It's good to see you smile again." He placed his arm around her, squeezing the breath from her lungs. "You should do that more often."

Taryn trained hard for close to three bells. She worked with the soldiers using swords and martial arts, complimenting them on their increased skill. Darius in particular showed great promise. He'd continued his training while she was gone; as a result, his body became leaner, more muscular.

Taryn wasn't the only one to notice, either. She often caught Ellie scurrying past the yard with a basket in hand.

Afterward, she relaxed with a hot bath and her daily dose of gossip from the maids. The court was in a tizzy because Lord Valen had proposed to Princess Sabina and she accepted. Taryn smiled to herself and sank beneath the bubbles, releasing a giggle. Poor Hayden.

Tarro arrived at the appointed time to escort her to Nena's house. Nerves fluttered in her belly and she worried over her attire, but Tarro assured her it was fine. The stiffness in his bow and curtness of his replies told Taryn he was annoyed with her. She hated deceiving him but couldn't afford for the court to know her real reason for visiting Armando.

The walk to Nena's hung heavy with silence; Tarro's reticence ate at Taryn. When he knocked on the back door, her confidence faltered.

As if he sensed it, Tarro reassured her, saying, "He's a man, like every other. There is no need to be anxious."

But he was wrong. Armando wasn't a man like any she knew. He was a whore, a very good one from what she'd been told. Taryn had little experience with men and yet was somehow expected to extract information from him. It was a doomed experiment, but she'd gone along with it to mollify her friends.

A small window opened and two dark eyes glared at them. A moment later, the door opened and Tarro greeted the doorman by name. Taryn smiled shyly, but he'd already lost interest in them and turned to chat with a young boy who wore what looked like women's pantaloons and nothing else. The pang of insecurity spread from her gut to her chest the farther up the back stairs they climbed. By the time they reached Armando's door, Taryn was shaking.

"Really, Princess. There is no need to be worried. Armando is the best."

"You know, it doesn't help to have his lover trying to make me feel better. Besides, I didn't come here for that."

Tarro's mouth gaped the same instant the door opened and quite possibly the most gorgeous man Taryn had ever seen stood before her. He wore loose breeches and a matching robe opened to reveal burnished skin so smooth it looked like toffee. He could've been wearing a clown suit and fruit basket on his head and still would've been perfect.

"Tarro." Armando's Summerlands drawl made love to the name and for one tiny moment, Taryn was jealous of her tailor. "Is this the woman you told me about?" Armando's gaze went to Taryn, surveying her from head to toe, every glance an invitation and lust-filled promise.

"I-I-I, uh, I'm Taryn." She thrust out her hand, forgetting the Aelans didn't shake hands upon meeting. Armando smiled and she swooned a little before snatching her hand behind her body. "Yes. I'm Princess Taryn and I wanted to meet you." Reminding herself who she was helped, but not much.

"Come in, please." He stepped aside, and Tarro turned to leave.

"Stay, Tarro," Taryn pleaded.

"I'm sorry, Princess, but I keep my love life separate from my work. I thought you understood this."

"I do. It's just…Tarro, get in here and close the door." A wall of ShantiMari rose around them and she took a steadying breath. "I might have given you the wrong impression. I didn't come here for, um, your skills. I need information."

Armando cut Tarro a glare and Taryn immediately apologized. "Please don't be angry with Tarro. He didn't know my reasons for coming to see you, and I'm sure if he did, we wouldn't be standing here right now."

Armando spun away and grabbed for the door, but Taryn blocked him with her power. "You will release me at once,

Your Highness." An evil glint hid in his dark brown eyes. "I don't know what it is with your family, but I am not a dog to be kicked around."

"I know you're not and I'm sorry. My mother and sister, they're not nice people, but I am. Really."

"You have an odd way of showing it."

"My love, please. The princess has only ever been kind to me. Won't you at least hear her out?" Tarro stroked Armando's arms, soothing him until the whore nodded.

"Thank you." Taryn breathed. "My mother and sister are why I'm here. They are taxing your people illegally and I fear are planning something horrific. If you have any knowledge you can share, I will forever be in your debt."

Armando shook his head and dark curls covered his handsome face. "I haven't seen the crown princess since just before the court left for Celyn Eryri. I'm afraid we parted on unfriendly terms. As for the empress, Nena is her favorite. I have never had the honor." The way he said the last word made it sound like bedding Lliandra was anything but.

"If you do hear anything, will you tell Tarro? He can pass the information along to me. I don't think it's wise if I'm seen visiting here regularly." Taryn took a step toward the door and paused. "One more question, if you don't mind? The Summerlands marriage tradition of piercing the groom's, um, body part—why?"

Armando indicated a tiny diamond in his ear. "To show the world you are taken. Why else?"

Taryn barely held her laughter in check. Poor Hayden. Sabina was cruel for allowing him to believe it was somewhere more intimate.

Taryn thanked the men and Tarro led her down the darkened hallways to the small sitting room where they entered the house. A buxom woman with flaming hair and wearing exquisite lingerie accosted them, much to Taryn's horror. She kissed Tarro's cheeks and patiently waited for an introduction.

When Tarro hesitated, Taryn curtseyed to the madam. "I'm Princess Taryn of House Galendrin."

The woman's mouth formed an *O*. "Your Highness. Nena never thought she would see you in her home. I trust everything was to your satisfaction?"

"Every moment."

"Excellent. Will Nena see you again, perhaps?"

"I certainly hope so. With such charming company, how can I stay away?"

Nena pinched Tarro's cheek. "She's a flatterer, this one. Were you visiting Armando?"

"She was. I just stopped by to say hello."

The young boy Taryn saw earlier rushed into the room and Nena made her apologies before leaving them alone. Once they were safely away from the house, Tarro asked quietly, "What did you think of my Armando?"

Taryn whistled and fanned herself. "I think you're one hell of a lucky man. Is it hard for you? Knowing what Armando does?"

"He comes home to me each night and I know he loves me, unlike his clients. To him, they are merely what puts food on the table. Sometimes, though, one of them will fancy themselves in love with him. That can be tiresome."

"You accept his profession with equanimity."

"I won't lie and say I like it." Tarro grinned and a blush crept into his cheeks. "But there are some benefits to having a lover whose job it is to perfect the art of lovemaking."

Taryn stifled an embarrassed giggle. "It's obvious you two have a deep respect for each other. How long have you been together?"

"Many seasons. I met him not long after he started working at the house. He was already one of Nena's boys by then, so there was no misunderstanding his duties. I fell in love immediately, but Armando was skeptical. When he was a lad, twelve seasons if that, pirates attacked his ship. They took him captive as a slave, but he caught the eye of the captain. He became that man's dog for four long seasons until one day he escaped. The thought of loving another man, or even a woman, frightened him. But I never gave up." Tarro's eyes glistened with unshed tears. "One day he said yes."

Taryn gazed at the imposing palace and wondered if she'd ever have the chance to one day say yes to Rhoane.

Chapter 41

KAIDA chased birds while Taryn strolled the orchard, the fragrant blossoms heavy with fruit. A sargot dropped on her head, causing her to swear out loud. At the sound of laughter high above her, she swore again.

"That's not appropriate language for a princess," Ebus taunted from a branch near the top of the tree.

"Do I even want to know what you're doing up there?"

He deftly made his way down through the branches, plopping beside her. "No, I don't think you do." Kaida ran to Ebus, licking his hand until he reached into his pocket for a treat. Once he gave her the scrap he had hidden, she leapt away to chase a butterfly.

"Have you forgotten she's a grierbas?"

Ebus looked at Taryn as if she were dimwitted. "Have you never seen what the others feed her? At least I keep it to her diet."

"I probably don't want to know that either, do I?"

"Not really. I wanted to talk to you about the boy, Gian." Ebus cleared his throat and asked, "May I speak freely?"

"Always." His behavior was strange, even for Ebus, and it worried her.

"What has Gian told you of his ordeal at Caer Idris?"

"Only a little. He's terrified of Zakael more so than

Valterys, even though they both tortured him."

"Zakael tortured Gian for nearly six cycles of the moon. What he did to the boy…" He sighed. "By all rights he should be dead, but he fought against the torture. Why? I can't tell you, but what I did learn at Caer Idris was that Zakael was looking for information about you. Your strengths, your weaknesses, how the Eleri felt about you, that kind of stuff."

"What did Zakael learn from him?" A sick feeling churned inside her. Faerie folk were much like Eleri in that they shared a bond with nature. If Gian spoke to the trees, he would know all manner of minute details about her Zakael could exploit.

"My source wasn't clear on this, but it was enough the boy felt he betrayed you. He tried on several occasions to take his life—each time Zakael prevented it. When it was clear Gian had nothing more to offer, Zakael took out his tongue, using clamps he pulled from the fire. He then threw him in a dungeon, leaving him for dead." Ebus sounded sad and disgusted at the same time. "Your brother is very dangerous, Princess."

"I'm aware of that. I think I know what kept Gian alive. Tell me, what do you know about the faerie life debt?"

"It is a very powerful oath. Gian must've bargained with Verdaine that if she let him live—he would find a way to repay you for his betrayal."

"But he had no idea I'd be at the castle or I would find him," Taryn argued.

"Funny how things have a way of working out, don't you think?" Ebus gave her a sideways glance. "About the time Gian lost his tongue, you set forth for Caer Idris."

"Poor Gian." Taryn sighed.

"There is nothing poor about that boy. He is richer than your mother and father combined. He has the love and respect of the greatest lady to walk this land," Ebus said simply.

"Flatterer," Taryn joked. "Now I understand why he was so reluctant to return to the vier. I need to find a way to let him know I value him but at the same time give him purpose. If I let Lords Tinsley and Aomori have their way, Gian will be nothing more than a well-dressed courtier who does nothing with his days."

"Do not discount the merits of being a courtier. Your young lordlings know more about the workings of this palace than even the chamberlain. Gian could serve you well as a spy, with the proper training," Ebus offered.

"What are you saying? I should let him play cards and croquet all day with Tinsley?" Taryn thought about the idea. "I suppose if it's what Gian wants…"

"I was hoping perhaps Your Highness would allow me to instruct the young lad in some of the finer aspects of espionage." His nose twitched again, his eyes brighter than before.

"What do you have in mind, Ebus?" The sick feeling in Taryn's gut mixed with a new sense of apprehension.

"I think I've proved myself to be loyal to you and it's no secret I'm getting on in years." He gave her a woe-is-me look. "Thieving doesn't hold the charm for me it once did, not with royal gold readily available for less work."

He cleared his throat at her look of alarm. "What I meant to say was I could take Gian on as my apprentice, and for a fee, train him how to be your personal spy. He's small and nimble, always a good thing for this profession. He isn't a servant nor is he a true courtier, which makes him amenable to both. Lastly, I think he's proved he possesses the courage to withstand any difficulty."

The idea had some merit, but Gian was so young. "I'll think about it."

"Of course, Your Highness. Now, if you'll excuse me, I believe your mother approaches." He leapt to a branch above her head and then scrambled up several more until he was completely concealed.

When Lliandra's voice sounded behind her, a wave of unease coursed through her already troubled stomach. This would be the first time she'd spoken to her mother face-to-face since their fight. Taryn braced herself for a verbal lashing.

"Daughter!" Lliandra strode to where she stood, arms outstretched. "What a pleasant surprise to find you here. I was just walking with my ladies. I do so love the scent of sargot blossoms in summer, don't you?" She took Taryn's arm in hers, strolling through the trees. "We can discuss your birthing day celebration."

The expected anger never surfaced. Instead, Lliandra described in minute detail everything planned for the grand affair. It was the party she should've given Taryn the previous season but couldn't because no one knew she existed. Lliandra was making up for lost time and her excitement was infectious. When Lliandra rushed off to speak with a cook or florist, Taryn forgot which, she was honestly looking forward to the event.

Lliandra left her with a command to join the court for dinner. Taryn avoided their formal dinners unless there was a feast planned, but that night Lliandra entertained Lord Aomori's parents and she wanted to make a good impression. Taryn hadn't forgotten Lliandra's accusation that Aomori had seduced her, but apparently, the empress had. She behaved as if the dinner meant the collapse of Talaithian society if it failed.

Exhausted, tired of political games, and wanting nothing more than to have a quiet night to herself, Taryn snapped at her maids while they dressed her.

Gian brought her a cup of spiced grhom, melting her anger. He always knew the right words to say or the perfect action to take with her. She was certain he conversed with

Kaida, although both denied it.

The fact was, she didn't want him to leave, but Ebus had a good idea of how best he could serve her. Considering Gian refused to leave until his life debt was paid, she had to do something with him.

When she asked whether he'd like to become a spy, he thought she jested with him, but the more she explained Ebus's offer, the more Gian became interested. The palace, while exciting, was too confining for a woodland faerie. Taryn understood that more than he'd ever know.

At dinner, Taryn insisted Gian sit between her and Tessa at the high table. Kaida curled at his feet, waiting for tasty bits of meat to find their way to her. Several of the gathered nobles gave Taryn disapproving looks, but she ignored them.

When Lliandra entered, she passed over Gian as if he weren't there. Marissa hurried to take her place after everyone else was seated. Before the meal concluded, she made her excuses, leaving the empress at a loss as to her daughter's behavior. Later, when wine had been flowing for quite some time, loosening courtiers' tongues, Taryn heard grumblings about the crown princess. It seemed Marissa's reluctance to participate in court functions was becoming regular fodder for the gossip mill. Of all the strange rumors bandied about, only one rang true.

Taryn was relaxing by the huge windows that overlooked the sea when Faelara sat next to her and took her hand in her own. "Gian is getting on well here. He and Eliahnna have devised a whole alphabet with signs for nearly everything in the palace," Faelara said.

"Ebus wants to train him as a spy." Taryn studied her friend's response, but Faelara only nodded, which meant she already knew. "Baehlon's watching you," Taryn whispered.

Faelara glanced at the big knight, squeezing Taryn's hand. "Stop it. You've done enough meddling. Let us decide whether we will be together."

They already were together, but playing coy. Technically, Baehlon had to ask Taryn's permission to court Faelara. She, in turn, needed Lliandra's permission to accept his advances. Taryn thought the tradition was chivalric, but idiotic all the same.

"Why do you suppose Marissa is acting so odd?" Faelara was expert at changing the subject from her relationship with Baehlon.

"She's pregnant. From what I can tell, no one knows, not even the empress. There's only one reason she'd hide a baby from her mother and that's if it's Zakael's."

Faelara's look of surprise amused Taryn. Their spies weren't absolute. "It certainly answers many oddities since we returned from Celyn Eryri."

"Whatever her reasons for keeping it a secret, I think we should honor them. If Mother found out from anyone but Marissa, it would be their head on a pike at the palace gate. I don't know about you, but I like mine right where it is."

Faelara swallowed hard. "You make a good argument for silence."

Myrddin approached and held his hand out for Taryn to take. "Would you honor this aging mage with a dance?"

They entered the quadrille and Taryn's spirits roused. It was one of her favorites.

"It's nice to see you smiling again." Myrddin lifted her with the strength of a young man and pirouetted before placing her softly upon the floor.

"So I keep hearing. You dance divinely."

"I can only imagine the horrors you've had to endure, but let's not speak of them. You made me a promise at Celyn Eryri, do you remember?"

A flush of warmth spread across her body. Not from her own doing, but Myrddin's. "I do."

"When the pressures of your position become too much, you can always find refuge in my tower. Any time." He tilted her chin until she faced him. "Will you at least let me provide a haven from all of this?" His dazzling blue eyes flashed toward the empress and back to Taryn.

"Yes." She grinned at his impertinence. "I would like that, actually. You probably have the most bizarre collection of artifacts anywhere on Aelinae. If you'll recall, in my former life it was my job to find such items."

"Then please, visit any time you like. Explore to your heart's content."

She spun into the dance and returned to Myrddin's waiting embrace. His generosity might be genuine or manufactured; for the moment, she didn't care. Everyone had ulterior motives and she was fed up trying to decipher who she could trust. For once, she was not going to question it and just dance because for the first time in much too long, she was content.

Chapter 42

FOR nearly two moonturns, Rhoane chased one lead after another, gathering little more information on the assassin or his master than he had when he left. Everyone associated with the pair died of mysterious causes. He learned of a baker in one village who provided rations to a lodger and a tailor in another town who made several sets of identical black clothing for an unknown client. Both ended up drowned in the local well. Another victim was found hanged in an apparent suicide, his connection to the assassin being nothing more than helping the fellow mend a wound. Disappointment clung to him like a worn cloak—he had hoped to have the assassin in chains upon his return.

Nena entered her room and grabbed her chest. "God's truth, Rhoane, one of these days you will stop my heart and then poor Nena will be dead."

He rose from the chair he'd been sitting on to kiss both of her cheeks. "It is good to see you, too."

She eyed him suspiciously. "You got the information you needed, yes?"

"Not as much as I would like. Do you have anything new to share before I return to the palace?"

"Of your shadow man, no, but I've had many visitors who might interest you. Your betrothed included," Nena said mysteriously.

"Taryn? Why would she come to see you?" Rhoane's insides flipped at the mention of her name. He couldn't imagine Taryn inside Nena's room, not without blushing rose red, at least.

"Not me—one of my best artists, Armando. Before you get the wrong idea, she came here for the same reason you visit. For information. As you know, Armando was a favorite of a certain someone you are close to. She may or may not inherit the Light Throne."

Nena gasped, putting a hand to her lips. "Did I say that out loud? Naughty Nena. Perhaps you should spank me."

Rhoane ignored Nena's taunt. "What information was Taryn after?"

"I don't know, but whatever it was, she didn't get it. She and Tarro were only in Armando's room for a few minutes. He would never betray the house rules or share anything discussed between the sheets. Believe me, we hear everything."

"That is why I come to see you. Who else has been here? You said many visitors." Rhoane tamped down his frustration at her playfulness.

"Don't rush me. Well, the empress herself stopped by. Unfortunately, it wasn't a social call." Nena touched her lips. "I actually miss her visits."

"Nena, please. I do not need to know any of this. Why are you purposely toying with me?"

"Rhoane, darling, don't tease. You know I'd love to toy with you, but now that I've seen your lovely betrothed, I can understand why you would follow that horrid Eleri edict that says you must mate for life. Still, if you ever feel you'd like to learn a few things, bring her to Nena. I can show you both ways to find pleasure you'd never think of on your own."

She dreamily touched the lace on her chemise and Rhoane cleared his throat. "Where was I? Oh yes, we had another

visitor, and this one you might find most interesting. Lord
Zakael. Seems he needs to find himself a Shadow Assassin
and thought this would be a good place to get information.
Who do you think told him to come here?"

Rhoane knew exactly who. "Did Zakael say why he was
looking for him?"

Nena shook her head and several curls loosened from
their pins. They fell around her face, making an auburn
frame against her olive skin. Her jade eyes regarded him for
a moment. "I can't be certain, but I think he wants to make
the assassin a deal. Not to kill the girl, but kidnap her. For
what, I can't say."

She shrugged. "That's all I know." She patted his shoulder
in a maternal, nonsexual way. "Be careful, my prince. You
know I've always loved you and so I will tell you this—if
Zakael wishes to find this assassin, your princess is in trouble."

"That is nothing new with Taryn, but I thank you for
your concern. If you will excuse me, I must hurry or I will be
the one in trouble." He kissed her cheek and jumped away
before she could grab him.

"You Eleri! Always the most beautiful are denied to
Nena. Remember what I said—bring your Taryn to me. You
won't regret it." Nena turned away for a moment and Rhoane
slipped from the room before she saw where he'd gone. Her
curses followed him as he leapt from limb to limb of the giant
tree that shaded the front of the house.

When Rhoane arrived at the palace gatehouse, he put a
finger to his lips. "My return is a surprise for the princess.
Please do not tell the empress or any of the others, lest they
ruin it."

The guard grinned at him. "'Tis a happy night for Her
Highness. She'll be most glad to share it with you."

Music drifted from the garden, indicating the party had
started. He raced to his rooms, startling Alasdair with his

entry. As he prepared for the grand ball, his valet brought him up to date on everything that happened since his departure, including the clandestine meetings Taryn and the others had.

At the mention of the woodland faerie, Alasdair's lips tightened to a hard line. The lad avoided Alasdair, for reasons he couldn't understand. Rhoane could guess at the reasoning but withheld his opinion until he could discuss the matter with Taryn. That she'd brought a faerie to Talaith was alarming in and of itself.

Rhoane settled his nerves with a shot of dreem. He fidgeted with the tops of his Eleri boots, folding them over the tight leather pants he wore, then pressing them against his thigh only to fold them once more. When he'd worried his boots enough, he fumbled with the collar of his silk court tunic, plucking at an invisible thread. The clothing felt strange to him, soft and too fine. He'd worn spun wool and rough cotton garments to authenticate his disguise, but the truth be told, he was happy to be rid of them.

"She will not care what you wear, my lord," Alasdair's lyrical voice said from behind him. "For she will not be looking at your clothing, but into your heart."

"It has been many moonturns since we have seen each other. I fear she has forgotten my face. Tell me true, how does she fare?"

Alasdair was tall for a woodland faerie, matching Taryn's height. He straightened his shoulders with a toss of his long black hair. "She takes up the sword each day and trains like a true Eleri warrior. Yet her heart is missing a crucial element. I am afraid she fades, my lord."

"No." Rhoane insisted. "She is not one to fade. I will not allow it."

Taryn wasn't in her rooms as he'd hoped. Their reunion was meant to be private, but he'd been delayed and the stop at Nena's further prolonged his return. Ellie's behavior intrigued him and when she refused to let him into the apartment, his suspicions were aroused that Taryn had found a new lover to replace him.

This thought, above all, tormented him the most. He knew it was based on fear with no validity, but Ellie's actions caused him no small amount of alarm.

"Let him in, you fool," Lorilee ordered from the sitting room.

Ellie opened the door, her eyes downcast.

"Surely there is no reason I am not welcome here?"

She gasped and shook her head. "No, my lord. It's just—" Her gaze traveled to the couch, where Saeko sat with a boy huddled in her arms.

From what Rhoane could see, his entire body trembled. "Who is this?" he asked as he knelt in front of the lad. "I am Rhoane. Are you a friend of Taryn's?"

The lad unfolded himself from the maid's protective arms and bowed with one leg extended, his left arm out to the side. He was Taryn's woodland faerie, not a boy at all.

"What is your name?"

"His name's Gian, but he doesn't speak, Your Highness." Lorilee's fingers flew in rapid movements and Gian nodded, pointing to Rhoane. "He says he is pleased to meet the beloved of his savior."

Rhoane stretched his thoughts and touched the lad's mind as was traditional. What he glimpsed in that moment of connection was enough to assure Gian no harm would come to him.

He hastily put up wards and warnings around Taryn's rooms, the whole time telling Gian he was safe. The faerie trembled, just from knowing Zakael and Valterys were near.

Kaida snuggled beside Gian, laying her head in his lap, a comforting protection Rhoane couldn't give.

Gian's presence unsettled Rhoane. Not because he was

a handsome young man staying with his betrothed, but he wondered again what sort of hell Taryn must've been through in his absence. The sheer horror Gian showed him sickened and disgusted him. If Lliandra had known what this young man had suffered at the hands of her past lovers, surely she'd not let them in the palace doors. But of course she would. Politics always came first for the empress.

His heart thrummed against his chest as he made his way down the stairs to the garden. It had been too long since he'd seen his betrothed. Their last parting was melancholy, to say the least. He approached the open doors that led to the lower garden, catching sight of Taryn. A swell of urgency caught him off guard. He leaned against a wall until his breathing calmed and his ears no longer pounded with the sound of his rushing blood.

All thought of what he'd say faded when he saw her face. Even lovelier than he remembered, she stood facing him, but was looking at someone to her left. Sabina and Hayden hovered close on either side of her, the Summerlands princess a dark contrast to the delicate beauty of his love. Candlelight danced along her silvery hair, catching in the crown that rested on her head. The diamonds shone like sunbursts in a field of stars. Tiny rays of light reflected off the gems woven into her white gown. She looked every inch the goddess she would one day become.

He opened himself to her and the emotions cascaded around him. Her outward controlled composure hid an undercurrent of anxiety. She laughed at what the gentleman next to her said, but was not truly listening. Her mind was distracted by thoughts of her missing betrothed. She mistook his absence as abandonment.

Guilt cut through him as surely as if it were an assassin's blade. He thought he was helping by leaving Talaith and yet his departure had broken her spirit nearly as thoroughly as his had been.

She turned and for one terrible moment, he saw her heartbreak etched clearly in her features. Her eyes, once so beautiful and blue and vibrant, were dull in her pale face. Even her Glamour was muted beneath her skin. Her gaze fixed on him with a questioning look crossing her features, as if she thought she saw a figment of her own making.

Then her smile, shy and unsure, beckoned him forth.

Chapter 43

TARYN couldn't believe what she saw. Rhoane stood in the doorway, leaning casually against a wall, watching her with a puzzled look. Sound evaporated and nothing existed except Rhoane.

He took a few steps toward her, then faltered. His brow pinched, a pained expression crossing his face, questioning. She moved and with that slight step, his body rocked forward. Then he was there, standing before her.

Words and thought deserted her; even her body seemed to be on the brink of shutting down. Nothing worked the way it should. Her legs wobbled as if made of jelly; her hands stayed limp at her sides. She'd thought of this moment since she left the vier. Now that it had arrived, she found herself quite unprepared.

Rhoane touched her cheek with the back of his hand, moving it up to caress her ear. "I remember you."

She closed her eyes, delighting in the roughness of his fingers against her skin. "And I you."

He kissed her, tenderly at first, unsure, and then with a passion that seared through her. Rhoane held her close and she inhaled the clean scent of the forest.

"Are you still my Taryn?"

"Forever, *mi carae*." She pulled away, searching his eyes.

"You have changed and yet you are the same."

"I am whole again. I have missed you." His lips were on hers and nothing in the world mattered but that he had returned to her. He held her face in his hands as if she were a precious, fragile thing. "I do not ever want to be apart from you," he whispered.

"Nor I you." She touched her lips to his, savoring the scent and smell of him, melting into the heat of him. Sound returned, of the party and other guests, music playing, people talking nearby. Sabina was laughing or crying, she couldn't tell which, and Hayden was welcoming Rhoane back to Talaith. She wasn't ready to share him. Not yet.

Taryn led Rhoane away from the crowd, her arm linked in his until they were hidden beneath the sargot trees. The sweet scent of orange and mango perfumed the air and she felt drunk with happiness. Prisms of light from her star crown played across his face. She could only stare at him, afraid what she saw was just a dream. "Are you truly back? You're no longer broken?"

"Yes, my love, I am no longer broken. I will tell you all about my journey later, when it is just the two of us. I hope that will be in one of our beds?" He raised an eyebrow, making her heart skip several beats.

"I've wished for this moment for so long. Now that you're here, I'm happy and sad, angry, and relieved. My faith in you has been shaken. I don't understand why you left me."

"I did not leave you, *mi carae*. It is difficult for me to explain and you have every right to be angry. When we are alone, I will explain everything, but for right now can you find a little bit of trust that what I did was for us? Always for us."

She started to protest, to argue it more, but he stopped her. "I would like to go out there with the other guests to celebrate your birthing day. As far as I am concerned, this is the most important day of my life. The second, actually. The first would be the day you stepped into the cavern." He gave her a crooked smile, melting her heart a fraction.

"As long as you promise to tell me everything tonight." She held out her marked hand.

He placed his runes on hers. "I swear it." A slight burn ran over their skin as he made the oath. If he'd been lying, he wouldn't have been able to touch her. He entwined his fingers with hers and they went back to the party. After they had made their way through the garden, fielding questions about his trip, for which he offered varying versions, he turned her toward the ballroom.

"Your Highness, may I have this dance?"

"I thought you'd never ask."

When they passed Lliandra, Rhoane bowed to her before spinning Taryn back into the dance. The empress scowled and Marissa turned away without looking at them.

"So, I wasn't the only one who didn't know where you'd gone," Taryn said.

"As clever as you are beautiful." When the music ended, he took two glasses from a nearby servant, handing one to her. "Lliandra was not aware I would be leaving."

They drifted to the balcony overlooking the sea. Tiny lights flickered just off the coast. Lliandra had sent an armada out to patrol the coastline as an added measure of safety for her party. Too many foreign dignitaries were in residence for her to take any chances.

"I'm surprised Marissa is still here. I can only assume it's because Mother commanded her to stay." At the mention of her sister's name, Rhoane tensed and a bitter taste filled her mouth. "Rhoane, we have to accept what happened at Gaarendahl and move on. Trust me, it isn't easy, but we have no other choice."

He breathed deep and his nostrils flared with suppressed

anger. "You are right, of course."

Taryn glanced over her shoulder at her sister and sadness washed over her. "It can't be easy using so much Mari to hide the pregnancy. She still hasn't told Mother."

Rhoane stared at her as if she'd just told him she kept a vorlock for a pet. "You know? Did Marissa tell you?"

At last, Taryn understood why he left court. It wasn't to leave her; it was to get away from Marissa's schemes. "She told you the baby was yours, didn't she?"

A look of confusion crossed his face and he nodded.

"Rhoane, she was pregnant at Gaarendahl. The baby can't possibly be yours." Marissa had tried to trap him into a life of agonizing guilt. Taryn wanted to hate Marissa, but could only pity her.

Anger coursed through Rhoane, so brutal it seared against their bonds. He gripped the balcony until his knuckles were as white as the twin moons. "She came to me after I returned from the vier and told me she carried our son. Baehlon warned me, but I still had faith there was some goodness in her. I made her swear an oath."

"She's chosen her path, Rhoane. You have to stop protecting her." He nodded miserably and Taryn wrapped her arms around him. Her ShantiMari embraced them until his breathing calmed; his fingers no longer clung to the wall. His moss-green eyes, so listless and full of pain only a short time before, regarded her as if for the first time.

"You have unlocked your Dark Shanti—the trinity is near complete." His lips quirked in the little half-smile that made her knees go weak. "It would seem we both have much to share about our adventures. I would especially like to know how it is you have a woodland faerie in your rooms and how he came to owe you a life debt."

"You have your secrets. I have mine. All will be revealed in good time." She tossed her hair over her shoulder, motioning to the ballroom. "Let's go in there with our heads held high. No one determines our fate except us."

Tessa intercepted them before they made it to the dance floor. Pale-faced and out of breath, she wheezed, "Have you seen Eliahnna?"

"Not since dinner. Why?" Tessa wasn't prone to dramatics and an alarm went off in Taryn's head.

"I can't find her. She was sitting with me in the garden, and then I got up to get cake and she was gone. It isn't like her to just leave like that so I went to her room because maybe she got tired. She wasn't there, or in here, or anywhere. It's as if she just vanished."

"I'm sure she's somewhere. Have you tried contacting her in here?" Taryn tapped her forehead.

"That's just it—there's nothing. No thought, no emotion, nothing. It's like I said—she vanished."

Taryn exchanged a glance with Rhoane. His voice was tight as he said, "Tessa, go tell your mother, calmly, to alert the guard that Eliahnna is missing. I am sure we will find her curled up with a book, but it is best to know. Taryn, you and I will gather our friends to look for her."

"Then what do I do?" Tessa asked.

"Stay with your mother and enjoy the party. Do not tell anyone of our concern or where we have gone," Rhoane said. "Now, go."

They found Faelara with Baehlon and sent them looking through the lesser used rooms. The palace was vast, with more rooms than Taryn could count. Hayden and Sabina went to search the libraries while she and Rhoane returned to the garden, quietly asking guests whether they'd seen the princess. Several remembered her sitting at a table with Tessa. A few thought she left with the Lord of the Dark. When Taryn heard Valterys's name, chills ran the length of her. "Rhoane, what if he kidnapped her?"

"We will keep asking. Perhaps they were mistaken." When more party guests confirmed Eliahnna had left with Valterys, Taryn's hopes sank.

"He's taking her to Rykoto as a sacrifice," Taryn told Rhoane.

"How can you be sure?" She told him about the scroll and he nodded. "All he needs is your sword and Rykoto will be released from his prison."

"I don't think he's trying to free Rykoto. Not yet. He needs something else and I don't think he knows what it is."

"Perhaps he found it and this is a way to lure you to the temple."

"Either way, we must hurry or Eliahnna will die. You go tell Mother whatever you need so she doesn't suspect anything. I'm going to get my sword." She sped off, but he caught up with her.

"You cannot go there. Leave this to Baehlon and me. We can handle Valterys."

"Not if Zakael is there. You need me, and Valterys needs my sword. That's two reasons I get to go."

"Taryn, think! If he has the last item and you take the sword, then he has all he needs to raise Rykoto."

"I know what I'm doing. He won't get the sword and Rykoto will stay imprisoned. Go find Baehlon. Bring Faelara as well. If he's hurt Eliahnna, we'll need her healing skills."

Taryn left him staring after her as she raced to her rooms, calling out instructions to her maids while she hastily grabbed her sword. The moonstone Brandt gave her winked in the light. She placed it inside the bodice of her gown and told Gian she would be gone for a while, to stay in her rooms with Kaida. Darius offered to lend his sword, but she commanded him to stay with her maids. As a soldier in her guard, he had to obey. Without wasting time to change clothes, she ran down the stairs to where the others waited.

Sabina and Hayden offered to go as well, but Rhoane told them to remain at the palace and make excuses to the guests for their disappearance. Under no circumstance were they to let Lliandra or Marissa know what was happening. They hurried to the farthest terrace, away from the party where only a few torches were lit.

"How the hell do you expect us to get there in one night?" Baehlon asked.

Taryn shot a questioning look at Rhoane. Since their flight at the cavern, she'd wondered why he never shared he could shape shift, but it wasn't the time to ask. "Baehlon, you go with Rhoane. Faelara, you're with me. Don't ask any questions—just get on." She took a few steps backward and transformed into the silver dragon.

Faelara stared in wide-eyed wonder. "Oh, Taryn, you're lovely." She curtseyed near to the ground before climbing onto Taryn's back, tucking her feet under the wings.

When Rhoane transformed, Baehlon swore under his breath but climbed on without another word. No one spoke as they flew toward the Temple of Ardyn. Taryn's dragon mind ran through several advantages she had in keeping her form once they arrived, but she needed to confront Valterys as a woman or the balance of Aelinae would be shifted irrevocably. Not necessarily in a good way.

Chapter 44

TINY dots of light flickered from the temple, which meant she'd been right. Valterys sought to fulfill his plan of sacrificing blood of the Light to the Dark god. She only hoped she was also right that her being there wouldn't be the key to releasing Rykoto.

Her talons had barely touched the ground when Faelara leapt off, urging them to hurry. With reluctance, Taryn shifted into her womanly form and yanked her sword from its scabbard while dashing up the stairs. The outer temple door creaked open as they entered and the group paused, waiting for discovery, but silence met them. They continued to the inner door and Faelara used her ShantiMari to slide it open soundlessly. One by one they crept into the cold temple and fanned along the outer wall.

Circular in shape, Taryn could see the entire area from where she hid behind a column. Eliahnna lay on a marble altar in the center of the room. Once white, it was now stained a sickening rust from past sacrifices.

It was an eerie repetition of nine months earlier when she'd found Sabina in a similar fashion, except this time she wasn't dealing with half-witted underlings. The miscreants were her father and brother. She gripped the hilt of her sword until her knuckles turned white. What was with her family?

Power hungry motherfuckers always ruining a good party.

Zakael patrolled the outer area, his ShantiMari swirling in a tempest around him. She could sense his lust for her. It wasn't the sexual lust she'd come to expect, but a lust for her blood. Suddenly, she wished she'd taken the extra minutes to change into proper fighting gear.

With as little sound as possible, she tore her gown at the knees and stepped out of the fabric. A cold wind whipped up her bare legs and she cursed her father, brother, and the mad god who drove her here.

Rhoane motioned for her to approach from the other side of Valterys while Baehlon kept an eye on the front. Taryn covered herself and Faelara in shadows, then snuck around the back of the temple. When they were all in place, Rhoane signaled for Taryn to address her father.

Valterys stood with his hands above the unconscious Eliahnna, a knife held between them. Blood smeared his face and clothes, and Taryn prayed fervently that it wasn't her sister's. He muttered indistinguishable words in an archaic language that teased her memory.

The floor began to shift. Raised edges in the tiles formed a labyrinth of sorts that led to a hole about the size of a gold coin. Flames danced up from the tiles and Rykoto appeared. His fire eyes and blood-smeared lips were a terrifying sight—a face Taryn knew all too well.

She stepped out from behind the column, holding her sword aloft. "Aren't you missing something, Father?"

Valterys paused in his chanting and the raised tiles slithered in a chaotic mess. Rykoto hissed when the flames lowered, his forked tongue slashing out of the fire. "Actually, you're just in time," Valterys said. The flames rose higher with his continued chanting.

Taryn tiptoed carefully around the tiles, avoiding the flames as she made her way to the altar. "Put the knife down."

He raised the blade higher, chanting in a louder voice, "Two sacrifices for our god."

Taryn edged close enough to touch Eliahnna's neck. She could feel a faint pulse, but not much more.

"Your sister lives." Valterys's laughter echoed off the marble floor around the columns.

The sound of steel clashing against steel rang out and Valterys jerked his head to the side, listening.

"You didn't think I would come alone, did you?" Taryn asked. She slipped around the altar to face Valterys. "And you honestly can't believe I'm going to let you hurt Eliahnna."

She swung her sword high, catching him in the shoulder. Valterys staggered back, gripping the wound. "I'm not armed!" He held the dagger out toward her. "You can't consider this a weapon."

With his attention distracted, the flames vanished with a lingering cry from Rykoto. Taryn lunged at Valterys, aiming for his legs, then his torso. He spun around, jumping into the air away from her. His movements were too quick to follow.

When she turned to find him, a fireball flew toward her. She sliced through it and dodged several more before she was able to pinpoint her father. She ran to where she saw a faint outline of his ShantiMari and sliced through his power, revealing him as he hid behind a column.

Faelara, see to Eliahnna. Get her out of here.

In his hands, Valterys held a heavy sword. When Ynyd Eirathnacht met it in the air, an electrifying jolt sizzled down her arm. "Now who's not playing fair? Using a Black weapon against me? For shame, Father."

He met her blows, striking at her again and again with his long sword. He would cut at her before leaping away, flying up to the ceiling or across the floor. She studied his movements, trying to anticipate his next move, but he surprised her each time.

Behind her, Baehlon and Rhoane fought Zakael, their ShantiMari spinning around the room as they fought with swords and power. Out of the corner of her eye, she saw Faelara take Eliahnna out of the temple. With her sister safe, Taryn fixed her attention on Valterys.

He crouched on a balcony near the top of the temple with shadows pulled over him. Taryn cloaked herself in darkness and focused on a spot just to his right. In an instant, she was beside him. "Nice view. It looks so much prettier from up here, don't you think?" As she'd hoped, he dropped his cover.

"Someone's been teaching you to use Dark Shanti, I see." He looked to where her voice had come. "Was it Anje? My cousin always was getting in my way. Such a shame his boy lived." He sliced randomly with his sword.

"Missed me," she said from right behind him.

He spun around, cutting the air with wild strokes. His eyes were flecks of steel set deep in his hardened face. "You can't win, Taryn. You should have stayed with me at Caer Idris."

"Why? So you could feed me to your lunatic god?" She danced away from him and met his attack with her sword. "No, thank you."

"I wasn't going to let him have all of you. Just a taste of your blood, nothing more." Valterys cocked his head as if listening for her footfalls, but her slippers made no sound on the balcony's marble floor.

A section of the temple exploded, rocking them backward. Rhoane roared a curse and his ShantiMari shot upward, through the torn ceiling. Zakael's laughter taunted the Eleri and then abruptly stopped.

Concern flicked across her father's face and jealousy warred with her anger. It was juvenile, really, to covet her father's love. Like Lliandra, Valterys saw her as a means to an end, not a daughter. A weapon for the mother, a sacrifice for the father. Her little-girl fairytale was that someday they might love her for who she was and not what she could do for them. Facing Valterys now, she burned any remnants of the storybook family she craved. It was never going to happen.

She threw off her cloak of shadows and assailed him with a vengeance. He met every thrust and parry with a strike of his own. Valterys raved, his ire cracking the balcony. Taryn lost her footing and fell hard on the temple floor while he floated in the air high above, laughing at his daughter.

Shoulder throbbing, ears ringing, she leapt back up into the air toward him. His look of surprise flitted across his face only a moment—he had gravely underestimated her. Like everyone else.

She attacked with her sword again and again. The air around them vibrated with a pinching viciousness. He gathered his power to him, stealing it from the sky down to the tiniest shadow. She pulled her own into Ynyd Eirathnacht. The sword jumped in her hand, excited to feel the strength of her ShantiMari.

It glowed white as she swung it out to the side in a broad slice at Valterys's legs. He faltered mid-jump and her sword caught the front of his leg above the knee. He cursed her, sending a ball of power slamming into her midsection, throwing her against a column. Sparks lit the backs of her eyelids. The wind whooshed from her lungs. She scrambled to keep herself from falling, to regain control.

Taryn? Rhoane's voice echoed in her mind and she struggled to answer him.

I am fine. Stay with Baehlon. The sound of their sword fight echoed around the chamber.

Her father's laughter taunted her as he sent another flaming ball of Dark Shanti at her head. She dodged it, jumping to the side to avoid his rapid-fire attacks. His sword pulsed black with a strange power Taryn didn't want to acknowledge. For the first time since she entered the temple, she knew fear.

Valterys was a master of the Black Arts.

The realization cut her deeper than she'd thought possible. How was it she could be related to such a monster? Marissa's words echoed in her mind, but she refused to believe she could ever be like them.

Valterys sensed the slip in her confidence and thrust the sword at her. A fierce light burned from the blade. When Ynyd Eirathnacht met it in mid-air, the force knocked Taryn to the ground. She rolled to her feet, gasping for breath. A searing pain shot through her vorlock scar, opening it anew. Valterys advanced on her, sucking her power.

Rhoane, he is stealing my power. How can I stop him?

Cut the thread. Only you can see it—it must be you.

Taryn searched frantically for a thread but saw only darkness. Valterys was almost upon her. She was weakening with each step. Ynyd Eirathnacht pulsed beside her and she spun it around like a dervish, making Valterys pause long enough for Taryn to spy a tiny sliver of inky black linking her to his sword.

With what little strength she had left, she sliced through the thread. A sharp bell clanged and she stumbled backward, as did Valterys.

The Black sword lost its glow as her strength flowed back into her. Taryn strode toward her father, anger roiling along every inch of her skin. He scrambled up, casting himself far into the air above her. She leapt up to where he bent double, catching his breath. Before he could raise his sword, she kicked him in the gut and then spun around to punch him alongside his head with her fist.

She moved with speed and precision through her karate moves, her mind empty but for Valterys. His movements were jerky as he held his sword out for protection. She cut through the black steel with all the force of her ShantiMari. It shattered with a deafening screech, tiny fragments raining down to the floor.

Valterys gaped at her, fear in his eyes. Rykoto laughed maniacally from his living grave far below.

"Tell him to shut up," Taryn said through gritted teeth. "Or I'll kill you." She held her sword at his throat.

"He wants your blood, Taryn. He won't stop until he has it. You are the only thing that can restore him to his former glory. Kill me if you must, but there will always be another."

He snapped his fingers and a staff appeared in his hands. He butted her scar with the end of the rod and she staggered back, breathless from the pain. "You're making this too easy." Blades appeared on each end of his spinning staff.

He advanced and she studied the rotation of the staff, pacing the timing. When he was two steps from her, she cut upward, slicing the weapon in two. Undeterred, he raised the broken pieces like clubs, ready to crush her skull. The next several heartbeats moved in slow motion. She swung her sword to counter his attack when Zakael appeared behind Valterys, his sword impaling her father through the chest. Valterys's shocked stare met hers. Zakael whispered in his father's ear before pulling his sword free and vanishing.

A sickening crunch of bone echoed in her head as her sword sliced through Valterys's neck. Ynyd Eirathnacht shrieked, as did her pendant. Rhoane's *cynfar* sang out to join them. Valterys's head bobbled once, then rolled off his body, falling to the temple floor. Taryn stared in calm silence as his body rocked forward and then it, too, fell through the air, landing in a heap on the altar.

It seemed to her she stared at the night sky for the span of ten lifetimes, when in truth it was no more than a moment. The stars blinked against their velvety blanket as they always had. The crisp air smelled clean where she floated above the temple. A light snow started to fall and she wanted to laugh. Snow in summer. But of course, this far north, it was perpetually winter. Something had been lost—hopefully much more had been gained.

She floated to the temple floor, stepping around her father's mangled head to where Zakael stood with his sword held aloft. She gently lowered it. "Why, Zakael?"

"You should have taken my offer. It's not too late." His eyes flicked to Valterys. "I would hate for that to be you someday."

Rhoane moved to strike Zakael, but Taryn stopped him. "There has been enough bloodshed this night. Take Valterys and leave this place."

"Taryn, do you think that wise?" Baehlon asked.

"What choice do I have? He is my father, too."

A soul wrenching scream from the temple entrance shattered the moment and they turned as one. Marissa stood in the doorway, surveying the destruction and the body on the altar. She gasped for breath, a hand on her swollen belly as she sank to the floor. Zakael rushed toward her, but Taryn ran past him, calling for Faelara.

Faelara knelt beside the princess and prodded her body with her fingertips. "What were you thinking, taking this risk?"

"I had to stop him," Marissa choked. Her eyes rolled to the back of her head and she groaned in pain. "Nadra help me."

A river of clear liquid ran beneath Marissa, and Taryn stared at Faelara. "It's early."

"About two moonturns, by my calculations. We'll need to deliver this baby here." She positioned herself between Marissa's legs and pushed the princess's gown over her knees. "Keep her with us, Taryn. I need her help to get this child out. Baehlon, get some snow and melt it until it's hot."

"I don't have that kind of power."

"Yes, you do. Now don't waste any more of my time. Zakael, make yourself useful and find me something to wrap the baby in once it's born. A cloak would suffice. Rhoane, help Baehlon with the water." Rhoane raced in one direction and Zakael in another, returning moments later with his wool cloak.

Marissa groaned louder and Taryn counted how long the pain lasted. "The contractions are close together. Can you see the baby's head?"

Faelara grinned. "I've been looking at it all this while."

Marissa grabbed Taryn's arm and squeezed. "Don't let him do it. You must stop him," she wheezed.

"It's okay, Marissa. Eliahnna is safe," Taryn reassured her sister.

"No, no." Marissa moaned, falling back against Taryn's lap. She soothed her sister while observing how Faelara maneuvered the baby's shoulders. Marissa cried out again and then went limp. Sweat rolled down her face and her lips turned an awful shade of blue.

Zakael ran off once more and returned with Taryn's discarded fabric. "To clean the baby," he said, offering it to Faelara.

"Thank you, Zakael. Just hold it for now."

Rhoane and Baehlon entered with a large ceramic basin filled with steaming water. At Faelara's furrowed brow, Baehlon explained, "The offering bowl."

Faelara nodded and indicated they set it down beside her.

The men watched with a mixture of awe and terror as Faelara shifted and pulled on the baby. Marissa screamed with each tug until finally the little thing slipped free. Faelara held him aloft. "It's a boy." She took the cloth from Zakael, gently wiping the newborn until his skin was pink and clean.

Marissa struggled to sit up, demanding her baby. Faelara

cut the birth cord, tying it with a thread of her Mari before handing the baby to the princess. Marissa beheld the child and half-sobbed, half-gasped. "Oh, Armando."

"Is that the child's name?" Faelara asked.

"No, he's the father," Taryn and Rhoane said in unison. A look of relief crossed Rhoane's face.

A thousand score of Eleri voices whispered in her mind, telling of the Black Princess's betrayal and deceit. Marissa's oath to Rhoane saw its completion. Her name would forevermore be a hideous curse to all Eleri.

"No," Zakael argued, his ShantiMari flaring with terrifying force. "This child is mine. He will be more powerful than even you."

"It is you who is mistaken, Zakael." Rhoane's power flared equally strong. "You know what happened at Gaarendahl. Were you aware Marissa told me this child was mine? She manipulated you just as she does everyone, even those who have shown her kindness." His stern gaze never left Taryn and a thrill rushed through her.

"Ask her yourself," Taryn challenged.

Zakael knelt beside Marissa and said with more tenderness than Taryn ever thought he could possess, "Marissa was with child long before your visit to Gaarendahl, and I am the only one who could have fathered him." He took the baby from Marissa, his eyes shining with unshed tears.

The crown princess wept quietly and lay back against Taryn, defeated.

Zakael searched the child's face, looking deep into his dull brown eyes. "No," he said, shaking his head. "You swore to me you'd been with no other."

A wildness entered his eyes and Taryn wrapped a protective arm around her sister.

"You swore, you stupid whore! He was supposed to be *my* Eirielle." With a grunt of disgust, he thrust the baby into

Marissa's arms. "This child has no ShantiMari. He is no son of mine." The venomous glare he gave Marissa made Taryn's insides quail.

The walls vibrated with Zakael's anger. His ShantiMari, deep grey and spinning in a fury through the open space, overwhelmed Taryn with its enormity. He'd withheld more than teaching while they were at Gaarendahl. His power, edged in the telltale signs of Black ShantiMari, was far greater than either Lliandra's or Valterys's.

"I hope you die a long, painful death in the fires of Dal Ferran, you worthless cur." Every word was like a hammer to anvil and Marissa flinched deeper into Taryn's lap with each syllable spat at her. "Never seek me out again, for certainly I will end your existence."

Zakael whirled once, transforming into a feiche. His powerful talons gripped Valterys's head before lifting into the air. It wasn't until he was a speck in the sky that anyone spoke.

"We must get Marissa and the baby to Talaith. It is too cold here for them to last," Faelara said, her voice trembling.

While the others made the necessary preparations, Taryn stroked her nephew's dark curls. He looked like his father in miniature. Marissa slumped in her lap, her eyelids fluttering closed, her breathing labored.

Taryn slipped into her sister's mind. Filth slid over her. She was disgusted by the savagery Marissa was capable of, but kept searching until she found what she needed.

You shouldn't have come here, Marissa.

You are an abomination who should be killed. Marissa's thought slammed into Taryn and she reeled against it.

You tried to destroy me, but you failed. You will never be Rykoto's queen. Zakael made certain of that when he killed Valterys.

There is no place for you in this world, filthy Offlander.

Rykoto will take me as his queen and you will obey my command. I never needed Valterys.

The Blood and Blade of the one who is and is not. *What is the third requirement to free Rykoto?* Marissa's face turned an ashen shade, her pulse barely more than a flicker. The others were about done with their preparations and time was running out.

Marissa gurgled a laugh, the sound sickening Taryn. *Even if I knew, I'd never tell you. But the phantom knows. Ask him yourself the next time he visits.*

Icy pricks roved up her arms to her neck. *Why does the phantom know? How?*

He knows everything about you. He's inside your mind, Taryn. Right now.

No, Taryn told herself. This was yet another ploy by Marissa to unsettle her. She shut out her sister's taunts and straightened her shoulders, warming her skin as she did.

These are just words. They can not hurt me, nor can you. All of your plans have failed, dear sister. You tried to destroy me, but I grew stronger. You tried to take Rhoane from me, but our bonds are unbreakable. You couldn't be me and so you tried to surpass me. Now all is lost for you. It was you who sent Valterys here with Eliahnna, but she lives. She will sit on your throne as the rightful Lady of Light.

Marissa gasped and shook her head, moaning. She'd risked her child's life to make certain no one stopped Valterys from killing their sister. Only Taryn's blood would release Rykoto, but her sisters' could strengthen him. Dangerously so. Valterys had sought Rykoto's release to gain immortality for himself and Marissa, but she'd betrayed him by telling Zakael their plan to overthrow first Rykoto, then Lliandra.

It never occurred to her Zakael would reject her because she never for a moment believed the child could be anyone else's. The gods would never be so cruel as to give her, the crown princess, a powerless bastard. It was inconceivable. Marissa was just as delusional as Zakael. They were a perfect match as far as Taryn was concerned.

I'm going to give your baby, a prince, to his father to be raised as a commoner. Taryn cooed in her sister's mind.

"Please," Marissa begged. "Have mercy."

You chose your path and now, I'm choosing mine. Tears rolled down Taryn's cheeks. *It should have been different, Marissa. We should've been allies. At least I can grant you one small favor. You'll be with Rykoto, but not as his queen. For all eternity, you'll be nothing more than an amusement. A diversion to keep his thoughts away from me.*

You've been playing a dangerous game, but you severely underestimated me. You are already close to death. It would be nothing for me to give you strength to make it to Talaith, but I promised you at Gaarendahl I would not have mercy a second time. I'm sorry, my sister.

Marissa opened her mouth to object and Taryn closed her mind around the faintly beating heart, commanding it to stop. A small cry escaped Marissa's lips before she slumped lifeless against her lap.

Taryn wept not just for the death of her sister, but for the innocent boy who would grow up never knowing his kin. Mostly, she wept for Rhoane and the anguish he suffered because of Marissa. In the end, she was right. Taryn was more like her than she'd thought. She didn't flinch from the truth. Instead, she embraced it.

Faelara took the child from Marissa's dead hands, cradling him in her arms. They wrapped Marissa in Zakael's cloak before Baehlon took her outside. Rhoane helped Taryn stand and when their eyes met, the sadness she saw in the mossy depths confirmed he knew what she'd done. She looked away, ashamed.

A rivulet of Marissa's birthing blood crossed in front

of her slipper. She followed it as it ran through the maze toward the center of the room. Her gaze traveled up the altar to where Valterys's headless body lay. Blood streamed down the side onto the floor. Blood of both Light and Dark. Taryn grabbed her sword, ordering everyone out.

"Taryn, there is no danger. Valterys is dead and Zakael is gone," Baehlon said, looking toward the still dark sky.

"Don't argue, just get out!"

He scowled at her but did as she asked, with Faelara right behind him. Rhoane hung back. "What is it?"

"There's no time to explain. Unless you want to be Rykoto's next meal, you'll do as I say and get the hell out of here." Taryn pleaded with him to leave. "You have to trust me."

Rhoane swore at the gods before storming out of the temple.

With the others out of harm's way, she stood over the hole in the floor and plunged her sword deep into it. She forced the trinity of power within her through the steel, chanting over and over. "This is a sacred space—let no harm befall anyone here. Rykoto will slumber in peace."

Ynyd Eirathnacht rose in song, with Rhoane's sword adding a deep bass from outside the temple. The melody they sang was ancient, from before the Great War. Taryn hummed with them, instinctually knowing the lyrics.

A white light, brighter than Nadra's brilliance, lit from the sword to every inch of the temple, cleansing it of Valterys's sacrificial stink. The trails of blood from Marissa and Valterys sizzled and popped before scorching to nothingness. The acrid smell burned her senses and she buried her face in her shoulder.

In his earthly cell, Rykoto shrank from her words and the song of her blade. He cursed her, damning her to several cruel fates. He, too, had underestimated her power and swore vengeance on all those she held dear. Her reply was to push her sword farther into the floor, her power pulsating harder until it touched Rykoto. He screamed against the purity of her light.

When the floor and walls shone white in the moonlight, she lifted the ceiling, restoring the temple to its original grandeur. Rykoto taunted her from deep in his prison. "Little girl, leave this place before it becomes your tomb as well."

"I don't fear you, Rykoto. I am Eirielle, the Child of Light and Dark. I am *Darennsai*." She jerked her sword free from the floor. "You have no power over me."

His answer whispered through the walls like the hiss of a trapped cobra. "You cannot hide from me, Eirielle. I will hunt you day and night. You will know no rest until your blood is mine."

"Hunt me, dead god. Chase me with your wicked words and fruitless visions. When we meet again, it will be the end of you." She glanced around the room, noticing for the first time the seals placed within each column. Five held only empty holes. "Sleep now, for I have business elsewhere."

Rykoto chuckled. "You grow stronger, little girl. Still, you are no match for a god." A blast of hot air shot out of the hole, singeing her bare legs. She cried out and Rykoto laughed harder. "Come back anytime. I like to play with my food before I eat it."

Taryn placed her hand over the steam, turning it to ice. She shoved it down the hole until Rykoto shrieked. When the ice froze over the hole, she set a seal into it, filling it with wards and alarms should anyone disturb it. Next, she went to each column, placing more wards on them. No one would remove or replace a seal without her knowledge.

On the altar, nothing but ash remained of her father. With a soft breath, she blew it into the night to scatter across the land. Marble gleamed white against the flickering torches.

It was as purified as she could make it.

"Sleep, Rykoto. Dream of your queen. Be at peace."

Facing the altar, she held Ynyd Eirathnacht in front of her and curtseyed low, her left arm extended to the side. "Great Mother, Great Father, honor me this day by keeping your son safe in his chamber. You have placed me upon this path for a reason and while I don't always understand your motives, I'll do my best to fulfill my destiny." She glanced at the empty columns. "I get the feeling the fun is just beginning. You sure know how to keep things interesting, don't you?"

A chill whipped her ankles and she cleared her throat. "I should probably be going, but Ohlin? If that offer still stands about giving me and Rhoane your blessing? I think we could really use it."

Warm air brushed her face and the visages of Nadra and Ohlin formed in front of her. Ohlin's eyes twinkled as he took the sword from her hand. "I do believe you're both ready. When all of this is settled, bring Rhoane to Dal Tara."

"You can't just do it here?"

"Your sister needs you more. The bonding can wait."

They started to fade and Taryn called out, "How do we get to Dal Tara?"

Nadra grinned impishly. "I'm sure you'll figure it out."

She stepped from the temple into the cold air, filling her lungs with its crispness. Rhoane swept her into his arms, holding her against him.

"We heard Rykoto's cries but were blocked from entering the temple."

The irritation at the gods' capriciousness dissolved beneath his powerful embrace. She'd missed those arms, that smell, him. "I'll tell you what happened on the way, but we need to get Eliahnna and the baby out of this damned cold."

Rhoane touched the crimson stain on her gown, sending his ShantiMari into her wound. She grimaced against the burn, holding her breath until he finished. Lightheaded, she swayed into him. Opening the wound had released some of the remaining poison into her bloodstream. "You can't fly injured."

"The dragon will finish healing me. We don't have time to argue. Let's go." She didn't know whether it was true, but hoped so.

"What do we tell the empress of her daughter's death?" Faelara asked.

Baehlon answered when Taryn could not. "We tell her the truth. She came here to save her sister. For whatever reason, she kept the child a secret from everyone, even her mother. I think we need to respect that wish. It will do no good to bring Lliandra a grandchild she will have to send away since male children can't inherit the Light Throne."

If her twin brother had lived, he would've been raised by Valterys. The thought repulsed her.

"Then we'll respect that tradition as well. I know the father. I'll take the child to him," Taryn said. Her sword glowed softly and the two dragons on the hilt shifted and fluttered their wings. The gems on the dragons sparkled in the moonlight: one silver, the other moss green. "I think Ynyd Eirathnacht wants us to swear an oath of silence about the child."

Rhoane placed a tentative hand on the hilt of her sword. When he noticed the changed dragons, he gripped the pommel hard, his eyes glassy. Baehlon followed and then Faelara placed her hand on the sword. They swore an oath of silence while Taryn wrapped their hands in her ShantiMari to bind their word to Ynyd Eirathnacht.

The baby's fingers and lips were a pale blue, even wrapped in Rhoane's tunic. "We must hurry if the child is to survive." Taryn handed Faelara the moonstone. "Tuck this inside, near his skin—it will warm him on the flight home."

Faelara cradled the baby tightly to her chest with one hand and with the other, clutched at Eliahnna. They wound their power around her, securing her to the dragon's body. Taryn took to the air with greater care than she had with just Faelara astride. The night was empty save for a snowy owl that ghosted through the sky close to the temple and then disappeared from their sight.

Chapter 45

THEY flew at breakneck speed, touching down just as the
sky to the west was beginning to turn from deep indigo to
rose and orange. Taryn's sole focus was to get them home
to warmth and safety. Rhoane instructed Baehlon to take
Marissa's body to the crypt while he and Faelara would return
Eliahnna to her rooms before informing the empress what
had transpired. Taryn agreed to meet them as soon as she'd
delivered the baby to Armando.

Her lips touched his downy hair and she transported
them through the city until she stood at the foot of the bed
Tarro and Armando shared. They lay together, arms and legs
entwined, a blanket covering most of their naked bodies.

She sent a gentle thought, waking them. They blinked
against the light that emanated from her, looking first at each
other, then her, incomprehension clouding their sleepy eyes.

Tarro jumped from the bed, covering himself with a
pair of loose-fitting trousers, but Armando lay against the
headboard, regarding her with the same sweet, brown eyes
as the baby. Tarro knelt at her feet, stammering his apologies
for not being prepared for a visit. She shushed him with
assurances he'd done no wrong. Armando slid from the bed,
moving toward her, his lean body naked and sensual. He
stared at the bundle in her arms with a look of curiosity and

confusion.

"I bring you a gift," Taryn said. Her voice was like that of Nadra: light, musical, utterly not her own. "This is your son, Armando. His mother traveled beyond the realm with his birth so it comes to you to raise him."

"I was not aware of any child of mine." His look was apologetic to his lover. Armando took Tarro's hand in his. "I am most careful in my work. I swear to you, I knew nothing of this." He denied it, but in his thoughts lingered the hope it was true. He had long wished to give Tarro a child they could raise as their own, a token of his love that marked their relationship as special from his work. Armando stroked the baby's curls, touching a finger to his cheek. "Who is the mother?"

"The child's mother must never be named." They shared a look that said he knew who it was. A pinch of disgust tightened his lips.

"Then he will have two fathers but no mother." He unwrapped the baby from Rhoane's silk tunic. "He will need proper attire and a wet nurse."

The look of pure devotion in Tarro's eyes tugged at something deep within Taryn. "You gave us a son." He gently took the naked babe from his father's arms. With a giggle, he said, "He certainly is yours."

"Perhaps it's not just the baby who needs proper attire." Taryn avoided looking at Armando's early morning erection.

Armando shrugged. "In my profession, clothing is a bother." He slipped on a robe, tying it around his waist. For the baby, he procured a soft blanket, bundling him tightly. "Tarro, we have a son." Tears welled in his eyes as he held the child close to his cheek, breathing in his scent.

"What will you name him?" Taryn asked. She stood on the floor and her voice was nearly her own.

They exchanged glances, saying in unison, "Percival."

"A princely name," Taryn said, approving. "I will see to it that you have a weekly stipend. This child will want for nothing as long as I'm alive."

"We have plenty of coin to take care of our child," Armando said defensively.

"Will you still work for Nena? I thought perhaps Percival would become your full-time job. If I can ease the burden for you only a little, it will gladden my heart."

Armando regarded her with mixed emotions. "Did you know all along?"

"I only learned tonight the child was yours. We were led to believe otherwise. May I visit him?"

Tarro answered immediately. "I'll bring him to work on occasion and, of course, his Auntie Taryn may come here anytime to see him. He should know the woman responsible for giving us our dream."

"My role in this must remain secret. Those who are aware of his birth have all sworn an oath of silence. If my enemies have knowledge of him, he can be used as a tool against me. Hide his birth well. Make up what story you will, but own that story until it becomes the fabric of truth in your life."

"As you wish, Great Lady." Armando inclined his head to her.

Taryn kissed her nephew's warm cheek. "Be well, little Percival. I will always watch over you, *mi carae*."

She left them as quickly as she'd come, speeding to the palace with a leaden heart.

The others were already in her mother's sitting room when she arrived. "Taryn. My daughter, are you well? Rhoane and Faelara have explained everything to me. Is Valterys truly dead?" Lliandra's tone gave away nothing and Taryn wasn't sure whether she was happy or sad to lose her past lover.

"Yes, he's dead." The mask of Mari wavered with Lliandra's grief, giving Taryn a glimpse into the struggle between her mind and heart.

"Poor, brave Marissa. She tried to save her sister and perished instead. Was there nothing you could do for her?"

The wind sucked from her and she staggered as if hit. "I'm sorry, Mother. I was busy with my father. Marissa's death is unfortunate, but our sister is safe."

Lliandra's cold blue eyes stared at her. "Unfortunate? She is a hero, you stupid girl. Because of her, we still have an heir to the throne. If you hadn't been so busy with your own ambitions, you could have protected Eliahnna better."

Cold rage ran through Taryn, and she pulled away from her mother to stare out the window at the churning sea.

Faelara stepped between her and the empress. "Your Majesty, Taryn was trying to save Eliahnna. Had we been but a moment later, Valterys would have succeeded in his plans. Without Taryn's help, we all would have perished."

Lliandra ignored Fae's plea. "You spent time with your father, yes? How do I know he didn't turn you against me? Wasn't it you just a fortnight ago who told me your sister was vile? How can you say that now? Without her help, you would have lost Eliahnna to that madman. To your father."

Taryn clenched her fists, tamping down her power. "You have no idea what you're saying, Mother. Your grief has clouded your judgment. I was not, nor would I ever be, aligned with my father or his horrid son. I serve Aelinae. Not the Light Throne, not the Obsidian Throne, not the Weirren throne. Aelinae.

"Tonight I saved an innocent girl from a brutal death. If you want to say Marissa should get the credit, that's fine, but don't you dare accuse me of things about which you have no knowledge." She glared at Rhoane and Faelara before leaving Lliandra's apartment without being dismissed.

She stormed to her apartments, ignoring the curious stares of servants and courtiers. Her maids scurried out of her way as she strode to her bedchamber. Their questions fell around her unanswered as she locked the door to her room and cradled Kaida in her arms. Gian crept to her bed, startling her. She'd forgotten she left him there before the party. She held up the blanket for him to crawl into bed with her and the grierbas. His small face was close enough she could see freckles on his nose that she'd not noticed before. He stroked her hair, murmuring quietly with his maimed mouth until her fury diminished and she fell into a fitful sleep. The last thing she recalled was Kaida asking the boy to move off her paw.

The funeral for Marissa was held at sunset. The nobles and courtiers who only the previous day had gathered to celebrate Taryn's birthing day now stood in silence as her sister's body was carried in procession from the garden to the crypt. The ceremony had been short, with Lliandra's high priest officiating.

Myrddin said a few words, as did several members of the Privy Council and other courtiers who were fond of the crown princess. Taryn chose to keep her mourning private, refusing the offer to speak.

Rhoane walked at her side, a grim expression on his face. Traces of the strain he'd been under were evident in the creases by his eyes. Marissa's lies had nearly destroyed him, but Taryn saw joy returning with every smile he gave.

She slipped her hand into his; he was hers, forever. If the events at the temple had taught her anything, it was to never take a moment of life for granted. It could end with a single touch of misplaced ShantiMari.

As the lid slid shut on Marissa's marble coffin, Lliandra

sobbed quietly. Eliahnna wrapped her arms around their mother and Lliandra leaned her head against her daughter's shoulder.

The girl regained consciousness shortly after they returned from the north, with no memory of what transpired at the temple. She'd been sipping wine in the garden when Valterys asked her to show him a particular flower that only bloomed on summer nights. At some point, Zakael joined them and the last thing she recalled was Zakael's face as he smashed his fist into her temple. Eliahnna swore that would be the last time anyone struck her. She told Taryn to expect her in the training ring each morning.

Marissa's death made Taryn the heir, but she refused the title. Eliahnna would make a far better empress. She just hoped it was what Eliahnna wanted.

Tessa had been distraught to learn of Eliahnna's capture and then Marissa's death. She'd tried so hard for so long to win her oldest sister's approval, it had become a part of her life. Now that Marissa was dead, Tessa tried to deal with the fact she would never have her sister's love.

Taryn took her hand, giving it a squeeze as they walked into the evening air. Birds sang in the trees and waves crashed on the rocks far below. Everything was as it should be, but for them, everything had changed.

Dinner that evening was a somber affair as they reminisced about the princess, as was the custom. Eventually, the conversation turned to other topics. The mood lightened with the court once again making merry with music and laughter. Lliandra sat on her great throne, observing the courtiers chatting about nothing to do with her daughter.

Taryn curtseyed low to the empress, showing her respect. "It pains me to see your grief, Mother."

Lliandra regarded her with tired eyes. Her mask of Mari was set firmly in place, but underneath it, Taryn saw the ravaged skin of someone who'd been crying all day.

"I know you don't share in this grief, daughter." She held up a hand to stop Taryn's denial. "Listen to them. They tell stories of a Marissa I never knew. They talk of happy memories, but are they of Marissa, or from their own lives? I must accept that part of what you've told me is true. I suppose I've always known it, but thought if I could love her enough, she would do right by my throne."

"You raised her to be a ruthless ruler, Mother. Don't pretend to be the victim here."

"I suppose you're right. I'm not the victim here, you are."

"Like hell I am. If that's what you think of me, then you don't know me at all."

"Lady Faelara told me in no uncertain terms how unfair to you I've been. I am unaccustomed to being spoken to so candidly. Except by you, of course. At first, I thought to punish her for the outburst, but your beloved cautioned me that if I were to harm Faelara, you would be quite vexed. It was a veiled threat, of course. You had, after all, just killed your father."

"I didn't kill Valterys. For reasons I can't even begin to fathom, Zakael did. I hope you don't think I'd ever hurt you."

"I would hope that's precisely what you'd do if I were anything like Valterys. You reminded me today that I wear this crown as a symbol for all of Aelinae, not just my own schemes or desires. If I'd listened to you, Marissa might still be alive."

"She chose her destiny. Now you must look to the future and do what you can to prepare Eliahnna for what comes next."

"Yes." Lliandra's eyes scanned the crowd for Eliahnna. "She will make a fine empress. She is wise and fair-minded. I used to be like her when I was younger." Lliandra chuckled. "Gwyn always told me I was too practical to be a good empress. I miss my sister very much. Taryn, promise me you'll take care of Eliahnna and Tessa when I'm gone." Her gaze slid back to Taryn.

"You have plenty of time to take care of them yourself. Let them know how much you love them. Teach them what you know of ruling. Above all, tell them you are proud to have them as daughters."

Lliandra snorted. "Is that what you've always sought from me? Approval?"

"Yes. And your love."

"Useless things." Lliandra waved her away. "Go—enjoy the evening with your friends. Let this be a celebration of life."

Lliandra clapped her hands, calling out for music, dancing, and wine. The crowd cheered and raised a glass to their empress.

Taryn drifted through the crowd as if in a daze. Useless things, love and approval. The empress might be right. Certainly they had caused her heartache, but more than that, love had given Taryn purpose. Without that, there was no hope.

Taryn had to keep the hope alive that she could somehow find a way to bring balance to Aelinae. With Zakael on the Obsidian Throne and Lliandra in failing health, the future of her home world was more precarious than ever.

She and Kaida ambled aimlessly through the grounds, eventually stopping at the crypt where Marissa's body was laid to rest. The cold marble was smooth against her skin when Taryn laid her head on the tomb.

"I'm so sorry," she whispered. "Your father was wrong, Marissa. You were of Light and Dark, but you could never be the Eirielle. Why couldn't you be content with the Light Throne? Why did you have to reach too far?"

She lifted the marble lid, using her ShantiMari to slide it

aside. Marissa looked serene in death, her pale skin a striking contrast to her dark hair. Taryn touched the place above her heart where she'd placed the sword at Gaarendahl. The wound had healed to a faint scar.

She sensed Rhoane's ShantiMari beneath her touch. He'd placed the oath on Marissa that Taryn heard in the temple. To the end, her sister had tried to destroy them. Taryn shook her head at the futility of Marissa's actions.

She embraced the anger that flowed through her, funneling it into Marissa's corpse. Every moment of anguish Taryn suffered at the hands of her sister, she forced into her power. Heat blazed up her arm and she squeezed her eyes shut.

She called on all her ShantiMari, begging mercy from the gods and goddesses, her immortal parents. Whether she sought to absolve Marissa or find forgiveness for herself, Taryn wasn't sure. All her pain, her anger, the confusion and mistrust she'd gathered over the past season, she released into the flames that burned her hands, but left no mark.

When at last the heat subsided, Taryn opened her eyes to see the destruction she caused. All that was left of her sister was a thick coating of ash. She produced a jar and funneled every last mote of ash into it before sliding the coffin closed. For good measure, she placed several wards over the lid to prevent anyone from discovering the princess had been taken. As an afterthought, she wove a delicate thread of Mari through the wards so that if anyone did open it, they would see a likeness of Marissa in perpetual slumber. Then she left the crypt for good.

A gentle breeze whipped Taryn's hair around her face when she stepped up onto the wall that surrounded a terrace overlooking the sea. She uncapped the jar, saying a prayer for her sister's immortal soul. "May you find the peace in death that eluded you in life." She upended the jar and the ashes were caught by the wind, scattering out across the ocean.

"It did not have to end this way." Rhoane stood a few feet from her. "I followed you to the crypt."

She threw the jar over the cliff, waiting until she heard the crash of pottery on the rocks below. "Whoever created the Shadow Assassin is skilled in the Black Arts and has access to court. Marissa caused enough pain in life. I can't let her be used against us ever again. This is the only way I can be certain of that."

"What she did to me—to us—she deserves nothing less." Rhoane sat beside her. "Marissa is gone, but the threat remains."

"Zakael." Taryn leaned against him, sorrow burrowing in her chest because nothing would ever be the same. "He won't soon forgive me for what happened at the temple. The battle is yet to begin, I fear."

"But not tonight." He took her hand, pulling her up beside him.

"We'll be okay, won't we?" Suddenly she was aware of his scent and the curve of his mouth as he smiled.

"Better than okay. We will be together as we were meant to be. Fly with me."

They leapt off the wall, transforming into their dragon shapes in mid-air. Taryn let out a cry that seared the sky and Rhoane followed suit. Kaida ran along the wall, barking and jumping until they were far from shore. They dove and spiraled together as if dancing through the air.

They passed over the oceans and lands as they had in her dream. When she saw the Narthvier, she knew where Rhoane was leading them. They shook off their dragon forms before touching the uppermost branches of the Weirren.

"Why did you not tell me you could transform into a darathi vorsi?"

"I did not know. A rune appeared one day and then a

short while later I felt compelled to become the great beast. It was then I found you drifting over the sea as a magnificent silver darathi vorsi."

She held her hand to his, their runes sparking against the night sky. "We still need Ohlin's bond to be complete." His fingers curled over hers. "Are you certain, Rhoane? These past few moonturns have not been pleasant for either of us."

"True, but we are as one, are we not?" She opened her mouth to argue and he pressed his lips to hers. "We both had doubts, yes, but we had faith, yes? We had hope."

"Yes, hope. Faith, trust, and—" She sat up, a thrill igniting her senses. "Glitter." She folded her fingers into a fist and opened them to reveal a mound of sparkling crystal shards. "We are capable of anything, you and I. But we are stronger together. Before anything else is spoken, before we even consider completing our bonding, there is something you must know."

The intensity of his stare unnerved her and she gripped the crystals for reassurance. "I do not possess the trinity, Rhoane." He started to argue and she continued, cutting him off. "When the phantom touched my soul, he did not stain me with his Black Shanti—he unlocked my own Black powers."

In the span of two long breaths, Rhoane's expression ranged from incredulity to confusion to denial to understanding, and finally acceptance. "Yes, yes that makes sense. The trinity is too confining. You must not be limited." He shook as he reached out to place his hand over hers, covering the glittering shards. Their runes illuminated and rose from their skin, flared rays brightened the space. "Do not see this as a defect, mi carae, but as a part of your whole perfection."

His lips rested against hers and warmth traveled to the place inside where the chill lingered. A shadow at the corner of her eye flickered and winked out. She opened her mouth fully, taking in Rhoane's heat, his power, his healing.

ShantiMari swirled in shades of pink to crimson with suppressed passion. Taryn withdrew from the kiss with heady reluctance.

"Are you ready to complete our bonding?"

"Now? It cannot wait?"

"It can, but trust me, you do not want it to." Rhoane's grin was answer enough. She transported them through the stars to Dal Tara, where Brandt and all of the gods and goddesses of Aelinae waited.

Rhoane blinked several times before covering his eyes against the brilliance of the gods. Taryn turned to him, her Glamour a radiant kaleidoscope of color shimmering beneath her skin. "Now what do you see?" she teased, reminding him of the first time she saw Nadra in the cavern.

"It is—overwhelming."

"You get used to it. Squint, it helps."

The gods wavered into recognizable forms and approached the couple. Brandt followed a step behind.

"Ohlin wishes to bond us, if this is what you truly want. Once he places his bonds, they are absolute and forever. Nothing and no one can ever unravel them. Are you sure you choose this path?" Taryn asked, her voice wavering the tiniest bit.

A little half-smile tugged at his lips. "I have wanted nothing else my entire life."

Ohlin stepped forward, chanting the ancient words of binding that would complete their union. He wrapped a multi-hued cord of power around their wrists, searing it into their skin. Taryn grimaced against the pain and stared in awe as Rhoane's skin rippled from his elbow to his fingertips with tiny moss-colored dragon scales. Silver frills flared out from her arm and then sank back into her skin. Their runes shifted and reoriented themselves, leaving several more ghost tattoos embedded against their Glamour.

When Rhoane lifted his hand away, a solid crystal dropped from their grip. Taryn bent to retrieve it, her attention momentarily captured by tiny buds sprouting from Rhoane's fingertips. A second later, they were gone. In place of her own hand, a galaxy of stars swirled and winked out, leaving her once more flesh and bone.

Brandt set the crystal into her palm and placed Rhoane's hand over hers. "Guard this well." He pressed against them until the crystal cut into her skin and she flinched. When he released their hands, the crystal had vanished.

"Where did it go?" Taryn flipped her hand back and forth, looking for a new rune or anything to indicate its existence.

Brandt tapped them on their chests. "In here. You created the dust from nothing and one day you'll have need of it again. But for now, keep it safe."

Taryn groaned and rolled her eyes. "Not you, too? Riddles? I am so bloody sick of riddles!"

Brandt chuckled and pulled her into a bear hug. "If I told you it was a planet you created, would you believe me?" he whispered and she jerked back to study his face. "I didn't think so." He gave a saucy wink and cluck to her chin before stepping aside.

Verdaine approached and placed a golden circlet upon Taryn's brow. A distinguished darathi vorsi head studded with topaz eyes and a larger gemstone above, the jewels burned with a fire in their depths. Once the metal touched her skin, an awareness tickled the depths of her memory and she looked at Verdaine in surprise. The goddess gave a slight nod and a wink before stepping in front of Rhoane. On him, she set a golden circlet studded with several oblong jewels in various colors. The same curious fire burned in the depths of the gems on his circlet as well.

"What—?" Taryn began, but Verdaine shushed her.

"Listen to Nadra. Quiet your heart."

Ohlin and Nadra took their hands in theirs, saying in unison, "Taryn and Rhoane, you are no longer. Darennsai, daughter of the sky, and Surtentse, son of the terrarae, return to your people and lead them to peace."

One moment they were standing on Dal Tara and the next they were back in the bower. Rhoane shook his head, flexing his marked hand. "Would you care to explain what that was all about?"

"It is their form of entertainment. You get used to it after a while. We could discuss the capriciousness of the gods, or we could make our own entertainment," Taryn said with a sly smile.

"I thought you would never ask."

They spent the night in their bower, solidifying their bonds over and over again with only the stars for a blanket.

As he brooded on the Obsidian Throne, King Zakael turned his gaze to the east. An all too familiar shudder of excitement ran through him when he thought of his true queen.

Marissa reached too high, wanting more than his throne. Her desire to sit at the side of Rykoto was easily dealt with, but Kaldaar—that was a problem. The increasing interest she showed in resurrecting the banished god became more than a nuisance.

Zakael sneered at the head of the fallen Overlord, encased in crystal and resting atop a cushion to the right of his massive chair. Disbelief and enmity shone in the misty depths of his father's eyes. The poor sod. He had no one to blame but himself. Neither he nor Marissa saw the potential right in front of them, instead looking to exiled and imprisoned gods for their immortality.

At least Zakael had made certain Valterys would never rule Aelinae, and Taryn had helped. In the single moment when he'd impaled Valterys upon his sword, she'd met his gaze and he knew. Knew in the core of his being that she understood his need. Without a moment of hesitation on her part, she made certain Valterys could never prevent them from ruling together.

All those moonturns ago when he'd first met her in the cavern, he sensed she was special. Then, when he studied her at Gaarendahl, and more recently when she was bound in the forest and trying valiantly not to give in to his charms, he perceived in her the same blackness that drove him. Their desires were one.

He stretched his mind toward the east and spoke an oath. Someday Taryn Galendrin, and all her power, would be his.

Glossary of Terms

Aelan (Ay-lan) ~ Any person born of Aelinaen descent. These are usually men and women descended from the Elder Gods: Nadra, Ohlin, Daknys, Rykoto, and Kaldaar. In modern times, Aelan refers to those not of another race.

Aelinae (Ay-lynn-ay) ~ A world created by Nadra and Ohlin. It is disk-shaped with waterfalls at the edge of the world, and volcanoes beneath it.

Aelinaen(s) (Ay-lynn-ee-an) ~ Of or having to do with Aelan culture.

Aergan (Air-gahn) ~ An ancient, valuable ore found in only a few places on Aelinae.

Air Faerie ~ Winged Faeries who call on the elements of air for power.

Anklam (Ahnk-lahm) ~ A city on the coast, south of Talaith.

Artagh (R-tah-g) ~ Related to the Eleri, Artaghs lack the Eleri Glamour, as well as the sophistication of the ancient race. They are rumored to be the best at making weapons and working with metals, especially the fabled Godsteel found only in the Haversham Mountains. Outsiders are often distrusted and it's rare to find Artaghs far from their caves.

Black Arts ~ A twisted version of ShantiMari that binds one's soul forever to the banished god, Kaldaar. Practitioners can be either male or female, but females become barren once they invoke the Oath of Fealty. Because of this, they are viewed as Brothers alongside the men.

Black Brotherhood ~ The oldest, most secret religion in Aelinae's history. Much of the Brotherhood is unknown to any except those who are counted among the members. Once a practitioner is invited to join the Brotherhood, they are challenged to a series of tests, many of which require virginal sacrifices. See also Vessel. Membership is often passed from one family member to another, but the terms must be satisfied before being accepted. Those who do not satisfy the requirements, or are not deemed worthy are destroyed.

Black Shanti and **Black ShantiMari** ~ See also Black Arts. This form of ShantiMari uses chaos to fuel its power. External and internal sources give practitioners their strength. They pull their power from the world around them, or the inner conflict people try to conceal. The use of Black ShantiMari is shunned by the Light and Dark, but there are those who have found a way to manipulate the strands of light and shadow into a woven tapestry of devastation that cannot be traced. These are Masters that even the Black Brotherhood fear.

Caer Idris (Care Ee-dris) ~ The ancestral home of The Overlord of the West. Currently, Valterys, Lord of the Dark sits on the Obsidian Throne.

Carlix ~ A sleek, winged feline who makes her home in the mountains known as the Spine of Ohlin. One of the first creatures to inhabit the planet of Aelinae. Often referred to for their flexibility and quick responses, the number of people who have actually seen a carlix is few.

Celyn Eryri (See-lynn Air-ee) ~ The mountain home of the Empress of Talaith. It is here the Light Celebrations take place every Wintertide.

Cockleberry ~ A yellowish fruit that grows in glens and

meadows throughout Aelinae. With a taste similar to blackberries, cockleberries are often used in pies and tasty treats.

Crystal Court ~ The accepted nickname for the court of the Empress of Talaith.

Crystal Palace ~ The accepted nickname for the palace in Talaith where the Empress rules. It's fabled walls are made from a thin layer of rock clear enough to see through, yet unable to be penetrated by weapons or ShantiMari. No one knows who built the great palace, or where the stone came from.

Cynfar (Sin-far) ~ The Eleri name for a talisman given to someone. Usually a pendant, it can also be a bracelet, earrings, or even a small stone. It must be kept close to the recipient for maximum benefit, hence the use of jewelry.

Dal Ferran (Dahl Fair-en) ~ The fiery pits of hell beneath Aelinae's surface.

Dal Tara (Dahl Tar-a) ~ A celestial resting place for the Gods and those they deem worthy. It is located in the second quadrant of the Meirdia Nebula.

Danuri ~ A Province located in the West. The second largest city to Caer Idris, Danuri is widely known for their wine and ale making skills.

Danurian ~ Anyone of Danuri descent.

Darennsai (Dar-en-sigh) ~ An ancient title given to Taryn by the Eleri. Most don't know the true meaning of the word, thinking of it as nothing more than an honorific bestowed upon her by the Goddess Verdaine. Only a few know the word means, Daughter of the Sky. Less an oath than a promise that one day Taryn will sit at the side of

Verdaine, as a goddess in her own right. The Eleri reject this idea.

Dark ~ The part of ShantiMari that is derived from the sun. Only men are skilled in the ways of the Dark, except for the anomaly. To have Dark powers does not automatically make one bad, or evil. There are many men who use their Dark Shanti for good.

Dark Master ~ A highly skilled practitioner of Dark ShantiMari.

Dark Shanti ~ The male side of ShantiMari.

Darathi Vorsi (Dah-rahth-ee Vor-see) ~ Aside from the carlix, *darathi vorsi* are the oldest creatures on Aelinae. Several thousand seasons ago they disappeared from the planet, but the Eleri hold the belief that one day they will return.

Delante (Day-lan-t) ~ A dance performed with a group of people.

Dreem ~ A whisky-like drink that ladies don't usually partake of.

Drerfox ~ Cousin to the fox, a drerfox is bigger, with fangs coated with poison. Their coats shimmer in the sunlight, blending them into the background, making them difficult to see during the day.

The East ~ A geographical location on the map indicating all lands, properties, kingdoms, etc east of the Spine of Ohlin. Includes the Narthvier, Ulla, Talaith, and the marshes near Kaldaar's Stones.

Eirielle (Air-ee-elle) ~ The one of prophecy. Said to be the destroyer or the savior of Aelinae, depending on which prophecy you read. Only one Eirielle is ever said to be created, but that doesn't stop those of the Light and Dark from trying to make one. The Eirielle is rumored to possess all the strands of ShantiMari: Light, Dark, Eleri, and Black. Although, the last is only known to the Brotherhood.

Eiriellean Prophecy ~ A collection of prophecies that record various oracles' visions and ramblings about the Eirielle. Throughout history, there have been those that decried the prophecies, and those that touted them as truth. Nearly everyone fears either version coming to pass.

Elennish (Elle-enn-ish) ~ The oldest language on Aelinae still spoken in the East and West.

Eleri (Ee-ler-ee) ~ A mysterious clan of elf-like men and women who live in the Narthvier. They stay within the borders of their forest and don't like outsiders coming on their land. The Eleri share a collective conscious, in that they can call on the wisdom of past and future Eleri in times of duress. The oldest race on Aelinae, they and the *darathi vorsi* share a common bond. Thought to be caretakers of the beasts, when the *darathi vorsi* disappeared, it was a time of great mourning for the Eleri.

Fadair (Fah-d-air) ~ The name Eleri have given to anyone not Eleri. It is meant to be used as a way to signify someone not of Eleri descent, but often it is used as a disparaging slur against non-Eleri.

Faerie Cakes ~ Small cakes light in texture, but filling. Made with sponge cake and jam, these are Taryn's favorite. Don't ever leave a plate sitting around or she'll eat them all.

Feiche (Fee-ch) ~ A large black bird similar to a raven, but faster and a bit bigger. They hunt in packs and are capable of taking down a small horse if so inclined.

Frost End ~ The time between Wintertide and Summer. On Earth, it would occur around April.

Gaarendahl (Gare-en-doll) ~ An older castle located between the Spine of Ohlin and the Summer Sea. It belongs to Valterys's family, but Zakael uses it most often.

Geigan (Guy-gan) ~ A warrior race of people. Dark in coloring, they are rumored to be the source of mating with the Sitari.

Glamour ~ A slight shimmering beneath the skin. Found only on Eleri.

Godsteel ~ A metal forged by the Artagh of Haversham. Stronger than any other metal, godsteel is unbreakable. Long ago, only the gods could wield weapons made of godsteel (hence, the name), but at least two swords have made their way into mortal's hands. Rhoane's and Taryn's. But there are rumors that a few other swords have been tainted by Black ShantiMari. Their owners are unknown at this time.

Grierbas (Greer-bah) ~ A large, wolf-like animal that makes its home in the Narthvier. Wild and territorial, grierbas keep away from civilizations, even avoiding the Eleri.

Grhom (Gr-om) ~ A spiced drink made by the Eleri. It has healing properties and gives strength through the many ingredients used to make it. Taryn likens the taste to a thick chocolate mixed with chai. Occasionally, the Eleri will add alcohol to the drink.

Gyota (Gee-o-tah) ~ In Eleri, *gyota* means 'destroyer'.

Harvest - The months during the season between Summer and Wintertide. On Earth, this time is referred to as Fall.

Haversham - A mountainous region where Artagh mine for gems, minerals, and the necessary metals to make weapons. Highly guarded, outsiders are not welcome in Haversham.

Hildgelt (Hill-d-gel-t) - A Danurian ornamentation made from thin layers of blown glass.

House - The family name by which most Aelans associate themselves. Every House has their own color and insignia. It is by these outward displays members of nobility and the court can recognize another's importance.

House Galendrin - Ohlin created this House for Taryn on her crowning day. This is the highest honor anyone could hope to achieve and has only been granted once.

Kalaith - The art of communicating with only a fan. Summerlanders have perfected this archaic language. It is often used as a form of seduction in the Summerlands.

Kiltern River - A river that runs north of Paderau to Ulla.

Lan Gyllarelle (Lahn Gill-a-rell) - A vast lake located in the Narthvier. Its waters are rumored to hold healing properties. The Eleri often hold ceremonies on the banks of the lake.

Lake Oster - Located between Talaith and Paderau, Lake Oster is often used as a stopping point for travelers. Fresh water and an abundance of fish refresh stores between the two great cities.

Levon (Le-von) - A sleek black bird. Faster than any other birds, the levon is a favorite form of transportation for those competent in transformation.

Light ~ A strain of ShantiMari found in females born on Aelinae. Not all women exhibit traits of the power, but are able to pass on Light ShantiMari to their daughters. Eleri females have Light ShantiMari, but their powers will differ from the Fadair's in that they use nature as a catalyst and Fadair use the air and sky. The Lady of Light is able to manipulate weather and has slight control over the sea.

Light Celebrations ~ A week long event featuring competitions of physical prowess. The celebrations began as a way to offset the dreariness of Wintertide.

Light Throne ~ The ancestral court of The Lady of Light, otherwise known as the Empress of Talaith. Also referred to as the Crystal Court. The actual throne is made of ancient oak from the Narthvier. Woven into the planks of wood is a thin layer of crystal.

Mari (Mar-ee) ~ The female side of ShantiMari. Also referred to as Light.

Mind-Speak ~ A form of communication used between two people within their minds.

Mount Nadrene (Mount Nay-dreen) ~ The holiest place on Aelinae, Mount Nadrene is where Nadra sent Taryn through a portal to Earth. It is also a cavern filled with glittering crystals and a large lake. Some believe the cavern is the birthplace of all the gods and goddesses of Aelinae.

Mowbat ~ A Summerland creature resembling a tiny winged squirrel.

Nadra (Nah-d-rah) ~ The Mother Goddess, she and Ohlin

created Aelinae.

Narthvier (Narth-veer) ~ A vast forest covering the north-east portion of Aelinae. The Eleri make their home in the Narthvier, or vier as some call it. The Eleri are protective of the forest and use veils to dissuade unwelcome visitors. Only the Eleri know how to raise the fabled veils.

Obsidian Throne ~ The ancestral home of the Lord of the Dark. The actual throne is made of the same oak planks as the Light Throne. Within the wood fibers is woven obsidian granite.

Offlander ~ Any person raised outside of the courtesies of court. The term is an insult of the highest order.

Ohlin (Oh-lynn) ~ The Great Father, he and Nadra created Aelinae.

Paderau (Pah-der-oo) ~ A vast city ruled by Duke Anje. Paderau sits between the Narthvier and Talaith, which makes it a busy port city for trading goods.

Paderau Palace ~ The home of Duke Anje and his family.

Privy Council ~ A body of advisers to the Empress of Talaith. The council is made up of senior members of the highest Houses. On occasion, as with Hayden and Duke Anje, a junior member can represent their House in council. Also included in the privy council are the High Priest, and captains of the guard or military.

Ravenwood ~ The less formal home of the Duke of Anje. When in residence, he oversees the local businesses.

Runyon Tree ~ A black, gnarled tree with sharp thorns embedded in its trunk and branches.

Sargot (Sar-go) ~ An orange-like fruit that tastes similar to a mango.

Seal of Ardyn ~ Seals created by the Elder Gods to keep Rykoto imprisoned in the Temple of Ardyn.

Shanti (Shahn-tee) ~ The male side of ShantiMari. Also referred to as Dark.

ShantiMari (Shahn-tee Mar-ee) ~ Two halves of the same whole. ShantiMari is a power found in all things on Aelinae. Within men and women, it manifests itself in varying degrees from no visible signs, to extremely powerful. Those in positions of great power will have more ShantiMari than those born to the lesser clans or Houses. ShantiMari is often referred to as Light and Dark, or female and male. Within the confines of ShantiMari are rules, or etiquette. The power can be culled from the smallest pebble to the stars themselves. Wielding more power than one is capable of controlling often leads to a painful death.

Shadow Assassin ~ Neither alive nor dead, Shadow Assassins were the elite force of Kaldaar's army. Only a powerful Master can create the demons.

Shadow Spawn, Shadow Soul ~ Nicknames given to the Shadow Assassin.

Sheanna (Shee-ahn-a) ~ An exiled Eleri. When an Eleri is *sheanna*, they are required to cut their hair and live outside the borders of the Narthvier until a certain amount of time has passed. Once they return to the Narthvier, they must complete the purification ceremony before they are considered to be Eleri once more.

Silden River ~ This river runs south from Paderau to Lake

Oster.

Sitari (Sit-ar-ee) ~ Blue skinned warrior women who live in a community devoid of men. Their island sits at the southernmost edge of Aelinae. It is rumored their preferred mates are Geigan males. Sitari women can be found in other kingdoms of Aelinae, usually scouting for the strongest to procreate with. Once coupling has been achieved, the Sitari return to their island. Male offspring are said to be sacrificed to their goddess.

Skirm (Sk-ur-m) ~ A banana-like fruit. The leaves of the skirm tree are broad and often used in cooking roasted meats.

Smelting Day ~ An annual celebration of Artagh to honor their god. The fires of Haversham burn brightest on Smelting Day, but no actual forging is done. Instead, the Artagh participate in dances and rousing songs around the flames.

Spine of Ohlin ~ The range of mountains stretching from the Temple of Ardyn in the far north to the Summer Seas in the south.

Summerlands ~ An island kingdom located south of Talaith in the Summer Seas.

Summer Seas ~ The body of water covering the entire southern area of Aelinae.

Surtentse (Sir-tants) ~ An ancient title meaning 'Son of the Terrarae'. Verdaine gives this honorific to Rhoane.

Sword of Ohlin ~ Also known as Ynyd Eirathnacht. Ohlin had the sword made out of godsteel for his daughter, Daknys. The bearer of the sword must be pure of heart and worthy of the weapon.

Sylthan Age (Sil-than Age) ~ The fourth century of Aelinae's time clock.

Talaith (Tal - eth) ~ The capital city of the East. Ruled by the empress, also known as The Lady of Light.

Temple of Ardyn (Ar-din) ~ Rykoto's temple and source of power. He was imprisoned here by Daknys and the Elder Gods after his defeat in the Great War.

Treplar (Treh-p-lar) ~ Round apple-like, spiky fruits from the Summerlands.

Trisp ~ A thick alcoholic drink.

Ulla (Oo-la) ~ A kingdom located in the far East of Aelinae. The Ullans are a tribal people, following their herds throughout the season. Ullan horses are of the finest stock.

Verdaine ~ (Vehr-d-ane) Daughter of Nadra and Ohlin, goddess of the Eleri.

Verdaine's Prophecy ~ When Rhoane was born, Verdaine prophesied that he would be exiled from his people until the *gyota* returned. His fate would be tied to the one who is and who is not for all time.

Veil ~ A mysterious barrier preventing outsiders from entering the Narthvier.

Vier ~ Nickname of the Narthvier.

Vorlock ~ A huge, lizard-like creature with heavy scales and a wide frill around its head. Vorlocks contain a poison that can kill a man or woman instantly.

Weirren (Weer-en) ~ The ancestral home of the Eleri King and Queen.

Weirren Court ~ The gathered nobility of the Eleri live among the many buildings interwoven through the ancient tree that makes up the Weirren.

Weirren Throne ~ Built into the oldest tree on Aelinae, the Weirren Throne is a living, breathing seat.

The West ~ Geographical area located to the west of Ohlin's Spine. Includes the kingdom of the Overlord of the West, Danuri Province, and Haversham.

Western Seas ~ The body of water located off the Western Coast of Aelinae.

Woodland Faerie ~ Faerie folk who make their home in the forests Aelinae, most commonly found in the Narthvier. Woodland faeries grow to be around three feet in height, although some are taller. They are the exception. Woodland faeries share a special bond with nature and can cultivate new species of living plants or animals.

Ynyd Eirathnacht (Inid Air-ath-nack-t) ~ The name of Ohlin's sword, currently in the possession of Taryn Rose Galendrin.

Cast of Characters

Adesh ~ Summerlander. A spice merchant in Talaith. Tabul's brother.

Aislinn al Glennwoods ap Narthvier (Ay-s-lynn) ~ Queen of the Eleri. Aislinn perished in a ShantiMari accident when Rhoane was a young man.

Alasdair (Alice-dare) ~ A faerie servant in the service of Rhoane. Brother to Illanr and Carld.

Alswyth Myrddin (Alls-with Mere-din) ~ Mage with exceedingly long life. Myrddin is the advisor to Empress Lliandra and is often far from court on assignments from the crown. No known children or spouses. No known House.

Amanda ~ Aelan. A young woman living in Talaith with dubious ties to Adesh the spice merchant.

Anje ap Paderau (Ann-jee ap Paw-der-oo) ~ Duke of Paderau, father to Hayden, husband to Gwyneira (now deceased). Anje is cousin to the Lord of the Dark, and third in line for the Obsidian Throne. His father was brother to Valterys's father. A prince in his own right, Anje renounced his Dark heritage to live with his wife in the Light. Descendant of House Djeba.

Aomori di Monsenti (A-more-ee di Mon-scent-ee) ~ A young Danuri lord fostering with Tinsley in Paderau. Descendant of House Monsenti.

Armando ~ Summerlander. Lover of Tarro. Whore in Nena's house. Marissa's favorite.

Ashanni (A-shawn-ee) ~ A mare Duke Anje gives to Taryn.

Baehlon de Monteferron (Bay-lohn de Mont-fair-on) ~ Danuri and Geigan knight employed by Empress Lliandra, sworn to protect Taryn and her House. Descendant of House Monteferron.

Bornu (Bore-new) ~ Summerlander. A young boy who works for Adesh.

Brandt Kaj Endion (Brant) ~ Aelan. High Priest of Talaith and advisor to Empress Lliandra, Brandt was commissioned with Taryn's safety when she was born. After his death, Nadra took Brandt to Dal Tara, (home of the gods), which allows Brandt to communicate with Taryn. House Arran.

Bressal ap Narthvier (Bress-all) ~ Eleri. Second Son to King Stephan and Queen Aislinn (now passed beyond the veils).

Carga ap Narthvier ~ Eleri. Daughter to King Stephan and Queen Aislinn (now passed beyond the veils).

Carina (Ka-reen-a) ~ Aelan. A member of Taryn's personal guard.

Carld (Car-uld) ~ A faerie maid in the service of King Stephan. Sister to Illanr and Alasdair.

Celia ~ Aelan. Minor noble and Marissa's favorite until she perished at the Stones of Kaldaar. Descendant of House Deltanna.

Cora ~ Aelan. A maid in the service of Empress Lliandra.

Daknys (Dak-niss) ~ Elder Goddess. Daughter of Nadra and Ohlin, she is worshipped by the Light and Dark in the central area of Aelinae.

Darius (Dare-ee-us) ~ Artagh, Eleri and Aelan. A page at Celyn Eryri who joins Taryn's guard.

Denzil de Monteferron (Den-zell) ~ Danuri and Geigan. A mercenary hired by Lliandra to patrol Talaith's docks. Brother to Baehlon.

Ebus (Ee-bus) ~ Race unknown. Spy employed by Taryn and Rhoane. Can see the Shadow Assassin.

Eliahnna Tjaru (Ee-lahn-ah Shar-U) ~ Aelan. Daughter of Lliandra. Her heritage is much debated since Lliandra has never publicly named her father. She is third in line to the Light Throne. Descendant of House Nadrene.

Ellie ~ Aelan. A maid in the service of Taryn.

Eoghan ap Narthvier (Eee-gan) ~ Eleri. Third Son to King Stephan and Queen Aislinn (now passed beyond the veils).

Faelara Dal Arran (Fay-lara) ~ Aelan. Daughter of Brandt, Faelara is currently a lady-in-waiting to Empress Lliandra. Her Healing skills are legendary, as were her father's. House Arran.

Faisal dei Tarnovo (Fay-sal) ~ Summerlander. Sabina's father and the king of the Summerlands. House Tarnov.

Fayngaar (Fain-gar) ~ Rhoane's stallion.

Gian ap Brenbold (Jawn) ~ A faerie found in Valterys's dungeon.

Gwyneira Tjaru ap Paderau (Gwin-eera ap Shar-U) ~ Aelan. Sister to Empress Lliandra, wife of Duke Anje, mother to Hayden. Gwyneira died after childbirth when Hayden was a young man. Houses Nadrene and Djeba.

Hayden ap Valen ~ Aelan. Lord Valen, Marquis of the province Valen, son of Anje and Gwyneira. Hayden is cousin to the heirs of the Light Throne and the Obsidian Throne. Descendant of House Djeba.

Herbret ~ Aelan. A minor noble in Talaith's court and one of Marissa's favorites until he perished at the Stones of Kaldaar. Descendant of House Gilfroy.

Illanr (Ill-an-or) ~ A faerie maid in the service of King Stephan. Sister to Carld and Alasdair.

Iselt (Ee-selt) ~ A blacksmith at Celyn Eryri with secrets and a past he's trying to hide. He is half Artagh and half Eleri.

Janeira (Juh-nair-a) ~ An Eleri warrior of great standing, excellent skill, and deadly capabilities.

Julieta ~ Younger Goddess. Daughter of Rykoto and Daknys.

Kaida (Kay-da) ~ A grierbas Taryn rescued in the Narthvier. Companion to Taryn ~ they have the ability to speak with each other in their minds. Kaida can track the Shadow Assassin.

Kaldaar (Cal-dar) ~ Elder God. Son of Nadra and Ohlin, worshipped by inhabitants of the Southeast until his banishment after the Great War. Kaldaar hasn't been seen in Aelinae in over five thousand seasons.

Lliandra Tjaru (Lee-on-dra Shar-U) ~ Aelan. Empress of Talaith, Lady of Light. Mother to Marissa, Taryn, Eliahnna, and Tessa. Lliandra is directly descended from the goddess Nadra. She is thought to be a just ruler who thinks of her subjects in all matters. House Nadrene.

Lorilee ~ Aelan. A maid in the service of Taryn. Sister to Mayla.

Marissa Tjaru (Shar-U) ~ Aelan. Crown Princess of Talaith, heir to the Light Throne, daughter of Lliandra and Esna (not named in books one or two). Descendant of House Nadrene.

Mayla ~ Aelan. A maid in the service of Duke Anje. Sister to Lorilee.

Margaret Tan ~ Geigan. Seamstress to Empress Lliandra, she often travels with the court. Her tailoring skills are said to be admired in all the kingdoms.

Marina ~ Summerlander. A maid in the service of Marissa.

Matilde ~ Aelan. Amanda's mother. Lives in Talaith with dubious ties to Adesh the spice merchant.

Nadra ~ Mother of Aelinae, Great Mother of all Creation. Along with Ohlin, Nadra created Aelinae. Mother to Daknys, Rykoto, Kaldaar, and Verdaine.

Nena ~ Race unknown. Owner of a house of prostitution in Talaith.

Nikosana ~ Black and tan Ullan stallion given to Taryn at the Light Celebrations by Duke Anje.

Ohlin (O-lynn) ~ Father of Aelinae, Great Father of all Creation. Along with Nadra, Ohlin created Aelinae. Father to to Daknys, Rykoto, Kaldaar, and Verdaine.

Oliver ~ Aelan. A servant in the service of Hayden, Lord Valen.

Percival ~ Marissa's child.

Phantom - An unknown entity manipulating Celia, Herbret, and Marissa. The phantom is thought to be an agent of Kaldaar.

Prateeni dei Tarnovo (Pruh-teen-ee) - Summerlander. Sabina's mother and the Queen of the Summerlands. House Tarnov.

Rhoane al Glennwoods ap Narthvier (Rone) - Eleri. First Son of Stephan, King of the Eleri, and Aislinn, Queen of the Eleri (now passed beyond the veils). At birth Rhoane was prophesied to be the Eirielle's protector. When he was old enough, he took an oath forsaking all others and devoting his life to upholding Verdaine's prophecy.

Rykoto (Ree-ko-toe) - Elder God. Son of Nadra and Ohlin, worshipped by inhabitants of the Northwest and of the Dark. Rykoto was imprisoned in the Temple of Ardyn after the Great War.

Sabina dei Tarnovo - Summerlander. Daughter of King Faisal and Queen Prateeni. Currently fostering with Empress Lliandra in Talaith. Sabina's ShantiMari was unlocked after the ordeal at the Stones of Kaldaar. Descendant of House Tarnov.

Saeko (Say-koh) - A maid in the service of Taryn.

Shadow Assassin - An unknown assailant stalking Taryn. He can 'disappear'.

Stephan ap Narthvier - King of the Eleri. Direct descendant from Verdaine.

Sulein ap Lorn (Sue-lain) - An Artagh living in Talaith.

Tabul (Tah-buhl) - Summerlander. Spice merchant from

Paderau.

Tarro (Tare-O) ~ Danuri. Assistant to Margaret Tan. Lover of Armando.

Taryn Rose Galendrin (Tare-in) ~ Daughter of Lliandra, Empress of Talaith, Lady of Light and Valterys, Overlord of the West, Lord of the Dark. Raised on Earth, Taryn grew up unaware of Aelinae, believing Brandt was her grandfather and only family. House Galendrin.

Tessa Tjaru (Shar-U) ~ Aelan. Daughter of Lliandra and Razlog (not named in books one or two). She is fourth in line to the Light Throne. Descendant of House Nadrene.

Timor (Tim-or) ~ Aelan. A member of Taryn's personal guard.

Tinsley Alcath (Tins-lee All-koth) ~ Aelan. A young lord with business ties to Duke Anje and is often at Paderau Palace. Descendant of House Alcath.

Valterys Djeba (Val-terr-iss D-jj-ay-ba) ~ Aelan. Overlord of the West, Lord of the Dark. Father to Taryn and Zakael. Valterys is directly descended from the god Ohlin. He rules his kingdom with a tight grasp on its economy and trade. His subjects think of him favorably. House Djeba.

Verdaine (Vare-dane) ~ Elder Goddess. Daughter of Nadra and Ohlin, she is worshipped by the Eleri in the Narthvier.

Zakael Djeba (Zah-K-ay-eel D-jj-ay-ba) ~ Aelan. Prince, heir to the Obsidian Throne. Son of Valterys and Troyanna (not named in books one or two). Descendant of House Djeba.

Thank You For Reading!

Dear Reader,

I hope you enjoyed *The Temple of Ardyn*. I have to tell you, I really love the characters of Taryn and Rhoane. Though many readers have written asking, 'When can we have more of Rhoane?' Well, stay tuned because he's going to have his own adventure in a novella coming out later this year.

Writing this series is a joy for me and hearing from you makes the experience all the more exquisite. I love connecting with you! You can always email me at TameriEtherton@gmail.com, or find me on Facebook, Twitter, Google +, Goodreads, and Pinterest. You can find more information about the books on my website, www.TameriEtherton.com.

Finally, I need to ask a favor. If you're so inclined, I'd love a review of *The Temple of Ardyn*. Loved it, hated it ~ I'd love your feedback. Plus, your review helps other readers find what they're looking for. Readers are the rockstars in an author's world. We love you, truly, madly, deeply.

Again, thank you for reading and being a part of Taryn and Rhoane's adventure.

Until next time, be amazing!

Tameri Etherton

Meet the Author

Rocker of sparkly tiaras, friend of dragons, and lover of all things sexy, Tameri Etherton leaves a trail of glitter in her wake as she creates and conquers new worlds and the villains who inhabit them. When not masquerading as a mom and writer, rumor has it she travels to far off places, drinking tea and finding inspiration for her kickass heroines—and the rogues who steal their hearts—with her own Prince Charming by her side.

To find out more about the author, visit her web site at www.TameriEtherton.com. Be sure to sign up for her newsletter to receive exclusives like advanced notice of upcoming releases, secret scenes, and other enticing tidbits about the Song of the Swords series.

There you'll discover the World of Aelinae where you'll find maps, glossaries, and a complete cast of characters to further your reading experience.

For more about the artist who designs the Song of the Sword covers, please visit Carol Phillips at RadianceWeb.com. Her amazing art will take your breath away.

If you enjoyed reading **THE TEMPLE OF ARDYN: SONG OF THE SWORDS BOOK TWO**, the adventure continues with **THE RUINS OF MALLAQAI: SONG OF THE SWORDS BOOK THREE**.

Look for it this winter.